Gold rose from his chair and approached the science station. "How bad is it? Are any of the ground stations in harm's way?"

Gomez consulted her sensors once again, then faced Gold, who felt a sense of mounting alarm as he watched her face suddenly drain of all color. "One of the lower-elevation ground stations is right in the path of the lava flow—and it's going to be engulfed in less than two hours."

"Two hours," Gold repeated, allowing himself to feel relieved as he turned the information over in his mind. "That should give us enough time to evacuate."

Gomez continued to look worried. "Maybe. As long as things don't get any worse."

A worm of apprehension turned in the pit of Gold's stomach. "What do you mean? How much worse could it get?"

"I'm reading the mother of all volcanic eruptions letting loose right now under Alpha Regio. It might set off a domino effect that ends up repaving most of the planet's surface—in the span of three or four hours."

"I'll start coordinating the evacuation plan," Corsi said.

Gold nodded to his security chief. *Oy. Looks like we might have arrived just in time for the half-billion-year barbecue.*

He reopened the audio feed to Ishtar Station. "Pas, I think we have a huge problem on our hands. . . ."

STAR TREK®
CORPS OF
ENGINEERS

AFTERMATH

Christopher L. Bennett, Randall N. Bills, Loren L.
Coleman, Robert Greenberger, Andy Mangels,
Michael A. Martin, and Aaron Rosenberg

Based upon *Star Trek®* and
Star Trek: The Next Generation®
created by Gene Roddenberry
and *Star Trek: Deep Space Nine®*
created by Rick Berman & Michael Piller

POCKET BOOKS
New York   London   Toronto   Sydney   Venus

POCKET BOOKS, a division of Simon & Schuster, Inc.
1230 Avenue of the Americas, New York, NY 10020

This book is published by Pocket Books, a division of Simon & Schuster, Inc., under exclusive license from CBS Studios Inc.

Library of Congress Cataloging-in-Publication Data
Aftermath / Christopher L. Bennett . . . [et.al].
    p.cm — (Star trek, corps of engineers)
    "Based upon Star trek and Star trek: the next generaltion created by Gene Roddenberry, and Star trek: deep space nine created by Rick Berman and Michael Piller"
    Contents: Aftermath / by Christopher L. Bennett — Ishtar rising / by Michael A. Martin & Andy Mangels — Buying time / by Robert Greenberger — Collective hindsight / by Aaron Rosenberg — The demon / by Loren L. Coleman & Randall N. Bills.
    ISBN-13: 978-1-4165-2576-9 (trade pbk.)
    ISBN-10:   1-4165-2576-9 (trade pbk.)
    1. Star Trek fiction. 2. Science fiction, American. I. Bennett, Christoper L. II. Star trek (Television program) III. Star trek, the next generation (Television proogram)
    PS648.S3A5 2006
    813'.0876208—dc22
                                                    2006049444

This Pocket Books trade paperback edition November 2006

10 9 8 7 6 5 4 3 2 1

Manufactured in the United States of America

These titles were previously published individually in eBook format by Pocket Books.

For information regarding special discounts for bulk purchases, please contact Simon & Schuster Special Sales at 1-800-456-6798 or business@simonandschuster.com.

CONTENTS

INTRODUCTION

Miracle Workers on Parade

For those of you who've been following the adventures of the Starfleet Corps of Engineers, welcome to the new face of the S.C.E. in print!

For those of you who are new, a simple welcome. You're in for a fun ride. What you've picked up is actually the eighth book to print stories of the S.C.E. in codex book form. The first seven, under the series title of *Star Trek: S.C.E.*, were published from 2002–2005; those, in turn, were reprinting the first twenty-eight eBooks that were available for download starting in the summer of 2000. We recently relaunched the eBook line under the more descriptive title *Star Trek: Corps of Engineers,* and have done likewise with the print volumes—and also moved them to trade paperback, where we can fit six to eight eBooks per volume, giving the reader more bang for the buck (and also keeping the eBook line from getting too far ahead of the dead-tree format).

It all started when then-Pocket Books editor John J.

Ordover called me up and said that Pocket wanted to develop an original line of eBooks that would debut alongside the new Microsoft Reader that was unleashed on a panting reading public in 2000. John and I hammered out the concept of the S.C.E., and then Dean Wesley Smith, Christie Golden, and I banged out three stories that introduced us to the crew of the *U.S.S. da Vinci.*

Honestly, I never imagined that six-and-a-half years later, it would not only still be a going concern, but some of the most fun I've had as a writer or an editor.

In 2001, *Star Trek: S.C.E.* became an eBook series edited by me (also with occasional writing contributions from me), with a new story coming out each month. A huge variety of authors have contributed over the years, providing an equal variety of stories.

You see, the Corps of Engineers tales aren't just about technobabble—the biggest concern expressed by readers reluctant to try it out. These are high-adventure problem-solving stories, where the solution doesn't just come from some piece of tech we made up on the fly (though it is sometimes a piece of tech the *characters* make up on the fly) to write our way out of a difficult situation.

These are also character stories. Over the twenty-eight eBooks that made up the seven volumes prior to this we've seen the people grow and change and be affected by their surroundings, whether it's Dr. Lense's post-traumatic stress (*Hard Crash, Oaths*), the Gomez-Duffy relationship (*Invincible, Wildfire*), Captain Gold's relationships with his oldest friend (*No Surrender*) and his family (*Breakdowns*), or the fallout from Corsi's one-night stand with Stevens (*Cold Fusion, Home Fires*).

And then, of course, there's *Wildfire*, David Mack's gripping tale that saw the *da Vinci* beset with an awful tragedy.

If you are new to the S.C.E., then this is a fine jumping-on point, because *Aftermath* represents a new beginning for the crew of the *da Vinci*. They've begun the process of moving forward from the tragedies of *Wildfire*, new crewmates have taken the place of those who fell, and the S.C.E. is continuing their mission of solving the galaxy's crises, whether it's cabochons that suddenly grow in size in San Francisco to the Venus terraforming project to a Ferengi with a time machine to a Dominion War salvage operation that comes back to haunt them to a bizarre distress signal from a black hole. We'll also see how the new crew members—in particular the new second officer, Mor glasch Tev—fit in with the old, and how the old move forward from the tragedy.

And hey, if you like what you see, check out the newly relaunched line of eBooks. As of the release of this book, there are three new titles out: *Turn the Page* by Dayton Ward & Kevin Dilmore, *Troubleshooting* by Robert Greenberger, and *The Light* by Jeff D. Jacques. They also serve as an excellent jumping-on point.

So sit back, and enjoy the ride. . . .

Keith R.A. DeCandido
Editor
New York City, 2006

AFTERMATH

Christopher L. Bennett

CHAPTER
1

"Danged Breen," Katie Huang complained. "They put a hole in my city."

Sanek, her new assistant, looked up at her as they worked their way down the slope, his bright orange hard hat clashing with his sallow skin. "The Breen put a great many holes in San Francisco. However, most of those holes have been filled."

"Yeah," Katie acceded grudgingly—or not so grudgingly, she decided as she caught a glimpse of the Golden Gate Bridge, now restored and reopened. She remembered how it had looked a year ago, after the Breen attack on Starfleet Headquarters—the north tower crumpled, the span missing a huge chunk in the middle. It was a miracle the bridge hadn't collapsed. Some had wanted to leave it as it was as a monument, but it was too valuable a thoroughfare, and too important a symbol of the City by the Bay, not to be restored to its former glory. As proud as Katie was of her fellow civilian builders and maintenance workers, she gave a silent thanks to the Starfleet Corps of Engineers, Earth Division, for their tireless efforts on the city's behalf.

"But that's just it," she went on. "All this time, and there's still this great big ugly scar in the middle of my town."

"That is more the fault of the geology than the Breen."

"They had sensors. They must've known about the underground caverns." The Breen had been indiscriminate in their attack, hitting parts of the city far removed from the military targets and costing many innocent lives. They'd even attacked the Starfleet Museum Center, destabilizing the ground beneath it and opening a sinkhole into which most of the complex had collapsed. The losses to art, culture, and science were incalculable, and Katie felt them keenly; but the massive blemish on the landscape had become her personal symbol for all of it, something that affected her on a visceral level. What had made it worse was that the continued instabilities had hampered efforts to clear and restore the site, so it still remained, even though the rest of San Francisco was as good as new.

"Still," Sanek said, "the ground is now stabilized and most of the wreckage has been cleared away. The new museum can be built soon. Perhaps the construction of a war memorial will be approved. I understand you humans are fond of such emotional representations."

Katie smiled at her new friend's very Vulcan sentiment. "Nothing wrong with a good emotional representation, Sanek. You should try it sometime."

He raised an eyebrow. "That would be illogical, as you well know."

Katie laughed and said, "I know, but you can't blame

a human for trying. I'm sure lots of humans think Vulcans would be better off if they let their hair down a bit."

"Just as many Vulcans think humans would be better off if they, to maintain the metaphor, kept their hair tied up."

That prompted another laugh. "Probably, yeah. But that's what keeps the galaxy interesting." They reached the bottom of the sinkhole and activated their sensor units. Not as versatile as Starfleet tricorders, they were still good enough to scan for remaining instabilities, gas pockets, salvageable artifacts from the museum . . . or organic remains. Even now, a few victims were still unaccounted for.

Sanek focused intently on his scanner, barely paying attention to his footing, and Katie smirked. "Don't trip over any android heads."

"I beg your pardon?"

"These tunnels are where they found Data's head a few years back."

"Assuming you are referring to Lieutenant Commander Data of the *Starship Enterprise,* I was under the impression that his head has remained attached to his person."

"This was his head from the past. He went back in time, it got knocked off, gathered dust here for five hundred years, and got put back on." She frowned. "So his head's twenty times older than the rest of him. I wonder what that does to the warranty."

"According to the records, that was a 'prank' on the part of some cadets from Starfleet Academy—another of your emotional representations."

Katie grinned. "That's the official story. Of course, time-travel evidence gets classified. Too dangerous, you know. Imagine the havoc someone could cause if they knew how to go back and mess around with the past." She noticed something on her scanner. "Hey, I've got some kind of . . . reading. It's coming and going . . . but yeah, it's there."

"What manner of reading?"

"I think it's some kind of subspace static," she frowned. "Under those rocks."

"Down here?"

"Hell, maybe it's some old communicator from the museum with a bit of power left. Better check it out, though—might be a priceless antique." Again, she smirked, showing what she thought of the odds. "Help me here." Together they moved the rubble out of the way, exposing the item.

It was a small spherical object, about the size of a golf ball, covered in dust. "It is not registering on my scanner," Sanek said. "Perhaps a Starfleet-issue tricorder would do better."

"No, we don't need to call in the troops every time a problem comes up." She reached toward it.

"I would not advise touching it. We have no way of knowing its function."

"Whatever its function *was*, if anything, it's been blasted by the Breen's energy dampers, dumped through a sinkhole, and buried under rubble for a year. It probably doesn't do much of anything anymore. Hey, look, it's even got a crack in it. Was that there a moment ago?" She reached a finger forward to indicate the hairline fissure. Her fingernail barely brushed it.

She never heard the blast that followed—though it rocked the whole city.

* * *

It's too quiet, thought David Gold.

He was walking to the bridge with Sonya Gomez, the same morning ritual he and his first officer had enacted every day until the *da Vinci* had been crippled in the incident at Galvan VI. This was their first morning back since then, and they'd resumed the ritual automatically, a natural beginning to the day when the repaired starship would launch herself out of dry dock once more. Around them the rebuilt corridors sparkled in mint condition; in the background the restored engines thrummed in perfect tune, supplying electroplasma for perfectly calibrated systems. *Shipshape and Bristol fashion,* Gold thought, remembering the phrase his old friend Jean-Luc liked to use in his antiquarian moments.

But it was too quiet. There was none of the pleasant bustle that had formerly filled the ship's compact corridors—whether that of engineers pursuing their projects, constantly making adjustments to push the systems just a bit more beyond dry dock specs, or that of crewmates and friends exchanging banter and giving friendly greetings as their commanding officers walked by. All the people they passed were subdued—the old crew members (agonizingly few) still recovering from the tragedy, the new ones still adjusting to unfamiliar surroundings. It would take time for them to get comfortable with each other, to mesh into a unit that Gold hoped could work as smoothly as the old crew—though not in quite the same way, to be sure. The *da Vinci* would never be truly the same again.

Gold wondered if his morning walk with Gomez would ever be the same again either. In the past, it had been an opportunity for small talk, for exchanging shipboard gossip and chatting about family and news and trivia, having more to do with friendship than duty. To Gold, it helped to compensate for being so far from his own family.

In fact, he hadn't been sure that she was going to show up for the walk at all. Among the many fatalities had been Kieran Duffy, the ship's second officer and Gomez's lover. It had seemed from the outside like a simple shipboard romance—until Duffy had popped the question out of the blue. Gold couldn't blame Gomez for being too *farblonzhet* to give him an answer. But then Duffy had sacrificed himself to save the ship, never knowing what her answer would've been. By her own admission, Gomez herself didn't know, either. One more loss to add to the list—the loss of closure. But for a time, Gomez had blamed Gold for Duffy's death, and, though they had settled that, at least, and regained a semblance of their former friendship, Gold knew that Duffy's death would always be a barrier between them.

Gold knew she'd worked through the worst of her grief, and was ready to resume her duties. But there was no telling how long it would be before she could take joy in them again. Which was a shame. She was generally a serious sort, a hardened pro, tough on herself, prone to worry; but underneath it all was a girlish innocence and playfulness, which manifested itself in a radiant smile that filled Gold with fatherly warmth. He missed that smile.

And it was still too quiet.

Naturally, just as he thought that, a jolt went through the ship, knocking him briefly off balance. As he and Gomez ran to the bridge, the captain reflected that he had some choice words for God about His sense of timing.

The bridge was bustling with activity as the crew

worked to analyze the disturbance. Yet even here it seemed too quiet, without David McAllan to announce "Captain on the bridge" as he always had. That shtick had annoyed Gold at first, but over time he'd grown accustomed to it, and now he'd give anything to hear it again. Better that than the memory of McAllan sacrificing himself, shoving Gold out from under a falling ceiling support—of the look on the young man's face in that last moment, meeting his captain's eyes imploringly, seeking assurance that he'd done all right. Until that moment, Gold had never realized the deep respect and devotion that had underlain young David's—his *namesake's*—insistence on announcing his captain's arrival.

Anthony Shabalala, McAllan's replacement at tactical, looked for a moment like he wanted to announce Gold, but couldn't bring himself to. They weren't his words to say.

So Gold announced himself. "What's all the tumult about?"

Lieutenant Commander Mor glasch Tev, the *da Vinci*'s new second officer, rose efficiently from the center seat and faced his captain. The stocky Tellarite barely came up to Gomez's height, but carried himself high and proudly. His monk's fringe of dark hair and the gray-frosted beard that framed his porcine features were groomed to machine tolerances. "Subspace shock wave, sir," Tev reported in a curt but surprisingly mellow baritone. "No damage reported, but I'm having Chief Engineer Conlon recalibrate the warp coils." Although no engineer himself, Gold knew well enough that the wave, moving through subspace instead of normal space, wouldn't have affected the *da Vinci* at all if the warp coils hadn't resonated with it and transmitted the shock to the ship. Any resultant misalignment would be minuscule, but if there was one thing Gold had already learned about Tev, it was that he was a perfectionist.

"Subspace shock?" Gomez asked with an air of dread. "Did a ship blow up?"

"The wave metric is wrong," Tev told her. "No engine signature, no magneton pulse." Efficient, too, to have evaluated and responded to the situation so quickly. "It reminds me of a warp-field collapse upon collision with a massive body, though."

The most massive body in the immediate area was the one where most of Gold's family, and a fair percentage of his species, lived. "Where did the shock wave come from?"

Tev's reply was prompt, but muted. "San Francisco, sir."

Gold stared for a second, then turned to Shabalala. "Get me Starfleet Command."

The city looked like a bomb had hit it.

Smoke and dust hung in the air, obscuring the sun. Buildings around the blast site stood empty, some burning, some teetering on the brink of collapse. Emergency crews, including S.C.E. units, worked with grim, determined efficiency.

It could've been far, far worse, thought Montgomery Scott as he surveyed the scene. The sinkhole region had still been largely unpopulated. And transporter grids, both civilian and Starfleet, had been able to lock onto buried survivors and beam them promptly to hospitals across the western seaboard. But dozens of people— cleanup crews, surveyors, geo-engineers, and gawkers—

were still unaccounted for. More than a few had been S.C.E. personnel. Scotty knew from experience—too much of it—that the number would likely fall as more information was gathered; but however low it went, it would still be far too many.

Perhaps the worst damage was to the spirit of the San Franciscans. Their postwar sense of security and comfort had been shattered in an instant. Thousands stood outside the force-field cordons, gazing on in fear or bewilderment or anger, while children cried and asked their parents why this was happening again, or whether another war had begun. Nobody had any answers for them. Scotty hoped to change that, with the help of his S.C.E. crews.

So far the one clear thing was that it hadn't been a bomb. Instead, in the middle of a new crater blown in the side of the sinkhole, there was . . . a *thing*. A stout domed structure eight stories tall, its fluid contours declaring an unearthly origin. The blast damage had been done by its impromptu arrival, rather than by any explosive reaction.

An image came to Scotty's mind—the distress signal from Intar months ago, showing the devastation wrought when the Omearan Starsearcher *Friend* had crashed into their capital city. The Intarians had been lucky, he'd reflected at the time, that the ship had been traveling relatively slowly. If a vessel that massive had hit at full impulse, a quarter lightspeed, it would've been a dinosaur-killer of a blast. That was why almost every spacefaring world—including Intar now, belatedly—had a damned good planetary defense grid. The Breen fleet that had attacked Starfleet HQ had sacrificed half its ships just to break through Earth's defense grid, even with the advantage of their energy dissipators.

"And that's what doesn't make sense!" Scotty insisted to the two men who walked through the disaster zone alongside him: Starfleet Admiral William Ross, the decorated Dominion War commander, and Cemal Iskander, the civilian Director of Earth Security. "My crews rebuilt that defense grid stronger and better than ever, upgraded with the finest sensors and countermeasures ever devised. No cloak ever made could slip by it. A Denebian dust mite could not get through, not without setting off every alarm from here to Neptune's nether regions. I'd stake my life on it!"

"I don't doubt you, Scotty," Iskander said. Indeed, the distinguished Turk had worked closely with Scotty in rebuilding the grid, and had proven a good sort to trade tall tales with, even if his faith kept him from enjoying a good bottle. "But then, how did it get here? Could it have stayed in warp until the actual moment of impact?"

"That would've set off the alarms even sooner."

"Could it have been *beamed* in somehow?" Ross asked.

Scotty shook his head. "A confinement beam strong enough to shove that much solid earth aside, that forcefully? That'd be a devil of a weapon in itself—why bother beamin' anything in with it?"

Iskander frowned. "Maybe as a warning—psychological warfare. Maybe this enemy wants to terrorize rather than simply destroy us—to cow us into accepting conquest, like the Dominion." He peered at the structure, though, as if expecting it to erupt at any moment. "But just dropping that in our laps as a statement isn't enough. The other shoe could fall any moment. That's why you've got to attack it now, Bill."

"And we know this is even a weapon, how?" came a

familiar, gruff voice. Scotty brightened to see David Gold and his team approaching.

Iskander was taken aback. "Look around you, Captain. . . ."

"Gold. David Gold. *Shalom*."

They shook hands. "*Merhaba*. As I said, look around. Our city is ablaze again. Does that look like a peaceful gesture to you?"

"In fact, it looks a little like the Starsearcher crash on Intar. That turned out to be an accident."

Right, Scotty remembered, it had been the *da Vinci* that he'd assigned to that mission.

"And how do you 'accidentally' slip through the most secure defense grid ever built, bypassing its every sensor mechanism?"

"I don't know, but my crew here is the most likely group to find out."

Iskander looked impatient. "Scotty, all respect to your people, but shouldn't they be working with the other S.C.E. teams on cleanup and ground stability? Even if we do risk the cautious approach," and his expression showed what he thought of that, "we have specialists who are better qualified to tell us about that thing."

"I can tell you one thing right now," said P8 Blue, startling Iskander, who'd overlooked her since she was down in crawl mode taking some low-angle seismic readings. The Nasat rose to full height to continue her report. "That object wasn't designed to arrive the way it did."

"We don't even know how it did arrive."

"We don't need to, not for this. The structure's not as badly damaged as the buildings around it, obviously, but it shows clear signs of stress. There are cracked support members inside, fatigue in several shell layers, and it's visibly crumpled at ground level." Scotty peered closely at its curves, but couldn't tell what was crumpled and what was intentional. But he wasn't a structural specialist like Blue. "The only reason it hasn't suffered worse is that it seems to be designed for a higher gravity than this, using dense materials such as cortenum."

"Then there's the inside," said Tev, holding up a tricorder with a cross-section display. "Clearly designed for habitation, but not for ferrying troops. The compartment size, corridor layout—they'd be too spread out, take too long to get to battle stations or exits. And there's nothing that looks like a weapon."

Good man, Scotty thought. Tev wasn't a tactical specialist like Fabian Stevens, but he was nearly as much a "Renaissance man" as Spock himself had been. Scotty had hand-picked him for this assignment, knowing only the best could hope to make up for Duffy's loss.

Stevens, however, looked a little annoyed, as though Tev had stolen his lines. "And the very fact that we can scan inside," he added, "means there isn't any substantial shielding."

"Obviously," said Tev dismissively. "More importantly, it suggests the structure wasn't designed for combat."

Stevens glared. "I was getting to that."

"What about life signs, though?" Iskander asked. "We can't get a clear read. They might be shielding the occupants."

"Or they could all have been killed on impact, and we're just reading residual heat and organic residue," Stevens replied.

"Besides," chimed in Carol Abramowitz, the team's cultural specialist, "if this structure were intended as a warning in itself, I doubt it would look so . . . placid and soft. Most species would symbolize aggression with sharper, more angular designs. And if something within it, rather than the structure itself, is the message, then it probably would've emerged by now."

Scotty beamed. "Cemal, there are no better specialists around for this sort of thing than this bunch before you. Explorin' dangerous alien whatsies, findin' out if they're safe and makin' 'em safe if they're not—that's what S.C.E. teams like theirs are all about. And there's no team I'd rather have here than this one. The best thing about this whole mess is that these lads and lassies are here to straighten it up. So let them do their job," he said, addressing Admiral Ross as well now. "Send them in."

"This was the team that brought back the old *Defiant* and averted a war with the Tholians," Ross told Iskander. "I have every confidence in them."

The director was hesitant. "We still don't know what dangers there might be in there. Surely this is a job for Starfleet Security."

"You rang?" Domenica Corsi strode forward, seemingly towering over Iskander, though they were comparable in height. She made her case just standing there. The security team behind her, and the sizable phaser rifles they all carried, didn't hurt either.

Iskander sighed. "Very well. I concur. But may Allah protect you all."

CHAPTER
2

The comm screen in the O'Brien household had been tuned to the newsfeeds ever since the disaster struck. But Keiko had grown tired of the images and taken Molly into her room to brush her hair. The nine-year-old had protested that she was old enough to do it herself, but Keiko felt a strong need to be with her children right now, to take care of them, to keep them close and at least *feel* like she was protecting them.

Besides, she knew what was coming. What Miles was about to do. And she didn't want to be in the room when he made the call, didn't want him to see her reaction.

Of course he came into Molly's room soon thereafter. The child fearlessly asked the question Keiko couldn't. "Are you gonna go help with the accident, Daddy?"

"That's right, dear. I just made the arrangements with Scotty's office, and they've given me an assignment."

"What about teaching your class?"

Miles shrugged. "The accident's kind of put things on hold today, honey. The Academy's not holding classes, so people can watch, and be together, and help if they can." He smirked. "Look at it this way—we both get the day off from school."

Molly pouted. "I *like* school. We're learning about subspace and warp engines, so I can be an engineer like my daddy!"

Miles wasn't falling for it. "And you like taking classes with that cute boy Masoud, don't you?" Molly blushed. "Well, maybe Mommy could invite a few of your class-mates over for a little home schooling today, how about it, honey?"

"Um . . . sure! That sounds fine!" Inwardly she winced. Why was she so bad at trying to sound sincere?

Of course Miles caught it instantly, peering at his wife in puzzlement. "Molly, why don't you go call your friends now?" He didn't have to ask the girl twice—she was out the door before he finished. "Keiko? What's wrong?"

She rose and turned away. "Oh, nothing's wrong. I'm just concerned about the . . . 'accident.' The attack. Whatever. I'm sure everybody is."

He put a reassuring hand on her shoulder. "Well, there's no real sign that it's an attack. The thing hasn't made any hostile moves—there aren't even any clear life signs from it. Anyway, Scotty's put Sonya Gomez's team on it, and I'm sure they'll clear it up in no time. I'm more concerned about the mess it's made of the city. There's damage all the way from Presidio Boulevard to the Marina. We may have to demolish some of the buildings that just got finished a few months ago, and there'll have to be a whole new geological survey, no telling what new instabilities the blast has caused, and—"

"Miles . . ."

"What?"

She quashed what she'd been about to say, and put on a calm face as she turned to him. "I'm sure you could do more good if you went ahead and started doing it, instead of standing here telling me about it. So why don't you just go ahead?"

He started to nod, but then sensed something from her and frowned. Trust him to be most sensitive to her feelings when she didn't want him to be. "That's not what you were going to say, is it?"

"It's all right, Miles—"

"No, it isn't." There was no anger in his voice, just pure openness and caring, which made it worse. "Honey, you know you can tell me anything." He tried so hard, Keiko thought, to keep things running smoothly, to avoid the kind of tensions they'd had in the past. The problem was, his efforts were undermining her efforts to do the same thing.

"It's nothing," she insisted. "It's silly and selfish and I don't want to bother you with it."

"Hey." He put his hands on her shoulders. "Nothing you think or feel is silly to me. Whatever it is, you can tell me. It's when we don't talk that things build up and cause problems." He gave her that adorable rakish grin. "Come on—if it's that silly just tell me and we'll have a good laugh."

He didn't seem to notice he was contradicting himself. It was the thought that counted, she supposed. Anyway, it was clear he wasn't going to drop this. She sighed. "I really didn't want to do this again."

"Do what?"

"Complain. I was always complaining back on DS9. You were doing an incredibly hard job in incredibly chaotic conditions and instead of being supportive I just kept whining about how unhappy I was."

"I never felt that," Miles said emphatically. "You had every right to be happy, to fill your own needs."

"But that meant going away from you, going off to Bajor. We spent so much time apart."

"It wasn't your fault. It was the place, that's all."

"That's just it! I was hoping that, once we came back to Earth, we could finally live a nice, quiet life together, concentrate on being close again."

"I want the same thing!" he assured her. "That's why I took the teaching job—so I'd have time for my family."

"And I do appreciate the intent, really."

"The *intent*?" he frowned.

"It's just that . . . no sooner did we get to San Francisco than you were off joining the repair crews, rebuilding the city. Or volunteering your time to help rebuild the defense grid."

Miles's gentle, understanding mood seemed to be fading, just as she'd feared. "Those were important jobs. They had to be done."

"Of course they did, but they weren't your responsibility anymore. Nobody ordered or even asked you to do these things. You promised we'd have a nice quiet life from now on, but you don't seem that interested in living one."

"I'm not doing these things for fun," he countered, his voice rising. "They *needed* every extra hand they could get."

"And I understand that, I do! But then there was the chaos from the gateways, and then the earthquake, and now this. Miles, every time there's a problem to fix, you go off and fix it, even though it isn't your responsibility. And I feel like I'm not seeing any more of you than I did back in the Bajoran system!"

"What are you saying? That I care more about my work than our marriage?"

"No, no, I'm not saying that."

"Everything I do out there, Keiko—every bit of it—is to keep you, Molly, and Yoshi safe. I can't do that by staying at home! This is what I have to contribute."

Now her voice was hardening despite herself. "I could understand that back on DS9. You were the chief of operations; you had an understaffed department in a remote outpost. But this is *Earth*, Miles. This is the capital of the Federation, the heart of Starfleet. There is more ability and brilliance concentrated here than anywhere else in the quadrant. You don't have to do it all yourself."

"So what do you want me to do?" he demanded. "Call up Starfleet and tell them I changed my mind? Back out of my commitment, my duty?"

"No. No, you've already made the arrangements; you have to go."

"Then why'd you dump this on me now?"

She gaped. "Because you *asked* me to! I didn't want to burden you with it. I *told* you you didn't want to hear it."

"Damn right I didn't! Too late now, though, isn't it?"

"Look, just—just go. They need you."

"That's right. They do." An awkward silence. "Good luck with Molly and the kids," he said curtly, and left.

Keiko winced and rested her forehead against the wall. "I *really* didn't want to do that anymore."

*   *   *

Sonya Gomez stared up at the alien structure with no idea what to do next.

Was there any more they could learn from outside? She couldn't think of a way. But did they dare attempt entry? Was it worth the risk? True, there wasn't any sign of hostile intent—not recognizably so, anyway—but who knew how they might react if they felt they were being invaded? If there was anyone there at all. And how could they know for sure unless they went in? But shouldn't they run every possible scan from outside to judge if it was safe?

She was thinking in circles, she realized. But her thoughts just seemed sluggish today, her creativity offline. *I've heard of writer's block—am I having engineer's block?*

Kieran would've had an idea. Kieran would've found some wisecrack to break the tension, make the problem seem smaller than it is and give us the confidence to face it. Kieran—

Kieran is gone. Stop it.

As if to drive the point home, Duffy's replacement—no, Commander Tev, she corrected herself, realizing she had to accept him on his own terms—approached her. "Commander, I recommend we proceed inside. There's nothing more to be gained by waiting."

She felt a twinge of resentment—who was this newcomer to tell her how to run an operation?—which fizzled in the face of her awareness that she wasn't doing so well on her own right now. And in the rather striking face of Corsi, a friend and proven veteran, who said, "I concur. If they don't want to come out and play, I say we start knocking."

"I've confirmed there's no match in the cultural databanks," Abramowitz added. "If there's more to learn about these people, we need to go to the source."

"True—Abramowitz and Faulwell should be on the team," Tev recommended.

"Sure, makes sense." Sonya nodded absently.

"One catch, though." That was Vance Hawkins, Corsi's deputy chief. "The readings show a synthetic gravity field over three times Earth normal in there. We'll hardly be able to move."

"Speak for yourself," Pattie chimed in (with actual chimes, no less, or at least that was how the Nasat's voice sounded).

"Ahh, I think I may have a solution for that wee problem," came Scotty's unmistakable brogue. "With some help from a laddie I think some'a you know. Obie?"

"Commander Gomez!" came yet another brogue, one Sonya knew. She turned, and was startled to behold a familiar face over Scotty's shoulder—a broad, rough, comfortably lived-in face, like an old teddy bear with its fur worn off from frequent attention.

"Chief O'Brien!" she exclaimed, her mood actually brightening a bit.

Stevens laughed. "Or should we call you 'Professor' now?"

"Fabian!" exclaimed Miles Edward O'Brien, heartily returning his handshake. "It's Old Home Week."

"Been too long, Chief," Stevens said, apparently forgetting his own question. "But that just means you've finally got some stories I haven't already heard a dozen times."

"Ahh, my life is boring now. *Good* and boring," he corrected quickly. "A cushy teaching gig, plenty of time for the wife and kids, no Jem'Hadar shooting at me . . ."

"You must be hating every moment of it."

"No!" O'Brien insisted firmly, even though Stevens

had been joking. "I've never been happier. Though, well, I'll admit it's nice to get back in the saddle for a bit, work alongside the old gang. Just for a bit, though." He sobered. "I just wish Duffy could be here too. I'm so sorry, Commander," he told Sonya.

"That's all right," she demurred, really not wanting to face it again. "So what are you doing here?"

"Well, there's a little project I've been working on lately—really some of my students came up with it, but I've been helping out. It's a sort of antigravity suit, designed to allow mobility in high-gee environments. The prototypes are a bit bulky, I'm afraid, but they should let us move freely in there."

"'Us'?" asked Stevens. "Are you joining the team?"

"With the commander's permission, of course. But you'll need me in there if the suits need adjusting or something."

"You mean like if they break down, as prototypes have a way of doing?" Corsi asked, skeptical as always of engineers and their experiments.

O'Brien seemed a bit intimidated by his first good look at the statuesque blonde, but then most people were. He recovered quickly, though. "Not on my watch, Commander."

"We're glad to have you, Chief," Sonya told him. Except why did it have to be O'Brien? Looking at him just reminded her of her days back on the *Enterprise*, when she and Kieran had first dated. But she kept that to herself. It wasn't his fault. It was just so frustrating—she'd committed to moving on with her life, but the universe kept throwing her reminders of what she'd lost.

Tev stepped forward. "Commander, will you be leading the team, or shall I?"

"If you don't mind, Commander," Scotty interposed,

"I'd like to borrow Mr. Tev here. Stevens too. Some of us should stay out here and do some brainstormin', try to figure out how this bloody big bauble did what it did. I have a few thoughts, but I'd like some strong theoretical minds to help me out—tactical minds, too, in case Cemal's right and this is some kind of attack."

Gomez nodded. "All right, that sounds fine."

"One more question, Commander," said Tev.

"Yes?"

He faced her squarely. "I was told I would be the *second* officer on this crew. Following your leadership. But you have yet to offer any. Will I have to carry that load for you? Not that I'm not capable, of course. I just need to know what's required of me."

"Hey!" Stevens cried. The whole team bristled, but he was the one who strode forward to confront the Tellarite. "You have no right to talk to her that way. She's just lost someone very special to her. Special to all of us."

"Then if she's not ready to resume her duties, she should still be on leave."

"You are *so* out of line!"

"I?" Tev replied in cool disbelief. "Which of us has the officer's pins, *Specialist*?"

"Fabe—it's okay." Actually it wasn't; Sonya was angry inside. In place of Kieran, who would've supported her and cheered her up and made it all better, they'd stuck her with this smug, coldhearted . . . But no, that was unfair to Tev. She couldn't let herself resent him just because he wasn't Duffy. She had to give him every chance. "Mr. Tev is expressing a valid concern. Giving me something to think about. A little bluntness is a good way to do that. I'd prefer you to do it in private in the future, Tev, but I appreciate your input." She smiled politely, extending a hand.

Tev glared at it as though she were making a rude gesture with it. "With your leave, Commander," he said stiffly, "we all have work to do."

She controlled her reaction tightly. "Dismissed," she said through clenched teeth. *Damn—why does this keep getting harder?*

Corsi squirmed within her antigrav suit, tugging at the collar. "Sorry if it's a bit snug, Commander," O'Brien said.

"It's not that," she replied. "Do we really need these cowls? They restrict head movement. Not good if something's sneaking up behind us."

"Well, without it your head would be three times heavier than normal. How easy would that be to move?"

"Point taken," Corsi said, and concentrated on tucking a loose strand of dirty-blond hair under the cowl. She checked over the rest of her security team—Vance Hawkins, Rennan Konya, and Ellec Krotine—to make sure they were properly suited.

Noticing her gaze upon him, Hawkins approached. "You sure you want us both to go in? Chief and deputy chief? I mean, shouldn't one of us stay behind in case . . . you know, if something should happen in there. . . ."

Ahh. Like most of the crew, Hawkins was still dealing with the losses they'd suffered. It had been particularly hard on security; only three of them, including Corsi and Hawkins, had come out alive. And Corsi doubted Hawkins's survivor's guilt was in any way helped by the irony that, after having been the *da Vinci's* resident punching bag on mission after mission, he'd come away from Galvan VI without a scratch.

"Listen, Hawkins," she said firmly. "Just because we

had a disaster last time out doesn't make it any more or less likely to happen this time. There's no reason to change the way we do things. We're security—we're always prepared for the worst, right?"

"Yes, sir," he replied, subdued.

"Besides—based on our track record, disasters only happen when *I'm* not there to stop them." Corsi had been in a coma during the worst of it, taken down by an alien light show that didn't even give her anything to shoot or kick at. Rationally, there was no cause to think she could've prevented things if she'd been conscious; but she just knew deep down that somehow she could've. *Right—like only Hawkins is dealing with survivor's guilt.* "So I'm sure as hell not gonna sit out here twiddling my thumbs."

"Me neither."

"Issue settled, then."

"Okay." They exchanged a look of mutual approval and support. Then Hawkins sidled closer and whispered, "One other thing, though."

"What?"

"It's about Konya. I mean, he's a nice guy and all, but . . . a Betazoid in security?"

Corsi smirked. "Hawkins, he *is* a Betazoid," she said in a normal tone. "Why whisper? He already knows what you think." Hawkins blushed, throwing a sheepish look at Konya, who waved back insouciantly. "All I can tell you is, he came through training with impressive marks, and recommendations from instructors I know and trust."

"Which doesn't necessarily mean anything out in the field."

"No. But we have to find out what he's made of sometime, so why not now?"

Hawkins granted her point, then awkwardly wandered over to Rennan Konya, whose large dark eyes met his expectantly. "Look . . ."

"It's all right," said Konya. "It's a perfectly understandable concern. Betazoids aren't known for our combat skills. I know I have to prove myself; I don't take it personally. Oh, and as for the other thing, don't worry—I can only read your surface thoughts. I'm not the most powerful telepath on Betazed."

"Then how did you know I was worried about that?"

"Because everyone is."

"Oh."

Corsi wondered if that made Hawkins more or less embarrassed.

"So," her deputy chief asked, "does that mean you don't feel people's pain? Is that why you can be in security?"

"Oh, I feel it, all right. My cognitive reading's average, but my empathy's just fine."

"Then how do you do your job?"

Konya looked at him contemplatively. "Why should causing pain and injury be necessary to preserve security?" he asked as though positing a topic for philosophical debate.

"Well . . . of course there's more to security than fighting. Crowd control, paramedic stuff, investigation—I bet you'd be great at interrogation, catching liars and such."

The lanky Betazoid shrugged. "I do okay."

"But if someone's coming at you and wants you dead, you have to fight back."

"Fight, yes. But inflict pain?" Konya shifted easily into a loose fighting stance. "Come on—attack me," he said, his tone as amiable and serene as ever.

Hawkins hesitated, so Corsi gave him a prompt. "Go on, Hawkins—I'd like to see for myself."

"Okay." Hawkins shrugged. "But you asked for it."

He didn't lunge blindly—Corsi had trained him too well. He read Konya's stance—some kind of judo variant, it seemed to Corsi, designed to turn his own attack against him with a minimum of effort. Sensible enough, given their difference in build, but Hawkins knew how to adjust to such tactics. *If the new guy wants to prove himself,* Corsi thought, *Hawkins will make him earn it.*

Moments later, he was on the ground, with Konya extending a hand to help him up. He took the hand, rose, then tried another throw.

And found himself facedown this time, his cheek a little scraped. "Ow," Konya said in sympathy. "Sorry, didn't see that pebble. Better than broken ribs, though, huh?"

This time Hawkins didn't try anything when he accepted Konya's hand up. "How?"

"Proprioception," Konya smiled. "The body's sense of its own position and movement. I've trained myself to tune into it, into the motor cortex rather than the cerebral cortex. I can feel the way your body moves as clearly as you can. I know your every move as soon as you start to make it, so I can evade it. I can sense your weak points, your most exposed moments. So I don't need to force my way through your resistance—I can find the attack that neutralizes you most effectively with the least damage."

"Neat trick," Corsi said icily. "But what if you're twenty meters away, a Nausicaan's about to disembowel your chief, and the only weapon you have is an antique plasma rifle that kills slow and burns like hell?"

Konya's calm wavered for the first time, the possibility clearly disturbing him. But he faced her squarely. "I'm committed to my duty, Commander, whatever the psychic cost to myself. But isn't good security procedure about averting such situations before they arise?"

"A nice idea in principle, but reality isn't so tidy."

"But if we're too quick to assume violence is necessary, will we try hard enough to find alternatives?"

Corsi loomed over him. "You want to avert violence, then you watch that lip, mister."

"Children!" The sharp bark came from Tev, who stood there with arms crossed, looking down his substantial snout at them even though they were all taller than he was. "If you're done playing, it's time to go."

Corsi had her expression composed by the time she turned to face the Tellarite second officer, but Konya's eyes widened at what she was thinking.

CHAPTER
3

The first thing Gomez realized when they entered the alien structure was that there were too many tall people on her team. O'Brien, Bart Faulwell, and three of the four security guards—the exception being Krotine, a wiry Boslic with golden skin and cherry-red hair beneath her gravsuit cowl—were nearly scraping their heads against the ceilings, and having to duck through doorways. "This may not have been designed by humanoids," Abramowitz observed.

"There are short humanoid species," O'Brien observed. "Like Ferengi, or Kaldun."

"But the corridors and doorways are wide and arched as well," Abramowitz went on. "And the door controls don't seem to be shaped for a humanoid hand."

"That makes sense, doesn't it?" Faulwell asked. "That high-gravity dwellers would be shorter than most species?" That was one blessing—O'Brien's gravsuits worked like a charm, making them feel they were walking in normal gravity—although the tight suits did restrict movement somewhat, and they had to keep a firmer grip on their tricorders.

"Not necessarily," Gomez said absently. "Long limbs would give you more leverage for fighting higher gravity."

"Sometimes," Pattie said. "But it's important to stay low so falls don't hurt as much. As for the leverage, well, you don't think all these legs are just for sex appeal, do you?"

Somehow Pattie's joke fell flat. In fact, all their conversation was feeling a little strange, full of awkward pauses, as though everyone's timing was off. Gomez realized what it was—everyone kept expecting to hear a patented Duffy wisecrack, and got thrown off when none came.

"You know, I think Stevens and Commander Tev were right," O'Brien ventured as they entered a new chamber. "This doesn't look anything like a troop carrier or any kind of military facility. There's practically no internal security." He looked down the length of the room, which contained several tiers of low tables facing a podium of sorts at the front. "And I'll turn in my teaching credentials if this doesn't look like a classroom."

"Then where are the chairs?" Corsi asked. "All this gravity and nowhere to sit?"

"Maybe they sit on the floor, like in Japan," Abramowitz suggested.

O'Brien grunted. "Keiko's decorated the house with a Japanese theme. Tatami mats, low tables, the works. Looks nice and all, and the kids love having things on their level—but my back hasn't been the same since." He threw Gomez a long-suffering grin. "The things we do for love, eh, Commander?"

"Wha—? Oh. Sure," she said distantly.

The grin changed to apology. "Oh . . . sorry, Commander. I didn't mean to hit a sore spot."

She offered an apologetic look right back. "It's okay, Chief. You're lucky you have someone like that."

"Well, most of the time," he grimaced. "Some days are better than others, and sometimes . . . but, well, that's nothing next to what you must . . . umm . . . I'll scout on ahead, if it's all right with you, Commander."

"Go on, Chief. Thank you."

"Hawkins, Krotine, go with him," Corsi ordered, coming up alongside Gomez. Once they'd gained some privacy, the taller woman asked, "Are you okay?"

Gomez frowned. "You mean, am I too distracted? Not showing enough leadership?"

Corsi bristled a bit, then reversed herself, speaking with a softness few people heard. "I mean, are you okay?"

Now it was Gomez's turn to be embarrassed. She'd forgotten—this wasn't just "Core-Breach" Corsi, the coldhearted, no-nonsense security chief. This was her friend Domenica, with whom she'd been through hell recently. (Come to think of it, after what had happened at Galvan VI, maybe it was time to retire that "Core-Breach" nickname—it wasn't very funny anymore.)

"I don't know, Domenica," she sighed. "I mean, I've grieved. God, how I've grieved. I got it all out, I worked through it like they say, I felt better, all . . . cathartized and everything. Is that a word?"

"Hell if I know. Faulwell's the linguist, not me."

"So I got through it, came out the other end, decided, you know, it's time to move on. Kieran's gone. I accept the loss. It still hurts like hell, but I accept it, and it's in the past, and what I need to do now is focus on the future. On rebuilding my life."

"Sounds like a plan."

"Yeah, but . . ." She gazed up at Corsi imploringly. "*I don't know how*. I look at my life, at the pieces that are left, and I don't know how to put them together into something new. They just . . . don't fit. Because there's this one huge piece that's missing, that's never going to be there again. And without that piece, none of the others make sense." She shook her head. "The strange thing is . . . even when Kieran was around, I wasn't really sure how he fit into my life."

Corsi smirked. "He wasn't exactly a standardized component."

"Yeah, I guess they broke the mold after they made him."

"After? I was thinking before."

Gomez glared . . . but saw a rare flash of humor and understanding in Domenica's ice-blue eyes. She was mocking her own past disapproval of Duffy, and thus in an odd way apologizing for it. Sonya accepted the apology with a look, knowing she wouldn't want to make a big deal out of it. "Whatever. All I know is, as little sense as our relationship made to me, my life makes no sense without it. I just don't know what to do next."

Corsi mulled it over. "Well, I'll tell you this, Commander: I've seen you take a meaningless jumble of parts and build them into something functional more times than I can count. Even if they were missing the most important piece, you found something that'd do the trick in its place, or a way to rearrange things so it wasn't needed after all."

"Yeah, but that's engineering. This is life, and emotion, and . . . it's not the same thing."

"So I keep telling you guys. Well, except for the emotion part. We all know I don't have any."

"Of course not." Gomez smiled.

"Well, maybe the thing to do is start with what's in front of you. You've got a job to do. A team to lead and protect. Maybe a city or a planet to keep safe. Focus on solving their problems—maybe it'll be a start to solving your own. At least . . ." She faltered, shrugged a bit. "At least it'll distract you from your own, and sometimes that's enough."

Gomez looked at her thoughtfully for a moment, until Corsi fidgeted and shook her head. "Hell, I don't know. First Stevens, now you—do I look like a counselor?"

"All right." Gomez clasped her shoulder briefly, but her voice was businesslike. "So we have this job to do. This place to explore."

"Yes, we do. And since you brought it up, Commander," Corsi went on, becoming all business again, "*do* we have any sort of a plan, or are we wandering aimlessly? A little more leadership actually wouldn't hurt about now."

Gomez accepted the chastisement. "You're right. We need to find the answers to some questions," she went on more loudly, taking in the rest of the team. "Like, where is everybody? We've found plenty of sleeping quarters, cafeterias, and the like, but we haven't seen any people."

"They *were* here," Konya said, "and not long ago." He gestured to his tricorder. "The DNA residue's still fresh, and there are still heat signatures in the floor, like someone was sitting or walking on it. Odds are they were here until just before the thing appeared—maybe even shortly after."

"Well, the building was damaged in the blast," Abramowitz said. "Maybe they evacuated."

"To where?" Corsi asked. "Out into the caverns? They'd have been spotted."

"Beamed out?" asked Pattie.

"Again, to where? And how could they do it unde-tected? Certainly no hostile ship could've gotten close enough to beam them without being intercepted first."

Gomez changed tacks. "Bart? Have you been able to get any information from their writing?"

The middle-aged linguist shook his head. "It's hard to translate writing without some context, without know-ing anything about the spoken language, the species doing the writing. I can tell you what symbols mean 'open door' and 'close door,' but extrapolating further meaning would take a lot of time, trial and error. I'll be more help if we can meet somebody who'll talk to us."

Gomez sighed. So much for constructive leader-ship—she couldn't accomplish much if the universe didn't give her anything to work with. "Okay, I guess we'll just keep looking. Maybe Scotty's team outside will have better luck figuring this thing out."

Blasted meetings, thought Scotty as he strode into Cemal Iskander's mobile command center, where he'd been summoned by the director. *Waste of time, the lot of them.* "I'm not a spring chicken anymore, y'know! I can't be bothered wastin' what time I've got left in meet-ings!" He barely noticed his transition from thinking it to saying it aloud, or cared much. One advantage of being a Living Legend, and just generally an Old Cuss, was that you could get away with telling people exactly what you thought, even when they outranked you. That was a lesson he'd learned from Leonard McCoy—

though come to think of it, Leonard had been just as outspoken at forty.

"I think you'll find this a productive meeting, Scotty," said Iskander, who sat behind a central desk filled with monitors and readouts, while Admiral Ross and Captain Gold stood nearby. "We've been contacted by someone with information about the alien construct. A member of a species called the Nachri. Ever heard of them?"

"Nachri . . . Nachri," Scotty repeated, the aspirated "ch" fitting neatly into his brogue. "It sounds familiar."

"Probably from history class," Gold told him. "If I remember right, they were a little before your time—a two-bit empire the Federation ran up against in the late twenty-second century. I think Starfleet had a hand in overthrowing their government."

"That's right," Ross said, reading from a file he'd called up on his padd. "That was before the Prime Directive was firmly established. Starfleet backed a rebel movement that drove out the dictatorial, expansionist regime and set up a representative government. They've pretty much kept to themselves ever since, declining to join the Federation, though we've had a friendly trade relationship the whole time. Yes, I remember now; they supplied some relief materiel during the war. Nothing combat-related, though; they've left that pretty far behind."

"So you'd say they're trustworthy?" Iskander asked.

"Worth hearing out at least," said Gold.

"That's my conclusion too. I have their representative standing by." He opened the comm channel. Replacing the Federation seal on the big screen was the image of a tall, sleekly built humanoid covered in short gray fur. His head was somewhat avian, with a beaklike muzzle underneath a pair of large eagle eyes, and topped by a triangular, pterosaurian fin. He wore a uniform and seemed to be seated on a starship bridge.

"My prayers to you all in your time of crisis," he began in a rich baritone. *"I am Captain Zakash of the Nachri Defense Group."*

Iskander returned the greeting and introduced the others with him.

"As I told your director earlier," Zakash went on, *"we observed the news broadcasts of the San Francisco catastrophe and immediately recognized the design of the alien structure. We are already en route to Earth and eager to offer our assistance against this enemy."*

"Enemy?" Iskander repeated intently. "So it is a hostile force?"

"Yes," he told them solemnly. *"Their species is named the Shanial. They are ruthless, hideous creatures, too alien to coexist with species like yours and mine."*

Scotty frowned at that, and noticed Gold doing the same.

"My people had the misfortune of encountering them early in our interstellar age, before we met the Federation. These large domes would mysteriously appear on our colony worlds, displacing the surrounding earth and atmosphere to produce a devastating shock—an opening blow against population, infrastructure, and morale. The structures are at once a kind of homing beacon and staging area, a ready-made base for launching their invasion when they arrive soon thereafter. This is why we immediately launched our Defense Group toward Earth—you have limited time before the invasion begins."

"I knew it," Iskander exclaimed, though his voice remained level; he was too good a Muslim to let anger overcome him.

"But why wait so long before attacking?" asked Ross.

"Presumably so that you will let your guard down."

"Then why get it up in the first place with this initial attack? Why ruin the element of surprise?"

Zakash fidgeted. *"Who can understand the motives of such alien creatures? They do not think the way we do. I concede we can only speculate about their motives, but their actions are clear."*

"How come we never heard about this Shanial menace?" inquired Gold.

"We fought a fierce war against them over two centuries ago," Zakash told him. *"It was that struggle that began our conquering period. We finally drove them from our space, but had become so used to fighting,"* he went on ruefully, *"that we just kept at it, finding new enemies to battle even after the original foe had vanished."*

"Vanished?" Gold echoed.

"Yes, Captain. They abandoned their strongholds, disappeared back to wherever they came from. I see now they were just biding their time. Perhaps seeing a prime target like the Federation, still weakened by recent warfare, has renewed their appetite for conquest."

"You see, Bill?" Iskander said. "It's as I've said. Now more than ever we must remain alert to enemies, to vultures hoping to prey on our weakness. The struggle to preserve our way of life is never-ending."

"Captain Zakash," Scotty asked, "do you know how they pull off their appearin' act?"

"Our scientists never fully determined that, but our analyses from the time are at your disposal. Together, hopefully, we can find a way to defeat them once and for all."

"And can you tell me . . . if these structures are designed for poppin' in and blastin' away the earth around them, how come they aren't built to handle such a shock? And how come they aren't defended? Surely after the first attacks, you'd have blasted the later ones as soon as they appeared."

Zakash had grown increasingly impatient as Scotty spoke. *"Director, why are we wasting time with all these questions? I'm sure my technical people and yours can work these side issues out later. Right now there is imminent danger."*

"I agree," Iskander said. "There's a time for analysis and a time for action. Captain Zakash, your Defense Group is welcome, as is your assistance."

"We should be there within three hours," Zakash assured him. *"Defense Group out."*

Iskander turned to Ross. "Admiral, I recommend doubling the size of our defensive cordon around the Shanial structure."

"I'll begin the arrangements."

Turning to Scotty, Iskander added, "And Scotty, you should pull your team out. It's too dangerous for them to be in there."

"Cemal, they've seen no sign of any danger. The place is abandoned."

"You heard Zakash. The Shanial could materialize at any moment."

"Aye, I heard what he claimed. Whether I believe him—that's another matter."

Iskander frowned. "Scotty, I admit we only have his word to go on, but it's a word we have no reason to doubt—and can't afford to ignore. And one thing is clear—we have been struck a harsh blow. Dozens of innocent people have been killed, including some of your own." He strode over to a window, gestured out at the onlookers. "Look at that crowd. The people are angry, afraid. Less than a year has passed since the war, and now we've been assaulted again. Those people aren't going to be content to have us sit around asking questions—they want us to *do* something that will keep them safe. And I intend to heed their voices. That structure is dangerous, and the people who sent it are dangerous. That much is certain. We can sort out the reasons why later, but for now we have to protect ourselves. Pull out your team."

"Not without a clear and present danger, Cemal. We've got a transporter lock on 'em at all times. If things get hot, we'll pull them out in a jiffy. But unless that happens, I say they're in the best position to give us some real answers. To confirm Zakash's story—or not."

"I agree," Gold said. "They're my crew and my responsibility." He shook his head. "Lord knows, after what we've been through recently my first impulse is to yank them out at the first sign of trouble. But if I did that they'd never accomplish a damn thing. They go into danger because that's where they're needed, where they can do the most good. If I forget that . . . I betray the memory of all the ones who gave their lives doing good for others. I say they stay, as long as there's a chance they can help."

Stevens and Tev absorbed the information Scotty passed on to them (and to the rest of the team, over the open comm) with very different attitudes. Tev hardly seemed interested, concentrating more on reviewing the blast analysis they'd been working on when Scotty was called away. "How can you be so stoic?" Stevens asked the older officer. "It's just been confirmed that we're about to be attacked! I don't know many Tellarites who'd take that sitting down."

"First," Tev responded, "I have a job to do, and histrionics don't help. Second, it's been *alleged*, not confirmed. I don't place stock in intangibles—only in what I can handle, test, and prove. Third, I've been sitting less than you have—I should talk to the captain about enforcing the physical fitness requirements."

Stevens gapèd, but restrained himself from saying what he wanted to say. Not only was Tev his superior, but Scotty was standing right there and he didn't want to look bad in front of the big boss. Indeed, Scotty was chuckling. "He has a point about one thing, lad—all we have is one man's word."

"But why would he lie?"

The S.C.E. chief shook his silvery head. "That's for him to explain, if it turns out he is. All I know is, his story feels as phony as Harry Mudd's handshake."

"Leave the politics to those who can understand it, Specialist," Tev told him. "What we have here is a delightful engineering puzzle. How does an eight-story building appear out of nowhere?"

"Delightful?" Stevens echoed in disbelief. "Dozens of people died!"

"As they did on Maeglin, Eerlik, BorSitu Minor, Kursican, Sherman's Planet, and many other places the *da Vinci* has visited. Tragic, of course, but it doesn't change what we do—solve the puzzles the universe gives us. You can't tell me you don't enjoy the mental achievement." He grinned. "Have I thanked you for this assignment, Scotty? It's a dream job, the chance to go out there, pit my mind against the strangest technologies, the toughest crises. So much better than that laboratory job I almost took. Wonderful luck, that this position opened up when it did."

To hell with respect for superiors, Stevens thought—the self-satisfied look on Tev's face as he said that was the last straw. "That *position* opened up because my best friend died!" he shouted in Tev's face. "You think that's good luck? Do you?"

"How good is your luck, Specialist?" Tev fired back. "You'll need it if you persist in that tone."

Stevens felt Scotty's hand on his shoulder, his grip surprisingly firm. "Settle down, laddie. Tev didn't mean it that way."

"Yeah?" Stevens said, struggling to control himself. "Well, he could show a little more respect."

"Respect for the dead?" Tev asked. "A strange custom, since they don't care one way or the other."

"How about respect for the loss their friends are going through?"

Tev was silent for a moment, studying him thoughtfully. Then he turned away. "Not my business," he said brusquely. "I didn't know the man—can't offer any meaningful sentiments. So let's drop it and get back to work, shall we?" He grew animated again. "We have a mystery to solve. How do you penetrate a defense grid that can't be penetrated?"

After a moment, Scotty's eyes widened. "Maybe you don't!" At the others' puzzled looks, he said, "Think about it, lads! If it's here, inside the grid, and nothing can get through the grid from outside—"

It hit Stevens. "Then it wasn't outside to begin with!"

"Rather," said Tev pedantically, "it must have been placed here before the grid was erected."

Stevens glared, but he had greater concerns. "Could the Breen have left it during their attack? Are these Shanial allied with them?"

"I have a suspicion, lad," Scotty replied, "that it was here much earlier than that. Ask yerself—where did it burst from?"

"The sinkhole."

"Aye, and what was there before the ground caved in?"

"The Starfleet Museum."

"Exactly!" Scotty smirked. "Since becoming a historical relic myself, I've taken quite an interest in museums. I used to visit that one all the time. There was a wealth of alien artifacts there, some of which nobody ever figured out the use of. I spent many a day tryin' to eke out some answers of my own from 'em. Many of 'em are gone forever, alas—but many were just buried under the rubble."

Stevens frowned. "So what are you suggesting? That one of them was some kind of, maybe a wormhole terminus that opened up to let the structure through?"

"Aye, that's one possibility. I'm sure we can come up with dozens, just standin' here brainstormin'. But as an ancestor o' Mr. Spock's used to say, it's a mistake to theorize ahead o' the facts. I say we go to the new museum, study their records of the missing artifacts, and see what we can find that might give us a clue."

Gomez, listening in over the comm, had winced when Tev and Stevens had gone at it. She hadn't known which side to take—certainly Tev's callous cheerfulness infuriated her as much as it did Stevens, but she couldn't condone an enlisted crewman talking to an officer in that way. She could feel the knot forming in her shoulders, followed by a twinge of despair when she remembered Kieran's massages were a thing of the past now. She was grateful that Scotty had broken it up, and changed the subject back to business. "Good idea, sir," she told him after his museum suggestion. "We'll start scanning in here for any evidence of wormhole generators, or similar equipment."

"Keep an eye out for symbols, too," Faulwell suggested. "Perhaps something at the museum has similar markings to the ones we're finding here. I'll upload what I've scanned so far to your tricorder, Captain Scott."

"Good lad."

"Commander?" That was O'Brien, calling from a nearby intersection. "I'm scanning something strange here. A subspace reading I didn't get before."

Gomez and the others gathered around him, confirming the readings on their tricorders. "Was it shielded?"

"Hard to say. Maybe just too faint to read from a distance." They homed in on the signal and began moving toward it, fanning out as much as possible to get a better sensor baseline. O'Brien frowned as his tricorder brushed the corridor wall. "Hang on." He placed the sensor array against the wall. "The readings are stronger in the walls themselves."

"Are they generating it?" Corsi asked, looking around suspiciously.

"No, I don't think so . . . more like the subspace waves are being channeled through them, isolated within them, so that we didn't read them in the corridors."

"Like a light pulse in a fiber-optic cable," Gomez said.

"Exactly. The cortenum in the wall is confining them. We thought it was just for holding up against the gravity, but it's more like it's functioning as a gravitic wave guide. I think this whole structure is designed to channel gravimetric energies—which probably means it can create subspace distortions, like a warp coil."

"It should've been obvious," Gomez said, chastising herself. "The cortenum."

"Not really, Commander. Cortenum's useless for warp drive without verterium in the mix. As far as we knew, it was just inert building material."

"So this isn't a warp engine—but it must be something similar."

"Something that went in a different direction from our science."

"Never mind the lecture, Professor," Corsi said. "Are you telling us this whole structure around us is active, generating some space-warping effect?"

Gomez studied her own readings. "It looks more like a resonance—like it's picking up emissions from somewhere else, the way the *da Vinci*'s warp coils resonated with the blast. The actual source must be what the chief picked up before."

"Which means," Corsi said, "that we're close to the source." With a glance, she put her security team on heightened alert.

Soon they came to a large, heavy portal. Sonya placed her hand against the surface—it was literally vibrating with gravitic energies. "Bart, the control panel?"

Faulwell examined the markings and made some efforts to open the hatchway, with no success. "I don't think we're authorized users," he said dryly. "Perhaps the P-38s?"

"Try it." Gomez nodded to O'Brien and Pattie, who extracted their trusty door-openers from their kits and went to work.

"Just call me P-38 Blue," Pattie muttered.

"Where are we?" Abramowitz asked. "Within the structure, that is."

Gomez studied her map. "Pretty much dead center. No clear reading of what's inside—it scanned like a solid mass."

"Maybe . . ." O'Brien grunted as he strained at the portal. "Maybe an equipment core . . . with just some maintenance crawlways inside."

"Then why the big door?" Abramowitz asked.

"You're the culture maven, you tell us," Pattie said, not panting in the least, since her speech apparatus didn't depend on breath.

"Anyway," Gomez continued, "whatever's in there is no bigger than the *da Vinci*'s bridge. It's probably pretty important, though, considering—"

She cut off as the door finally sprang open. They gazed inside, to behold . . .

A huge indoor plaza, nearly as wide and high as the whole structure they were in, its roof supported by tier upon tier of heavy columns. Through the spaces between the columns could be seen large domelike buildings, braced with flying buttresses and holding thousands of windows, many lit from within. Between the buildings ran roadways that stretched into the distance.

They all just stared dumbly, until Corsi glared at the impossibility and cracked, "So—is that a city in your pocket, or are you just happy to see me?"

CHAPTER
4

The team advanced cautiously into the city—indeed, that was the only word for it. Corsi left Konya and Krotine to guard the door. Looking back, they saw that it was one of numerous such portals in a domelike structure some six meters high and twelve wide, serving as the base of one of the many columns that bore the weight of the roof twenty-five meters above.

"Are we . . . still on Earth?" Abramowitz asked as she gazed wide-eyed around her.

"Maybe it's an illusion," Hawkins suggested. "A holodeck simulation."

"I'm not reading any photonic fields or projections," O'Brien told him. "As far as the tricorder can tell, this is just what it looks like—a whole city, kilometers wide."

"And I'm getting plenty of life readings now," Corsi warned. "Nothing the tricorder recognizes. And something's making it hard to pin down positions."

"Must be the cortenum in the walls," Sonya said, "scattering the signals."

"I don't care how it works, I just don't like it. I'm going to be predictable here and suggest extreme caution."

Naturally, it was then that the shooting started. "You think?!" O'Brien cried as he ducked behind a column.

Corsi let her tricorder drop, trusting her eyes more, watching for the source of the beams. More blasts came, from a low angle, and she returned fire, but not before one particle stream hit Vance Hawkins in the leg. He cried in pain and dropped. Corsi afforded him a brief glance—he was moving, but still in the line of fire. "Konya! Get Hawkins to safety. Krotine, cover fire!"

Sonya struck her combadge. "Gomez to Gold, we need emergency beam-out!" Nothing. "Gomez to Scott! Gomez to Starfleet HQ, come in, emergency!" Nothing and more nothing. "Damn—we're cut off!"

Fabian Stevens was no racist. He'd never approved of the occasional wisecracks he heard about the Tellarites' resemblance to Terrestrial pigs. Few people in this day and age meant anything truly malicious by it, but even the casual jokes and swine-related nicknames struck Stevens as insensitive and disrespectful to an entire species (though, come to think of it, that attitude in itself was probably unfair to pigs, who were surely perfectly decent sorts once you got to know them). Indeed, that was part of what had prompted his interest in Tellarite culture, his desire to learn about their full depth and texture as a people. (Said interest, of course, had led to a rather unfortunate incident in a bar, thus providing Kieran Duffy with one of his favorite stories to tell.)

Even with his personal dislike of Tev, Stevens still would've objected to anyone making a porcine slur against him. Generally he could never resist a bad pun, but he'd never even *think* of accusing Tev of hogging the glory, or of saying there was something not quite kosher about him. No, the thought would never cross his mind.

Nonetheless, the metaphor came to him unbidden: As they surveyed the exhibits in the Alien Technologies wing of the new Starfleet Museum, Tev looked as happy as a hog in a wallow. His deep-set eyes gleamed as they roved over alien devices whose function remained unknown, burning with the desire to dissect them and extract their secrets. He clearly had great enthusiasm for the S.C.E.'s work, and Stevens figured he deserved some credit for that. But it seemed to be the only thing Tev *did* give a damn about, and Stevens didn't see any way he could work with the man. Let Tev go off on his own one-man team—he sure seemed to think he could do it all himself. Probably everyone would be better off that way.

At least Tev spreads the wealth around, Stevens thought. As if condescending to his own crewmates weren't enough, he was now haranguing the museum's assistant curator, a bearded, professorial man named Sutherland, about the inaccuracies in some of the artifact descriptions. "He can never resist telling anyone how brilliant he is, can he?" Stevens asked Scotty.

The older man shrugged it off. "Och, you know how it is with Tellarites. Honest to a fault. To them, courtesy and tact are just other words for lies. I find it refreshing myself."

"Why am I not surprised?" Stevens said.

"And modesty's no different. Tev's just bein' forthright about himself. If it comes off as superior, it's because, bottom line, he *is* one o' the very best. What, ye think I'd assign anything less to fill poor Duffy's shoes?" Stevens winced, and Scotty peered closer. "Och, I get it. Of course this isn't about his bein' a Tellarite."

"Of course not. I like Tellarites. They tell it like it is, just like you say. Makes them a very . . . dramatic people."

"What it's really about, then," Scotty went on, "is that he's not Duffy."

"It's not just that. He's the *anti*-Duffy. Duffy was a nice guy, easygoing, friendly. He made the team like a family. It's not just—with all due respect, sir, it's not just technical know-how that makes a good team member."

"Are you sayin' I chose badly, then?" When Scotty wanted, that avuncular twinkle in his eye could become a cutting laser. Stevens fidgeted under it for a moment, until Scotty chuckled and released him from the stare. "Fabian, lad, let me tell you somethin'. If I gave you a second officer like Duffy was, you'd keep expectin' him to *be* Duffy. Which would not be fair to him—or her— and would be terrible for the team, because you'd keep on strivin' after a rapport that's gone forever, and you'd never find your stride again. This way you can make a fresh start, and find a new balance."

"You make it sound so easy," Stevens said. "But then, what would you know about it? Someone on the *Enterprise* crew died, they always managed to come back to life. Hell, you were resurrected twice! What, did you guys do the Grim Reaper a favor or something?"

Scotty's anger returned, for real this time. "Don't you dare tell me I never lost anyone, Mr. Stevens! I lost dozens of good people on the *Enterprise*. Engineers like Harper, Compton, Watkins, and Cleary. Friends like Gary Mitchell and Bob Tomlinson. My own nephew died in my arms! Aye, I'm blessed that a few of my closest friends are still with me, but when I woke up from that transporter beam, it was like almost everyone I'd ever known had died all at once. So don't you presume to tell me I don't understand what it means to lose someone!"

They were both very quiet for a time after that. Finally Stevens met Scott's eyes in silent apology and entreaty, and asked in a very small voice, "So how do you manage it?"

The anger in Scotty's eyes turned to a deep sadness. "I'm afraid experience is the only way. You just have to get through it and out the other side."

"But then what do you do?"

Scotty smiled understandingly. "You find something new. Something to build, something to fix . . . something to give yer life meaning. That's why I took Admiral Ross's offer to join the S.C.E.—better than wallowing in nostalgia."

"But how meaningful can it be if it's going to be lost sooner or later too?"

"It doesn't have to last to have meaning, lad! Every moment it brings you a sense of accomplishment, of success, of makin' entropy's work just a wee bit harder—that's all the meaning you need."

Scotty clapped Stevens's shoulder, and the younger man smiled in thanks. Then he shook off the moment. "Okay, that's all well and good. But how do you fit Tev into that equation? He's just impossible to get along with." Stevens saw that Tev was starting back toward them, and lowered his voice. "I don't see myself building anything useful with him. There's no way he could be part of any rapport."

"That's what I thought about a certain Vulcan when I first met him oh, a lifetime or four ago. Not to mention a certain doctor with such a mouth on him I wondered he hadn't been kicked outta Starfleet the first day." He winked. "Tension's a force like any other, lad. The trick is simply findin' how to make it useful."

Stevens was skeptical, but said nothing, since Tev was arriving. "Despite the mislabelings," the Tellarite told them, "we can be confident nothing's missing from the AT collection that fits our parameters."

"Aye," Scotty sighed. "'Twas a long shot."

"Not necessarily. Alien devices aren't always recognizable as such." He showed them a padd containing a lengthy catalog of items and their descriptions. "A list of all missing alien artifacts, even those not clearly technological." Stevens groaned inwardly at the added work. At least this was one difference between Tev and Duffy that should work in his favor: Tev seemed to revel in research. He'd probably be glad to carry most of the workload himself.

Indeed the Tellarite did throw himself eagerly into the research, but it didn't make things any easier for Stevens, since he had to struggle to keep up, checking items that Tev then double-checked. When his pace flagged, the second officer prodded him to work harder, which, on top of his constant kibitzing of Stevens's conclusions, just made the human more and more frustrated. Only Scotty's weather eye upon him kept him from erupting. He just couldn't understand how this kind of tension could produce any beneficial results.

Just as Stevens was becoming convinced they were on a wild-goose chase, Scotty perked up as something in the catalog caught his attention. "Hang on a minute!"

"Sir?"

Scotty showed the padd to the curator, Sutherland. "Can you show us where these are kept?"

"Ah, yes, the Cabochons. This way, please. We, um, have them in storage. Much of the museum is still under construction, and the, ah, flashier items tend to take priority. A shame, really—I've always felt they were an intriguing mystery."

Stevens was feeling the same way about now. "Sir, what are these . . . Cabochons?"

"Ah," Sutherland said. "A set of small crystal spheres discovered on a dead planet in the Beta Aquilae sector in the 2180s, by the starship *Knossos*, I believe. Presumably created by that planet's civilization, but the planet had suffered some total cataclysm, wiping out all other signs of their presence. To this day we don't know by whom they were made, or how, or even what they're made of."

"Aye," Scotty said intently. "They canna be scanned clearly due to some kinda low-level subspace interference."

"And what does that tell us?" Stevens asked.

"I'm not sure." Scotty frowned. "There's something on the tip of my mind, something familiar about the interference patterns."

Sutherland led them through the museum archives, finally reaching a shelf from which he extracted a box not much bigger than a standard engineer's tool kit. He opened it to reveal a set of fourteen glassy orbs of various sizes, though none larger than a racquetball. Stevens peered into their deep red interiors, intrigued by their inner facets, which seemed to extend to infinity. "I don't get it. I thought we were looking for missing items."

"Ah, but two of them are missing, including the largest one," Sutherland told him sadly. "These were all we could recover."

Tev was scanning them with his tricorder. "The interference pattern *is* familiar, Scotty. It reminds me of the subspace shockwave that hit the *da Vinci*."

Scotty examined the tricorder readings, a gleam coming into his eye. "No doubt, laddie, but that's not what I saw in it. Look closer—doesn't that remind you of anything else?"

Tev frowned. "Some kind of primitive warp equation—Alcubierre, perhaps?"

"More like Van Den Broeck."

"What are you talking about?" asked Stevens.

"I take it," Tev said pedantically (and predictably), "that you're not up on the history of warp theory."

"I'm a hands-on kind of guy, Commander. I leave theory to the ivory-tower types."

"Ahh, that's how I used to think," said Scotty. "But once I woke up from my seventy-five-year nap and saw how much learnin' I had to catch up on, I figured I might as well brush up on the basics.

"Ye see, lad . . . the problem with the earliest warp theories is that generatin' the warp bubble would've taken more energy than the universe contains." Scotty chuckled. "This was before Cochrane figured out how to tweak the subspace geometry and change the constants. Anyway, one o' the proposed solutions was to make the warp bubble dimensionally transcendental. Big as a ship on the inside, smaller than an atom on the outside."

Stevens's eyes widened. "Of course! If the Shanial structure was in a microwarp bubble like that, and the field collapsed . . . my God, it'd be just like what happened. It'd expand from a point to full size in an instant, blasting away everything around it with incredible force."

"Aye. The microwarp equations turned out to be useless for propulsion—for one thing, you'd be smaller than a wavelength of light and couldn't see a thing—so they were abandoned when subspace theory came along. But who's to say they couldn't be used to shrink somethin' into a *static* microbubble?"

"You mean . . . like a subspace compression!" Stevens interpreted. "Like that time on DS9 when they shrank the *Rubicon* by folding most of its mass into subspace."

"Aye," Scotty chuckled. "I heard about that. A wild tale, that one. I never would've believed it if we hadn't run into such a trick back on the old *Enterprise*—a scoundrel name o' Flint shrank the whole ship down into a trophy for his shelf. Lucky for him he froze us in time, too, or you can be sure I'd'a sent a phaser beam right up his haughty snoot."

Stevens smiled politely. Even though he'd seen plenty of strange things himself, he felt Scotty's yarns always had an air of the tall tale about them. Tev simply ignored them both and focused on the problem at hand. "So you're saying the Cabochons are some kind of static warp-field generators, containing these microbubbles?"

"Aye. It all fits. Which means they cannot be part of a Breen attack—they've been on Earth for two hundred years already."

"But that was about when the Nachri drove off the Shanial," Stevens countered. "Maybe they've been lying in wait all this time. Maybe they're the kind of species that thinks in the long term."

"Maybe," Scotty said with a skeptical squint. "But consider for a minute, lad, what might happen to a static warp bubble if it were hit by . . . oh, say, the Breen's energy-damping weapon?"

That brought Stevens up short. The Breen weapon had had a devastating impact on the Allies' forces, dissipating ships' energies into the subspace dimensions, rendering them powerless. "It would probably break down the field. But no, wait, if that were the explanation, this would've happened months ago."

"Unless the fields were only destabilized." Scotty didn't need to say more—this was practice, not just theory. Unless stabilized by exotic particles such as tetryons, a warp field was as shaky as a house of cards, prone to collapse if jostled by too much mass or energy. "Buried under the rubble, things would've been pretty quiet for 'em and they could've stayed semistable indefinitely. But if one of 'em was dug up, handled, even exposed to too much sunlight, it could've been the straw that broke the camel's back."

Sutherland was fascinated, and moved in to examine the Cabochons more closely. "You mean . . . these—"

"*Don't touch that!*" Scotty hissed. "Have ye not heard a word we've been sayin'? If those Cabochons were destabilized as well, they could be bombs waitin' to go off!"

Sutherland jerked away and began a careful retreat on tiptoe, promising to notify the authorities.

"But they've already been handled since the attack," Stevens said. "Dug up, cleaned, brought to the museum—"

"The fields may have been only partially destabilized," Tev replied. "Any further stimulus would worsen the instability. There's no telling when the point of collapse could be reached."

"We've got to beam them into space." Stevens reached for his combadge.

"It won't work," said Tev. "Even this close we can't scan the Cabochons, only their interference patterns. Impossible to get a transporter lock. We'll have to remove them physically."

"Can we do that?"

"If we're careful enough, hopefully," Scotty answered. "But that still won't solve the whole problem." He met the others' gaze solemnly. "There were *two* Cabochons missing."

The massive columns provided excellent cover against the Shanial's fire (assuming it was the Shanial). Unfortunately, the team was cut off from the exit, which had closed anyway when Krotine had come through to provide cover fire for Konya. It would take more work with the P-38s to get out, which would leave them exposed to the attackers' particle beams.

Konya had dragged Hawkins behind a column and was scanning him with a tricorder. "It's not too bad," Hawkins said with a grunt, critically appraising his own leg wound. "But it . . . shorted out the gravsuit. I can hardly move."

"I know," Konya said. "I can feel it all. Here—for both our sakes." Konya concentrated for a moment. An intense pain arced through Hawkins for a split second, leaving a relative numbness in its wake. "Wha—what did you do?"

"A feedback trick—temporarily overloaded your pain receptors. Only lasts a few minutes, though."

"Thanks. Maybe you should've been a doctor instead of a security guard."

Konya studied him. "You have an unusually high sensitivity to pain, did you know that?"

"Well, I can't actually sense other people's pain to compare. But I'm not surprised."

"And yet you went into a line of work that constantly exposes you to pain and injury. Why didn't you do something safer?"

"Sometimes I ask that myself," Vance smirked. "Here I thought my bad-luck streak had finally broken—but no, first day back, I get shot." Noticing Konya's dark eyes appraising him, Hawkins searched for a serious answer. "Sometimes I wonder if it's worth it. But bottom line—it is. If it protects other people. So I'm not going to let a little sensitivity stop me from doing what's worth doing."

Konya smiled. "Then we have more in common than you thought."

Behind another column, Gomez and Corsi were pinned down. Corsi was saving her shots, carefully aiming at the sources of fire, but the shooters moved deftly through the maze of columns. Gomez glimpsed broad, squat bodies with numerous limbs, and no clear vital spots such as a distinct head. Abramowitz had guessed right—they were not humanoid.

"We come in peace!" Gomez cried for the fifth time, hoping the hoary first-contact mantra would reach the attackers' ears (if any) over the gunfire, and get translated into terms they could understand. "We mean you no harm!" she continued, though it was hard to say it with conviction when she saw Corsi's expression.

Still the shooting continued. "Bart! Any chance of a translation?"

Faulwell shook his head. "They're not using any

known grammar. They're too alien." Most humanoid species, by virtue of similar neurological evolution, spoke languages following several dozen basic grammatical structures. This was why universal translators could usually get a grip on an alien language in mere moments. The pattern even held for certain energy beings that had presumably evolved from humanoid ancestors. But these Shanial represented a separate evolutionary track. Deciphering their speech would be a slower process—if they ever got a dialogue going.

"Konya!" Corsi called. "Can you reach them telepathically?"

"I've been trying," the Betazoid replied. "No more luck than Faulwell, for the same reason. Their brain structure's hard to read, and they don't seem to be 'hearing' me."

"Damn. Commander? Any suggestions? Commander?"

"I don't know." Gomez met Corsi's eyes pleadingly. "I can't decide. What if . . . what if I choose wrong? I don't want to lose anyone else."

Corsi grabbed her shoulder. "And we don't want to lose you, Commander. So get a grip! If you need a slap in the face I'm willing to provide it."

Gomez gritted her teeth and tried to think of something. Fortunately (or unfortunately?), just then Pattie called, "Commander, I have a thought."

"Go ahead, Pattie."

"It doesn't seem like anybody's shooting at me."

"Feeling left out?" Abramowitz quipped.

"Not particularly. But maybe they don't see me as a threat. I'd like to try getting closer, so I can try to convince them to stand down."

"But then they might *start* shooting at you," Gomez said.

"With antiquated particle beams like those? My carapace can handle a few hits."

Gomez hesitated, but Corsi raised a hand threateningly, and only half-jokingly. "Okay, Pattie. Go."

A moment later Pattie rolled out from behind a column, curled up into pillbug mode and wheeling herself forward. Well, actually *backward*—she propelled herself by flexing her carapace plates outward one by one, rolling herself along in a continuous reverse somersault. Which made sense, given that the Nasat, a people prone to conflict avoidance, had evolved the ability for the purpose of retreating from danger. What Pattie was doing now would probably qualify her for psychiatric evaluation on her own world, but then, Sonya wondered, was it any saner for the rest of them to be here?

Indeed, Pattie advanced unmolested—if anything, the attackers were trying to avoid hitting her. Peering around the column, Sonya saw them gesturing to her as though waving her to safety. She vanished from view . . . but the shooting continued.

After a few more moments, Corsi scowled. "Now what? Commander, should we signal her?"

"No, that might turn them against her. We just have to hope she can get through to them somehow—or find a way to overpower them."

Corsi shook her head. "Nasat aren't the overpowering type. I hope she hasn't gotten in over her—"

She broke off, realizing the shooting had stopped. *"Pattie to away team,"* came her voice over their combadges. *"My head is just fine, Commander Corsi. And I think cooler heads have prevailed—though maybe 'heads' isn't the right word."*

CHAPTER
5

"*It's a stretch, Scotty.*" On the comm screen in Sutherland's office, Director Iskander shook his head. "*You're asking me to believe that what happened this morning is a delayed reaction to something that took place nearly a year ago. That these microwarp fields were somehow weakened, but fourteen of them managed to stay intact throughout extensive handling while one other erupted after being buried quietly for all that time.*"

"We don't know what set it off, Cemal. It could've been dug up by an excavator, subjected to rougher handling than the others. Or it could've just been hit more directly by the Breen weapon, so it was closer to the bursting point."

"*And what about the sixteenth one? If it was buried in the rubble with the other, why didn't it go critical and expand too?*"

"You know I cannot answer that. It could've been

blown farther away in the attack. Maybe some souvenir hunter found it and carried it off to parts unknown."

"Or maybe this isn't some bizarre accident, but a carefully planned attack."

"Cemal, their interference patterns *are* fluctuating! A destabilized warp field would look just like that."

"And is it the only thing that could?"

"No, but—"

"Scotty, if this were just an accident, why would Captain Zakash claim differently? Why bring a whole fleet here for a wild-goose chase?"

"I can think of a reason or two to bring a fleet to Earth," Scott said darkly.

"And it would be a pointless exercise, given the level of defenses we have now. The Nachri fleet is small, underpowered, little more than an orbit guard."

"Maybe," Scotty said. "One thing, though—the planet where yon Cabochons were found? It's in the space once controlled by the Nachri Empire."

"Well, that makes sense. They were the first victims of the Shanial. Perhaps these Cabochons were how the enemy struck—they snuck these harmless-looking baubles onto other worlds like Trojan horses, and then burst out to attack."

"Except there was nobody in this one. Cemal, there's something that Zakash isn't telling us, as sure as I'm standin' here."

"Maybe so, Scotty. But I can't afford to ignore the possibility that we're under attack. And Zakash is our only source of information about the Shanial—at least until your team makes contact again."

"But can we afford to ignore the possibility that I'm right? That there are fifteen other time bombs waiting to go off? Even if you're right, if these are Trojan horses o' some kind, surely that's all the more reason to get them off the planet right away!"

Iskander needed to consider only briefly. *"All right. I'm still not convinced they have anything to do with this matter, but we should take precautions. Can your people manage to move them without setting them off?"*

"It won't be easy. It's as delicate a job as I've ever had to do—but we'll figure out a way."

"This is most interesting news, Director Iskander," Zakash said to the human on the viewing globe. "These . . . 'Cabochons' could explain a great deal about the Shanial's method of attack. Once we arrive, our science teams will be glad to cooperate with yours in analyzing this technology."

"As a precaution," Iskander told him, *"we're having them removed to a secure research facility in our asteroid belt. I'll try to arrange clearance for your teams."*

"A wise precaution," Zakash said, trying not to display the flush of excitement that ran through him. "The Shanial are a cunning foe, devious and secretive. I do not wonder that they've managed to convince some of your people that this attack was a mere accident. That is how they weaken a foe—by sowing confusion and doubt."

"Yes," the human replied with a conviction that delighted Zakash. *"The Dominion was the same way, eating away at us from within. We should have learned by now not to fall for such tricks again."*

"I have faith in your clarity of thought, Director," Zakash said. "We shall arrive within a standard hour. Defense Group out."

Once the globe went dark, Zakash clapped his fists together in triumph. "Trusting fool. Did you hear, Jomat? They're taking the crystals off the planet!"

"Yes," his first officer replied, "it should make obtaining them much easier."

"And once we have them, what a weapon we will wield against our oppressors!" He rose, addressing the whole command deck crew. As the moment of battle neared, it was important to remind them of their cause, to motivate them to succeed. "Imagine what we could achieve—an army could be smuggled in a pendant. A warfleet, an invasion force could slip through a planetary defense grid as easily as a clump of space dust. The simple reexpansion would be devastating, as we've seen today! Our forces could destroy an entire city simply by arriving there—the rest would simply be cleanup! The whole Federation will soon be at our mercy!" Zakash basked in the crew's cheers.

But Jomat moved closer to speak privately. "Don't lose proportion, Captain. Our enemy is the ruling party, not the Federation."

"It was the Federation that put them in power two centuries ago, that supports them to this day," Zakash snapped. "The party's alliance with the mighty Federation cows the people into submission, reduces them to a passive shadow of the glory that was Nachros. The rhetoric of democracy they borrowed from the Federation lets them create an illusion of freedom, of legitimacy." The captain let his voice rise loud enough for the rest to hear. "Theirs is a Federation of hypocrites, Jomat. They claim such high ideals, and yet they persistently ally themselves with brutal and corrupt governments—the Klingons, the Romulans, the Son'a—anyone who suits their own interests, while turning a blind eye to their brutality and corruption, condoning it in the name of 'diversity.' That makes them our enemy—the enemy of all downtrodden peoples. That is why we must create a new Nachri Empire, one that enforces justice rather than paying lip service to it."

Again the crew cheered; again Zakash basked. Jomat observed their adulation. "They would follow you into Death's own fortress," he said.

"Yes," Zakash sighed. "It's most heartening."

"Just take care to remember it is a means and not an end."

The captain glared at his first officer. "I lead our people where they wish to go. To the defeat of our oppressors, the restoration of our lost greatness. I am nothing without their support—and without the cause we all share."

"Of course, Captain," Jomat said in a yielding tone.

"Good. Now—ready the kinetic missiles and FMS drones. The first shot of the revolution is about to be fired!"

Bart Faulwell was having a great time, though he was the only one. Deciphering the Shanial language, so he told the others, was a rare challenge for him, the kind he rarely faced in this age of near-instant computer translation. Not only that, but he was presented with a type of grammar and concept arrangement new in Federation experience, one he was having to learn as he went, and could no doubt produce a fascinating paper about. "I feel like Bowring or Sato in the pioneering days of Starfleet," he beamed.

"I'm sure we're all happy for you," Gomez told him dryly. "But are you actually getting anywhere useful?"

"Oh, we're making a lot of progress," the bearded linguist told her. "The key was recognizing how their anatomy affects their worldview—like the way that Syclarian journal on BorSitu Minor became easier to translate once I realized that their anatomy led to a circular mode of writing. So much of the way we see things is based on a fixed sense of bilateral orientation—a definite forward and reverse direction, a right wing and a left wing, and so forth. With their radial symmetry, they see things much more flexibly. You can reverse direction and still be making progress, have foresight and hindsight at the same time . . . and most questions have more than two sides in their minds. I doubt they ever invented the true-or-false test."

Gomez gazed over at the Shanial, considering his words. The two emissaries who parlayed with Faulwell and Pattie (they seemed most comfortable with her nearby) were apparently among the leaders; Faulwell had introduced them as Matriarch Varethli and Designer Rohewi. It was in fact impossible to pin down a front or back to them. Each Shanial had a barrel-shaped torso supported by four squat legs at the base. Extending from the upper part of the torso were four longer limbs, which arced tarantula-style to the ground, terminating in four thick, mutually opposed digits; these served as arms or additional legs as necessary. Atop the torso was a domelike head containing four eyes at the compass points, and above them four large ears, which seemed to be used in echolocation. There were only two mouths, but Gomez couldn't decide whether to think of them as being on the front and back or on the sides. Though the heads didn't turn, Gomez could see the eyes rotating within their sockets to track her movements, proving that the Shanial were watching her as well.

"So if they don't take sides," Corsi asked, "what were they doing shooting at us?"

"Just because they have a multivalued logic doesn't mean they won't protect themselves," Faulwell said. "As far as I can tell, they thought we were Nachri, and they're afraid of Nachri."

"But why would they think that?" Gomez frowned.

"Same reason they weren't afraid of me," said Pattie. "Because you're bipeds."

"I get the strong impression," Faulwell added, "that the Nachri are the only humanoids they've ever met. They didn't know that it's the dominant sentient form in the galaxy."

"How could they not know?" O'Brien asked. "With subspace technology like this, how could they not have been spacefarers?"

"There's a more important question," said Corsi. "Why are they afraid of the Nachri?"

Faulwell shrugged. "I'll need to improve the translation before we can get any clear answers."

"Fine," Gomez said. "You do that." She turned away, planning to leave him to his work.

But the linguist sidled over to her and spoke softly. "Commander, I just want you to know . . . nobody blames you for your . . . moment of indecision before. We've all been through so much lately—"

"That's okay," she replied curtly, not really wanting to discuss it.

Faulwell studied her. "I remember something you told me back on Evora. That no matter what losses we endure, we're survivors, and fighters. We've all lost people before, and we've dealt with it, and moved on, because we had our duty to keep us going."

"I said that?"

"Words to that effect."

She was quiet for a moment. "Well, I didn't know what the hell I was talking about."

Faulwell blinked. "Well . . . it brought me some comfort. Then, and now."

"It was just words."

The linguist smiled. "Words are powerful things. Especially when they come from a leader. We all look to you to give us strength, Commander. You've never let us down yet."

But who can I look to? Sonya thought. Outwardly, though, she just gave the older man a tight smile and said, "Thanks, Bart. Get back to your translations now—we really need them." He nodded and moved off, accepting the words. *Are the words really enough, with no certainty behind them? How can I lead when I don't know where to go from here?*

It was refreshing to get her hands dirty.

Paradoxically, Keiko found it cleansing to get down on her knees and work with some good honest soil. It had come from life, and it sustained life—what could be more pure?

Molly and her friends had gone over to Masoud's place, and Keiko had decided she needed to get out of the house. So she'd left little Kirayoshi with Aunt Midori and gone over to the rebuilt Academy grounds to visit Boothby. Naturally the wizened groundskeeper had no patience for mere social visits, so he'd wasted no time putting her to work, recruiting her to help him tend some of the more exotic floral displays. Balancing the needs of plants that had come from dozens of worlds, evolved under radically different conditions, so that they could coexist in a single bed without dying or killing each other was an ongoing challenge, and Keiko was always as glad to help out as Boothby was to have an expert xenobotanist as a volunteer. The work struck Keiko as a sort of metaphor for what the Federation strove to achieve, and she figured that was why Boothby worked so hard at it—not that she'd ever extract such a sentimental admission from the old grouch.

"Careful with those windsingers!" Boothby scolded. "Plant them the wrong distance apart and the chords interfere—sounds like a transporter accident." A Talosian windsinger was a cluster of wire-thin stems, each terminating in a single metallic-blue leaf seemingly too large for it to support. They trembled in the slightest breeze, and the air rushing across the leaves' microserrations created a haunting chimelike sound that rose and fell in pitch with the changing airflow. It actually did sound somewhat like a transporter chime, Keiko realized. The ancient Talosians had planted them on a number of worlds during their spacefaring age, thousands of centuries ago. Past Starfleet crews had reported hearing such chimes on dozens of the worlds they'd visited, even coming to expect them as part of the ambience of alien planets. Sadly, late in the twenty-third century those same Starfleet explorers had unknowingly spread a botanical plague that had killed off most of the windsingers. Starfleet's botanical gardens were one of the few places—aside from Talos IV, Keiko presumed—where windsinger chimes could still be heard. Now they'd bred a strain that hopefully would be hardy enough to survive unprotected in Earth's biosphere. Keiko would've liked to be involved in that work, but she'd been too busy trying to build a nice, quiet family life with Miles. At least she got to participate in this small way.

Still, she realized her preoccupation with this morning's argument was causing her to make mistakes. "I'm sorry, Boothby," she sighed. (Somehow it had never occurred to her to ask his first name. Assuming he even had one.) "I just . . . had a fight with Miles this morning."

Boothby grunted. "I thought you'd resolved not to do that anymore," he said, with a touch of "I told you so" in his tone. "How'd he screw it up?"

"It wasn't him," she insisted. "Well . . . not really." She fidgeted under that glare that would brook no nonsense. Boothby's visage was as rough and gnarled as a Denevan millennium tree. Nobody knew how old he was. He'd mentioned being Martian by birth, which narrowed it down to under two hundred and seventy, but people said he'd always been here and the Academy had just grown up around him. Anyway, however old he was, his eyes looked older than Q, and certainly a thousand times wiser. They had a way of digging right down to the roots of your problems.

"I mean, most of the time Miles is the perfect husband and father. We have just the life we want, a quiet life where we can focus on being a family. No more space battles, no more religious fanatics, no more invasions."

"And then these Shanial have to come along and screw it up for you. How inconsiderate." She didn't ask how he knew their name. He was Boothby, after all.

"It's not just them, whoever they are." She laid out the gist of her argument with Miles—how he kept finding reasons to spend time away from her, kept taking on responsibilities that weren't his.

"So you don't think he's serious about your marriage?"

"No, that's just it—I know he is. That's why it's just so frustrating. Before, back on DS9, I always knew he was devoted to me, but circumstances just kept keeping us apart. I just thought that back here on Earth, things would be . . . easier."

"So your marriage can only work when the conditions are perfect? Sounds like a pretty fair-weather relationship to me."

"No, of course that's not it."

"Then what is it?" Boothby asked piercingly. "If you don't think your marriage is in trouble, what's upsetting you about his little jaunts? Don't you want him to help out? You think he should just sit back, mind his own damn business?"

"You make it sound so terrible."

"Well, how should it sound? You tell me."

Keiko sighed, making the windsingers squeal a bit. "I don't know. I shouldn't feel this way about it. Miles is right; the work he's doing is important. And I don't know anyone who's better qualified to do it. I just . . . wish it wouldn't happen so often. I hoped being back on Earth would be like it was when I was growing up—peaceful and safe and serene."

"And then you came back to San Francisco and found the aftermath of a war zone."

Keiko acknowledged it silently. "It was like coming to DS9 all over again. The devastation, the loss, the pain all around us. I didn't want to have to endure any more of it. But Miles threw himself right into the thick of it. Again. Every day he was away, dealing with the aftermath. And every night it was all he would talk about.

"And it just keeps coming back, over and over. I just feel so helpless, like I can't get away from it!" Unthinkingly, she snapped one of the windsinger's slender stems. The wiry filament cut into her fingers, drawing blood. "Oh! I'm sorry," she began, but Boothby was already pulling out his pocket first-aid kit, tending to her cut and ignoring the broken plant.

"Seems easy enough to fix," Boothby said as he sprayed the wound with antiseptic sealant. "Just ask Miles not to talk about it. Find other topics. Join a book club or something."

"It's not that easy."

"Why not? Is he that hard to shut up?"

"No, that's not—I mean, that's not the problem."

Boothby met her eyes. "Then what is it that makes you feel so helpless?"

She realized where he was leading her. "The crises themselves. It's not that Miles is doing something about them," she said, discovering it as she said it. "It's that I'm *not*. My city, my planet, is in trouble, my neighbors are hurting, and I can't do anything to help them. My husband is an engineer, a builder—a soldier when necessary—he can *do* something substantive about these disasters. I can see it in his eyes, hear it in his voice—he has a purpose. He's scared, just like the rest of us, but he handles it because he knows how he can help. But I'm just a botanist. What can I do to help in a disaster, or a war? What can I do aside from sitting around and being afraid for the people I care about?"

Boothby quietly finished tending to her hand, and then gave it a surprisingly tender squeeze, matched by a rare smile. Then he grunted and turned back to his work. "You ask me," he groused, "the Breen gave me quite enough to do when they attacked. This place was in ruins. All my plants died from the fires, the radiation. Trees I'd tended my whole life, that I'd grown up with, blasted to kindling. Rare specimens from a hundred worlds vaporized. And did the Breen care? Hell, no. The plants never did anything to them, but they killed them all anyway, just innocent bystanders that got in the damn way.

"That's the part of war people don't talk about much. Sure, the loss of life is horrible—the Breen took a lot of my friends that day. And the property losses, okay, those are bad too. But it's a damn sight easier to rebuild a lecture hall or an office complex than it is to regrow a Gordian oak or a sahsheer crystal. And who got stuck doing the hard part? Me, that's who!" Boothby shook his head. *"Humph.* I should talk—at least I still have a breathable atmosphere to do my work in, and soil that isn't poisoned. Other worlds the Dominion invaded, they weren't so lucky. Look at Cardassia—it'll take decades for all the dust and the smoke from the fires to settle out of the atmosphere. Their plants are starving for light across the whole planet. The acid rain is poisoning the water, too. A century from now there might be nothing alive on Cardassia larger than a vole. Who's going to clean up *that* mess? That's what I'd like to know."

Boothby turned back to his work, muttering under his breath, while Keiko pondered silently. Then she hugged him and kissed his cheek. "Thank you, Boothby—you're a lifesaver."

CHAPTER
6

Faulwell had gotten the translation algorithm to a point where normal conversation with the Shanial was possible. The rendering was only approximate, not to mention delayed, since Bart was filtering it through his tricorder and modifying some of the translator program's word and grammar choices. "Trust me, it's better this way," he'd insisted. "Our grammars are so different that a more literal rendering would just be too awkward. Good translation is more about capturing the overall sense of the material, choosing whatever phrasing conveys that sense best even if the specific words are very different."

"Come clean, Bart," Pattie had joked. "You're just trying to give yourself more to do."

Still, Faulwell's system seemed to work, though Gomez was concerned about what might be lost in the translation. "We never knew of other worlds," Matriarch Varethli told them. "The ceiling hid them from us."

"Ceiling?" asked O'Brien. "Have they always lived indoors? No, that's silly, how do you evolve indoors?" He corrected himself. "Underground, then?"

"I'm not sure the word came through right," Faulwell said. After some discussion with the Shanial, he reported, "I think she means clouds. Sounds like their world has a dense, constantly clouded atmosphere. They couldn't see the stars."

"But you know about the stars now? About space travel?" Gomez asked.

"Yes," said Designer Rohewi, the darker-hued male who was apparently Varethli's partner, though whether professionally, politically, or personally was unclear. "The Nachri came through the clouds. We learned from them that other worlds existed, that vessels moved between them."

"But they didn't just bring knowledge."

"No," Varethli told them, her four arms (upper legs?) twitching in agitation. "They killed many Shanial. They sought to align us in one direction."

"Sorry," Faulwell interposed, "I think that's a metaphor for trying to conquer them."

"They wanted our technology," Rohewi continued. "We and they did not progress the same way. They, like you, used subspace for travel, to find new worlds for their growing population. Our population grew as well, but we made our own new territory by creating subspace pockets."

Rohewi, apparently the lead engineer of the Shanial and innovator of much of their subspace technology, began to explain the specifics. It wasn't long before the engineers caught on to the nature of the microwarp bubbles. "Like a subspace compression," O'Brien grimaced. "Just great. I'm tiny again. I hate it when that happens."

"But how could they have warp technology without spaceflight?" Corsi asked.

"I can see how they might just have a knack for it," Faulwell mused. "With their flexible sense of direction and movement, their ability to reconcile opposites, I bet they have an intuitive understanding of the subspace dimensions, the way they're curled up inside space and vice versa at the same time." The others stared at him in surprise. "What? I'm a linguist surrounded by engineers. I listen to the jargon and pick up the meaning."

Apparently there was a whole network of microbubbles, externally encased within stabilizing crystals, yet connected to each other through subspace wormholes, one of which the team had passed through to reach this city, the hub of the network. "The Nachri wanted the microbubbles as a weapon," Rohewi explained, "to smuggle armies and fleets, or destroy cities through their reexpansion."

"We would not do this," Varethli said. "To destroy those you disagree with, rather than finding a new way forward for both, is insane."

Gomez smiled. As Bart had said, their multivalued logic kept them from seeing things in black-and-white terms. If two sides clashed over something, they could just reorient their perspectives and negotiate a settlement. It apparently made for a very peaceful society.

"We sought a common orientation with them, but they would not change direction. The Nachri began to destroy our world! They thought it would make us do what they wanted. But this was a direction we could not move in. So we turned inward. We encased what we could within subspace pockets, intending to hide within them until the threat was gone."

"So you've been living in these pockets for two hundred years?" Sonya asked.

"No," replied the designer. "Resources and power are finite. And we knew our world would take millennia to recover. We compressed the time dimension as well."

"You mean . . . for you, hardly any time has passed?"

"Days."

Gomez's eyes widened. That meant that the devastation these people described, the destruction of their entire world, was not something that they'd studied in the history books—it was a firsthand experience, the memory still fresh. Something was indeed being lost in the translation—the anguish and grief the Shanial must be enduring. She couldn't read their body language, so she'd had no idea. "I'm so sorry," she whispered. "We, too, have suffered many great losses in recent times. Though nothing as great as what you've lost. I . . ." She trailed off. She had no idea what she could say to them that could sound remotely meaningful.

"Gratitude," Varethli said simply.

"But the course has altered," Rohewi said. "Time is uncompressed again. The emergence of one pocket back to the outer universe has reconnected the network to normal timeflow. And clearly we are not on Shanial anymore."

"What caused the pocket to emerge?" O'Brien asked.

"An abrupt power leakage into subspace weakened the stabilizing crystal. We do not know the cause."

"May I take a look at your readings? I have an idea about that."

Once O'Brien got a feel for their readouts, it didn't take long. "Just as I thought—looks like they were hit with the Breen's energy-dampers. These crystals we're in must've already been in San Francisco when the attack happened."

"Probably in the museum," Abramowitz said.

"My God," Gomez said. "How many of these crystals were there?"

"We only managed to generate sixteen," Rohewi replied.

"And have the others suffered similar power drains?"

"Yes. We are searching for a way to reverse them, with no success."

"We believed it was a Nachri attack," Varethli added, "which is why we reacted defensively to your entry. But now we see it is you who needs defense." She paused, dealing with unreadable emotions. "We mourn the loss of life our accidental emergence caused."

"Not your fault," O'Brien assured them. "We're all just delayed victims of a war that already ended. That's the way war always is—goes on killing long after the fighting's supposed to have stopped."

"But the tragedy will be far greater," Rohewi said, "if we cannot halt the power drain of the other crystals."

"You said it," Pattie chirped. "If a complex this size underwent instant reexpansion, the blast would totally destroy San Francisco—and blow enough dust and smoke into the stratosphere to cause a global ice age."

"Wait," said Rohewi, studying his readouts. "The other crystals show anomalous readings."

"Are they about to rupture?" Gomez asked.

Rohewi absorbed the data for a moment. "Borderline, but holding. They seem to be in motion, but something from outside is damping its effects."

Abramowitz turned to Gomez. "Do you think Scotty and the others have found them?"

But Gomez addressed the designer. "You said the other crystals. Not this one?"

"No. We remain stationary."

"We need to get in contact with our people right away. Can you arrange that?" she asked the Shanial.

"You must return to the facility you came here from," Rohewi told her. "Sending a signal through our warp field would require altering its geometry, and it is too tenuous to risk that."

"Okay, let's go."

"May we accompany?" Varethli asked. "Perhaps by combining our knowledge we can solve this crisis. We have only just discovered the richness of the universe beyond our clouds—it would be tragic to die before getting to explore it."

"It's always tragic to die," Gomez muttered. "All right, come on."

The matriarch and the designer came up alongside her as she strode toward the exit. Despite their bulk, they made excellent time, and she had to jog to keep up. She tweaked the antigrav suit a bit to reduce her weight some more. "Is there really a Federation of hundreds of worlds, coexisting in peace?" Varethli asked.

"Yes, there is."

"And all these peoples are different?"

"Well, most of them are humanoid like us, but yes, there are many different kinds."

"Amazing. When we entered these pockets, all we knew of was the Nachri and their empire. Now there is a great union of worlds in which the Nachri play no part. While we have locked ourselves away, standing still in time, so much has happened, so much has changed. Perhaps we were too hasty to cut ourselves off from the universe. It is not as dark a place as we had thought."

Gomez chose not to argue the point. She simply fell back to the rear of the group, and let Faulwell and Abramowitz monopolize the Shanial. But soon O'Brien fell back alongside her. "The gravsuit working okay, Commander? I saw you fiddling with it earlier."

"It's fine, Chief. Thanks." She let him see the readouts on the wrist panel, knowing a fellow engineer would need hard data.

O'Brien nodded approvingly at the readouts, but kept pace with her. "It's always something, isn't it, Commander? Goes with the job, I guess. Do well fixing one crisis, they send you to fix the next one. Some reward, huh?"

"It never ends," Gomez murmured, more to herself than to him.

"Be glad it doesn't," O'Brien said, catching her eyes intently.

"What?"

The chief fidgeted. "I don't mean to intrude, Commander . . . but I've known people who . . . well, after suffering a loss, or a bad crisis, they . . . maybe were too ready to see it end. To give up."

"'To take arms against a sea of troubles, and by opposing end them'? Is that what you mean?" Gomez smiled reassuringly. "Don't worry, Chief. I'm not suicidal. I'm just. . . ." She searched for a word. "*Stuck.* I feel like the Shanial—frozen in place while the universe is going by around me. I want to get back in motion again, but I just don't see how."

"Sure you do. Just take one step forward, then the next, and so on. You're just not letting yourself do it."

"And what would you know about it?"

He shrugged. "Been there. I once . . . well, I once went to prison for twenty years."

Gomez stared. "Chief . . . I haven't *known* you twenty years."

"It was a virtual prison—twenty years of memories dumped into my brain in a few hours. But it felt real. By the end of those few hours, I was a changed man. I'd gotten used to thinking I'd lost everything. And I . . . well, let's just say I sank into some pretty deep despair.

"Then I came out, and I found the life I'd lost was still there. I could have it back—my wife, my daughter, my friends, my career, my youth, everything. But the despair still had its grip on me, and so I didn't reach out to take it. I even—" He broke off.

Gomez shared an understanding look with him. "I guess it got pretty rough for a moment or two."

"Yeah," he acknowledged. "Anyway, well, I've never had much use for headshrinkers, but I have to admit, Counselor Telnorri did help me understand how depression works—how it tricks you into thinking there's no hope, blinds you to everything you've got in your favor. And I realized something else, too—life's short, and you never know how long happiness will last. So you need to make the most of every moment you have. Don't let yourself miss opportunities—don't let yourself fall into a rut, or worse."

"That's just it," Gomez said. "I thought I'd learned that already, after Sarindar. It was even that decision that made me . . ." She sighed. "Made me start things up with Kieran again."

"So you tried it that way, and it ended badly. It's no wonder you'd have second thoughts after that. But let me ask you something, Commander: Did it end that way because of anything *you* did wrong?"

"No," Gomez had to admit. "There was nothing I could've done."

"There you go. The problem wasn't in your approach—so if it ain't broke, don't fix it."

He makes it sound so simple, a part of Gomez scoffed. But she was beginning to recognize that voice for what it was. *That's because it* is *simple,* she told herself. *You can't succeed if you don't try—so you might as well try.*

She gazed up ahead at their newfound friends, who were chatting enthusiastically with Faulwell and Abramowitz, pumping them for information about the galaxy. "Look at the Shanial," she said. "They lost their whole world, just days ago by their count. And yet they're excited about all the new worlds they've suddenly discovered."

"I guess it's like Mr. Faulwell said. They don't see much difference between backward and forward. So a setback can become an advance, with just a little shift in perspective."

"Do you think humans can learn that?"

O'Brien smiled encouragingly. "I've seen it happen."

"Are we there yet?" Stevens asked.

He, Scotty, and Tev were aboard shuttlecraft *Haley* (on loan from Starfleet HQ), transporting the Cabochons to Vesta Station in the asteroid belt. The *da Vinci* could've gotten them there faster, but Scotty had insisted on a shuttle; not only would it mean fewer people were at risk, but the shuttle had less mass and fewer energy sources to jostle their microwarp bubbles. The starship was escorting the shuttle, but from a comfortable distance—just within transporter range, in the slim hope of being able to save the crew if the crystals ruptured.

Even though Tev had done most of the work design-ing the stasis-field apparatus that now encased the Cabochons and cushioned them against external stim-uli, the Tellarite had insisted on sitting in the front of the shuttlecraft alongside Scotty, relegating Stevens to the back, and incidentally putting him right next to what were currently the deadliest *objets d'art* in the known galaxy. Of course it would only make about a femtosecond's difference in how soon he'd be killed, but it was the principle of the thing.

So Stevens had decided that if Tev was going to stick him in the backseat like a little kid, he might as well act the part. He was tired of being at a disadvantage, letting Tev make him angry and frustrated. It was time to take back some control, redefine the terms, and start giving as good as he got. He couldn't fight back openly without getting himself cashiered out of Starfleet; but there were always passive forms of resistance, and humor was one of the most tried and true. If Tev took himself so blasted seriously, then Stevens's best option was to stop taking him seriously at all.

Besides . . . it's what Duff would've done.

"Are we there yet?" he asked again, for the fifth time. "I'm hungry."

"Quiet back there, or I'll turn this thing around," Scotty shot back with a grin.

"We can't risk going faster, or the engine emissions will overwhelm the stasis," Tev said, apparently missing the joke. Well, to be fair, he couldn't be expected to know hoary Earth clichés. "At this rate we're several hours from Vesta." He turned to skewer Stevens with his deep-set eyes. "So perhaps you should consider tak-ing a nap."

Ouch! Stevens realized he may have underestimated his opponent. Well, that just made it more interesting.

As soon as they emerged from the hatch, Gomez hit her combadge. "Gomez to Scott."

"Commander Gomez, this is Director Iskander," came the reply. *"Where have you been? Is your team all right?"*

"The team's okay, sir, but we have an emergency. Where's Scotty?"

"Captain Scott is escorting the alien artifacts off-planet. We've discovered there's a risk—"

"We know, sir, that's the emergency. The crystal containing the largest Shanial city is still on Earth somewhere, and they can't stabilize it. If it reemerges like the first one, San Francisco's off the map and Earth becomes another Cardassia. We need to find that missing crystal, fast!"

"Wait. You've been with the Shanial?"

"We have their leader and their chief engineer with us now."

"Are you able to talk freely?"

"What? Of course, sir. There's something else, you have to warn the Nachri off. They lied to us; they invaded the Shanial for their technology, destroyed their world when they refused. They must be trying to steal it again."

"And the Shanial told you this?"

"Who else?"

"Commander, it's their word against the Nachri's, and they're the ones who blew a fresh hole in San Francisco. I want you to place them under arrest."

"Sir, that's not necessary. They're not the enemy.

Please, warn off the Nachri. At least let us talk to Captain Scott and our people."

"*These Shanial are a deceptive people, Commander—you're letting yourself be swayed by them. Bring them in for interrogation so we can evaluate their claims.*"

"We don't have time! We need to work with them to stop the deterioration, before it's too late."

At that moment, a division of armed agents rounded the bend in the corridor—Federation Security, not Starfleet. "*Cooperate with the agents, Commander,*" Iskander instructed. "*Even if this threat is real, I don't trust the Shanial to be in control of this power.*"

Gomez cursed to herself. "What was that, sir? I'm losing your signal, it must be the subspace instability." Catching on, O'Brien started making a *kkhhhhhh* noise. She glared to make him stop—not only was it entirely lame, but it was threatening to make her giggle. She just cut off the badge. "Come on, back inside!"

"What about Scotty and the rest?"

"Good question," Gomez said grimly.

"Da Vinci *to* Haley," came Gold's voice over the comm.

"*Haley.* Scott here."

"*Folks, we've been hailed by the Nachri Defense Fleet. They're in-system, and volunteering to have their lead ship join the escort.*"

"Tell 'em to keep their distance," Scotty warned. "We don't want any unnecessary emissions clutterin' up our space."

"But we could use their help at Vesta," said Stevens. "They've dealt with these Shanial before."

"Aye, so they say," the Scotsman answered skeptically.

Tev said, "It might be wise to have another set of transporters for backup."

"Like that's going to matter. Och, very well, they can approach to maximum transporter range. *Gently!* Tev— any chance o' raising shields?"

The Tellarite's stubby fingers were already at work on his console. "If I ramp them up gradually enough. Stevens, keep a close eye on that stasis field. If it fluctuates more than—"

"I know what to look for. Sir."

"You'd better."

"Watch out," cried Gold, *"they've fired something!"* Moments later, the shuttle rocked, and Stevens's heart tried to abandon ship through his throat as he watched the readouts fluctuate.

"My God," Scotty gasped. "Shuttlecraft to Nachri ship," he hailed desperately. "We surrender! Hold yer fire! Repeat, *hold your fire!*"

"Scotty, what are you doing?" cried Stevens. "We're in Sol System, there are hundreds of starships around to defend us!"

"One ship or a thousand, it doesn't matter—they don't dare fire, not around the Cabochons. Those Nachri have us with our britches down. We have to surrender!"

The *da Vinci* shuddered under another hammer blow. The Nachri had attacked them at the same time as the shuttle, and were continuing their assault even after the shuttle's surrender. "What are they firing, anyway?" Gold demanded.

"Some kind of kinetic missiles," Shabalala answered.

"They're shooting *cannonballs* at us?"

"At eighty percent of lightspeed. They hit with incredible force. And they're hard to track at those speeds, even with subspace sensors." Another blow interrupted him, but Gold didn't need further explanation. Few starships or torpedoes traveled much faster than a quarter lightspeed in normal space—relativistic effects made it troublesome, and it was more efficient just to go to warp. And natural objects rarely reached a fraction of such speeds. So the sensors weren't really calibrated for this.

"Can we return fire?"

"I can't lock on for sure," Shabalala told him. "They're jamming sensors, and using some kind of decoy drones, giving off the same emissions as their ship." Before the attack, Shabalala had been confident in his threat assessment, reporting that the Nachri's shields were downright primitive, a simple point-defense system supplementing their polarized hull plates. Now he and Gold were learning the hard way that their own technology wasn't really superior to the Nachri's, just specialized in a different direction—and therefore it had its own limitations. Gold would make sure the crew remembered that lesson in the future—provided there was one.

"We can't fire anyway," Shabalala added. "The discharge could set off the Cabochons."

"Damn. That's what the Nachri are counting on," said Gold. "They'll keep firing until we retreat—so we have to retreat."

CHAPTER
7

"*Gently,*" hissed Chief Scientist Mansee as the crew grappled the Starfleet shuttlecraft into the cargo bay. "One untoward bump could destroy us all in a nanosecond."

"Then perhaps you shouldn't hover over the crew and make them so nervous," Jomat suggested. He seemed relaxed, even cheerful, but it was more of a resigned calm—an acceptance that his fate, one way or the other, was out of his hands.

Mansee couldn't be so calm—the drawback of knowing just how probable it was that they were about to die, not to mention the precise technical details of how and why it would happen. He drew the first officer aside. "Is the captain mad, firing weapons around those things? We came to liberate our people, not get ourselves ground to molecular dust!"

"Freedom requires risk, Mansee," came Zakash's deep

voice, making the scientist cringe. "There is no safer place than a prison, provided you accept your bondage. You are sheltered, provided for, rescued from the peril of having to make choices, to bear responsibilities, to make mistakes. Rejecting that security, fighting against it to claim a hard, uncertain existence out in the cold . . . well, you have to be a little insane to do that." The captain smiled charismatically. "Our people will never be free without lunatics like us to show them the way. And since I'm your leader, I must be the maddest one of all." He moved in close to Mansee, looming over him. "See that you remember that."

"Yes, sir."

"Good man!" Zakash clapped him on the shoulder, almost knocking him down. "Now let's go claim our prize."

Zakash's strategy, Jomat had to admit, was extremely effective, provided it didn't kill them. The Starfleeters understood the delicacy of the situation and knew better than to put up any struggle. They obligingly opened the shuttle's rear hatch as he, Zakash, and Mansee approached. But the shuttle's three occupants stood in the doorway, blocking it symbolically at least. "If you value your lives at all, you won't tamper with the Cabochons," said the central figure, establishing himself as their leader—confirming the impression Jomat had already gotten from his advanced age and considerable girth. Surely someone that well-fed was a member of the ruling elite. Jomat recalled seeing him with the Earth official and the admiral—Scott had been his name. The Tellarite behind him, also well-fed and showing moderate age, was presumably next in the hierarchy, and the young, skinny human was surely a mere subaltern.

Zakash smirked. "And what exactly were you planning to do with them, if not 'tamper'? Our military scientists have been attempting to re-create this technology for two centuries. Federation arrogance aside, we are the ones best qualified to neutralize the threat."

"Aye, 'qualified' enough to nearly blast us all to our rewards with that daft attack! No thank you. We don't need *that* kinda help."

"Wait, I seem to be missing something," Zakash frowned. Then he brightened. "Ahh, yes. It was the part where you had any say in the matter." He signaled the guards to advance and bodily move the Starfleeters aside. He had Scott brought over to him as Mansee delicately entered the shuttle to examine the stasis generator. "We are a once-glorious people, now downtrodden into virtual slavery by tyrants your Federation put into power. We are not the ones who have anything to lose here."

The human met his gaze with equal confidence, his own devil-may-care cheer making Zakash's seem a pale imitation. "I must say I'm impressed, Zakash. Most fanatics let their followers do all the dyin' for them. How refreshing to see a leader who's willing to be one o' the very first to die."

Zakash smiled back, unintimidated. "Then maybe I'm not a fanatic. Maybe not every government the Federation backs is ethical, and maybe not everyone who fights it is insane. Maybe they simply have good reason to be desperate. You should think about that."

"Aye, you're revoltin' because o' your oppressive rulers, who revolted against their oppressive rulers, and so on and so on. You're just more o' the same, if you ask me."

Zakash's retort, if any, was cut off by Mansee's return. "Their stasis generator is excellent, but the crystals are very unstable. I think we can move them to the lab using antigravs—provided we shut down all nonessential power to minimize emissions."

"Very well," the captain nodded. "That means the brig will be offline, so seal the Starfleeters in their shuttle. They won't risk firing engines or weapons, or using their transporters."

"If ye're goin' to try stabilizin' the Cabochons, at least let us help," Scott insisted.

Zakash decided quickly. "Since we have a common interest in this at least, very well. *You* may help, Scott. The others stay in the shuttle."

"Scotty, no!" the young subaltern cried.

"Pipe down, Mr. Stevens. We're hardly in a position to bargain. Both of you, do your duty. Understood?"

"Aye, sir," the Tellarite replied crisply. The one named Stevens nodded more reluctantly.

"Good," Scott said, and he allowed the guards to escort him to the lab while Mansee delicately began moving the stasis generator.

As soon as the hatch shut them off from the Nachri, Tev spoke. "Let's get to work, Stevens."

"On what?"

"Our escape plan, of course. You heard the captain."

Stevens frowned. "When did he tell us to escape?"

"'Do your duty,'" he said. Stevens stared blankly. "Something they teach at the Academy. 'The first duty of any prisoner is to escape.'"

"I thought our first duty was to the truth."

"And we truly need an escape plan. Unless you prefer Nachri hospitality?"

"No," Stevens conceded, hating it when Tev was right.

"Good. Now what do we have to work with?"

"One Type-8 shuttlecraft and all its systems. None of which we can use without setting off the Cabochons."

"For now. If we get an opportunity, I want us ready."

"And what about Scotty? How do we get him out?"

"Captain Scott can fend for himself."

Stevens was shocked. "Just like that? All that man's done for you and you'd just abandon him?"

"We can only work with what the situation gives us," Tev replied coolly. "Do you really think two engineers can fight their way through hundreds of trained warriors to retrieve the captain?"

"No," Stevens was forced to admit.

"That's why Scotty ordered us to arrange our own escape."

Stevens grimaced. "Understood. But you could try being a little less cold about it."

Tev sighed with impatience. "Look, Mr. Stevens. You don't like me, I don't like you. Fine. Can we just stipulate to that and work together?"

Stevens *really* hated it when Tev was right. "Okay. Now what have we got?"

With outside help not an option, Gomez had turned the group right back around—fixing the Shanial tech from the inside was the only choice now. "I do not understand," Varethli told her as they hurried to the control room. "Why can we not get help from outside?"

"Bureaucracy," O'Brien said, his tone conveying volumes.

Faulwell frowned. "I'm not sure how to translate that."

"Oh, it's a universal constant."

Gomez made another attempt. "Some of our leaders believe you attacked us. They . . . they're afraid," she finished simply, honestly. "So they don't see the real danger. I'm sorry."

"I understand," Varethli said. "Just as we feared you when we first saw you. Yet now we see you offer us hope, and the chance to discover a rich new universe beyond our dreams. Fear blinds us all. It is in balance."

Faulwell listened carefully to her original words. "I think that means 'don't worry, we're even.'"

"Sadly, the warp fields are not in balance," Rohewi said as they reached the main console and surveyed the readouts. "The external stabilizing field is now the only thing holding the other warp fields from collapse. They are being subjected to emissions . . . scans of some sort."

"Scotty wouldn't be that reckless," O'Brien insisted. "Would he?"

"With Scotty," Gomez replied, "it can be hard to tell. But I don't think so."

As usual, it fell to Corsi to propose the worst-case scenario. "Maybe the Nachri have captured them."

"If so, we face even greater urgency," Varethli declared. "They will risk much to obtain this technology, putting us all in grave danger. More—if they do break our secrets, they will do to other worlds what they did to ours. This is not a direction we wish to travel in."

"The resonances are affecting our field stability," Rohewi interrupted. "Oscillations are worsening! I am trying to compensate."

"With what?" O'Brien asked, trying to interpret the displays. "Looks like tetryon fields."

"Yes."

"You'll never get enough particle density built up at the warp interface in time. Can you generate more massive exotics, like verterons?"

"What are verterons?"

"Never mind."

"Commander," Corsi suggested, "perhaps we should begin evacuating the Shanial."

"To where?" Gomez asked. "If this thing goes up, the whole planet's devastated. And we'd never be able to beam enough people off-planet in time."

"The other warp fields' oscillations are worsening," Rohewi called. "Resonance is increasing."

"Can we at least sever our link with them?" Sonya asked. "Maybe we can't save them, but we could at least save the Earth."

"It would not halt our own field decay. We—" He stopped. It was hard to tell, since they had eyes all around their bodies, but it seemed that he and Varethli exchanged a significant look. "Yes. There is a way. A way to prevent the collapse of *all* the warp fields."

"Well, what is it?"

"We can reduce our interface with normal space to zero dimension."

Gomez's eyes widened. "But that would mean pinching the warp bubbles off completely—severing your connection with our universe. You'd be trapped in here forever, adrift in subspace."

"It is the only way," Varethli said.

"But sooner or later your resources will run out," O'Brien cried. "You'll die!"

"We can place most of our people into temporal-stasis pockets, increasing the resources for the rest. Those will search for ways to reconnect us."

"Once we lose our link, it may be impossible to restore," Rohewi said. "But there are other sources of energy in subspace. We may be able to tap into them and prolong our existence indefinitely. Perhaps even expand our pocket universe to greater size and complexity."

"But you'd still be alone," said Gomez. "You've only just discovered the universe, and now you have to lose it. You never even got the chance to know what it's like." *Just like I never got the chance to know . . .*

Varethli took Gomez's hand in one of her own very alien ones. "Your sympathy moves us. But do not grieve. The universe does not always let us move in the direction we wish. So we simply move forward in another direction. It is still progress. It is better than standing still, yearning for the path we cannot take. Only the dead stand still."

"Systems ready," announced Rohewi. "Collapse is imminent. If you do not wish to be trapped with us, leave now!"

"Go," Varethli told them. "Go forward in your path, as we will in ours. Go forward and live!"

Something in Sonya still resisted. She needed time, it demanded, time to linger in her memories, absorb her losses, indulge her regrets to the fullest. Anything less would seem like a betrayal of those she was losing, had lost. But now another part of her spoke up—the real betrayal would be to lose herself along with them. Life pulled inexorably forward, and staying in one place, letting herself be trapped in the past, wasn't living at all. She had to *move*. "Move. Move, move, move, people!" And she ran, faster than she'd ever run in her life. And it was exhilarating.

*   *   *

"You're crazy. It'll never work!"

"The equations are basic. Brilliantly simple. There's little that can go wrong."

Stevens grimaced. "Famous last words."

"Besides," Tev said reasonably, "you've seen the proof of concept yourself, with the *Rubicon*'s subspace compression."

"Yeah, but that was down to toy size, not subatomic size!"

"That's the only scale on which the Van Den Broeck equations can work. Besides, it means we can slip right out through their hull like a quantum black hole, at most leaving a tiny leak they'll barely notice. Since they don't have full shields, we can get away cleanly."

"Yeah, but we won't be able to see where we're going."

"We only need to go a few kilometers."

"But generating this field would collapse the Cabochons, guaranteed! You want to just kill Scotty?"

"I don't want to kill anyone. But if we use this, it means that either Scotty's neutralized the danger himself, or the Cabochons are collapsing anyway and we have a split second to escape."

Stevens stared. "Tev, you are depressingly pragmatic."

"I thought you preferred solid realities over intangibles like theories and ideals."

"So I contradict myself," Stevens shrugged. "I'm not as large as you—well, as your ego—but I contain multitudes."

Suddenly a strident alarm sounded outside. The two engineers tensed. "Are the fields collapsing?" Stevens asked.

"I can't get a reading. Even the interference is gone! I can't read the Cabochons at all!"

"What does that mean?"

Suddenly there was a knock on the window. They looked up—to see Scotty making urgent faces at them, mouthing *Let me in! Hurry!*

Stevens wished shuttle hatches wouldn't open so slowly. But Scotty, showing unexpected spryness, clambered onto the hatch before it touched the ground. "Have ye got an escape ready?" he demanded.

"Yes, sir!" Tev replied crisply.

"Then use it now!"

"But the Cabochons—" Stevens began.

"Not a problem. *Go!*"

The shuttle jerked as Tev applied the new field equations. The warp engines weren't designed to shape this kind of field, and the crew felt every instability. But then it snapped into place, and everything was calm. Stevens didn't feel any smaller—but there was nothing outside but blackness, with a few intermittent flashes as the odd high-frequency gamma ray fluoresced against the warp envelope. After fifteen or so seconds, the shuttle began to vibrate again. "Field's destabilizing," Tev said. "Shutting down."

And the *Haley* popped back into normal space just a kilometer or so off the *da Vinci*'s starboard flank. Tev showed no surprise as he angled the shuttle around on a docking approach. "Oh, don't you dare tell me you meant to do that," Stevens moaned.

"Believe what you will," Tev replied cheerfully.

Scotty reviewed the console readouts. "You made your own microbubble! Very clever, lads."

"Well . . ." Stevens decided to be big about it. "I can't take the credit. It was the commander's idea. Tev, I have to admit, I could never have pulled off anything like that."

"Well, of course. I am a craftsman. You are a mechanic."

Stevens stared at Tev for a moment, then shrugged it off. "Fine. If you need me, I'll be at my anvil, pounding horseshoes." He moved over to Scotty, throwing him a *what's a guy to do?* look, but the S.C.E. chief just shook his head and chortled. "So tell us, Scotty, how'd you solve the Cabochon problem?"

"Och, I wish I could take credit, but all I know is, they just suddenly shut down. The interference vanished and all that was left"—and he reached into the pocket of his old-style uniform jacket and pulled out a handful of Cabochons—"was a pile o' pretty baubles. I managed to salvage a few for the museum. The Nachri are welcome to the rest—they went to all that trouble for 'em, after all," he laughed.

"But sir, how did you get away from the Nachri?" Stevens insisted. Scotty just glared at him as though it were a stupid question.

CHAPTER
8

"I was a fool," Cemal Iskander said as he gazed up at the Shanial dome, now the only physical evidence, aside from the empty Cabochons, that they had ever existed. "I can't believe I was so blind."

"It's understandable, Cemal," Scotty told him. "You had no way of knowin' who were the good guys and who were the bad guys."

"But I was far too quick to condemn the Shanial. I presumed them guilty, accepted the Nachri's lies that supported my prejudice, and refused to listen to the true innocents. Maybe if I had, they wouldn't have had to make such a sacrifice. At least some of them could've been evacuated in time."

"Or maybe not. They only had minutes to spare by that point."

Iskander shook his head, unappeased. After a long pause, he sighed. "You know that *jihad* doesn't truly mean 'war,' right? It's the struggle to defend what's right. Sometimes, yes, that means defending your community against invaders or oppressors. But the greater *jihad* is the one we wage every day against the weakness, doubt, and folly in our own minds. Scotty, I got so caught up in the lesser *jihad* that I failed in the greater. And so I violated one of the most basic commandments of *jihad*, never to strike against a nonaggressor. That makes me no better than the fanatics of past centuries who twisted the rhetoric of *jihad* to justify their betrayals of it."

"Cemal, you're bein' too hard on yourself. Aye, you made a mistake. We're all entitled to a few. What really matters is what you do *afterward*. You can wallow in regret and second-guessing, or you can move forward and build something new out o' the ashes, better and wiser than you were. From what I've been told, that's likely what the Shanial are doing right now—tryin' to build their pocket universe into something bigger and better. Who knows? There are other domains in subspace, whole other universes we cannot even reach yet. Maybe the Shanial will be able to travel between 'em, invent a whole new type of exploration."

"Maybe," the director said quietly.

"And look around you—folks are rebuildin' this city, just as they did before. 'Tis a cliché to say that life goes on, but the fact is, it does."

"And you should know, eh, Scotty?" Iskander teased, smiling a bit at last.

He looked up at the structure again. "I'm going to propose keeping this here permanently, as a monument to the Shanial's sacrifice, and to those who were tragically lost."

"That'd be a real *mitzvah*," said Captain Gold, coming

up alongside them. "You should make it a museum of their world—send archaeologists there, learn what their civilization was like before the Nachri attack."

"You're right. I'll talk to Admiral Ross, see what can be arranged."

"And what have we heard from the Nachri about all this *mishegoss,* anyway?" Gold asked.

"They insist Zakash is a rogue," Iskander told him. "That their legitimate government and military had no involvement in the attack. They've asked us to return him to Nachros for trial. Given Zakash's own claims to be leading a revolutionary movement, I suspect they're telling the truth."

"About that, probably," Gold said. "But people generally don't revolt against just, benevolent, fairly chosen leaders. If you ask me, the Federation should send observers to that trial, make sure it's fair, and do some general fact-finding—and think about whether we really want them as allies."

"I'll see to that myself." Iskander nodded.

"What's so funny?" O'Brien demanded, breaking off from recounting his adventures.

"I'm sorry, Miles," Keiko chuckled. "It's just . . . I know how you feel about being small. After the *Rubicon* thing," she told the S.C.E. team, "he had Dr. Bashir measure him every day for a week to make sure he was back to normal." The others laughed, and O'Brien fidgeted. "Don't worry, honey," Keiko teased wickedly. "You know I'd still love you whatever size you were."

After a moment, O'Brien gave in and accepted her good-natured teasing. Then he led her aside from the others. "The thing is, Keiko . . . I haven't exactly been big in other ways today. I'm . . . sorry about this morning."

"No, Miles, that's okay, I—"

"No, I mean it. I've been thinking about this. You're right, sweetheart—I haven't been spending enough time with you and the kids lately. I've been forgetting how precious the time we have is—how we need to make the most of every moment. So I'm going to be a different man, starting now. No more volunteer work—my time is for my wife and children." He broke off. Keiko didn't seem as happy as he'd expected she'd be. "What's wrong?"

"Oh, Miles . . . the fact is, I've realized something too. I don't begrudge you the time you spend helping people. On the contrary, I admire it! I just felt bad that I couldn't do the same. So I . . . I've applied for work at an agricultural lab. They're working on engineering fast-growing crops, high-yield oxygen producers, and other new flora for the planets that were hit hardest in the Dominion War, like Cardassia Prime and Gaylor VI. It's a way I can make a tangible difference, help rebuild the same way you do." Those beautiful eyes gazed at him apologetically. "But it means *I* won't have as much time for you and the kids." She studied him, waiting for an answer. "Miles? Are you okay with this?"

"Well . . . I mean, sure, it's . . ." He hugged her. "Keiko, I'm proud of you."

"And I'm proud of you."

"It's just . . . are we *ever* going to manage to have that nice quiet life together?"

She smiled. "Life always seems to have its own plans. We can only make the most of what time we do have."

O'Brien smiled. "I'm free tonight. What did you have in mind?"

Her smile was much wider, and promised a greater adventure than the one he'd just lived through.

Gomez gazed wistfully at the hastily departing O'Briens. "I'm glad somebody's had a happy ending today."

Corsi studied her. "And what kind of ending has your day had, Commander?"

Gomez pondered. "Bittersweet, I guess. I'm sad for all the people who lost loved ones today, and I'm sad for the Shanial. But they've all shown me something."

"What?"

"How to rebuild. How to start putting the pieces together. It doesn't matter if you don't know what they'll be when they're assembled—you just have to go ahead and start doing it, or you'll never find out."

Corsi pursed her lips. "I'm starting to think we're driving the engineering metaphors into the ground here."

Gomez laughed—her first laugh in quite some time. "You're right. That means it's probably time to wrap this up and go home."

"One more thing, though—did they ever find that last Cabochon?"

Gomez shook her head. "Could be anywhere. Buried underground where we'll never find it; sitting on some construction worker's shelf somewhere; blown out into the Pacific when the first Cabochon erupted. Maybe it wasn't even still on Earth. It doesn't matter now; it's just a harmless crystal."

"I know . . . but I hate loose ends."

"You'll just have to live with this one."

"I guess so."

Corsi and Gomez then beamed back up to the *da Vinci*, both of them ready to face the S.C.E.'s next mission.

ISHTAR RISING

Michael A. Martin & Andy Mangels

CHAPTER
1

Thirty-nine Days Ago

This place is the closest I've ever come to hell.

Dr. Pascal Saadya gazed through the viewport at the heat-distorted vista that lay before him. The terrain was typical of Venus: Fractured rock surfaces flattened by the ninety-bar atmosphere stretched toward the walls of a steep canyon whose details grew indistinct with distance in the smoglike haze. He knew the lethal heat of the planet couldn't penetrate Hesperus Ground Station's reinforced duranium hull—at least not so long as the shields remained operational. Nevertheless, tiny beads of sweat formed on his upper lip.

Venus was a terraforming challenge unlike any other. She was a deadly foe, and his body refused to be convinced otherwise.

"After spending six years overseeing Project Ishtar," said Adrienne Paulos as she inspected the instrument panel beside Saadya's, "it's hard to believe you've never been all the way down to the surface before."

Still looking out through the viewport, Saadya imagined he could feel the atmosphere of Aphrodite Terra pressing down on the ground station's structure, like the hand of some merciless god inexorably closing into a fist.

He forced the image from his mind.

"The big-picture theoretical work requires a global perspective, Adrienne," Saadya said, "and that's rather difficult to achieve down here beneath the clouds. Like trying to forecast Earth's weather from the bottom of the ocean. How are the force-field generators holding up?"

"Everything in the ground network is still looking nominal," Paulos said, then turned toward the pair of Bynars who ran the computer console to her immediate left. "How do the atmospheric numbers and the probe network data look?"

1011 and 1110—known to the predominantly human crew members of Project Ishtar as Ten-Eleven and Eleven-Ten—spoke in their customary smooth, collaborative manner, each finishing the other's utterances.

"According to the probe data—"

"—and our last round of chaotic atmospheric motion simulations—"

"—the force-field generator network should succeed in lifting the bulk of the atmosphere from this valley—"

"—all the way to the superrotational region of the cloudtops—"

"—and safely disperse it there."

The first step to setting this place to rights is to blow all the excess atmosphere off this Gehenna of a world.

Saadya felt awed by the powers now at his command. Using only directed force fields, they were preparing to displace a mass comparable to that of the Indian Ocean, moving it about as though it were furniture.

Saadya smiled. "Let's do it, then."

Paulos, the Bynars, and the rest of the crew—both in the ground station and up in the orbital facility—continued their work with resolve and professionalism. Within eight minutes, the force fields had pushed an immense swath of superheated, compressed carbon dioxide gas to an altitude of about sixty-nine-point-two kilometers above the canyon floor, where it came into contact with the fast-moving layers of the atmosphere, a torrent of noxious Venusian air that circled the entire slow-turning globe in a mere four Earth days.

The theory had been worked out superlatively. The numbers were right, as confirmed by the network of orbital satellites and the millions of tiny, interconnected probes that floated through the atmosphere. The force-field generators, the bulk of whose hardware was distributed among several hundred staffed and automated ground stations, were working to perfection.

Perfection. He smiled.

Then Saadya was momentarily struck speechless when the force-field generator network's computers became confused by the chaotic motions of the upper atmosphere and began feeding an ocean of ionized carbon dioxide—air displaced by the mass that Hesperus Station's energy fields had moved—straight back at the station dome with nearly the force of an asteroid impact.

"Abort!" shouted Paulos. The Bynar duo struggled to bring the forces the team had unleashed back under control, with no immediately apparent success.

From somewhere behind Saadya's instrument panel, one of the dome's support trusses groaned ominously.

Paulos evidently heard it, too. She cursed, then began speaking rapidly into a comm panel. "Ishtar Station, initiate backup force fields across the entire ground network."

Damn! Saadya thought. *This cock-up will take us weeks to set right.*

A moment later, the local force field collapsed and in-rushing atmosphere rang Hesperus as though it were a colossal church bell. The impact rocked the station, throwing Saadya to his knees. The Bynars fell like dominoes, though Paulos somehow managed to remain at her console.

The atmosphere must have breached the outer hull, Saadya thought, swallowing panic.

Braces and beams shrieked in protest, responding to the irresistible heat and pressure bearing down on them from just outside the inner hull. The exterior viewport shattered as though the angry god's fist had abruptly closed. Saadya's ears popped from the sudden change in pressure. Something hot seared his cheek.

Clinging to her console, Paulos shouted to be heard over the surrounding din and chaos. "Beam everyone on Hesperus the hell out *now!*"

Saadya's concerns about work setbacks now struck him as trivial. *This planet wants to kill us all,* he thought. His flesh began to crawl as though inundated by soldier ants, and he wondered if this is what flash incineration felt like.

Then a faint, semimusical tone reverberated in his ears, faded briefly, then returned to build into a labored crescendo.

To Saadya, the overstrained transporter's keening wail had never sounded so lovely.

Today

"Computer, run program Saadya Ishtar Endgame One."

From within the small holodeck, Dr. Pascal Saadya carefully opened an interior hatch and stepped out onto the rugged northern plains of Ishtar Terra. Black, gravel-strewn soil, so far able to support only intermittent patches of scrub vegetation, crunched beneath his boots.

As he always did whenever he ran this scenario, the terraformer reflected anxiously on the six years of his life he had already devoted to Project Ishtar, immersed in its monstrously complex theoretical and preparatory work.

I've survived the wait for six years. Surely I can wait a little longer to finish turning this world into the garden it is destined to become. Once the team finishes replacing the equipment that Aphrodite Terra devoured.

The air, already pleasantly warm, caressed Saadya's face, running its insubstantial fingers through his close-cropped, black-and-gray hair. The scent of wild strawberries wafted on the gentle breeze. He breathed the sweetness deeply into his lungs.

Saadya looked into the brightening sky and smiled. The moon—or rather, iron-gray Mercury, Venus's new surrogate natural satellite—presented a wide, gibbous disk as she descended slowly near the eastern horizon. *Right where I want her to be,* he thought. *Just where she will* need *to be if I am ever to take Ishtar all the way to completion.*

Turning toward the west, Saadya watched as the morning sun climbed over the steeply sloping prominence of snow-capped Maxwell Montes. The golden sun looked bloated, noticeably larger than it appeared when seen from the small village of his birth near Madras, India.

That was, of course, because Venus lay over forty million kilometers closer to the Sun than did Earth.

The grin on Saadya's dusky face intensified as he contemplated the enormity—and the sheer *rightness*—of this project. He gazed into an azure sky, now forever free of its crushing blanket of carbon dioxide. The clouds gathering on the southern horizon promised gentle, life-giving rains. This, he reflected, was how Venus should have been. *How she* will *be, by the time Project Ishtar is finished.*

Saadya wasn't the least bit startled by the sonorous voice that suddenly began speaking directly behind him. "I certainly must give you credit for ambition, Dr. Saadya."

He turned toward the sound, allowing the rising sun to warm his neck and shoulders. Before him stood three hologrammatic representations of men whose faces were especially familiar to scientists in Saadya's line of work.

"Good morning, Dr. Seyetik," Saadya said, bowing slightly toward the distinguished, gray-bearded man who had just spoken. "Please call me Pascal." This Saadya added despite the fact that the late flesh-and-blood version of Dr. Gideon Seyetik had always addressed him with the utmost formality, a forced politeness that Saadya attributed as much to contempt as to envy. Saadya knew well that the real Seyetik's ego had been colossal, restless, and fragile in the extreme. During his long life, Seyetik had produced a seemingly endless stream of papers, books, paintings—and refurbished worlds. Blue Horizon, New Halana, and the scores of other planets Seyetik had terraformed would stand for ages as monuments to that ego—masterworks painted on planetary-scale canvases, displayed in galleries of cosmic proportion.

True, Saadya had not tamed quite so many harsh worlds as had Seyetik. But then, even the great Seyetik had never set his sights on that mother of all terraforming conundrums: Venus. *Which of us, then*, Saadya wondered, *has the greater ego?*

One of the other two men who stood beside Seyetik spoke up. "Ambition is a fine thing, Gideon," said Dr. Kurt Mandl, the second member of the trio, his Federation Standard colored with a thick Teutonic accent. The rising sun gleamed against Mandl's bald pate. "For instance, reigniting the fires of Epsilon 119 must have required ambition in no small measure."

Seyetik cast a wry look at Mandl. "There's ambition, Doctor, and then there are pipe dreams. Starfleet has been trying to terraform Venus for how long now? Twenty-five years, on and off? Trying to make this hellbeast of a planet habitable would put even *my* talents to the test."

"You make a fine argument for a new approach to the problem," Mandl replied, offering Saadya a fatherly smile. "Perhaps the problem with some of the previous Venusian terraforming notions was that they weren't *sufficiently* ambitious." To the third man, who had not yet spoken, Mandl added, "No offense intended, Carl."

The man Mandl addressed appeared to have scarcely heard his colleague's comments, so enthralled was he by his surroundings. He breathed deeply of the air. Then, speaking to no one in particular, he said, "This really is Venus. As it will appear after the terraforming process is finished."

Saadya enjoyed the awed look on the dark-haired man's face. *This is how Surak might have looked had he lived long enough to witness peace finally breaking out on Vulcan. Or Einstein watching Cochrane accelerate the* Phoenix *past warp one.*

"That's correct, Dr. Sagan," Saadya said.

The twentieth-century planetologist squinted at the horizon, examining the brightening sky the way a jeweler might inspect an intricately cut gemstone. "I can't see any trace of the parasol you must have used to cool the atmosphere down. And you appear to have greatly increased the Venusian rotation rate. I can see that you're pretty far along in the process. It must have taken millennia to—"

"You'd do best to think of our surroundings as a mere thought experiment rather than a true picture of the final result, Dr. Sagan," Seyetik said. "Our young host hasn't pulled off his prospective miracle just yet."

Carl Sagan trained his curious gaze upon Saadya. "So what we're experiencing is actually some kind of . . . simulation?"

Saadya felt his face flush with embarrassment, but he recovered swiftly. "Yes, sir. But it is an extremely accurate one. My staff and I will make it a reality very soon. The key to that reality is dealing with its complexity."

"Ah," Sagan said. "Number crunching."

Saadya nodded, trying to imagine the primitive state of computing during Sagan's heyday. "To that end, the Bynars on my research team have increased our computational resources by orders of magnitude."

Sagan looked puzzled. "Bynars?"

"Bynars or no Bynars," Seyetik said to Saadya, apparently relishing the mellifluous sound of his own voice, "there are some extremely delicate calculations at play here. Needless to say, the state of the terraformer's art has evolved far beyond the use of giant beach umbrellas and atmospheric bombardments of blue-green algae." Seyetik's eyes met Sagan's as he made this last comment.

Dr. Sagan reddened, but was far too gentlemanly to rise to Seyetik's bait. Saadya knew well that Sagan had been among the first twentieth-century planetary scientists to seriously advance the notion that Sol's second planet might be made habitable. Back then, however, the mechanisms available for inducing such large-scale climate change were necessarily both primitive and prohibitively expensive. Sagan's suggestions that Venus's superhot atmosphere might be cooled down using giant spaceborne parasols and through the introduction of high-altitude microbes had eventually proved far too slow and difficult to work in actual practice.

Looking abashed by Seyetik's boorishness, Mandl broke the ensuing silence. "Whatever we have accomplished in the field of terraforming during this century, Dr. Sagan, we owe in large part to you, sir. We stand humbly upon the shoulders of giants."

Dr. Sagan smiled back at the older man, seemingly mollified. But he also appeared to be working very hard to ignore Seyetik.

Seyetik looked oblivious to this as he turned back toward Saadya. "Dr. Sagan might be interested in hearing how close your terraforming project came to utter destruction only— How long ago was it? A few weeks?"

Thirty-nine days, Saadya thought, gritting his teeth.

He was beginning to regret having programmed the station's holographic Seyetik simulacrum to be so faithful to the original.

Saadya noticed a moment later that both Sagan and Mandl were looking expectantly in his direction. "I will admit that Project Ishtar has suffered its share of setbacks recently," he said at length. "What worthwhile scientific enterprise hasn't?"

Sagan nodded, then resumed scanning the horizon and the distant, snow-bedecked steepness of Mount Maxwell. "The amount of energy you'll need just to cool down the atmosphere is incredible. The number of megajoules required must be—"

"Billions and billions," Seyetik said with a smirk.

Sagan sighed. "I never, *ever* said that. Why does everyone feel obliged to make that same pathetic joke every time they talk to me?"

Saadya felt obliged to steer the conversation back toward matters scientific and technical. "Actually, I'm taking the opposite approach, Dr. Sagan. I've chosen to thin the Venusian atmosphere by heating it up, rather than by cooling it down."

"So you must be planning to thin the atmosphere by blowing most of it off into space," Sagan said, looking intrigued. "But how?"

"Shaped force fields," Saadya said.

Sagan seemed disappointed. "Oh. Magic, then."

"Clarke's Law," said Mandl, shaking his head but maintaining a good-natured smile. "'Any sufficiently advanced technology is indistinguishable from magic.'"

"But only if that technology actually *works*," Seyetik said. "Terraforming Sol Two is no mere feat of legerdemain. It is an act of creation worthy of the gods themselves."

No pressure, Saadya thought, suppressing a nervous laugh.

Seyetik wasn't finished. To Dr. Mandl, he said, "But at least there are no hidden indigenous life-forms here on Venus that might compromise the project. Such things put quite a crimp into your terraforming efforts on Velara III, did they not?"

Dr. Sagan looked horrified. A storm cloud crossed Mandl's face. "There was no way to foresee that," Mandl said before lapsing into a moody silence not unlike Sagan's. Saadya had read the papers Dr. Mandl had written nearly a dozen years ago, after the partially terraformed planet Velara III had turned out to be the home of a subterranean species of sentient crystalline life.

Saadya knew all too well that such discoveries were the stuff of a terraformer's worst nightmares.

Seyetik raised a hand in a gesture of truce. "Forgive me, Dr. Mandl. I know that the scanning technology your team had available then did not permit the detection of the native fauna until it was nearly too late."

Mandl appeared content to forgive Seyetik's behavior. "Such are the limits of technology."

"Technology can be a finicky thing, indeed," Seyetik said, nodding. "But failures of vision on the part of the powers that be have scuttled more good science than all of technology's glitches and gremlins combined."

"The Federation Council," Saadya said, realizing too late that he had been thinking aloud.

"Exactly," Seyetik said. He seemed to be warming up to full lecture-hall mode. "Governance is about resource allocation every bit as much as terraforming is. Unfortunately, the Federation has other resource priorities."

Saadya swallowed hard. "The Council will resume

giving the project its full support," he said, "once the war damage on Betazed is put to rights."

"Let us all hope so," Mandl said, nodding sympathetically.

Seyetik mirrored Mandl's expression, but somehow made it look mocking. "Indeed. Let's hope they don't make you wait in line behind all the *other* places that need rebuilding after the war. Don't forget the beating that Benzar took. Or Durala V. Or Sybaron. Or Ajilon Prime. Hell, they're even sending aid to Cardassia. I hope with all that going on the Council can still afford to throw you a few scraps."

Saadya grinned. "As long as I have the assistance of the Bynars, you'd be surprised at how little else I need."

As if cued, two high-pitched voices issued from Saadya's wristcom, disrupting his train of thought. *"Dr. Saadya?"* said 1011 and 1110, uttering their words in alternation.

"Speak of the devil," said Seyetik, a look of mock surprise blossoming across his face.

Saadya raised his wristcom. "Saadya here. Go ahead."

"We are receiving an incoming communication."

"It is from the Central Processor Pair—"

"—on Bynaus. They wish to confer—"

"—with you—"

"—immediately."

The uncharacteristically jangled cadence in the Bynars' tandem speech told Saadya at once that the news couldn't be good. "I'm on my way," he said, already walking toward the holodeck door.

"I'll keep my fingers crossed for you, Dr. Saadya," Seyetik called out as the hatch opened.

"Computer, delete—" Saadya paused on the threshold. He had been about to instruct the holodeck to delete the insufferably egomaniacal scientist. Then he smiled grimly as he realized that that description might just as easily be applied to Saadya himself. He was, after all, trying to accomplish the impossible.

"Computer, end program," he said finally. Mandl, Sagan, Seyetik, and the transmogrified Venus all vanished like morning mist as Saadya strode quickly into the corridor.

Saadya trotted onto the orbiting station's observation deck, which faced the planet, whose bilious yellow cloudtops seethed some three hundred and fifty kilometers below. Ishtar Station currently straddled the slow-moving day-night terminator of Venus.

Despite his hurry, Saadya spared a moment to glance at the clouds that concealed a surface that couldn't have differed more from his terraformed-Venus holodeck scenario. Below that dense, poisonous atmosphere lay a surface whose temperature would quickly melt lead—and which could just as quickly destroy the string of tiny ground stations that lay along the equator, as well as their human crews, should their force-field generators suffer catastrophic failures of the kind that had burned up Ground Station Hesperus. The tiny planet Mercury was not in orbit around Venus, as had been the case in the holodeck scenario; the battered, iron-rich world still cleaved to the same sunward track it had followed since time immemorial. Here, in the unmodified reality of the inner solar system, the barren little planet would soon appear as an evening star, a bright dot visible only briefly between the setting sun's waning glare and Venus's gradually darkening western limb.

I know we can make my *Venus a reality,* Saadya thought. *All we need is more time. And perhaps a small miracle or two.*

Adrienne Paulos cleared her throat, interrupting Saadya's reverie. One of Saadya's senior research assistants, the young Denevan had apparently materialized out of nowhere, as had the holodeck planetologists. He couldn't help wondering if this was a subtle hint that she, too, was destined for greatness.

When Saadya turned toward Paulos he immediately saw the stricken look on her face. "I see Bynaus didn't waste any time giving you the bad news," he said as they began walking together toward his small private office.

Paulos shook her head, and a shock of blond hair popped up from where she had pinned it back. "They won't talk to anybody but you, Pas. But you don't have to be a Betazoid to guess what they have to say. They're pretty grumpy."

"Well, you know how Bynars hate to be kept waiting when they have data they want to upload." Saadya smiled weakly. Though she returned the gesture, it was clear to him that his studied nonchalance wasn't reassuring her in the least.

1011 and 1110 stood sheepishly beside the office door, their pale, hairless heads bearing identical worried frowns.

"The Central Processor Pair remains—"

"—waiting on the open channel. We surmised—"

"—that you might wish—"

"—to speak to them—"

"—in the privacy—"

"—of your personal workspace."

Saadya thanked the diminutive computer experts and motioned for Paulos to accompany him inside the small, cluttered room. The office was dominated by a small viewport that faced Venus, several shelves sagging beneath the weight of dozens of ancient-looking hardbound books, and a battered desk topped with a veneer of half-billion-year-old Venusian igneous rock.

Two aged Bynars glowered at Saadya from the computer terminal sitting at the desk's center. *"Your latest report contained little of use to us,"* said the Bynars, who spoke in an impatient tandem.

Saadya sat before the monitor and silently counted to five before responding. "Terraforming is often not subject to exact timetables, Honored Processors. There are always unknowns that require time to iron out."

The elderly Bynars nodded, though their expressions did not soften.

"That is as may be. However, time—"

"—has been at a premium for us—"

"—ever since our primary star—"

"—went nova."

Saadya was well acquainted with the 2364 Beta Magellan supernova. It had threatened not only the planetary computer network upon which the entire Bynar civilization depended, but had also nearly extinguished all life in their solar system. During the latter phases of the Dominion War—when Project Ishtar hadn't been able to count on the unwavering support of either Starfleet or an understandably preoccupied Federation Council—Saadya had turned to the planetary government of Bynaus for help. Still recovering from the decade-old Beta Magellan disaster, the Bynars had been happy to lend their computational personnel to

Saadya's Venusian terraforming effort—so long as the data it yielded proved useful in their own long-term ecological recovery efforts.

"Please be patient," Saadya said. "I've only been working with the Venusian environment for six years, after all. That's hardly a drop in the ocean, so to speak, of the planet's four-billion-year history. Nevertheless, we are very close to being able to implement an accelerated terraforming program. It will be only a matter of a few weeks before we can begin making permanent physical changes to the planet."

The Bynars appeared unmoved by Saadya's entreaty.

"You have promised imminent success before—"

"—but it seems that you are also—"

"—on the verge of disaster. Need we remind you—"

"—that the Bynar pair we lent you—"

"—could easily have perished when the shielding—"

"—collapsed in your surface facility?"

Saadya ground his teeth together involuntarily. He and Paulos had both nearly died that day as well. "That's why I had Ishtar Station maintain a constant transporter lock on all of us. 1011 and 1110 were in no more danger than I was myself. Ask them yourself."

The Central Processor Pair sniffed as one.

"We do not wish to continue—"

"—placing them at risk—"

"—indefinitely. Not in the furtherance—"

"—of a project that appears rapidly—"

"—to be approaching a rather hazardous—"

"—dead end."

"What are you saying?" Saadya said, a foul taste appearing in his mouth.

The Pair's black eyes flashed.

"We will recall our Calculation Team—"

"—in another two of your weeks. Unless—"

"—you can give us a tangible reason—"

"—to refrain from doing so."

A black hole yawned open in the pit of Saadya's stomach. "You know I can't guarantee—"

"We have never asked you—"

"—for guarantees, Dr. Saadya. However—"

"—our resources are limited—"

"—and our world's ecological problems—"

"—remain vast. If—"

"—you are indeed as close—"

"—to a breakthrough as you say, then—"

"—two more weeks should afford you—"

"—ample time."

The screen abruptly went blank.

The office remained silent until Paulos cleared her throat and said, "That certainly went well. There's only one problem."

Saadya nodded. "A two-week deadline will put us on a completely impossible schedule. We'd never have enough time to finish the chaotic Hadley-cell atmospheric modeling, to say nothing of the lithospheric response simulations."

"Not if we want to maintain a margin of safety when we activate the entire planetary force-field grid for real," Paulos said, leaning against the bookcase. She clearly hadn't forgotten the near-catastrophe that had resulted the last time their numbers had failed to jibe closely enough with the unpredictable vicissitudes of the real world.

"What if we were to ask the Federation Council for some additional short-term help?" she asked.

Saadya shook his head wearily. "It would probably take at least two weeks just to get a formal request in front of the Science and Technology Committee. No, Adrienne. I'm afraid we're on our own." *And that could mean that six years of work is about to get tossed right out the airlock.*

He realized glumly that none of Seyetik's projects had ever come to such an ignominious end.

"Then what we really need," she said, "is more Bynars to help Ten-Eleven and Eleven-Ten with the number-crunching."

"That's not funny." Saadya said, scowling. *How could she make jokes at a time like this?*

"No, I'm serious, Pas. So the authorities on Bynar are being stingy. Why can't we look elsewhere for what we need?"

Saadya sighed in resignation. It was obvious that she was determined to draw this out. "Look where?"

"The last time I checked," Paulos said, "there was a Bynar pair working as civilian observers aboard a Starfleet Corps of Engineers ship. One of those retro-looking *Saber*-class jobs."

Despite having served in Starfleet decades ago, Saadya hadn't kept up with the starship configurations of the past several years. These days, he wasn't sure he could distinguish a *Saber* from a *Sovereign*.

But he cautiously allowed hope to rise within him anyway. "What ship?"

"The *da Vinci*, I think."

The da Vinci. The name triggered a sudden avalanche of memories. *What spectacular luck.*

"Would you do me a favor, Adrienne?" Saadya asked.

"Shoot."

Saadya grinned. "Find out if David Gold is still in command of that ship."

CHAPTER
2

Captain David Gold headed straight to his ready room the moment Pascal Saadya had finished making his somewhat oblique request for assistance.

"So he didn't say what help, precisely, he was hopin' you could provide?" said Captain Montgomery Scott, the Starfleet Corps of Engineers' official liaison, and Gold's immediate superior, from the small computer terminal on the ready room's desk.

"Not exactly."

Scott offered a good-natured scowl. *"Typical. But you also say he's one of your oldest friends."*

"That's right."

Gold thought he saw a wistful look pass across Scott's face. *"Old friendships are something I can appreciate,"* Scott said. *"But I have to be honest with you, lad—I'm not thrilled about Saadya's plans to play billiards with the inner solar system."*

"Haven't you played a bit of planetary pool yourself, Scotty?" Gold said. "I seem to remember reading about a tide-locked planet that you once helped spin up to something resembling an Earth-normal day-night cycle."

Scott sighed. *"Aye, I have to admit to helpin' the Dumada put the planet Rimillia to rights. But that was a very long time ago—very nearly came to a bad end for millions of people."*

"You're not saying you regret it, are you, Scotty?" Gold said, grinning.

"Not at all. But that mission did give me a healthy respect for the forces of nature." Scott paused contemplatively for a moment before continuing. *"I suppose I must seem hypocritical."*

Very deliberately, Gold adopted a demeanor of wide-eyed innocence. "Perish forbid I should even *suggest* such a thing."

Scott appeared to have come to a decision. *"An old commander of mine once warned me that I ought to be more tolerant of fresh ideas. All right, then. Far be it from me to stand in the way o' progress. Besides, maybe havin' an S.C.E. contingent watchin' over the critical phases of his experiment will keep Saadya's haggis out of the fire. Just give me a detailed report once all the shoutin's over."*

"Thank you, sir," Gold said, smiling. After Scott had signed off, Gold tapped his combadge. "Wong, this is the captain."

"Aye, sir," came the conn officer's response.

"There's been a small change in plans. Best speed back to the Sol System." The *da Vinci* had only just departed Earth a few weeks earlier. "And tell everyone to bring their suntan lotion. We're in for some warm weather."

"*Sir?*"

"We're off to Venus. Gold out."

"Dropping into a standard equatorial orbit," said Lieutenant Songmin Wong, still working the conn station.

"Very good, Wong," said Gold, sitting in the command chair at the center of the *U.S.S. da Vinci*'s busy bridge. He stroked his chin with his biosynthetic left hand as he stared contemplatively at the amber, cloud-shrouded world that already half-filled the main viewer.

He couldn't help but recall that it had been in a similarly hellish planetary atmosphere that he had lost his hand not very long ago. But Galvan VI had cost him a good deal more than that—half his crew had died there, and the *da Vinci* herself had very nearly been pulled down to a fiery demise in the superdense core of that gas-giant world.

So many good people lost, he thought, his mind conjuring faces out of the broad swirls of the cloudtops. He would never forget McAllan, the tactical officer who had always insisted on such spit-and-polish formality on the bridge—and who had died while pushing Gold away from several collapsing bridge ceiling support beams. Or Barnak, who had been immolated along with most of his engine-room crew while saving the ship from an imminent warp-core breach.

And Duffy, whose sacrifice had saved not only the *da Vinci* but Galvan VI's resident global civilization as well, a race of energy beings who called themselves the Ovanim.

If any force in the universe could have restored those lives in exchange for his own, he'd have struck the bargain in a heartbeat.

The turbolift doors hissed open directly behind the captain, interrupting his grim meditation. He turned and watched his first officer, Commander Sonya Gomez, enter the bridge. Trailing behind her was Lieutenant Commander Domenica Corsi, chief of security, and Lieutenant Commander Tev, the ship's new second officer.

Gold glanced over his shoulder and observed Gomez and Corsi watching the screen, apparently enthralled by the spectacular image displayed there. Tev merely glared down over his flat Tellarite nose at the viewer, his blunt, hirsute face a study in disdain.

If the tableau on the viewer provoked any Galvan VI-related unease in Gomez or Corsi, neither officer revealed it. Instead, both women seemed momentarily awestruck, like children seeing the Grand Canyon or the Valles Marineris for the first time.

"Venus," Gomez said. "I've never taken the time to come here before."

Gold smiled, thinking of all the denizens of New York City who had never managed to fit a visit to the Statue of Liberty into their hectic schedules. His New York–bred wife, Rabbi Rachel Gilman, had yet to make the brief trip downtown to the reconstructed monument.

"I haven't been here since I took dense-atmosphere flight training back at the Academy," Corsi said, her gaze captivated by the lethal, deceptively placid-looking cloudtops. "It's funny how little the planet has changed since then. Considering how long terraforming efforts have been going on here, I mean."

"That's why we're here," Gomez said. "To help the Ishtar team fix whatever seems to be holding the project back."

"How long has the project been under way?" Corsi said.

"It's been six years and change since Pascal Saadya took the reins," Gold said. "And Starfleet had been studying the whole Venus-terraforming concept for a couple of decades before that."

Gomez whistled, evidently surprised. "Six years. That seems like sort of a long time for one of Dr. Saadya's terraforming jobs."

Gold nodded. "Dr. Saadya told me that preparing and testing mathematical climate models has taken up the lion's share of his time up until now. But he claims that the numbers phase of the work is finally coming to an end. So the time has come, at long last, to apply a bit of elbow grease and start turning the nuts and bolts."

Corsi made a face. "I wonder how he was able to sit on his hands for such a long time and do nothing but . . . *calculate*."

Gold shook his head and allowed an impish grin to spread across his face. "Maybe six years sounds like a long stretch to you and me, but Saadya can be a patient cuss when he needs to be."

But it's never taken him more than four years, tops, to renovate an entire planet from soup to nuts, Gold thought. *Strange.*

"I've read some of Dr. Saadya's papers," Gomez said, sounding impressed. "He's already terraformed a couple dozen pretty inhospitable planets. He'll probably go down in history right alongside some of planetology's real legends, like Gideon Seyetik and Carl Sagan."

Gold maintained his grin. "That's what Pas always believed. I can already tell that the two of you are going to get along great."

Gomez's jaw dropped. "You know him personally?"

"Before he went full-time into the business of re-creating the heavens and the Earth, he was a junior science officer aboard the *Gettysburg*. We struck up a friendship there and we've tried to keep up with each other's careers ever since. But before yesterday I hadn't heard from him in years."

He only seems to get in touch when he needs a favor from Starfleet. Or has an extremely farshtinkener tsoreh *of a problem that he needs somebody else to fix in a hurry.*

"Saadya's project is obviously suffering from some fundamental efficiency problems," said Tev, shaking his head dismissively at the image displayed on the screen. The *da Vinci* was quickly approaching the planet's night side.

"I'm no planetologist," Corsi said, apparently in reluctant agreement, "but maybe Dr. Saadya has bitten off more than he can chew with this project."

Gold shrugged. "We'll find out soon enough." He couldn't help but wonder whether Corsi was right. Had his old friend finally taken on a world that even his great talents couldn't tame? *Pas certainly hasn't lost any of his* chutzpah. *Nobody can take* that *away from him.*

"Faugh," said Tev. "Some truly egregious errors have been committed here, despite Saadya's alleged 'patience.' Otherwise the terraformers wouldn't have destroyed one of their own key ground stations."

Turning to face the Tellarite, Gold said, "I'm sure Dr. Saadya will be delighted to accept your keen engineering insights, Tev. And that Project Ishtar's problems, whatever they may be, will soon be in the most capable of hands."

Tev nodded to Gold, clearly accepting the compliment with what passed for good grace among Tellarites.

Though Gold knew his praise sounded superficially sarcastic, his words were, in fact, utterly sincere. Despite Tev's lengthy inventory of personality deficits—vanity, arrogance, and overweening conceit predominating among them—none of Tev's crewmates could dispute his technical brilliance.

"Ishtar," Gomez repeated, still staring at the hothouse planet. The *da Vinci* continued moving languidly toward the terminator that demarcated one end of the long Venusian night. "I know that name's from some old myth or other."

"Mesopotamian," Corsi said. "Assyrian and Babylonian, mostly. She was a fertility goddess. They used to call this planet Ishtar all over the ancient Middle East."

Gold's eyebrows lifted in surprise. "Have you started working Abramowitz's side of the street, Corsi?"

The security chief shrugged. "I guess I got interested in ancient cultures back at the Academy around the same time I was memorizing Sun-Tzu's *Art of War*." Gold wondered briefly if, in turn, Abramowitz, the ship's cultural specialist, had secretly cultivated some unarmed combat expertise that she was keeping to herself. *Go figure*, he thought.

"This is simply an N-class world with a toxic, reducing atmosphere," Tev said. "Perhaps this so-called Project Ishtar is less than efficient because the humans running it have chosen to waste so much of their time and energy on romantic superstitions and unproductive tale-telling."

Gomez scowled. "Romantic or not, most of us humans find 'tale-telling' a rewarding pastime. And a lot of fun to boot."

"I am not here to have 'fun,'" sniffed Tev. "I am here to repair what others have broken."

"I'm sure we'll all have a positively delightful time," Corsi said, deadpan.

Standing behind the tactical console located at the rear of the bridge, Lieutenant Anthony Shabalala interrupted Tev's response. "Ishtar Station is coming into view, Captain."

On the screen, the exterior running lights of the half-kilometer-long Ishtar Station had become visible, peeking out from beyond the dark side of the planet's terminator.

"Hail them, Shabalala," Gold said, grateful to get back to business.

"Aye, sir," the tactical officer said. "Hailing frequency open."

A moment later, the noxious cloudscape vanished from the screen, replaced by the face of a dark-skinned man who appeared to be in his early sixties. When Pascal Saadya saw Gold he smiled, displaying his even, brilliantly white teeth.

"David! It's good to see you again, my old friend."

Rising from his command chair, Gold returned Saadya's smile. "Likewise, Pas. What can we do for you? I know it has something to do with assistance for your terraforming project, but our last conversation was a bit, ah, vague." As, Gold thought, was the initial message Saadya had sent him the previous day.

Saadya's smile faltered for a moment, but quickly recovered much of its wattage. *"I'd prefer we discuss that in private, if you don't mind. Could we meet aboard the station?"*

Something's got him rattled, Gold thought.

Aloud, he said, "My first officer and I will beam right over."

*　　　*　　　*

It was long past midnight as the schedule was reckoned aboard Ishtar Station, and most of the staff had already retired for the evening. But Pascal Saadya wasn't one who tended to waste much of his precious time sleeping. He regarded the dearth of other people in the vicinity of his office principally as an absence of distraction.

Saadya was beside himself with both joy and relief as he watched Gold and his first officer materialize on the transporter pad near his office. The joy was sincere and heartfelt, for it had been too many years since he'd seen his old friend David in person. The relief stemmed from what Saadya had heard about the crack team of engineers David commanded.

Particularly his Bynar pair.

"I have to tell you, Pas," David Gold said after the initial greetings and pleasantries were exchanged, "my boss wasn't keen on diverting the *da Vinci* here."

Leaning against the side of his cheerfully disordered desk, Saadya steepled his fingers. "Ah. Montgomery Scott. A true traditionalist. Tell me, what specifically bothers him about the project?"

Saadya watched as Gold's eyes strayed to the cloud-tops that were visible through the office viewport. "Captain Scott seems to have more than one objection."

Saadya did his best not to scowl. *Deliver me from the Starfleet brass and their retrograde thinking. And they say* Venus *spins backward.*

"For instance?" Saadya asked carefully.

Gold appeared to consider his words for a moment before speaking. "For starters, he's not thrilled with your plan to tow Mercury into a new orbit around Venus."

Saadya chuckled. "I see. No doubt because I wish to tamper with the familiar early-morning skies of his youth. Unfortunately, it's a step I will have to take eventually if Venus is ever to take her rightful place as Earth's twin world."

Gold offered Saadya a blank look, then gazed toward Gomez. The *da Vinci's* first officer appeared to understand.

"You need to create tidal effects," she said. "You're planning to jump-start the Venusian core by generating a magnetic field to keep out hard radiation."

Saadya felt a broad, involuntary smile cross his face. "Mercury will also stabilize the Venusian rotational axis over multimillion-year timescales."

Gold's eyebrows rose as the true enormity of Project Ishtar appeared to sink in. "You've taken on quite a job, Pas," he said at length. "No wonder it's taken six years just to get through the number-crunching phase."

"I do not believe in taking half-measures, David. Of course, one mustn't get ahead of oneself. These steps won't be taken until after the atmospheric reconditioning is completed."

"And there, I'm guessing, lies the problem," Gold said, nodding. "And the reason you've asked the S.C.E. for help."

"Precisely," Saadya said, trying to keep the edge of desperation out of his voice.

"I'm not sure exactly what we can do for you, though," Gomez said. "The *da Vinci* doesn't carry a lot of atmospheric processing equipment."

"I know," Saadya said. "But that's not why I asked you to come. What I need is your crew's computational brilliance, to tie up the final loose ends of our atmospheric dynamics simulations. Particularly that of your resident Bynar pair."

Gold and his first officer reacted in a manner that

Saadya didn't expect—they cast distinctly uncomfortable looks at one another.

The captain was the first to break the ensuing silence. "Ah, Pas, something's happened that you obviously weren't made aware of."

Saadya felt the emotional scaffolding behind his smile begin to crumble. He struggled not to show any anxiety. "What do you mean? You *do* have a Bynar pair serving aboard the *da Vinci,* don't you, David?"

"*Had* a Bynar pair," Gold said.

A pit of despair opened in Saadya's belly. He couldn't keep his eyebrows from vaulting heavenward. "They're gone?" He trailed off in confusion. For a brief, irrational moment, he wondered if the Central Processor Pair on Bynaus had discovered his plan to draft a second Bynar pair and recalled Gold's Bynars out of sheer spite.

"One of our two Bynar crew members was killed on an away mission earlier this year," Gold said quietly.

Without that Bynar pair, Saadya thought, *there truly is very little these people can do to help save Ishtar.*

"Pas, how the hell did you even know we *had* a Bynar pair on board?" Gold said. "Your Starfleet membership card lapsed a long time ago."

Hearing no heat behind his old friend's words, Saadya offered him a rueful smile. "Surely you've spent enough time around us technical types, David, to know that we're nothing if not resourceful."

"You forgot to mention sneaky and underhanded," Gold said, returning the smile. "But it's reassuring that you don't seem to be quite sneaky and underhanded enough to steal current information. Anyhow, we've just got the one, now."

Saadya's brow wrinkled. "Just the one what?"

"Bynar. After 111's death, 110 decided to stay on board. He's going by the name Soloman now, and he's our resident computer expert."

Hope rekindled within Saadya. *All right. If I can't have access to another Bynar pair, perhaps a solo Bynar will do in a pinch.*

Aloud, Saadya said, "I thought Bynars always stayed in bonded pairs."

"They generally do—*if* they expect to integrate back into Bynar society," Gomez said. "Single Bynars tend to be pariahs among their own people."

Saadya briefly considered whether a Bynar social leper might succeed in expediting the computational efforts that were taking up so much of 1011's and 1110's time these days. *Surely they wouldn't let a social stigma affect a working relationship,* he thought. *Not on something as important as Project Ishtar.*

"Soloman," Saadya said aloud, parsing the name's evident meaning. "Doesn't that name seem vaguely insulting to you? It sounds like a reminder of what he's lost."

"He's never complained about it," Gold said, his tone growing defensive. "We both sort of arrived at it together."

Gomez cocked an eyebrow and adopted an almost lecturing tone. "In fact, I think the name helps him deal with his single status successfully. And it might even give him a perspective on information technology that's completely unique among Bynars."

Fascinating. A Bynar who stands astride both Bynar and human experience, Saadya thought, hope returning. *Perhaps he could be useful in ways I haven't even anticipated yet.*

Saadya held out his hands in a placating gesture. "Forgive me, David. I did not mean to criticize your crewperson's choice of nomenclature." He sighed. "Will you help us?"

"No offense taken, Pas," Gold said. "And as long as the *da Vinci* is in the neighborhood, you'll have all the engineering and material support we can spare. Commander Gomez will supply you with whatever you need. Including the able assistance of Soloman."

Saadya felt his smile broaden. "Thank you, David. You may well be the salvation of Team Ishtar's efforts."

Perhaps I won't need that second Bynar pair after all. Maybe one individual will make all the difference.

If not, he knew he had run out of other options.

CHAPTER
3

Gold was pleased to see that the *da Vinci's* senior staff was already assembled when he and Gomez arrived together in the starship's main briefing room at 0758. Present around the irregularly shaped table were Tev, Soloman, tactical systems specialist Fabian Stevens, and structural systems specialist P8 Blue. The former three individuals already were seated, while Blue sat in her specially modified chair at the end of the table. Also present were Corsi, cultural specialist Carol Abramowitz, cryptography expert Bart Faulwell, and Dr. Elizabeth Lense, the *da Vinci's* chief medical officer.

A few hours earlier, Dr. Saadya had supplied Gold and Gomez with copious amounts of data regarding Project Ishtar, intended to bring the *da Vinci's* staff up to speed as quickly as possible. From the intent manner with which most everyone was studying their padds, Gold intuited that his people were still doing as much last-minute homework as they could cram.

"Good morning, everybody," he began as he sat at his usual spot at the head of the table. "As I'm sure you've all already noticed by now, the project we're going to assist Dr. Saadya and his team with is pretty heady stuff."

Corsi's earlier expression of awe had been replaced by a furrowed brow, a change no doubt caused by prolonged exposure to cold, hard data. As usual, the security chief didn't mince words. "It looks pretty damned dangerous, sir," she said, setting her padd down on the table. "If everything doesn't go perfectly to plan, it's going to be a real challenge just keeping everybody on the team alive."

Gold tried to muster a smile, but failed as recollections of Galvan VI sprang to mind unbidden. "That's why I invited you to the party." He took a seat, then faced Dr. Lense. "And you, too, Doctor. As Corsi has pointed out, this project is liable to suffer a catastrophe during its next phase—unless everybody involved is *very* careful. Lots of people could be injured."

Lense did not look enthusiastic. "Anybody exposed to that witch's cauldron of an atmosphere for more than a couple of seconds will be way past my ability to help."

To break the pensive silence he sensed was about to engulf the room at that statement, Gold nodded to Gomez, signaling her to begin the technical briefing.

"The real dangers are hard to evaluate objectively," Gomez said, still standing as she looked over the figures on her own padd. As she continued, Gold noticed that she, too, now seemed haunted by memories of the hell-world where her lover, second officer Kieran Duffy, had died. "Venus isn't the most human-friendly environment in the solar system, so any approach to terraforming it is certain to involve some unavoidable hazards."

Gold admired his first officer's talent for understatement. With a temperature of around four hundred and eighty degrees Celsius, Venus's surface was the hottest in the solar system, except for the sun's photosphere. Flesh would vaporize in moments, and its surface pressure of ninety bars would just as swiftly crush humanoid bones—or a Nasat exoskeleton—flat. *"Venus" and "friendly" shouldn't even be used in the same sentence.*

Corsi seemed to be having similar thoughts. "Doing the work from orbit seems to me a surefire way of avoiding the worst of those hazards," she said dryly.

Gold silently conceded that the security chief's point was an excellent one. Why subject anyone to unnecessary risks on that pressure cooker of a planet?

"Unfortunately, the whole project depends on a large number of networked ground stations," Gomez said. "The equipment and software are pretty complex, and only some of these facilities can be automated by slaving them to other stations. But somebody's got to run and monitor at least the key surface stations."

"What about using telepresence?" Faulwell said, a skeptical frown creasing his boyish features. "I'd think that techies in a nice, safe orbit could run the equipment remotely just as easily as people on the ground could."

"Amen," Corsi said.

"That's because your respective specialties involve word puzzles and brute force," Tev interjected testily, addressing both Corsi and Faulwell, "rather than the fluid dynamics of N-class planetary atmospheres."

Gomez quickly interceded, prompting Gold to wonder what pungent reply Faulwell had been about to deliver to the second officer. "It's a good question, Bart. But that superheated carbon dioxide ocean that separates us from the planet's surface makes ship-to-ground communications pretty spotty. Also, the atmosphere is filled with literally millions of tiny, reinforced probes. They're in constant subspace contact with each other, the ground stations, the satellite network, and Station Ishtar up in orbit. That web of transmissions can create interference problems with high-bandwidth communications as well. But without it, the force-field generators can't stay ahead of the atmosphere's chaotic motions."

Stevens spoke up. "I think somebody had better point out that the superrotational zone"—at the blank looks from Corsi, Lense, Abramowitz, and Faulwell, he quickly added—"that's the turbulent atmospheric layer that circles the planet once every four days, can play hob with a transporter beam. Those people at Hesperus Ground Station were lucky they were able to beam out before the atmosphere flooded in and flattened the place."

"That's a potential problem, I'll admit," said Gomez. "But the project scientists have already provided a lot of good atmospheric data that will help us compensate for that, as well as information on beaming through the gaps in their force-field nodes. When you're talking about moving an entire planetary atmosphere the way the Ishtar team plans to do it, you can't afford either comm glitches or transporter foul-ups. So even though it's dangerous, I'm afraid we're stuck with the up-close-and-personal approach."

Looking overwhelmed, Faulwell set his padd on the tabletop and pushed it away as though it were a plate filled with writhing Klingon *gagh.* "Can somebody please explain to me *exactly* what we're getting involved with here? Preferably *without* all the columns of figures. Any language will do. Even Tellarite." He glanced playfully at the second officer.

Tev snorted. "Linguists. Perhaps we should have arranged the data into rhyming stanzas for your benefit."

"All right," Gomez said, putting up a hand in an apparent effort to encourage Bart and Tev to bury the hatchet. "Remember, this mission is as much about data processing as it is about making brute-force changes to the planet." She gestured toward Soloman.

"I will help coordinate the data-flow between the probe network and the ground stations on a full test of Ishtar's hardware and software," the slight Bynar said, his hands primly folded on the table beside his padd.

"What's involved," Gomez continued, "is a complex, planetwide network of surface-deployed devices designed to thin out and cool the Venusian atmosphere. Rather than using slower methods, like giant orbiting 'parasols,' Dr. Saadya is using a radically different approach: His plan is to use specially shielded, tandem-operated field generators to create a partially gas-permeable force field. The overall operation will follow a carefully orchestrated meteorological plan. But the field will constantly adjust itself to adapt in real time to observed changes in air pressure, temperature, and velocity as it envelops the entire planet and slowly expands outward toward the sunward side."

If Stevens repeats that crack about "Venus enlargers" I overheard him make last night, Gold thought, *I'm putting him on report.*

Stevens merely sat listening attentively, his eyes twinkling with suppressed mischief, as Gomez continued. "The goal is to push the bulk of the atmosphere far enough away from the surface so that the sun will heat it even further, blowing most of it off into space in a matter of days."

"Pas was never one for taking the slow road if he could avoid it," Gold said.

Gomez continued. "The net result is a quick reduction of both the atmospheric pressure and the greenhouse effect, in the direction of something considerably more Earth-like than what's there now. The process should knock hundreds of degrees off the planet's surface temperature virtually overnight."

"Sounds too good to be true," Corsi said.

Tev waved his padd before him, and spoke in a throaty rumble. "The theoretical work appears sound. What remains to be proved is whether or not it will work in practice." Gold wasn't certain, but he thought he heard grudging admiration in the Tellarite's tone.

"For all that effort and danger, I still don't see how it's going to turn Venus into another Earth," said Lense. "The planet still takes, what, three months to turn on its axis."

"One hundred and seventeen days," said Pattie.

"Whatever. It's still a problem. Along with the planet's complete lack of free oxygen, or even a magnetic field. Think of all the radiation-related health hazards that alone will create for anybody trying to live on the surface."

"TANSTAAFL," Abramowitz said.

"Excuse me?" said Gold.

"A very ancient homily that every good scientist or engineer ought to remember. 'There Ain't No Such Thing As A Free Lunch.'"

"Exactly," Gomez said, nodding with apparent enthusiasm. "Remember, folks, the initial 'big blowoff' we're assisting with here will only be the first step in a many-years-long process. Adding in the appropriate amounts of nitrogen, oxygen, and surface water will come next, from comets barged down from the Kuiper Belt. Huge surface-mounted impulse engines will be set up to try to speed the planet's slow, retrograde rotation up to an approximately twenty-four-hour cycle, like that of Earth or Mars."

Pondering the planet's bizarre backward spin, Gold wondered what it would be like to live on a world where the sun rose in the west and set in the east. *Probably not the place where Rachel and I will want to retire,* he thought wryly, *warm weather notwithstanding.*

Gold listened as Gomez continued: "Using similar techniques, the planet Mercury can be relocated into a lunarlike orbit around Venus, where its tidal effects on the planet's core should create a radiation-repelling magnetic field. The Federation Council will probably provide increased resources for these later steps once Saadya and his team achieve a successful blowoff."

"And no doubt Starfleet Command will be persuaded then to schedule a return engagement for the S.C.E.," Gold said. "And the *da Vinci.*"

Gomez smiled enthusiastically. "One can only hope."

A broad grin appeared on Stevens's face as well. Turning toward Gomez, he said, "You sound like the president of Saadya's fan club, Commander."

"Well, it's hard not to admire what he's already accomplished all over the quadrant," Gomez said. Gold wasn't certain, but he thought she might be blushing. "What he's about to achieve here—essentially rebuilding Venus into a duplicate of Earth—is nothing short of extraordinary."

Gold looked around the room, gauging the reactions of his staff. Other than Corsi's skeptical frown, he saw nothing but nods of agreement and murmurs of assent. Even Tev looked uncharacteristically upbeat.

"That's it, people," the captain said, rising to adjourn the meeting. "The journey of a thousand miles begins with a single step. I trust that all of you essentially know what you have to do to assist Team Ishtar. Commander Gomez will organize the teams who will report to Dr. Saadya and his staff. Let's get to work."

As the crew filed out, Gold thought, *And I, as usual, will do what any other good cat-herder would do in my place: do my best to stay out of the way of the technical wizards.*

Unless something goes seriously mish-mosh *down there.*

CHAPTER
4

The outlines of four humanoids and one wider, smaller mass shimmered for a moment in the air, before the members of the engineering team solidified on the transporter platform. Saadya was waiting for them, and as he stepped forward he adjusted his well-worn lab coat.

"Welcome aboard Ishtar Station again, Commander Gomez," he said, extending his hand to the young, dark-haired woman who stood in the small group's center.

The woman stepped off the platform, followed by the others. Smiling mischievously, she took his hand. "It seems like it's been . . . hours, Dr. Saadya." She gestured to the others behind her. "This is our second officer, Lieutenant Commander Tev, and our tactical systems specialist, Fabian Stevens."

But it was the pair to Gomez's right that held the better part of Saadya's interest. One was the Bynar, and the other most closely resembled a giant pillbug. *I've never actually stood so close to a member of the Nasat species,* Saadya thought, suppressing a revolted shudder. Gomez introduced the Bynar as Soloman, and the giant insect as "Pattie" Blue.

Saadya guided the group out of the transporter room and into a corridor. "I'm sorry that my lead assistant, Adrienne Paulos, won't be able to join us for this dry run. She's down on the surface overseeing some repairs at Ground Station Sukra."

He pressed a panel next to a doorway, and the door slid open, revealing a large room. "This holodeck features an exact re-creation of Ground Station Vesper, although it could really be just about any of the stations. They're all built essentially from the same design. We have a skeleton crew at each of the stations presently, so that as many of our personnel as possible can engage in these simulations." He swept one arm wide as a gesture for the others to enter.

They filed in and saw a number of workers bustling away at computer terminals, checking padds and gauges, and generally looking very busy. Then several of them moved aside, giving the *da Vinci* team an unobstructed view of the far end of the room.

Saadya turned just as Gomez's jaw dropped open and her features took on a look of surprise. *Damn. I forgot to tell them!*

Everything about Saadya's operation had seemed very well-designed, if a bit overly cautious in terms of resource consumption. Despite the obviously budget-conscious philosophy at work here—or perhaps because of it—Gomez was impressed as she viewed the ground station's holographic representation. The simulated viewscreens faithfully displayed the brown-yellow swirls of noxious wind that billowed high above the compound. *Or at least the ones that go whipping across the sky over the* real *ground stations,* she thought.

Then some of Saadya's workers moved to other stations, revealing the rows of computer banks arrayed farther into the room.

And the two diminutive Bynars who were working amid this compact maze of silicon, cortenide, and polyalloy.

Gomez realized with a start that her mouth was hanging open, and she shut it with a snap. Sparing a quick glance over to Soloman, she gave Saadya a sharp look. "You neglected to tell us that you already had Bynars working on this project. Or are they holograms as well?"

Saadya's features darkened slightly, and he looked apologetic. "No, they're quite real. I'm sorry. I thought I had mentioned something about this to Captain Gold." He gulped. "I hope their being here won't present a problem."

Stepping forward, Soloman furrowed his expansive brow slightly. "It will not be a problem for me, Doctor," he said. "Certainly, the mass of information the three of us will be able to process will be far greater than anything I could manage by myself, and will also greatly exceed their tandem capacities as a dual processing unit." Soloman glanced at Gomez, and she saw a bit more trepidation in his eyes than his words communicated. However, he intended to be professional about it, which was her primary concern. *Let's just hope those two Bynars have the same intention.*

Clearing her throat softly to table this line of discussion for the moment, Gomez gestured around the room. "Which stations do you want us to take?"

Saadya clapped once, gaining the attention of everyone in the room, except that of the Bynars, who remained fixated on their computer screens. They had yet to look up or acknowledge anyone else's presence in the room. "Everyone, this is the engineering team from the *da Vinci*. As I briefed you all before, they're here to help us run this simulation, and if all—*when* all works out properly, help us implement the actual atmosphere reduction programs we'll be running on the ground." He looked back at the assembled S.C.E. personnel and added, "These fine Starfleet officers have had all of Project Ishtar's schematics since yesterday, which means that they're already familiar with the broad ideas if not every aspect of the actual implementation. Those of you who were assigned partners, please help bring them up to speed on the operational specifics."

As technicians came forward to introduce themselves, and the other members of the team moved toward them, Gomez put a hand on Soloman's shoulder. The small, slight Bynar looked up at her, his eyes guileless. "Are you sure you're all right with this?" she asked, taking care to keep her voice low.

He cocked his head marginally, as if considering the question, then nodded. "Yes. Even though I am no longer bonded, I am still one of them."

I certainly hope so, Gomez thought.

As soon as Saadya brought Soloman near the Bynars, they turned. As if controlled by a single mind, both pairs of eyes narrowed. Gomez could see that the Bynar pair had not been as surprised by Soloman's presence as he had been by theirs. *Did Saadya* purposely *keep the existence of these two Bynars from us, or was it just an oversight?* Gomez wasn't certain—in fact, she hated to question the motives of someone whose work she so admired—but she intended to discuss this with the captain once she returned to the *da Vinci.*

The Bynars—she couldn't tell which was 1011 and which was 1110, even though Saadya had just introduced them—began speaking to each other, voices high-pitched and chattering, and definitely *not* in Federation Standard. She hadn't heard the sound since 111 had been aboard the *da Vinci,* discussing technical issues with 110. She could hear the same type of data-stream in their sounds as she had heard from some ancient pre–World War III communication devices they had studied while at the Academy.

Abruptly they stopped, and both of them looked at Soloman. One of them spoke again, in a slower code.

Soloman sighed. "Of *course* I can still understand binary language. I am not mentally deficient. I am unbonded due to an accident that befell my mate."

The Bynars looked surprised. One spoke, in English now. "Why have you—"

"—not bonded again—"

"—with another?"

Soloman looked as if he was about to sigh again, but Gomez was relieved to see that he didn't. "The reasons I have not rejoined with another Bynar are not germane to this mission. My personal decisions have nothing to do with atmospheric pressure, force-field mechanics, wind vectors, planetary realignment, or any other aspect of this terraforming project."

The Bynars looked up at Saadya with concern showing in their features. "That is not—"

"—an acceptable answer. How—"

"—do we know that—"

"—he is not infected with a virus—"

"—which will be transferred—"

"—to us if we link with him?"

Soloman's voice got a bit louder, and more stern. "You might at least look at me when discussing me, please." Once the pair had returned their gaze to him, flinching slightly, he continued. "I am alone because my partner, 111, was killed on a mission. She was brave and beautiful and able to process data as quickly as any Bynar in the upper cluster. When she was killed, I felt that if I were to re-bond, it would dishonor the memory of her that I carry within my heart."

The Bynars blinked once, then twice, then chattered at each other in a stream of code. Seeing that Soloman was making every effort not to wince or evince other emotions, Gomez wanted to rap them on the top of their bald little heads. Within moments, they had stopped again.

"We will attempt to—"

"—work alongside you—"

"—as long as you do not—"

"—try to infect us with your—"

"—perverse lifestyle."

Gomez had to bite her tongue to suppress a snort. Luckily, Dr. Saadya spoke up quickly. "It is my understanding that 110 is one of the most *capable* Bynars that has ever worked with Starfleet. I have no doubt he will be an excellent coworker."

The two Bynars turned away and stepped back to their workstation, tapping the touch-sensitive monitor. A bright multicolumn stream of data began pouring downward on the screen. They began their codelike chatter almost immediately.

Soloman looked up at Saadya, who guided him toward another station located several paces away. The scientist resumed pointing at a few panels, and Soloman appeared to understand his tasks very quickly.

Gomez cast an evil-eye glance at the backs of the other two Bynars' crania. She didn't think of herself as someone who often felt vindictive, but these two had been indescribably rude to her friend and colleague.

All thirteen stations had been linked, and the simulation was going well. *No, perfectly,* Pascal Saadya thought, allowing himself a wide smile behind the hands steepled in front of his mouth. He moved from bank to bank, as the many technicians monitored the programs that were regulating the endlessly shifting interactions between the simulated force fields and the *faux* Venusian atmosphere. Between the presence and advice of the Starfleet engineers, all the preparatory work that Team Ishtar had done, and Saadya's own elated vigilance, the feeling of success in the room was almost palpable.

Suddenly the Tellarite bellowed, "Faugh!" Pandemonium followed.

"We have a cascading node failure commencing northward along meridian number thirty-eight!" said Shaowa Isyami, her usually reserved voice raised in alarm.

"The field is buckling at points 0456 and 0892," chimed in Kent Laczmyr. "Now points 2487 and 4511. Now 4582."

As Kent bleated numbers, those around him pressed on the screens, trying to correct the problems.

"Major power surge at Helel Ground Station. Shields are— Oh my God! We've lost her!"

As Saadya rushed toward the monitors, the acidic winds above the chamber—lifted tens of kilometers high by the coordinated force fields—howled and rushed down at them in seconds. "Reinforce the fields at all junctures," he yelled. "Concentrate power at points 8242 and 2983!"

But it was too late. The ceilings and walls groaned, and bolts began to scream as they scraped out of their sockets. Even as the station began to collapse around them, Saadya called out, "Computer, freeze program."

Instantly, the holographic chaos went both still and silent.

Saadya looked around the room toward the people at their stations, a grim look on his face. Some of the technicians were rattled by the holographic disaster around them, bringing things too close to home for those who had witnessed the final moments of Hesperus Station at close range.

"Any idea what went wrong?" he asked, running his hand up and through his hair. "Anyone?"

The Bynars stepped forward.

"We believe that—" said 1110.

"—the presence of a—" added 1011.

"—contaminant in our—"

"—thought processes—"

"—caused a miscalculation—"

"—which allowed us to—"

"—deploy an incorrect—"

"—vector. We have been—"

"—shamed."

Saadya's eyes widened. *The Bynars are admitting they were wrong? Or* are *they?*

He saw Gomez cast a nasty look toward the Bynars, and she stepped forward. "Doctor, I suggest we take this data back to the *da Vinci* to study it, and that your people do the same here. How soon can you have another simulation prepared?"

Time was running out, but Saadya knew that it would be many hours before this data was analyzed. "How about 0830 tomorrow? Would that be a good time?"

"I think so. I'll discuss it with my engineers."

Saadya saw Soloman step away from his console to rejoin his Starfleet companions. He didn't even glance at his fellow Bynars, until one of them spouted a few short syllables of code at him.

Then Soloman squared his shoulders and stalked out of the holodeck, some of his coworkers trailing after him.

Saadya gave an apologetic look to Gomez as she, too, left. And then he counted to ten. And then twenty. He couldn't afford to make 1011 and 1110 angry, nor could he risk losing the help of the third Bynar if the project was to stand any chance of success before Bynaus and Starfleet recalled the lot of them. *What* did *those two say to Soloman, anyway?*

Saadya counted to forty, just to be sure he wouldn't blow up before he turned back around to face his technicians.

CHAPTER
5

"They called you a *what*?" Dr. Elizabeth Lense leaned forward, her hands splayed on the desktop.

"Singleton."

Lense looked at Soloman, her eyebrows raised. She was trying very hard not to look amused, realizing that cultural differences gave the term much greater weight on her friend's homeworld. "And this is an offensive slur on Bynaus?"

"The *worst*." Soloman slumped back in a chair on the other side of her desk, looking for a moment like a petulant, wounded child. "A singleton is not just a person who is unbonded; it is someone who is *incapable* of being bonded. It is a *rejected* person. Someone who cannot fit into our society. A perversion."

"But you know that isn't you, Soloman," Lense said. "You *were* bonded, and as far as I know, you fit into the society on Bynaus just fine. Not only that, but you are one of the few Bynars who's integrated yourself into an outside society: Starfleet. You have to understand that their taunts are nonsense."

Soloman sighed and opened his mouth to speak, then closed it again. After a clear moment of reflection, he finally did reply. "I understand that I am not fully the singleton that they have identified me as being. But their comments do give me cause to wonder whether my decision to remain alone does not stem from my fear that I may not be able to become bonded again."

Lense wasn't able to stop herself from a brief laugh, though she quickly smiled in an effort to let the Bynar know she wasn't laughing at him. "Sorry. I don't mean to laugh, but you really have been picking up new traits from living among us humans. That's a very human response, whether it comes from the death of a significant other, divorce, or a breakup. Everyone wonders whether they're tainted, whether anyone will ever want them again. That's just something that seems to be built into close human relationships." She leaned back in her chair and propped her elbows on the chair arms. "*Trust* me on that one. I know from personal experience. You go through the five stages of grief, and then—if you *want* another relationship—you just have to get back on the horse."

Soloman looked at her quizzically. "The horse? What does a Terran riding animal have to do with human relationships?"

"It's a metaphorical horse, Soloman. When you're learning to ride a horse, if it throws you off, you have two choices. You can either leave and never learn to ride, or you can get back on the horse and try again, until you get it right. That's what relationships are like."

He nodded. "Were you ever . . . thrown off the horse?"

"Oh yeah," she said. "Almost everybody who comes out of Starfleet Academy has a doomed romance or two in their history. For example, I've got a short-lived marriage and an ex-husband in my past."

"You've never mentioned that before."

"No need to. He's off in some other area of Starfleet and with luck, I'll never have to see him again." Lense put a fist under her chin and regarded the diminutive Bynar for a moment. "So, do you *want* to get back on the horse?"

Soloman thought a bit before answering. "I do not think so. My relationship with 111 was what made me complete then. Now, I feel that I am complete on my own. I do not feel that I need another person to be the"—he smiled—"the zero to my one."

"Then *that's* what you need to remember when those rude little Bynars aboard Ishtar Station start in on you again," Lense said, returning the smile. "You've worked very hard to forge an individual identity for yourself, and it's one that both respects the memory of 111 and helps you grow on your own."

The Bynar's features brightened for a moment, and then a cloud seemed to pass over his face again. "While this solution may help me on an emotional level, I am also concerned about our interaction on a physical level."

Lense didn't want her mind to go where that statement had led it, so she asked, "Could you *clarify* that physical part, please?"

"It seems to me that the most effective way to accomplish the task ahead of us in the next few days is to allow a physical data link among the three of us. This would process information faster and reduce the margin for error. And by subjugating our personalities to the link, it would—"

"Okay, let me stop you right there," Lense said, interrupting Soloman. "First, as I understand it, your entire culture and language are dependent on two integers: 0 and 1. By introducing a third element into that equation, don't you risk blowing a circuit at the very least? I seem to recall from some medical texts that Bynars who tried a three-way link suffered permanent brain damage. A few even died. There's a sound physiological reason why your people aren't called *Trynars*, Soloman." He started to speak, and she held up a hand, palm outward. "I'm not finished yet. You came to me for advice, so listen to what I have to say." Once it became clear she had his full attention, Lense continued. "Second, it seems to me that tonight's show-stopping error came from the paired Bynars. *They* made the fubars that brought the simulation down because they were so busy condemning you that they didn't pay close enough attention to what they were doing. So the best way to eliminate those sorts of errors next time would be for them to get over their petty prejudices. Third, how can you even entertain the idea of subjugating your personality? You have come a *tremendous* distance in establishing your individuality. And that individuality may bring you the solutions that have eluded your paired counterparts so far. Maybe not tomorrow, but someday.

"Finally, I'm concerned that your joining in any way with this pair might erode whatever protective emotional 'scar tissue' you have accumulated while grieving the loss of 111. The process could leave you even worse off emotionally than you were right after 111 died. As this ship's chief medical officer, I can't allow you to harm yourself physically or emotionally if I can help it. And Starfleet has given me the authority to help it, let me assure you."

Soloman looked at her expectantly, watching as she settled back in her chair. "May I speak now?" he asked. When Lense nodded, he continued. "I am aware of these dangers, and yet, as a great Federation diplomat once said, 'The needs of the many outweigh the needs of the few.' This mission needs to succeed for the benefit of the many. It is not just for the sake of my commander and shipmates, nor for Dr. Saadya and his terraformers." He leaned forward as if to emphasize his point. "I need to succeed for my own people, for Bynaus. It has only been about twelve of your years since the star in our system went nova and wiped out the memory banks of Bynaus. It's been only slightly less time than that since a quartet of Bynars hijacked the *U.S.S. Enterprise* and used it to transfer the core data of our civilization back to our inert planet. Bynaus is still a world in turmoil and recovery. My people still desperately need to learn all they can about terraforming and ecosphere reconstitution techniques."

Almost absentmindedly, he reached up to scratch the skin around the chip implanted into the side of his head. "No matter what the cost, I will not allow my estrangement from the ways of mainstream Bynar society get in the way of my duty to my homeworld. Just as I would sacrifice myself for my friends here on the *da Vinci*, so too will I sacrifice myself for my planet if need be."

"You don't need to be either a pariah or a martyr to your people to help them," Lense said. "You need to find a solution to Project Ishtar's problems that accomplishes your goals in a way that only *you* can accomplish them. You. As an *individual*. Thinking outside the numbers, as it were."

Soloman regarded her in silence. Lense wondered whether she had made her point effectively, or if the message had been lost. *Time will tell*, she thought.

CHAPTER
6

Soloman squared his shoulders and walked forward toward the pair of Bynars. He had spent most of the night reflecting on his discussion with Dr. Lense. He was determined to find a way to make the situation work, and he would not allow himself to get the worse end of the bargain.

As the two Bynars stared at him through baleful eyes, he spoke. "Reflecting on the events of yesterday's trial, it occurs to me that if we create a three-way datalink, we might be able to sift through the data more quickly and accurately."

"You want us to—"

"—allow you to—"

"—link with us?" The looks on their faces had now switched from contempt to incredulity.

"We think that's a great idea." A voice from behind Soloman forced all three Bynars to look to the side. It was

Fabian Stevens, with a pair of the regular Ishtar Station scientists. "Several of us discussed that option earlier, and we believe that Soloman may be on to something."

"It is *possible* for the three of you to link, isn't it?" asked a sallow-skinned female scientist.

"It is—"

"—theoretically possible—"

"—but hardly an—"

"—optimal situation."

"What *is* optimal in our situation?" the woman asked with a smile. "Why don't you guys try it for this simulation and see if it works?"

Soloman looked over at his fellow Bynars, and saw them opening and closing their mouths like fish stranded on a beach. Finally, 1011 said, "We will attempt it—"

"—this once, but we—"

"—do not expect it to—

"—be a success."

Minutes later, the holodeck simulation began again, with most of the same scientists, technicians, and engineers in the same places they had occupied the previous day. Soloman and the two Bynars synchronized the signals to the interfaces on the sides of their heads and the data buffers they carried on their belts.

The high-speed multiplex language of the Bynars suddenly filled his senses in every fashion, jolting Soloman into a reality from which he had been removed for far too long. The code-language used by 1011 and 1110 began as a low-pitched whine, and Soloman began to speak back to them.

As they talked, numbers scrolled on viewscreens in front of them. Not only were they keeping track of the columns directly in their sight, but the linked-mind synchronization meant that a residual sense of the columns being studied by the other two Bynars maintained a palpable presence in the consciousness of each.

Soloman had not spoken like this—had not shared data in this fashion—since before 111 had died. The act had never seemed so intimate before, but perhaps that was because as an adult, he had never linked with anyone other than his bond-mate. Now, the linkage seemed not only intimate, but also euphoric. The information poured in a torrent from the computer screens to their eyes to their brains to each other to their mouths to their ears to their brains . . .

He had not noticed the higher pitch that 1011's and 1110's chatter had reached until he felt the connections being severed. One by one, faster and faster, he was being blocked. His mind raced to find an entrance, but like a dam constructed midstream in a river, the paired Bynars were now methodically—and quickly—obstructing him. The revulsion they felt at his presence in their link was so strong it almost appeared as a color; not a vibrant bright or dark, but a swirling, muddy, grayed tone.

Soloman spoke to them in their language, trying to impress upon them the need to cooperate, but it was too late. He felt his ejection from the link like a physical blow. Indeed, his body reacted as if it had been shoved, and Soloman fell backward, his arms pinwheeling as he fell to the deck.

His mind still reeling from his expulsion, Soloman became aware that the holodeck simulation had been halted once again. And Dr. Saadya did *not* look happy as his gaze settled on all three Bynars.

*   *   *

Domenica Corsi was no happier about the *da Vinci* crew's involvement in the terraforming project now than she had been when Captain Gold and his staff had first discussed it. She hadn't expressed it out loud—though she and Stevens had discussed it late last night—but she didn't feel that altering Venus to support terrestrial life was a priority that the Federation should be expending time and energy toward. As intriguing as Project Ishtar was, thousands of M-class planets already existed, as well as countless other N- and K-class worlds that could be terraformed with far greater ease than this one.

Stevens had countered her concerns by noting that the proximity of Venus to Earth was clearly a large part of the reason behind Saadya's efforts. Fabian's explanation accounted for why Mars hadn't been completely terraformed before Venus, if only in an emotional way; Mars was the god of war, and that world had always been called "the angry red planet." Stevens had argued that the romance of Venus—the goddess of love—probably played an unconscious role in all the decision making.

Of course, it was fairly common knowledge that it had been the discovery of native Martian microbes in the twenty-first century—and not romantic notions of gods and goddesses—that had jumped Venus to the head of the terraforming line. *Even I know that,* Corsi thought, smiling just a little. *Fabe may have the tactical instincts of Garth of Izar and the soul of a poet, but what he doesn't know about planetology could fill a library.*

But whatever her personal feelings and misgivings, Corsi knew she had an assignment to fulfill. After the second test run had failed earlier today, she had decided to watch the next simulation from Ishtar Station's holodeck, instead of just looking over the data after it was collected. She wasn't the only *da Vinci* crew member here either; Fabian, Captain Gold, and Dr. Lense were also present, stationed throughout the room and observing discreetly over various shoulders.

Fabian approached Corsi and spoke in a low tone. "So, what do you think?"

"I think Saadya's done the best he can with what he's got," Corsi admitted. "But I still have to question the need in the first place." Under her breath, she quietly added, "To tell you the truth, I'm also pretty much at a loss to understand most of the theoretical science they're using, too. Weapons I know, and I even get the force-field applications they're using. But this kind of planetary science is way out of my specialty." She offered a wry smile, and added, "I mean, what do I *shoot* if something goes wrong?"

Stevens chuckled. "You got me there. But somehow I don't think weapons fire is going to help much if the atmosphere suddenly decides it doesn't *want* to be repositioned."

Corsi's eyebrow rose, and she nodded slowly. Something had been nagging at the back of her mind, and it had finally crystallized. Looking across the room, she saw Dr. Saadya and waved him over.

"I have a concern, Doctor," she said.

"Well, now's the time to voice it," he said, obviously feigning an air of conviviality. She could tell he was hiding a tremendous amount of stress. Or attempting to hide it.

"You're using the linked force fields to push the atmosphere upward, but asymmetrically, correct?"

He nodded. "Yes. Pushing the gases into space on the night side of Venus will not allow them to dissipate. So, we are forcing them to flow toward the sunlit side, where the heat will help burn them off. The overall shape of the combined force fields will be similar to that of a pear."

"So, the stress from the atmospheric pressure will be greatest on the sunlit side, under the apex of the wide part of the pear?"

Saadya smiled. "Exactly. The strain of the dataloads being carried by the dayside ground stations, atmospheric probes, and force-field relays will also be greatest."

Corsi nodded slowly. "So, once you start the process, it's all or nothing, right?"

"That's what all these simulations are for. If it doesn't go smoothly, we risk the destruction of some of the surface stations, almost as if the atmosphere were a tidal wave crashing down." Saadya looked around the room, beaming. His gaze stopped for a moment on the Bynars. The pair was now working at one area, while Soloman was set up nearby at a similar station. Assisting, he had told Corsi, with the Bynar pair's dataloads in a "merely superhuman" capacity, rather than trying once again to engage in a three-way link with them.

"With luck," Saadya said, "this will be the final simulation."

"Have you planned a retreat?" Corsi asked.

"*Excuse me?*" Saadya looked momentarily bewildered.

"If there is a problem, do you have any way to reverse the procedure safely during the blow-off?"

Now Saadya blanched. "*Reverse* it? Not precisely, no."

"Well, I think it would be a good idea to run some simulations for that possibility," Corsi said, noting from the corner of her eye that Stevens was nodding.

Saadya regarded her for a moment, silently. Then, with a curt nod, he said, "Yes, well, thank you for that bit of advice, *Security Chief* Corsi. But I think I'll take it up with the engineers if we can't perfect our calculations on this run. In the meantime, I prefer to look at this project somewhat more positively than you do, rather than with a defeatist attitude." He began to turn away. "If you'll excuse me, Commander, I think we're ready to begin."

Corsi watched him walk away toward some of his technicians. She turned to Stevens, and in a low voice said, "*That* could be a big problem. If he hasn't built in enough margin for error, he'd better hope there *aren't* any more errors. Otherwise, we just might find ourselves trying to run from that tidal wave."

Perfection, Saadya thought forty-five minutes later, as a cheer rang out across Ishtar Station's holodeck. This time the simulation had not only gone without a hitch, it had also moved the bulk of the holographic Venusian atmosphere into space with minimal strain on either the force-field network or the ground station shielding. And it had done so with vast amounts of power to spare.

As his technicians cheered, hugged, and mobbed each other happily, Saadya scanned the room. Catching the eye of the dour security officer he had spoken with earlier, he gave her a large grin, and an exaggerated thumbs-up sign just as someone popped a champagne bottle.

Corsi smiled back politely as glasses clinked and the spontaneous cheers, applause, and embraces continued.

After the demonstration he had just delivered, surely even the hard-nosed Lieutenant Commander Corsi had to be a believer now.

Tomorrow, his work here—the real, nonvirtual work—would prove just as successful as had today's demonstration. And he would enter the history books as the man who tamed Venus.

CHAPTER

7

It seemed to Soloman that the transporter took an extraordinarily long time to reassemble him inside Ground Station Vesper. He wasn't surprised, however, given the unusually dense Hadley cell—in essence, a hemisphere-spanning bubble of slow-moving, superheated, convection-lifted carbon dioxide—that had been observed hanging directly over the station for the past several days.

The moment the transporter beam released him he tapped his combadge. "Soloman to *da Vinci*. I have arrived safely." Aware that the safe operation of the transporter depended upon perfect targeting of the narrow gaps between the networked force-field nodes, Soloman hoped that no hasty departures would be needed. In that eventuality there was no guarantee that the "node gap" necessary for transport would be available.

"Understood, Soloman," responded the voice of Cap-

tain Gold, somewhat distorted by its passage through the thick atmospheric blanket. *"We're maintaining a transporter lock on you and everyone else in your ground station. And we're prepared to assist Station Ishtar in evacuating any of the other ground stations, if they should run into any serious problems. Just in case."*

"Acknowledged," Soloman said. "However, the last round of simulations indicates that you might be taking an overly cautious approach." *I hope.*

"Maybe so. But considering what became of Ground Station Hesperus, Gomez and Tev are recommending we wear a belt and suspenders both. Gold out."

From directly behind him, a pair of voices spoke up.

"So. You have—"

"—come back—"

"—to shame—"

"—us further."

Turning to face 1011 and 1110, Soloman felt his face flushing to a temperature that rivaled the air outside the station dome. Nevertheless, he remained determined not to react overtly to the expressions of naked contempt etched across the smooth, pallid faces of his fellow Bynars.

Only then did Soloman notice the presence of members of the ground team's human staff.

"Listen, guys," Adrienne Paulos said, looking tired and harried as she scowled at each of the three Bynars. "I don't know what sort of grudges you're carrying around and I don't care. But in spite of our success in the simulator yesterday, our margin for error is still *way* too slim to allow for anybody's private hissy fits. Understood?"

The Bynar pair said nothing. They merely continued staring impassively at Soloman.

"I came here to assist Dr. Saadya with work that will

benefit our people, as well as the people of Earth," Solo-man said carefully, his eyes alternately boring into 1011's and 1110's. "I trust that my conspecifics feel the same way. Unless I missed the point of all those atmo-spheric simulations we've been running in preparation for today's task."

The Bynar pair continued their stony silence. Moving as one, they turned their attention to a tandem console situated amid a complex cluster of computer terminals that lined the small room's cramped center. As one, the pair began interfacing with the computer, speaking to it in high-pitched, rapid-fire ululations of vocalized ma-chine code.

Soloman felt a surge of envy for the rich dataflow in which the other Bynars immersed themselves with such apparent ease. *So much like what 111 and I shared—*

With a supreme effort of will, he forced the thought from his mind, as though purging a computer of a dam-aged file.

"I'm glad that's settled," Paulos said, a sour half-smirk crossing her face as she crossed to one of the other nearby consoles, where a trio of human techni-cians busied themselves with similar tasks. She quickly examined her readouts, then paused to confer with the other human staff members.

Feeling even more awkwardly alone than usual, Solo-man took his seat at a console adjacent to the one being used by the Bynar pair, neither member of which deigned to look in his direction. Working in silence, Soloman summoned several columns of figures to the touch-sensitive display screen.

Turning his chair slightly away from the other By-nars, Soloman was relieved to note that only the other humans now lay within his immediate line of sight. Let

1011 and 1110 think whatever they wanted about him. He was determined to put their ill will out of his mind, concentrating instead on monitoring and checking their dataflow, which roared through his terminal like the desert winds of Bynaus.

Then he noticed one of the human technicians, a female, glancing at him and shuddering, evidently involuntarily. Though the incident occupied only some small fraction of a second, Soloman thought the woman might have tried to do a better job of concealing her revulsion.

The woman's reaction brought to mind a warning that Fabian Stevens had once given him. Some humans, Stevens explained, felt uncomfortable around members of the slight, large-brained, computer-dependent Bynar race. "Creeped out" was the expression he had used to describe this unconscious flinching reaction.

I truly am at home nowhere, Soloman thought, sparing a quick glance at his—thankfully preoccupied—Bynar brethren.

"Aphrodite Ground Station ready," declared a voice carried over the comm speakers. The scratchy message instantly brought Soloman's entire concentration back to the mission before him.

"Helel Ground Station, check," another distant voice reported.

"Ground Station Sukra, ready to go," came the next.

One by one, each of the thirteen remaining staffed ground stations, distributed at even intervals around the planet's equator and along its prime meridians, reported their status to the central surface-based hub at Ground Station Vesper. Each of these facilities were virtually identical, and each now stood ready to link its technological capabilities to all the others.

1011 and 1110, looking through Soloman as though he weren't even present, exchanged nods with Paulos and one of the other human technicians.

Soloman swallowed. The moment of truth was fast arriving.

Paulos punched a key on her console and leaned forward. "Paulos to Ishtar Station. Vesper reports ready as well. All other stations showing green for go."

"Saadya here. Everything looks good from up here."

Soloman felt his pulse beginning to race, and his rate of breathing increasing. This was no simulation.

Then he noticed 1011 and 1110 watching him with narrowed eyes.

"Try to—"

"—keep up—"

"—with the dataflow—"

"—singleton."

Say nothing to them, Soloman thought, trying to ignore the slur.

His jaw tightened as he returned his attention to the ranks of marching figures. So far, nothing in the sensor readings appeared to necessitate making any new adjustments to the force-field network parameters. Field strengths were holding, and remained in balance. All was proceeding as planned, and the numbers attested to it.

The behavior of numbers, unlike that of flesh-and-blood beings, had the virtue of being understandable, logical, and predictable. But the figures were moving so very quickly. Nearly as fast as the dataflow to which he and 111 had been long accustomed . . .

Concentrate on the numbers. Nothing exists except for the numbers.

Saadya's voice came over the speakers again, via a

somewhat atmosphere-distorted signal. *"I wish I could be down there with you, Team Ishtar."*

"We've been over this a million times, Pas. You've got to delegate. And who better to get a God's eye view of things than you?"

"All right, Adrienne," Saadya said, still sounding wistful. *"I promise to stay up on Ishtar Station and just watch. Now go ahead and raise the roof."*

Soloman saw from his readouts that the so-called "roof-raising" was already well begun. He stared into his terminal, whose edges soon grew indistinct and vanished altogether, leaving nothing in his sight but the figures that expressed the shape, ebb, flow, and strength of the force-field network that strained and flexed in its effort to cage the broiling Venusian sky.

Wading alone into the rapid information torrent, Soloman exulted wordlessly in his ability to let the numbers occupy all of his concentration. He no longer had time to consider his outcast status, nor to ponder the enormity of what he and Team Ishtar were undertaking as they guided the bulk of the Venusian atmosphere away from the planet's surface and toward the endless gulf of space.

But somewhere deep within him burned the persistent hope that these understandable, logical, predictable numbers would take no unexpected turns into chaos.

Pascal Saadya stood in his office, having had far too many cups of coffee to remain in his padded chair for very long. He leaned against the transparent aluminum window, watching the stately yellow world that turned below him.

"*The force fields are networking nicely,*" said Adrienne, her voice crackling with static no doubt exacerbated by the increasingly complex interplay among Project Ishtar's artificial energy fields, atmospheric probes, and the planet's high-pressure, acid-laden air. "*We're detecting no node failures, power surges, or significant deviations. And the probe network shows the atmosphere behaving exactly as the models predicted.*"

So far. Saadya stood in silence, his mouth forming a grim slash as he stared down at Venus. After having worked so long and hard planning for this day, he could scarcely allow himself to taste of his triumph now that it had finally arrived.

Then he saw it. The first tangible, undeniable sign of his success. Venus, a world that had been utterly changeless for hundreds of millions of years, now appeared to be . . .

. . . *bulging.*

Saadya grinned, elated. *It really* is *working!*

With most of the *da Vinci*'s senior staff present, the small bridge seemed crowded enough to make David Gold reminisce about his youth. He recalled the time he had stuffed himself into a small hovercar along with eleven other first-year Starfleet Academy cadets.

Gold sat in the captain's chair, watching the forbidding hellworld that filled the viewer, along with everyone else present. The tension in the air was palpable, and he realized too late that his biosynthetic fingers had dug themselves completely through the upholstery at the base of the chair's left armrest. *Instinct can get too big a push from technology sometimes.*

He hoped Pas stopped to consider such things occasionally.

"The procedure seems to be working well," Tev said, grunting in apparent disbelief as he leaned over the engineering console.

"Has anybody noticed the predicted expansion effect yet?" said Gomez, who had situated herself at one of the science stations, across the bridge from Tev. "It's already measurable and it's steadily increasing. Looks like those newest atmospheric models were pretty accurate."

Gold turned and glanced around the rear of the bridge. Abramowitz, who stood between Corsi and Stevens, watched the forward viewer closely, squinting as if to tease out every possible detail.

"Looks the same as ever to me," Abramowitz said. "Of course, I suppose I must be the proverbial untrained eye."

"Then consider this your training," Stevens said. "Keep watching the cloud bands near the equator. We're in for quite a show."

Corsi remained silent, her body taut as a bowstring. Her gaze was riveted to the screen as though she were seeking a target onto which to lock every weapon in the ship's arsenal.

Gold turned back toward the screen and continued watching in silence. At first he thought it was his imagination, but as the minutes piled up, he knew there could be no denying it.

Venus was *growing,* especially in the middle.

"Look at that," Corsi said.

Abramowitz whistled. "I'll be damned."

Gold pushed a button on the arm of his chair. "Gold to Saadya."

"*Saadya here. Ishtar is finally rising, David. I'm glad you've come to assist in her ascent.*"

"Me, too, Pas." Gold watched as the planet's atmosphere continued pushing outward and upward, like a river flooding and overflowing its banks. The normally slow-moving cloudtops had begun whipping themselves into a frenzy, and golden streamers of gases were reaching spaceward, delicately tapered fingers probing the shallow shoreline of the cosmos. As they rose, the plumes of vapor lengthened, attenuated, and vanished in brilliant, thousand-kilometer-long streaks of auroral blue, violet, and magenta, scattered and ionized by the fierce onslaught of the solar wind. The rising gaseous traceries began appearing—and vanishing—faster and faster as the force-field network gradually ramped up its power output, pushing oceans of atmosphere to higher and higher altitudes.

Through the gathering brilliance of the ionized atmospheric "blow-off," Gold could see that the planet's sweltering carbon dioxide blanket had to be dissipating at a phenomenal rate, like a balloon whose air was being abruptly released. He could only watch in wonderment.

Gold was startled, just for an instant, by an alarm Klaxon from the science station from which Gomez was monitoring the proceedings. Noting that his channel to Saadya was still open, he momentarily interrupted the audio feed.

"Report," Gold said, turning his chair toward his first officer.

"This can't be good," Gomez said. "Maybe Dr. Saadya should have spent more time running geological simulations."

"Why do you say that?"

"I'm reading a massive geological upheaval occurring

beneath the tessera of Alpha Regio. About twenty degrees south latitude."

"What could be causing it?" Gold wanted to know.

"We know that the Venusian surface lacks plate tectonics," she said, lifting her gaze from her readouts. "And that causes the planet to experience torrential eruptions of liquid magma every half-billion years or so because of the seismic stresses that accumulate without there being any plate motion to relieve them."

Gold blinked at her. "And this has exactly what to do with the price of *halvah*?"

"My point is that the last time this happened was about five hundred million years ago. Venus is due for another large eruption right about now."

"Give or take ten million years," Stevens quipped.

Gold scowled. "That's a little too much coincidence for me to believe in."

"I agree," Tev said. It occurred to Gold that he'd never heard the Tellarite use that particular expression before. "The likely culprit is Project Ishtar itself."

"You mean the force-field network is setting off quakes?" asked Gold.

Tev shook his head impatiently. "Only indirectly, by causing a precipitous change in air pressure at the surface datum."

Gold rose from his chair and approached the science station. "How bad is it? Are any of the ground stations in harm's way?"

Gomez consulted her sensors once again, then faced Gold, who felt a mounting sense of alarm as he watched her face suddenly drain of all color. "One of the lower-elevation ground stations is right in the path of the lava flow—and it's going to be engulfed in less than two hours."

"Two hours," Gold repeated, allowing himself to feel relieved as he turned the information over in his mind. "That should give us enough time to evacuate."

Gomez continued to look worried. "Maybe. As long as things don't get any worse."

A worm of apprehension turned in the pit of Gold's stomach. "What do you mean? How much worse could it get?"

"I'm reading the mother of all volcanic eruptions letting loose right now under Alpha Regio. It might set off a domino effect that ends up repaving most of the planet's surface—in the span of three or four hours."

"I'll start coordinating the evacuation plan," Corsi said.

Gold nodded to his security chief. *Oy. Looks like we might have arrived just in time for the half-billion-year barbecue.*

He reopened the audio feed to Ishtar Station. "Pas, I think we have a huge problem on our hands. . . ."

CHAPTER
8

As Domenica Corsi and Fabian Stevens piloted Shuttlecraft *Kwolek* toward Venus, Commander Sonya Gomez sat just behind the cockpit, studying the readouts on the small display in front of her. *This is going to be close,* she thought, her entire body knotted with the tension that only an urgent engineering crisis could create.

She swiveled in her chair and looked back at P8 Blue, who was sitting in the specially constructed slope-backed chair near another small bank of instruments.

"How are those numbers holding up, Pattie?"

"It's going to be a rough ride, but we should be able to make it through the force fields with minimal loss of structural integrity," she said.

Seated beside Pattie, Lieutenant Commander Tev lifted his gaze from a tactical display and spoke toward the cockpit. "Commander Corsi, make sure you approach the force-field boundary at exactly the calculated angle. Miss it by the smallest margin and you could bounce us off the field lines and back into space."

"Or it could be even worse," Pattie said, clattering her mandibles for a moment and making a strange sound that Gomez translated as her version of *splat!* "To coin a phrase, we might be squashed like a bug."

Gomez smiled at the self-deprecating humor, but Corsi only grunted in response, obviously concentrating on her flying. A little humor certainly didn't hurt, given the unrelenting grimness of their current situation.

One of the project's technicians had provided them with the vibrational frequencies of the force fields, so that they could penetrate them and try to get down to Aphrodite Station before the approaching lava flow destroyed it. *If that hasn't happened already,* Gomez thought. Recent sensor readings had revealed that the lava was moving toward the ground station far more quickly than had originally been apparent. And the *Kwolek*'s passage through the topologically complex, interlacing force-field network was bound to be tricky, even with the vibrational frequency data. And once down, they might have only seconds to effect any sort of rescue, most likely a hastily improvised one.

"Aphrodite Station, this is Shuttlecraft *Kwolek*. Please respond." Gomez keyed several panels on the touchscreen, modulating back and forth across the gamut of usable frequencies, but all that came through was a crackle of static. There wasn't even an amplitude spike to imply that anyone might be trying to respond. *This rescue mission might be completely in vain. But there's no way of knowing that for certain except by making the attempt.*

"Sensors still show nothing," P8 said. "But I'm reading some very strong subsurface rumbles, with shear waves, compression waves, and crust motions I've never seen before."

Great, Gomez thought. "What do you make of it?"

"I think the lava inundation could accelerate even further," P8 said. "We're running out of time."

"Doing my best," Corsi said through clenched teeth. The forward windows revealed only noxious yellow and brown gases that confounded any sense of direction. If one tried to measure the *Kwolek*'s motion by the available visual cues, the shuttle might as well have been standing still.

Judging from the feel of the inertial dampers in the deck plating, Gomez knew that Corsi had slowed the shuttle considerably in the last few seconds. Tev checked a panel and announced, "Three hundred meters to outer force-field boundary. Two hundred fifty. One seventy-five. Seventy-five. Fifty. Twenty-five."

The atmosphere outside the forward windows had grown so dense, thanks to Project Ishtar's force fields, that they had the look of a solid wall. Gomez reflexively checked her shoulder harness as Corsi and Stevens flew the *Kwolek* toward that apparently impregnable barrier at a steeply decelerating rate.

"Make sure our shield frequencies still match Project Ishtar's," Gomez said.

"Checking," Pattie said, tapping at her console with multiple extremities. "We still have a positive match."

"Confirmed," said Tev. "But we still don't know exactly how passing through multiply interleaved force fields will affect the shield-frequency compatibility."

"That's easy for you to say," grumbled Corsi, turning to glance at Tev.

"Eyes on the road, Dom," Stevens said.

"Force-field boundary now ten meters from ventral hull," Pattie said, then continued counting down quickly. "Now!"

For a moment, the *Kwolek* was suspended in the air, like a fly caught in amber, and then it was pushed downward with tremendous force. Gomez grabbed the edge of her console even as her body slammed upward against the harness. The shuttle's engines and inertial dampers both let out a sharp whine before the ship wobbled, then finally steadied and quieted.

"Now *that* was a ride," Stevens said with a grin.

"Did the fields close up all right behind us?" Gomez asked.

"Yes," P8 replied. "That jolt we felt was from the superpressurized gases that followed us through the aperture for a nanosecond or so."

The viewscreens were clearer now, though the air was tinted a dingy goldenrod hue, as though saturated with pollen. Gomez tried the communicator again. "Aphrodite Station, this is Shuttlecraft *Kwolek*. Please respond." As before, nothing issued from the console speakers except a burst of background static. Gomez smacked her palm against her leg in frustration.

"We're getting low enough to see something," Stevens said, pointing forward.

"That doesn't look good," said Corsi, unnecessarily.

As they descended further, the forward windows presented a relatively unobstructed view of Ground Station Aphrodite—or rather, what was left of it. The roughly disk-shaped, twenty-meter-diameter facility had been built on a small mesa-like bluff. Part of that bluff had crumbled, and had taken a substantial section of the station's external pressure dome with it.

And surrounding the partially shattered mesa was an almost blindingly bright, white-hot magma sea.

"There's no way anything could still be alive down there," said Tev matter-of-factly.

"We don't know that yet," said Gomez. "We have to find out for sure. Take us in closer, Domenica."

"That lava flow is getting closer, too," P8 said. "It's almost reached the facility's main level."

"The sensors are still being confused by the ionized atmosphere," Tev said. "So unless the survivors get outside, a transporter lock's out of the question."

Gomez nodded grimly. "Then we're going to have to get them out some other way."

"They can't go out in this soup without being immolated," Stevens said. "Even the best environmental suit wouldn't last more than a few seconds out there."

Corsi glanced at Gomez. "Even if we could get them outside in EV suits, where am I supposed to land this beast? The roof's too unstable. It's barely able to hold up its own weight, let alone ours."

Gomez studied the partially collapsed roof, which was glowing a dull red in the places where the Venusian atmosphere had begun to melt it. A structure that looked a lot like a water tank sat precariously on the roof's far edge. Was there some way to make use of that?

"I think I know what to do," P8 said, rising from her chair. Gomez noticed that the Nasat also seemed to be examining the station's roof very carefully. "And *I'm* the only one who can do it."

"What do you have in mind?" Gomez wanted to know.

Pattie's gaze grew intense. "First, I'll need some of our construction tools. . . ."

CHAPTER
9

As the shuttle hovered scarcely more than three meters above the station's damaged roof, the air below it shimmered for a moment. The transporter beam dissipated with agonizing sluggishness, finally leaving P8 Blue standing on the roof, her hard carapace exposed to the worst Venus had to offer. Strapped to her back was a large duranium locker that contained—she hoped—everything she needed to rescue whomever she found here.

In addition to the oppressive, caustic air—which, fortunately, Project Ishtar's force fields had thinned just enough for her to survive, at least temporarily—P8 could feel the intense heat from the magma that was surrounding the building. But she knew that as bad as it was for her, it would be far worse for anyone who lacked the advantage of her carapace. The natural membranes covering her eyes allowed her to see where she was going, and she wouldn't need oxygen for quite some time. She ran to the edge of the roof, then scuttled over the side, her eight hands having to work harder than she expected to maintain a grip on the structure's smooth polyduranium alloy.

As she came perilously close to the ground—and to the rising tide of detritus-speckled lava—she found the airlock's hatch controls. It was a bit tricky entering the code from an upside-down orientation, but she managed, then crawled into the airlock as the door hissed open. Once inside she punched a button on a keypad, feeling greatly relieved once the hatch closed smoothly behind her.

The airlock's fans had only begun pumping out the Venusian air, enabling the Nasat to speak. Fortunately, the tympanic membrane with which her body produced sound did not require her to exhale any of her precious oxygen. Tapping her combadge, P8 said, "I've entered the outer airlock. Can you read me?"

A moment of silence passed, then another, and finally a crackling voice came through. It was Gomez. "—es we re—you—"

"Your signal is weak, but at least we can communicate." She saw the green light that indicated the outer airlock's atmosphere was now breathable, as well as the air beyond the inner lock. She realized that at least some of the internal bulkheads must have closed in time to prevent a complete environmental compromise, like that suffered by Ground Station Hesperus. There might be survivors here after all. But with the Venusian atmosphere now cooking many of the station's interior spaces as well as the external ablative shielding, it was only a matter of time before the interior bulkheads succumbed to the inevitable.

Just like the da Vinci *hull did at Galvan VI.*

The ground rumbled, reminding P8 of the rising tide of lava outside, a danger that threatened to render all other hazards moot.

Putting thoughts of the *da Vinci*'s all-too-recent mission to the back of her mind, she said into her combadge, "I'm going in," and opened the interior airlock and exited into a hallway. She found the air stale and ozone-laced, but at least marginally breathable. *Life support must be down,* she thought. Only a few of the lights were working. She passed what appeared to be someone's personal quarters. The doors were open, but she didn't see anyone inside.

"Hello? Is anyone here?" Her voice echoed in the corridor. Breaking a tricorder out of the sealed tool kit she carried, she activated the device. A smile came to her mandibles almost immediately. Tapping her combadge, she said. "I read eight life-signs, the entire station's complement. They're all grouped together. They seem to be stressed by failures in the air-recyclers and other life-support equipment."

"—*opy that,*" Gomez's voice crackled.

P8 made her way into the main control room, but nobody was there. She noticed that anything that wasn't bolted down had been thrown about by the seismic disturbances. The groundquakes had obviously hit this place hard.

Up a short set of stairs, she saw movement through the broad window of what she assumed was an office. Squeezing her bulk up the stairs, she pounded on the door. Through the window, she saw a group of technicians clustered together in the dimly lit room. Four were fully conscious, two were a bit wobbly, one appeared delirious, and another was unconscious and bleeding from a laceration above his right eye.

When one of them opened the door, P8 entered and set her locker down on the floor. Opening it, she said, "We don't have much time. I need each of you to get into these EV suits, and quickly."

As the workers scrambled to don the lightweight emergency suits she pulled from the locker, P8 explained how to seal them. The first man to finish suiting up began pulling the unconscious man into a second suit, while a woman assisted her delirious co-worker.

"How are we going to get out of here?" a woman asked, eyeing her suit skeptically. "These things won't last long outside, even if the air *is* a bit thinner now."

P8 wondered why it had taken so long for someone to point that out. But there was little time for explanations. She decided to keep it brief. "If I could get you outside, we might get a transporter lock on you all, if not for all the ionic distortions out there." To the skeptical woman, she added, "And you're right—you couldn't survive long outside, even in an EV suit."

"Then how—"

"Is that tank on top of the building what I think it is?" P8 interrupted, wishing the *da Vinci*'s sensors had been working reliably enough to have already answered her question.

"It's water," said one of the men. "Mostly for equipment coolant and radiation protection."

P8 nodded, picking up a small tool kit and a phaser rifle from the locker's interior. She maglocked the tool kit to her belt and slung the weapon over her hard-carapaced shoulder. "Tank looks to be intact, too. But we'll need to test it, and quickly. Can you drain it from in here?"

The man looked puzzled, but answered in spite of that. "Yes."

"Then do it!" P8 couldn't remember the last time she had pushed her tympanic membrane so hard. But her shout—or perhaps the phaser rifle on her shoulder—seemed to have the desired effect. One of the technicians immediately entered a command into a nearby computer terminal.

If this doesn't work, we may all be dead very soon.

Another two minutes passed before everyone had completely suited up and checked all seals and connections. P8 then led the group out of the office, with two of them carrying their injured companion. On the main control floor, several inches of water had already accumulated on the deck, flowing down through a hatchway at the room's far end. From the rush of sound coming from the room beyond, P8 gathered that the bulk of the drainage was headed elsewhere.

Let's just hope the water inside that tank wasn't the only thing keeping it from being flattened by the atmospheric pressure out there, she thought.

The group made its way through the hatch and into a room that reminded P8 of the engineering section from some low-tech, pre-Federation Earth starship. From the ceiling, a series of pipes dripped water—the remnants of the contents of the rooftop tank.

P8 shouldered the phaser rifle and trained it on the area around the pipes. The phaser beam cut through the structure, and a neatly circular section of roof about a meter and a half in diameter fell to the deck with a clatter and a splash.

"Get everybody up there," P8 yelled. "Into the tank!"

One of the men protested, shouting from within his EV suit. "I still say this is crazy!"

P8 nodded. "Maybe. But it's your best chance to stay alive."

Using a set of wall-rungs and pipes, the first pair of workers reached the hole and climbed up. P8 could hear a hollow gong sound as they clambered within. Using the flashlight mounted on her middle right arm, P8 shined a light up into the hole. The first two men's arms emerged from the aperture, and they began pulling up the others.

P8 slung the phaser rifle over her back and grabbed the unconscious scientist, then started to carry him up the walls, bringing up the rear of the party. Balancing carefully, P8 handed the man up to the others, then clung to the lip of the hole for a moment.

A fast search of her toolbox yielded a small magnetic grapnel, which she aimed down at the section of metal she had just cut away. She aimed, fired, and the flukes made contact. Pulling on the grapnel with four of her limbs, she quickly took possession of the metal disk.

Using the phaser to weld the disk back into place took barely another two minutes.

The building shook, as though the molten rock outside had grown tired of being ignored. The already sloping floor suddenly listed even more sharply. Tortured metal creaked and groaned, and P8 could hear a hard wind keening outside. *The roof is going.*

P8's combadge crackled. The voice belonged to Commander Gomez. "*—ting rough out there, Pattie. How's it comi—*"

Keying her combadge, P8 said, "We're out of time, sir. Please hit the switch." *And hope my welds hold.*

"*—ou got it, Pat—*" came Gomez's scratchy reply.

The tank suddenly rang as if something massive had

struck it, and then a hum engulfed it, vibrating the polyalloy walls as the *Kwolek*'s tractor beam—usually used for construction projects—separated the tank from its rooftop moorings.

But there was no inrush of hot carbon dioxide gas. The air was stale but remained breathable. The tank's seams—including the ones P8 had just created—were holding, at least for the moment. She hoped they wouldn't fail until after the *Kwolek* had lofted the tank to an altitude where the temperature and pressure would allow Ground Station Aphrodite's staff to rely on their environmental suits for survival.

The tank was buffeted from side to side by the increasingly powerful winds. Despite that, P8 Blue felt certain that her plan was going to work. *As long as Corsi doesn't smack into the force fields at the wrong angle on her way back out of here.*

"I'll be damned," Stevens said with a big grin, looking up from his instruments. "We just caught ourselves eight humans and a pillbug."

Gomez grinned back. "Tractor beam status?"

"Holding steady," Tev said.

"Headed for orbit," Corsi said, anticipating Gomez's next order. "Course laid in for Ishtar Station. Quarter impulse."

As they rose through the air, Gomez adjusted one of the console viewers to get an aft view. Below the *Kwolek*, Ground Station Aphrodite was crumbling and melting into nothingness, shaken apart by groundquakes and consumed by the molten mantle of Venus.

Corsi piloted the shuttle swiftly upward, passing the

swirling ochre cloud bands, moving slowly but deftly through the force-field network, and finally grazing the edge of space, where Ishtar Station's crew managed to beam the people being ferried in the tank to safety.

Gomez keyed the companel and spoke. "Gomez to Captain Gold. We've just completed a rather . . . unorthodox rescue. All crew members of Aphrodite Station are out of danger."

"Good work, Gomez. Now we just have to save the rest of the planet."

Gold's words struck her hard. As Tev beamed P8 Blue back aboard the *Kwolek*, Gomez's earlier jubilation had abruptly died. After all, not even both the *da Vinci*'s shuttles could pull off Pattie's little trick at all the other ground stations, even if the Nasat engineer could be in two places at once. The planetary force-field network still remained dangerously stalled, geological upheavals threatened to engulf still more of the planet's crust in very short order, and the transporters remained unable to haul the people stranded elsewhere on the surface out of harm's way.

Gomez knew that solving those problems had to take priority now that the Aphrodite team was out of immediate danger. *Otherwise,* she thought, *what about the dozen other staffed stations down there? And what happens to Soloman?*

She watched in silence as one of her instruments displayed a schematic of the intricately fluctuating nodes and energy lines that made up Project Ishtar's force-field network. *Problem Number One,* she decided, scowling at the image.

"You still there, Gomez?" said Gold over the still-open channel, his voice free of static now that the shuttle had

made low orbit. Gomez realized with a start that she'd been woolgathering.

"Captain," she said, suddenly galvanized by a new idea. "I think we may have to try something *really* risky next. . . ."

CHAPTER
10

The columns of numbers that speed-scrolled across Soloman's screen were suddenly anything but understandable, logical, or predictable. The mathematical constraints of the force-field network were quickly taking on characteristics that reminded him of one of the chaotic *drad* cacophonies to which Carol Abramowitz was so fond of listening. It took all the speed his hands could muster to continue feeding revised force-field parameters into the system in time to prevent a chain reaction of node failures that would have brought half the planet's dense atmosphere crashing down onto their heads with nearly meteoric force.

And the numbers continued to change at an ever-accelerating rate.

Soloman felt a hard, rolling shock radiating from somewhere beneath his chair. It wasn't unlike the jolt one might feel aboard a starship during a phaser attack.

Groundquake! he thought, nearly falling out of the torrent of numbers that roared past his eyes.

A gabble of nearby voices engulfed him, those of the startled human team members mixing with the shriller-than-normal ultrarapid codespeech of the paired Bynars, who seemed to be struggling every bit as hard as Soloman was to make sense of the swiftly altering datastream.

Then he heard someone shouting above the din. The voice belonged to Adrienne Paulos, who was frantically giving instructions to her technical staff. "Keep those equatorial force-field nodes stable! If the z-axis keeps drifting, we'll have another Hesperus on our hands."

Or any number of Hesperi, as Fabian might say. Soloman thought this was an odd time for the tactical specialist's wry sense of humor to start rubbing off on him.

The ground station rumbled and groaned, but stopped shaking within a few moments, at least for the time being. But the vocalizations of the other two Bynars remained shrill—almost panicked, to Soloman's sensitive ears—as the team continued concentrating on maintaining the wayward force fields.

"Incoming message from upstairs, Adrienne," someone said. The voice belonged to one of the human technicians, a male human who was working somewhere out of Soloman's field of vision.

The on-site team leader acknowledged by opening up a comm channel with an audible snap. "Ground Station Vesper here. Go ahead, Ishtar."

A furious blast of static preceded Dr. Saadya's reply. *"Adrienne, are you and your team all right?"*

"We're all in one piece. But we've picked up some pretty severe seismic activity down here."

"We've detected it, too. It's centered around Alpha Regio, near Ground Station Aphrodite."

His mind still shooting a numeric rapids, Soloman spared a moment to make a quick calculation. Alpha Regio lay over two thousand kilometers to the southwest of Ground Station Vesper. Whatever subterranean forces had been roused there must be powerful indeed.

"How close is Aphrodite to the epicenter?" Paulos wanted to know.

"Near enough to interfere with our transporter locks there." Saadya's voice was getting progressively more obscured and distorted by static, presumably from air that was being rapidly ionized by large-scale volcanic eruptions. *"We can't raise them at the moment. We can only hope they weren't leveled outright."*

"Dear God," said Paulos. "Don't tell me we just happened to execute Project Ishtar on the same day the Big One finally decided to give the planet's crust a complete pave-over."

"I don't know what to tell you," Saadya said, an edge of barely contained panic in his voice. *"Except that the da Vinci has sent a shuttle down to rescue the Aphrodite personnel before the station is inundated by the magma flow itself. In the meantime, you and your team have to do whatever it takes to keep the force-field network up and running."*

Soloman knew that without the force-field network, Aphrodite's fate would be sealed, along with that of the rest of the ground stations. There was no way Vesper or any of the other surface facilities could outlast Aphrodite for very long. Should the force-field nodes collapse while still holding millions of cubic kilometers of atmosphere in high-altitude suspension, the abrupt release of kinetic energy as the atmosphere resettled would scour away every structure on the planet's surface within minutes. The protective shielding would be pulverized and everyone inside would be reduced to vapor without leaving so much as a bone or a tooth to be buried. Soloman shuddered at the thought.

The numbers. Don't lose your grip on the numbers.

"Understood," Paulos said, replying to Saadya with an unsteady voice. She, too, must have worked out the consequences of failure. "Let's hope that shuttle can do some good. In the meantime, it's all we can do just to hold the force field in place, without either expanding or contracting it."

The drift of the numbers racing past Soloman's eyes quickly confirmed that any attempt to use the force-field network to continue moving the atmosphere outward would greatly increase the risk of causing a catastrophic collapse. And the team had never tried reversing the motion of the force fields to create a controlled settling of the atmosphere. Therefore the force fields had to be maintained right where they currently were, half-expanded, so near the fast-moving seventy-kilometer atmospheric layer that it took all of Soloman's concentration just to continue following and reacting to the perpetually changing figures—figures that constituted an increasingly imprecise mathematical model of a complex system that was rapidly descending into chaos and entropy.

Soloman spared a quick look toward the console where his paired, data-efficient brethren worked, their strident voices keening in near-desperation.

Even they *are beginning to fall behind. How can a crippled singleton hope to do any better?*

His head beginning to throb with the fruitless effort of following the figures, Soloman knew that he should not have allowed the bigotry of 1011 and 1110 to affect him to such a degree that he was thinking of himself with the slur "singleton." He was also rapidly becoming convinced that if another single bit of data were to impinge on his consciousness, his head would surely explode.

His combadge chose that precise moment to speak. *"Gold to Soloman."*

Please, not now. "Soloman here."

"We're monitoring your situation closely."

For reasons that puzzled him, the captain's remark struck Soloman as humorous. He made a mental note to ask Dr. Lense, or perhaps Fabian, about that later. Assuming, of course, that he would be alive later.

"Thank you, sir," was all he could think of to say in response.

"I'll give you the bad news first, Soloman," Gold continued. *"We can't beam anybody back from any of the surface stations at the moment, and the orbital lab is in the same fix. The 'holes' in the force-field net that we beamed you through to get you down there are completely closed up now. And the volcanic activity at Alpha Regio is causing too much high-altitude ionization to risk using the transporter at long range anyway; the high-speed atmospheric layer is spreading it around like a* yenta *repeating gossip."*

Soloman nodded. The seventy-kilometer superrotational layer could blanket the entire planet in volcanic fallout in just four days—and that was without the extra heat-induced acceleration factor already introduced by the force-field network itself. The entire atmosphere was becoming thoroughly ionized by now. "I understand," Soloman said. "May I infer that you also have some good news to deliver, Captain?"

Soloman thought he heard Gold chuckle, though he couldn't be certain. *"Gomez just evac'd Ground Station Aphrodite with the* Kwolek*."*

Someone from Ishtar Station must have just relayed the same news to Paulos's team, since a brief cheer went up among the busy human technicians.

Gold continued: *"Gomez thinks that the engineers might be able to reestablish transporter locks on the other ground stations, at least intermittently."*

"That would certainly be welcome, sir." There was no trace of irony behind Soloman's words. "But how can that be done without allowing the force-field network to collapse entirely?" Clearly that wasn't desirable so long as maintaining the force fields remained essential for keeping all of the ground personnel alive.

"Nobody said this was going to be an easy job, Soloman."

"Captain, we have our hands full just keeping the force fields from collapsing and swamping everyone down here with an atmospheric deluge."

Throughout this exchange, Soloman continued trying to maintain his grasp on the numbers as they ebbed and flowed across his monitor. His hands fluttered quickly across the keypad, feeding revised instructions to the network, the human technicians, and the other Bynars.

His head was pounding, as though it contained a small animal that was determined to escape. The Bynar pair's tandem dataspeech had risen to an almost ear-splitting screech. The sound resonated across a gap in Soloman's being, forcibly reminding him of the easy informational intimacy that had been forever ripped from him on the day 111 had died.

If only 111 were here now. I'm certain the four of us,

working as paired pairs, could maintain some measure of control over these variables.

And he could feel that the datastream was eluding him. He was rapidly losing his hold on the numbers. He knew that soon he would input a parameter-change incorrectly, causing two or more of the wavering force-field nodes to fall into each other. A chain reaction would quickly ensue, probably faster than even the paired Bynars could react to it. Implosion would follow a fraction of a second later.

And minutes after that he and everyone else who remained on this planet would be reduced to their constituent atoms.

"Just hang in there for as long as you can, Soloman," Captain Gold said. *"Gomez is on her way with the cavalry. I'm sure you and her team will find a solution that everyone can live with. Gold out."*

The comm channel closed, but the cramped control room was anything but silent. The shrill elegance of the datasong the other Bynars sang as they interfaced directly with the linked networks of atmospheric probes and force-field node controls filled Soloman's soul with melancholy and longing. He wanted desperately to join in their ululations.

Switching on his console's voice interface, he opened his mouth, adding his voice to the piercing soprano chorus of the paired Bynars.

A Klaxon wailed as a force-field node suddenly collapsed. The first collapse was followed immediately by another. One of the human technicians yelped in terror. Soloman quieted, deactivating his voice interface. He resumed using his hands to input a series of lightning correction factors even as the Bynars altered their dataflow to counterbalance the ebb and flow of the field lines. Somehow, the three of them managed to transfer power in the correct amount, reconfiguring the remaining nodes to compensate for the rapidly accumulating errors. The network was holding steady.

At least until I make my next mistake, he mused sourly. Without a direct interface like that of 1011 and 1110, an otherwise easily avoidable error seemed all but inevitable.

It was intolerable. *How can humans be content to dwell* outside *the flow of the numbers, merely looking in at them? How can they deal with streams of data without knowing the joy of swimming* through *them?*

His skull felt as though it were expanding, until it seemed to him as big as all of space. He began to wonder whether he would suffer a brain hemorrhage before his processing incompetence cost everyone on the planet their lives. Dr. Lense's stern warning returned to haunt him: *There's a sound physiological reason why your people aren't called* Trynars, *Soloman.*

A static-shredded voice spoke from his combadge. "Kwolek *to Soloman.*"

"Here," he replied curtly, wary of splitting his concentration even by a small amount. The numbers continued to elude him until all he could follow was their general shapes and outlines. *Useless.*

He recognized the voice that responded as that of Fabian Stevens. *"You don't sound so hot, Soloman."*

"We're . . . having some technical problems down here."

Commander Gomez's voice replaced that of Stevens. *"You don't say. How is the force-field network holding up?"*

"Barely. But that could change at any moment. The force-field data is changing faster than the team can cope with it."

"Even with three Bynars working the problem?" replied a chiming, static-distorted voice that Soloman recognized belatedly as belonging to P8 Blue.

Soloman glanced over at 1110, who happened to be looking his way at that exact moment. The other Bynar made no attempt to hide his revulsion.

"We work optimally in pairs rather than in odd-number groups," Soloman said.

"As our captain might say, 'optimal, schmoptimal,'" Gomez said.

"Excuse me?" Soloman said, trying to ignore the rhythmic throbbing in his temples.

"I mean we're going to have to wing it, Soloman."

"Wing it *how*, exactly, Commander Gomez? Has there been a change of plans?"

"We need to find a way to deactivate the force fields— safely—if we're going to have any chance of getting everyone off the surface. But first we have to lower the volume of atmosphere that hasn't been pushed high enough yet to be blown off into space."

Ice slowly crept up the length of Soloman's back. "I understand, Commander. But the force fields have distributed the atmosphere asymmetrically toward the sunlit side, and that makes running the process in reverse extremely complicated. We never ran any simulations of that procedure."

"I hope Dr. Saadya recalls that I suggested he do just that before this fiasco started." This time the voice belonged to Lieutenant Commander Corsi, who sounded extremely unhappy. Soloman was content not to be the target of the security chief's clearly audible anger.

He noticed that the numbers had begun drifting again. His eyes felt as though they were about to launch from his head like a pair of photon torpedoes. "I'm not quite sure *what* I should be improvising, Commander Gomez."

"If we all knew the outcome in advance, Soloman," Stevens cut in, *"then it wouldn't be improvising, now, would it?"*

Soloman knew that his people weren't noted for their real-time improvisational skills. They were far more comfortable with laying out and following carefully planned, methodically executed lines of code.

But he could also see that he was rapidly losing control of the numbers. He felt certain that even the basic mathematical shapes and outlines would soon elude him. At least two more critical force-field nodes were in imminent danger of becoming unstable, threatening a lethal chain reaction.

"So much detail," he said as the numbers took wing. It took a moment for him to realize that he had spoken aloud.

"Don't sweat the details, Soloman."

Soloman's head throbbed painfully as the numbers on the screen continued dancing away, seeming almost to mock him. "This entire project *is* details, Fabian."

"No situation is completely about the details. There's always a bigger picture, if you look carefully for it. Try to think outside the numbers."

Hadn't Lense told him nearly the same thing? But hearing Stevens repeat the doctor's words made them no more comprehensible. His head pounding, Soloman glanced once more at the paired Bynars, who were immersed in the dataflow that seemed about to wash them both away.

He watched them from *outside* the digital stream, he realized, much as a human might.

Waves of pain coursed through his skull, making him

wonder if his efforts to keep up with his paired brethren were finally beginning to kill him, as Dr. Lense had warned, even without an actual three-way organic datalink.

Ground Station Vesper shook and rumbled again, as incalculable pressures sought release from far beneath the Venusian crust.

Pressure, Soloman thought, kneading his crumpled brow. *Somehow, I must release the pressure.*

Seized by a sudden inspiration, Soloman released the specifics of the numbers from his attention, allowing them to sail away like ships passing over some abstract mathematical horizon. *Think only of the bigger picture.*

Closing his eyes, he stood, leaning forward across his console to maintain his balance as the planet continued its intermittent lurching and bucking. Then he fixed his gaze upon 1011 and 1110, whose attention had been attracted by his sudden movement. The Bynars looked askance at him, their dark eyes hooded beneath their smooth, pale brows. Soloman noticed then that even Paulos and the trio of human technicians had paused briefly in their labors to look in his direction, their curiosity and hope as evident as their fear.

"I believe I may have found a solution," Soloman said, the pain in his skull still oscillating like a pulsar. It took all the effort he could muster to keep himself from resuming his fruitless chase of the force-field parameter figures.

The Bynar pair appeared to be about to make a tart response when Paulos chimed in, stepping on their words. "We're listening, Soloman. We don't seem to have many good alternatives left. Or a lot of time either."

Soloman nodded, struggling to master his own rising fear. Tapping his combadge, he said, "Commander Gomez, I will require your assistance, as well as that of the *da Vinci*. But everything will have to be done quickly. . . ."

CHAPTER
11

"Two of the equatorial force-field nodes just failed," Stevens reported. "The rest of the network seems to be trying to compensate, but there's a time-lag while the Bynars reinterpret the atmospheric models and decide which of the remaining active nodes to reinforce, and by how much."

Great, thought Gomez, her knuckles white as she clung to the armrest of the seat directly behind the two pilot's stations. The little shuttle lurched and bucked, and Gomez watched anxiously as Corsi piloted the *Kwolek* through swirls of dense, hot vapor while brief but intense cloudbursts of concentrated sulfuric acid sluiced the hull.

On its way planetward once again—following the same parabola whose upward arc had just enabled the orbiting Ishtar Station to beam the rescued Aphrodite personnel to safety—the *Kwolek* dived swiftly through

Venus's upper atmosphere. Normally, the Venusian air at this altitude—around eighty kilometers above the surface—would be somewhat calm, a relatively thin haze of carbon dioxide gas and the occasional minuscule sulfurous particle. But with the upward push that Project Ishtar's force fields were imparting to the lower atmospheric levels, the air at this height was far denser than usual, and had been whipped into a frenzy of chaotic motion. The effect was only intensifying the deeper the shuttle dived toward the upper edge of the planet-girdling force-field network.

"Some stretch of weather we're having, isn't it?" Stevens said, glancing out through the forward viewport, whose transparent aluminum was already beginning to show signs of scoring from the increasingly caustic atmosphere. Stevens sat in the secondary cockpit chair, where he worked the console to Corsi's immediate right.

Corsi said, "Better keep *your* eyes on the road, Fabe, or you're walking back to the *da Vinci*."

"I may have to let you handle the driving by yourself, Dom," Stevens replied, not sounding chastened in the least. "Say the word once we reach optimal distance from the field's equator."

"When we get there, you'll be the second one to know," Corsi said, apparently adjusting the sensors in an attempt to use the nearest free-floating atmospheric probes as navigational aids. "I just wonder why Soloman's 'optimal distance' had to be the one place on this planet where winds are strongest."

"Chalk it up to Finagle's Laws," Gomez said.

"We're receiving more revised force-field specs from the Bynar," Tev announced. His rotund body was wedged into one of the port-side chairs, his attention riveted to the console display before him. P8 Blue stood nearby, leaning forward to reach her own customized display. Gomez noticed that her tough, chitinous carapace was marred by sootlike streaks, apparently singed during the rescue of the Ground Station Aphrodite team. Fortunately, the Nasat seemed to be in no pain.

"Good," Gomez said, refocusing her own attention on the small science console beside her. A new stream of data was marching across the display, moving faster than she could read it, let alone interpret it.

The little ship lurched again, even harder this time. The external noise baffling did little to mitigate the howling of the corrosive Venusian winds.

"Full stop relative to the planet's surface," Corsi announced. "I'm keeping station nearly at the dead center of the superrotational layer, just like Soloman asked. I just hope he knows what he's . . . what *we're* doing."

An alarm on Gomez's console suddenly revealed three more key node failures, even as Soloman's force-field reconfiguration data continued to appear. Soon the node collapses would spread uncontrollably throughout the system, leading to an irreversible planetwide collapse. *With the data changing this quickly, if Soloman doesn't know what he's doing, then nobody does.*

The whine of the shuttle's overtaxed station-keeping thrusters soon drowned out the keening of the wind as the small vessel struggled to maintain its position. Normally, the winds at this altitude topped out at around three-hundred and fifty kilometers per hour, a respectable velocity. But thanks to Project Ishtar's atmospheric "blowoff," the air here was currently moving at perhaps four or five times that speed. As the shuttle jumped and bucked, Gomez began to wonder whether the engine nacelles would fall victim to shearing forces.

If we still had the old shuttles, we wouldn't have been able to pull this off, she thought grimly. The *da Vinci*'s previous shuttlecraft, the *Franklin* and the *Archimedes*, were lost at Galvan VI, and were replaced during the *da Vinci*'s recent overhaul with the *Kwolek* and the *Shirley*. Both were fresh out of the shipyards, with the most up-to-date shielding and toughest hull alloy Starfleet science had to offer—*and*, Gomez thought, *much better able to withstand this mess.*

"A pity we couldn't keep station in the clear-air zone around twenty kilometers closer to the surface," said Pattie, her vaguely crystalline voice sounding like the peal of a bell. "The temperature and pressure are greater down there, but the wind problem would be negligible."

"Fantasizing about the impossible is no help," Tev said, his porcine countenance sour. "If we were down that deep, we would be too far from the force-field network to do it any good."

"We'd also be on the wrong side of those fields," Corsi said. "Not a very good place to be if the whole thing really does come crashing down."

The *Kwolek* rumbled, its various overtaxed systems shrieking in a chorus of technological agony. Gomez could only hope that the procedure they were about to undertake would be finished before even Starfleet science's best gave in.

A burst of static issued from the comm system, followed by the voice of Soloman, evidently still doing his best to help Team Ishtar keep everything together down at Ground Station Vesper.

"*Soloman to* Kwolek. *Have you received the new data?*"

"Yup," Stevens said. "Along with the targeting coordinates. We're ready to tie our deflectors into the equatorial nodes you specified. Assuming we can spare the power, anyhow."

Doing her own quick mental calculation, Gomez looked significantly at P8 Blue and Tev for their input.

"It will be close," Pattie said, looking up from her console. "But I believe we can spare the required shield power with enough of a safety margin to avoid destroying the shuttle. At least until the *da Vinci* arrives to take over for us."

It would have been nice to have the luxury of waiting until the *da Vinci* arrived before beginning the process of propping up the force-field network from the outside. But given the larger ship's current position in its orbit, that simply wasn't an option.

"What's the *da Vinci*'s ETA?" Gomez asked Stevens.

"About one minute and thirty-eight seconds. With maximum output to the network and minimal shielding for us, our shield generators and thrusters ought to hold out for nearly twice that long."

Tev snorted. "Shuttlecraft shield generators were not designed to take this sort of punishment. I don't like this one bit."

"Neither do I," Corsi echoed, though she remained intent on her flying. "Any more than I like placing the *da Vinci*'s first and second officers both into harm's way at the same time."

"Not your call to make, Domenica," Gomez said gently. "Especially when so many other people are still in danger." *I just hope you learned the true meaning of stubbornness when you tried to make Tev and me stay behind.*

Soloman's static-laden voice came over the comm channel once again. *"There's so much pressure. So much pressure.* Kwolek, da Vinci, *please help.* . . ." Soloman trailed off again into the ionized hash of subspace background noise.

Gomez recognized the fear and desperation in the Bynar's voice. And though she wasn't happy about having had no opportunity to check his figures before acting on them, she knew she could afford to deliberate no longer.

"Fabian," she said, "hook our shield-generator output into the network grid, and give it every erg Soloman asked for."

There. I've rolled the dice. If chance smiled upon their efforts here, the prize would be the lives of the dozens of people still trapped on the planet's broiling surface.

If not . . .

Gomez watched as Stevens nodded, deliberately entered a brief command sequence into his console, then tapped the EXECUTE button.

Then the *Kwolek* lurched again, as though dropkicked by a giant. Gomez heard the sickening sounds of rending metal competing against the noxious Venusian wind's renewed fury.

CHAPTER
12

"There's so much pressure. So much pressure. Kwolek, da Vinci, *please help. . . ."*

"Hang in there, Soloman," said Captain Gold, leaning forward in his command chair. *I shouldn't have let them replace the whole seat after Galvan VI. I only use the edge of the damn thing anyway.*

Gold watched the viewer like a raptor stalking its prey. The darkened limb of the planet gave way to the bright, crescent-shaped terminator. The ochre-and-black swirls of the uppermost cloudtops rose to greet the *da Vinci*'s prow. The ship shuddered as she entered a region of increasing atmospheric turbulence.

Gold turned his chair toward the aft section of the bridge, where Lieutenant Anthony Shabalala busied himself at the tactical station. "What's our ETA, Shabalala?"

"We should be within visual range of the *Kwolek* any second."

"There!" Lieutenant Wong cried out. Gold spun his chair forward in time to see his conn officer pointing at the viewer. Near dead center, the acid-scoured hull of the shuttlecraft was now intermittently visible through the endless churn of the harsh Venusian clouds.

"Her hull is buckling and they're losing power," Shabalala reported. "Their shield generator can no longer support the collapsing force-field nodes. But at least all the life signatures aboard the shuttle are holding strong."

"Good. Wong, bring us to within five klicks of the *Kwolek* and hold our position there."

"Aye, sir," said Wong as he executed the order.

"Shabalala, inform Gomez that the cavalry has arrived."

Shabalala scowled. "I'm having trouble raising them, Captain. Their comm system may have suffered some damage. Wait a minute, I'm getting something. . . . Dr. Saadya is hailing us from the orbital station."

"On screen."

The shuttlecraft's intermittent image was abruptly replaced by the static-distorted visage of Pascal Saadya. The unsmiling planetologist seemed to have aged at least a decade during the past hour or so. *Watching your life's work circling the drain can do that to a man,* Gold thought, feeling an intense surge of sympathy for his old friend.

Saadya wasted no time on pleasantries. *"David, the force-field network is fluctuating so severely now that we're having trouble maintaining contact with the ground stations. And we can no longer raise your shuttlecraft."*

Gold put on what he hoped was a reassuring smile. "Don't worry, Pas. Some of my best engineers are aboard the *Kwolek,* and I'm sure they're still coordinating with Soloman and your ground teams to work the problem."

"Captain, I believe I can establish a transporter lock at this range," Shabalala said. "I recommend we beam the *Kwolek*'s crew to safety now."

"*No!*" Saadya shouted, his voice nearly breaking. "*Don't you see? They're working in real time with an extremely fluid and volatile data situation. You'll drop the entire Venusian sky right on top of the ground stations if you interrupt what they're doing!*"

But I can't just let this planet eat my shuttle crew either, Gold thought, feeling miserable. He was grimly aware that neither Soloman nor anyone else on the surface could be beamed up unless and until the forcefield network—along with the bulk of the atmosphere it had raised but not yet consigned to space—was brought down safely. As long as the force fields remained in a state of chaotic flux, they couldn't maintain the directed-energy-permeable "holes" necessary for safe operation of the transporters.

He also knew that he had been told precious little about the specifics of the *ad hoc* plan that Soloman and the shuttle crew were presently trying to carry out. There simply hadn't been enough time to go over it in detail. All he really knew about the scheme was that it was heavily dependent upon calculations made on the fly by Soloman, who was working under what might charitably be called less than ideal circumstances.

But Gold trusted his people and their talents implicitly. And he recognized that this was an occasion when it was best that he stay out of their way as much as possible—and to intervene only if circumstances made doing so absolutely necessary.

"Sir?" Shabalala said, dragging Gold harshly back into the here and now. "The *Kwolek*'s hull—"

Coming to a decision, Gold interrupted the tactical officer. "Steady. Extend our shields and structural integrity field to cover the *Kwolek,* and use our tractor beam to help them maintain their position relative to the shield nodes they're feeding power into. And use the deflector dish to back the *Kwolek* up with as much power as they can safely take."

"Aye, sir," Shabalala said, and set about entering commands into the tactical station with impressive speed.

Let's just hope we can hold the shuttle together long enough to finish up whatever Gomez and Soloman have started.

"Thank you, David," Saadya said from the viewer, his image rolling and twisting before it broke up entirely. The atmospheric turbulence was obviously growing ever more intense. *Not a good sign,* Gold ruminated. *This plan has* got *to work.*

He suddenly realized that he had no concrete idea of what success would actually look like. After all, not only had no one ever attempted a project quite like Saadya's, nobody had ever tried to force such a thing into an abrupt about-face right in the middle of the proceedings. Literally anything could happen now.

And my crew is still stuck out there, above it and below it.

The pressure, Soloman thought as he cradled his head between his long-fingered hands. His cranium felt as though it had tripled in size. The figures on his screen no longer held any meaning whatsoever. He was beginning to see double, and had begun to wonder if he was dying.

Ground Station Vesper shook again. The lights failed, to be replaced moments later by the dim red illumination of the emergency backups. Someone screamed during the momentary darkness. Soloman thought it was one of the Bynars, bereft of even the cold comfort of the computer system. Soloman's own console appeared to be dead, even though the emergency power was functioning.

Soloman closed his eyes, desperately wishing for the ordeal to end, one way or another. The calculations were done, transmitted, and received, and there was no way to refine them further. Even if he could, he wasn't certain how many of the atmospheric probes— the source of the preponderance of the climate and force-field data—were still functioning, given the high-altitude ionization being caused by the volcanic surges. The force-field network would either behave as he had asked it to behave, or else it would wander further into the unpredictable provinces of mathematical chaos.

And kill everyone on the planet, probably including the shuttle crew as well.

The pressure. The people up on the shuttle should have all the data they need. It's up to them now to relieve the pressure.

CHAPTER
13

No pressure, Soloman, Stevens thought, recalling one of the last intelligible words he'd heard the little Bynar utter before the storm-tossed atmosphere cut off communication between the *Kwolek* and Ground Station Vesper.

He hoped he hadn't misplaced his faith in Soloman's ability to improvise. Maybe the Bynar's facility with numbers was only an asset in situations that required one to *go* by the numbers.

This certainly wasn't one of those instances.

The sound of rending, shearing metal jolted Stevens out of his reverie.

"I told you this vessel couldn't stand up to this sort of punishment for long."

"Shut up, Tev," Gomez and Corsi said in a synchronized harmony that would have put a cadre of Borg drones to shame. Pattie's tinkling laughter was barely audible over the roar of the wind.

"Excuse me?" the Tellarite said, a now-familiar dudgeon inflecting his voice.

There was a loud bang, as though something had struck the hull. An alarm Klaxon sounded, and the readouts on Stevens's console suddenly changed. Numerous amber and orange warning lights suddenly shifted to a far friendlier green hue.

Stevens watched a grin spread slowly across Corsi's features like a Venusian sunrise. "The *da Vinci* has just arrived. And they're supplying all the power we'll need to finish this."

"How can you tell—" Stevens interrupted himself, watching the rhythmic pulsation of the energy-intake readout that monitored the main power coupling. "Morse code. Our comm system must be down."

Stevens turned in his seat, hoping to share a triumphant smile with Gomez. He was surprised to see a dour expression clouding her face.

"That's great," she said. "But we're still out of contact with Vesper. We can only hope that those last figures Soloman gave us are still precise enough to get the job done safely."

"So do we maintain power for the full duration?" Stevens asked as he quickly rechecked the numbers. Soloman's last batch of figures had required the *Kwolek* to bolster several key force-field nodes for another eight minutes and twelve seconds.

Gomez sighed. "We don't have any other choice. Not if we want to keep the sky from falling."

Corsi's sharp intake of breath caught Stevens's attention. "What's wrong, Dommie?"

For once, the security chief didn't seem ready to summarily execute him for using her family nickname. A quick glance at his own scanner readout told him why.

A large portion of the force-field network was suddenly twisting itself into an entirely unexpected shape.

Stevens felt a sharp pang of regret at having encouraged Soloman to improvise.

"Captain!" Shabalala shouted from the tactical station.

Startled, Gold turned his chair around almost quickly enough to cause a whiplash. He saw at once that Shabalala's dark skin had suddenly gone gray. "What is it?"

"The force-field network is . . . *changing.*"

Turning back toward the main viewer, Gold said, "Show me a schematic."

The static-marbled image of the *Kwolek,* held fast in the complex web of energy radiating from the *da Vinci's* main deflector dish, vanished. It was replaced by a simple orange-and-black wire-frame representation of the planet and the constantly fluctuating force-field lattice that surrounded it. Gold looked to a position on the daylit side, about twenty degrees south of the equator, where concentric rings marked the epicenter of the volcanic activity that had already radiated out across the surface in every direction for several hundred kilometers. Noting that the late Ground Station Aphrodite now lay well within the still-spreading volcanic hell, he mouthed a silent prayer of thanks that his people had reached the Aphrodite team before the lava did.

Then he saw that several other ground stations still lay in harm's way, the nearest of them perhaps another hour or two away from immolation.

Unless his people could find a way to work around the force-field network, all those people—Soloman included—were going to die. They would *all* expire, one small crew at a time, as each station slowly succumbed to the unleashed furies of the Venusian interior. *The same way Galvan VI slowly ate away at my ship, killing people off one by one. . . .*

Gold cut off those thoughts and forced himself to study the lines that represented the field network itself, in response to Shabalala's report. All across the schematic of the planet, the crisscrossing meshwork of field lines—the energetic meridians and parallels that connected hundreds of force-field generation nodes and covered the entire globe—appeared to have maintained a fairly stable, if lopsided, overall shape. The north-south field lines drew shapes that resembled overlapping slices of a strangely oblate orange, bulging out farthest across the planet's sunward side, which was the only place from which the atmosphere could be successfully "blown off."

But Gold saw a glaring exception to this general pattern: the portion of the force field that lay above the precise center of the volcanic eruption. Here, the lines of force were actively moving, twisting, and taking on a cylindrical shape that slowly rose above the rest of the world-girdling force field. It extended ever upward, like a tenacious plant determined to pierce the clouds and reach the sun.

"My God," Shabalala said, his voice pitched scarcely above a whisper. "The network must be malfunctioning."

From the forward ops station, Ensign Susan Haznedl said, "I don't think it is, sir." A lithe young human with strawberry blond hair, Haznedl had recently taken over as the primary operations officer. Two of the *da Vinci*'s ops personnel had died at Galvan VI, and the other transferred off, so Haznedl was new to the S.C.E. "The motions of those field lines are too—well, *orderly*, sir. I've never seen a failing deflector shield roll itself up into a funnel shape like that."

Shabalala asked, "You're saying somebody could be changing the field's shape deliberately?"

"I think so, yes."

Gold said nothing, focusing instead on the tale unfolding on the main viewer. As he watched, the single elongated tube of force split itself into two, then four, then eight and more progressively narrower tubes. He quickly lost count of the tubes, so quickly were they appearing, bringing to mind a sped-up recording of living cells dividing *ad infinitum.* He was, however, able to see that the bases of the force-tubules seemed to plunge themselves deeply beneath the planet's surface—

—piercing the exact center of seismic and volcanic activity with almost surgical precision.

Gold smiled. "Haznedl, try to get me a *real* visual on what's going on down there."

Also smiling, the young woman turned back to her console and said, "Yes, *sir.*"

The tactical display vanished, replaced by a hash of static that slowly gave way to a grainy, computer-enhanced image of the Venusian dayside, no doubt relayed down either directly from Ishtar Station or from one of the many automated support satellites that ringed the planet. The resolution was poor, but understandably so given the current local weather.

Gold quickly found the spot where the force-field network had morphed itself into such peculiar shapes. Although the fields themselves were invisible, the material that was rising with projectile speed along the narrow, rapidly multiplying vertical tubes of force was quite noticeable. The material became white-hot as it shot through the cloudtops and into space, passing at least one hundred kilometers above the highest-altitude layers of the atmospheric "blowoff."

The pitiless brightness of the sun made the nature of the ejected material immediately apparent. Recalling what Soloman had said about needing to relieve pressure, Gold looked around the bridge. He spent a moment watching the awestruck faces at each station as everyone present seemed to grasp the enormity of what they were witnessing.

The main mass of the lava flow was being diverted from the remaining ground stations and flung into a high orbit about Venus. No one seemed able to pry his eyes from the viewer as the molten material continued to be blasted hundreds of kilometers away from the greenhouse-desiccated world below.

The molten material continued trailing fire across the ochre sky, slowly turning dark as it exited the funnel-shaped, spaceward terminus of the reconfigured force-field network, gradually surrendering its heat to the airless void.

Haznedl finally broke the silence that had engulfed the bridge. "Somebody," the ops officer said, "has obviously figured out how to turn the force-field network into a colossal mass driver."

"Looks like the pressure may finally be off," Shabalala said, still looking awed. "The lava's being funneled off into space."

Shaking her head, Haznedl said, "This is truly amazing. I've never seen anything like it."

Gold sat back in his chair. "Just another day at the office for the S.C.E., Haznedl."

CHAPTER
14

Pascal Saadya stood alone in his darkened office, staring down at the great yellow world through the wide transparent aluminum window. As he looked upon the daylit face of Venus, an old joke sprang to mind: *What's the difference between God and a terraformer?*

He spoke the punch line aloud. "God doesn't think he's a terraformer."

The bulk of the force-field network—along with more than eighty percent of Venus's original hothouse atmosphere—had been carefully and safely lowered nearly an hour earlier. The vast majority of the atmospheric probes remained intact and functional. According to a quick report from the ever-busy Adrienne Paulos, all of the Project Ishtar ground crews, as well as the *da Vinci* personnel who had provided emergency assistance, were finally out of immediate danger. However, all but a handful of the ground staff had been evacuated up to

Ishtar Station, where they would remain pending a detailed appraisal of the damage sustained by the surface facilities arrayed across the Venusian surface.

Saadya was all too keenly aware that he owed an enormous debt to David Gold and his ingenious engineering team. As well as to one extremely insightful and courageous stray Bynar. *Without their help, my ambition and haste would have killed dozens of good people. And laid waste to years of meticulous research.*

Saadya watched silently as Soloman's improvised force-field mass driver continued its work, helping the planet continue to disgorge copious amounts of its fiery insides upward past the limits of the atmosphere and into the infinite gulf of space.

The "Big One"—the global volcanic conflagration Venus experienced every half-billion years or so—had indeed come, thanks to the internal stresses Project Ishtar had unleashed. But unlike earlier occurrences, the current lava flows would not engulf the entire planet. The damage would remain localized around a Greenland-size area, where a pancake-dome volcano had arisen in response to Soloman's inspiring job of force-field tailoring.

The door chime sounded. "Come," Saadya said.

He remained facing the planetary fireworks display as the door hissed open, admitting a harsh shaft of artificial light from the outer corridor. From the shape of the trio of shadows that fell across the carpet, he guessed the identities of his visitors at once.

"Hello, David. Soloman. Adrienne. I'm glad you came. I think that watching the fires of creation all alone isn't nearly so satisfying as sharing the experience with others."

He expected Gold to make a characteristically acerbic

remark. But when he turned to face his old friend, he saw only wonder on his face, which—like those of Soloman and Paulos—was turned toward the cosmic drama unfolding far below.

"It's incredible, Pas," Gold said. "And beautiful."

Spread into long, thin strands that Saadya estimated each measured no more than a few meters across, the ejected Venusian mantle material was rapidly cooling as it arced over the western horizon toward the night side, encircling the planet in a great ellipse along its equator. Of course, these "strands" were nothing of the sort; they were assemblages of billions of separate congealing objects, many of them no larger than a human hand, some as small as dust grains. But aligned as they were in speed and direction, they presented the long-distance appearance of solidity, as did the various-size particles that composed Saturn's voluminous system of rings.

Paulos must have been thinking along exactly the same lines. "It's a ring system. Forming right before our eyes."

Saadya squinted at the purple-and-ochre horizon of the nightward terminator. Was he seeing the telltale signs of uneven clumping of some of the ejected material?

"Perhaps," he said. "But it might not remain in annular form for long."

"What do you mean?" Gold asked.

"Just that we may have witnessed Venus in the throes of childbirth. She may have begun to spawn a moon of her own."

"If that's true," Paulos said, looking thoughtful, "then we have a baby to name."

"Eventually," said Saadya. "It could take centuries for the accretion process to settle down on its own." *Unless we find a way to help it along.* He dismissed the thought as soon as it occurred to him. *Will I never tire of playing God?*

"It'll still need a name," Gold said. "How about Venus Victrix, after the Roman bringer of victory?"

Shaking his head, Saadya resumed watching the planet. "I think a more appropriate name might be Venus Felix."

"Who's that?" asked Paulos, frowning. "The Roman bringer of housecats?"

"The bringer of good luck, not cats," Gold corrected. "Though there are members of my family who might argue that there's no real distinction between the two." The captain turned toward Saadya. "There's more to what you've done here than mere *mazel*, my friend. Getting Project Ishtar to this point wasn't dependent upon luck. To suggest that isn't fair to you, Dr. Paulos, or the rest of your team, for that matter."

Saadya smiled grimly, then faced Gold again. "You're right, David. But I'm being even more unfair to *your* crew." His eyes lit on the diminutive Bynar, who so far had yet to utter a word. "Particularly you, Mr. Soloman. You stand astride the worlds of Bynars and humans. And because of that unique outlook, you accomplished what no one else could—you rescued everyone on Venus from my hubris. I thank you."

Soloman nodded, though he seemed uncomfortable with the praise. "It would be wrong to completely discount random chance and contingency, Dr. Saadya. The unorthodox data-handling the situation forced upon me involved a good deal of guesswork."

"Skillful estimates aren't the same as lucky guesses," Saadya said. Soloman looked skeptical, but didn't seem inclined to argue the point.

Gold shrugged. "Call it luck, or skill, or even kismet if you have to. You've still had several very lucky outcomes here, even without completing the atmospheric 'blowoff.'"

Saadya was speechless for a moment. "Lucky outcomes? Name one."

"For one, no one's dead, or even badly injured."

Saadya drew scant comfort from that fact, then felt a paroxysm of guilt at his own callousness. "Including your shuttle crew?" He realized he'd been so focused on the specifics of Project Ishtar that he'd given little thought to the injuries David's brave engineering staff might have suffered while flying through the atmosphere's superrotational layer.

Gold made a dismissive gesture. "The shuttle took the worst of the beating. Dr. Paulos here has taken the liberty of letting us tow the *Kwolek* to one of your docking ports so Gomez and Tev can kludge a few quick repairs together before the *da Vinci* shoves off. Tev says your shuttlebay has a smidge more elbow room than ours."

"It seemed like the least we could do, since our own hardware apparently caused at least one of the shuttle's hull breaches in the first place," Paulos explained, holding a dark, lumpy, baseball-size metallic object out for inspection. "It seems the *Kwolek* ran over one of our little reinforced atmospheric probes. Looks like that's what damaged her comm system when the *da Vinci* arrived to bolster her power reserves."

Saadya winced. That was yet another low-probability eventuality he hadn't spent a lot of time considering. "My God," he stammered.

"It's just a scratch," Gold said. "I'm sure Tev can buff it right out."

But Saadya wasn't buying Gold's breezy denials. He

understood only too well the peril of an untoward encounter with a projectile that was plated with a duranium/rodinium alloy. "Your shuttle crew nearly died trying to save this project. Only to see it fail in the end."

"Quit punishing yourself, Pas," Gold said. "It isn't as though we didn't know you were using atmospheric probes. It was *ahftseloches*."

"*Ahftseloches*," Saadya repeated, smiling fractionally. "Inevitable bad luck. I thought you said you didn't believe in that."

"Inevitable bad luck is the only kind of luck I can usually rely on," Gold said, staring at his left hand as he flexed and clenched the fingers. Saadya wondered if this was the hand that had been replaced after the recent shipboard accident he'd heard about.

Gold continued, "But bad luck, inevitable or otherwise, doesn't always *end up* badly. For example, Project Ishtar might actually be on firmer footing now because of what happened today."

Saadya could scarcely believe his ears. "That hardly seems likely, David."

"Listen to him, Pas," Paulos said, gesturing toward the window and the plumes of ejected material that continued streaming into space. "In just a few hours, we've relieved maybe a quarter of a billion years of seismic stress from the planet's interior. We'll be thankful for that little boon when the time comes to attach banks of impulse engines to the crust so we can spin this puppy up to a Terran-style diurnal cycle."

"And if a spanking new moon really has just *plotzed* itself up out of the belly of Venus," Gold said, "then maybe you won't have to tow Mercury out of its orbit after all. Scratch one more huge item off the 'to-do-later' list, Pas."

"I imagine Captain Scott will be delighted to hear that particular detail," said Saadya.

"There you go. Terraforming while you wait."

Saadya chuckled, though his mood remained dour. "There's still no denying the fact that this was a near-catastrophe. Or that I bear complete responsibility for it. I'm sure that's how the Federation Council and your Captain Scott will interpret the day's events. That was certainly how the Central Processor Pair on Bynaus reacted. They've decided that Project Ishtar is 'a waste of their finite time and scarce resources.' In fact, 1011 and 1110 have already been reassigned, and will return to Bynaus just as soon as the transportation arrangements are made."

"I'm sorry to hear that," Gold said. The little Bynar who stood beside him appeared anxious to speak, but held his tongue.

"You still have the rest of Team Ishtar," Paulos said. "We've gathered a lot of good atmospheric data to guide us through the next 'blowoff' attempt. The Federation Council is sure to be interested in tha—"

Saadya interrupted her. "It's possible that Bynaus is right about Ishtar, Adrienne. Perhaps what happened here today was a sign that my approach has been all wrong from the beginning."

"With respect, Dr. Saadya," Soloman said, finally interposing himself into the conversation, "I believe that Bynaus can be persuaded to resume its support for your efforts to remake this planet. My homeworld stands to learn a great deal from the geological information gathered by your ground stations during the crisis. Should you choose to share it with them, that is."

Saadya suddenly realized that he'd been concentrating so intently on the Venusian sky that he hadn't given adequate thought to whatever secrets still lay beneath its immobile, atectonic crust.

He resolved to review those data in detail as soon as possible—and discover precisely what it was he had to bargain with. There was so much to do. . . .

"If you're looking for signs and portents, Pas," Gold said with a gentle smile, "maybe you should consider today's events as a hint that only one major change needs to be made to Project Ishtar."

"And what's that?" Saadya asked.

"Slow it the hell *down*. Even God takes billions of years to cook up planets. And it's not as though there's been any sudden shortage of galactic real estate, the Dominion War cleanup efforts notwithstanding."

Saadya mulled over Gold's suggestion, and wondered what Dr. Seyetik would have said to such advice. *Slow down. Not a bad idea, perhaps. I could start by not rushing to the holodeck so often for browbeatings by Seyetik's ghost.*

Of course, without a pair of Bynars crunching numbers for Team Ishtar, a severe slowdown would be the project's only option—other than closing up shop entirely. To his surprise, Saadya felt great reluctance to consider that final option. His gathering despair warred briefly with his omnipresent desire to tinker as the gods themselves might do.

The gods appeared to be winning. Gods, after all, could afford to be patient.

"Perhaps," Saadya said, "I only need to make sure I'm headed forward. Regardless of the speed of my progress."

He paused, turning to gaze once more upon the clump of coalescing, impact-heated matter that was now growing noticeably near the western horizon's edge. He decided to indeed dub the nascent satellite Victrix-Felix, as a reminder that luck had prevented catastrophe today just as surely as had anyone's skill. Even that of Soloman.

Gods and planetologists alike sometimes have to bend knee at the altars of chaos, luck, and even ahftseloches. As did starship captains, Saadya suspected.

When Saadya finally spoke, his voice was lowered nearly to a whisper. Gesturing toward the scene of primordial creation outside his window, he said, "Perhaps what happened here today is a sign that new beginnings are in order."

After Captain Gold said his farewells to Saadya and Paulos, and beamed back to the *da Vinci,* Soloman remained aboard Ishtar Station. He had busied himself alongside Paulos and her frantically busy staff ever since the careful lowering of the force-field grid had allowed the Ground Station Vesper crew to be beamed up to the station, along with many of the other surface-based personnel. As he walked the length of the orbital complex, heading toward the docking port where the *Kwolek* was moored, he realized he wasn't entirely certain why he'd opted not to beam back to the *da Vinci* with the captain.

Perhaps he was merely stalling. He knew, after all, that Dr. Lense would want to examine him—and interrogate him about his informational ordeal with the other Bynars—the moment he returned to the *da Vinci.*

Soloman entered the corridor adjacent to the docking port. He saw 1011 and 1110 approaching from an adjoining corridor, as though summoned by his thoughts.

He saw in their hard, dark eyes that their contemptuous feelings for him had softened not at all.

"So you—"

"—are still—"

"—aboard—"

"—Ishtar Station."

Soloman found their grasp of the obvious just as keen as ever. Trying to maintain a guarded expression, he said, "As are both of you, I see."

"Only—"

"—temporarily."

"Bynaus has—"

"—summoned us—"

"—home."

Home. From the smug manner with which 1110 had delivered that word, Soloman knew it had been intended to wound. As long as he remained a singleton— an informational cripple and a social deviant in the eyes of his people—he knew he could never again use that word to describe Bynaus.

Then a completely unaccustomed feeling abruptly seized him. His facial muscles grew involuntarily tight and he heard a rhythmic, high-pitched, hiccuplike noise start up and repeat itself spasmodically.

Nearly three full seconds elapsed before Soloman realized that *he* was the source of the sound.

The other Bynars watched him in evident perplexity as he surrendered himself to the fit of laughter. Their disgust swiftly gave way to fear, and they quickly withdrew down the corridor as though certain that he had gone mad.

Perhaps I have.

Uncountable moments later, Soloman's laughter faltered, slowed, and finally ceased. He felt limp and wrung out. But also strangely joyful.

Bynaus rejects me, even though I have accomplished things that linked Bynars clearly cannot. That new moon forming over Venus proves it.

But something more fundamental vexed him: Try as he might, he could feel no sorrow over having lost Bynaus. Especially a Bynaus that would embrace the likes of 1011 and 1110.

"Hey, what was *that* all about?" said Fabian Stevens, whom Soloman belatedly realized must have been standing for quite some time behind him in the open hatchway leading to the docked shuttle. The nearby sounds of Bynar conversation and hysterical laughter must have made him curious.

Soloman instinctively raised his shields. "I merely had to conclude some . . . unfinished business."

The tactical specialist eyed him suspiciously for a moment, then shrugged in apparent resignation. "I understand. It's a Bynar thing, so you probably don't feel comfortable talking about it with any of your human friends."

Soloman thought about that for a moment. Were he still bonded to 111—and had circumstances not forced him to improvise with Project Ishtar's data in a most un-Bynar-like fashion—he would no doubt have agreed with Stevens's assessment.

Now he wasn't so sure. He only knew that the disapproval of Stevens and the rest of his shipmates suddenly mattered to him far more than any amount of opprobrium his fellow Bynars could heap upon him.

Just as Stevens was starting to turn back toward the hatchway, Soloman came to a decision. "Fabian . . ."

Turning back toward Soloman, Stevens asked, "Is something wrong, Soloman?"

"Yes. No. I don't know."

Stevens smiled. "Well, only three choices. That narrows things down a bit. How can I help?"

"I would be very interested . . . in hearing your advice on some of my . . . unfinished business."

Still smiling, Stevens gestured toward the waiting shuttle. "Well, the *Kwolek* is finally spaceworthy again. You can pour your heart out to me about whatever happened between you and your fellow infophiles while Gomez and Tev pilot this heap back to the *da Vinci*."

Soloman nodded, then followed Stevens through the docking bay and into the *Kwolek*'s narrow passenger compartment.

Stevens turned toward the cockpit, where Gomez and Tev were apparently going through their preflight checklist. The debris-ringed planet Venus loomed in the forward window.

"If you guys won't be needing me for a while," Stevens said, "I need to speak with Soloman back here for a bit."

Tev grunted, sparing only enough of his attention to glare briefly at Stevens. Compared to 1011 and 1110, Tev's casual belligerence seemed downright cuddly.

"We're doing fine up here, Fabe," Gomez said, pausing only briefly in her complex data-entering tasks. "You already performed your miracle on the tactical systems. And I think Tev and I won't need any help getting us back home."

Home.

Not Bynaus, but home nevertheless.

As he and Stevens took a pair of aft seats, Soloman realized he was no longer dreading his upcoming debriefing with Dr. Lense. In fact, he was beginning to feel great anticipation for it. He had a feeling it wouldn't take very long at all.

I have come home, a solo man, but one with many friends, he thought. He decided that this was probably all he needed to say to her.

Ishtar Station's docking clamps released the shuttle with a muffled clunk. The *Kwolek* glided slowly forward on its thrusters.

Soloman noticed that Stevens was regarding him with an incredulous grin. "You're *smiling,* Soloman. Mind if I ask why?"

"Because we're going home," the Bynar said, and then proceeded to explain.

BUYING TIME

Robert Greenberger

CHAPTER
1

No sooner had Susan Haznedl's head hit her hard pillow than the door to her cabin swooshed open. Dantas Falcão, her roommate and the ship's new medical technician, entered their small cabin, shook her mane of dark brown hair, and began unzipping her duty jacket before she even cleared the frame.

"What a shift." Falcão grinned at her new friend, showing nearly perfect white teeth set against olive skin. Haznedl sighed, since all she wanted was some sleep. Clearly her roommate was too energetic to let *that* happen. Propping herself on an elbow, she made a face that told Falcão to elaborate on her statement.

"Starfleet may think they're done with the refit," she said, slipping into her nightclothes. "But we're constantly recalibrating the medical sensors, so something's wrong."

The *U.S.S. da Vinci* had been nearly destroyed a few

months previously and had been only recently returned to active duty. Half the crew was lost in the ter-
rifying hours trapped within a gas giant star, and both
Falcão and Haznedl were among the replacement
crew. Haznedl had had roommates on her previous
posting, the *U.S.S. Burbank,* but none had Falcão's ex-
citability.

"At least I've gotten to meet more of the crew," Falcão
continued, brushing her shoulder-length hair. "Dr.
Lense insisted on fresh medical workups for everyone,
to keep the databases current. We'll be done by tomorrow, I figure. Hey, let me ask you, have you been able to
get the story on Bart Faulwell?"

Haznedl blinked. "I've talked to him in the mess a
couple of times. Seems like a good guy, very hardwork-
ing. Why?"

"I find him very attractive," her roommate replied.

"Songmin tells me that Bart's been in a long-term relationship with an officer on Starbase 92 for quite some
time, so you're out of luck." Haznedl was referring to
the alpha shift conn officer, Songmin Wong, whom she
sat next to on the bridge, and who had been on the ship
since the Dominion War. He had proven a useful source
of shipboard gossip. "Do you like older men?"

Falcão plopped herself at the foot of Haznedl's bed,
causing the ops officer to groan inwardly. She liked Falcão, she did, but wasn't up for a lot of girl talk right
now. Sickbay was not the only area experiencing shake-
down concerns. She thought ops was acting sluggishly
and had spent her entire shift tracing each circuit to
find the problem, with little success.

"I like all kinds of people, truth to tell. Well, good for
Bart," she said and then seemed thoughtful for a moment. "What about Sabrina Simon?"

Haznedl rolled her eyes and knew it was going to be a long night.

The following morning, Haznedl was once again concentrating on the operations diagnostic. According to the tricorder, the console was operating within Starfleet specs, but instinctively she knew that something was wrong when they left the Sol system a week ago. She tapped some controls and focused the tricorder on a particular junction grid. *A-ha,* she thought. There was something amiss—one of the isolinear chips was in danger of burning out, causing relay signals to intermittently die out before completing their connection.

Tev, their new second officer, was pacing the rear of the bridge, watching the alpha shift go about their business. Tellarites had a reputation for being arrogant and blustery, but Haznedl had served with a few in her time, and none fit that stereotype. Tev, however, more than made up for that. He always seemed to know one thing more than the station officer, and didn't hesitate to share that knowledge. True, those bits of knowledge had come in handy; she just didn't want to acknowledge it to his face. On the one hand, she knew he, like Haznedl and Falcão and the other replacement crew, was just trying to fit in, but on the other, he was too smug for his own good.

At tactical, Anthony Shabalala was frowning at an incoming signal. He toggled a control and beckoned to Tev.

"We have a signal from Starfleet. I've already alerted Captain Gold," he said crisply.

"Very good," Tev said, his voice deep and mellow. He

always sounded like that, but managed to slip in a superior tone whenever possible. "He and Commander Gomez should be en route, so he can take it in the ready room."

"I've already routed it there, sir," Shabalala said.

"Of course you have," Tev said. "Carry on."

Shabalala and Haznedl exchanged looks and brief smirks before Tev, now taking the center seat, could see either of them, at which point they put their poker faces back on.

Moments later, Gold and Gomez entered the bridge and immediately went to the ready room together. They were in there for several minutes, and Haznedl went back to focusing on her repairs. The faulty chip had been replaced, and now she was tracing other circuits.

Finally, the captain reentered the bridge. "I'd like to see the S.C.E. staff in the conference room, Tev," Gold said, then turned to the fore of the bridge. "Wong, set course for Ludugia, warp five."

"Yes, sir," Wong said. That got a pleased nod from the captain and then he was gone, headed to the observation lounge.

"That's not far from Ferengi space," Wong said.

"Yeah, it is," Haznedl replied. "Wonder if this is one of their scams."

"Hey, not all Ferengi run scams, you know."

Haznedl grinned. "How would *you* know?"

"Well, let's just say I've come across a few lately," Wong said, a gleam in his eyes.

Minutes later, Gold took his place at the head of the curved meeting table. To his right sat Sonya Gomez, to his left, Tev. Dr. Elizabeth Lense, Domenica Corsi, Fabian Stevens, Carol Abramowitz, and Soloman filled out the sides of the table, with P8 Blue in her specially modified chair opposite Gold. To the captain, the odd part was expecting the late Kieran Duffy to be on his left and seeing Tev's porcine features instead. He chastised himself for not moving past Galvan VI where Duffy and half the rest of his crew met their deaths—it wasn't fair, especially to Tev. Rachel, his loving wife, had told him it would take time. She just never said how much time.

"We've gotten a signal from Starbase 9," the captain said once everyone was settled. "Commander Uthlonicam reports complaints from several trading ships regarding navigational hazards near the asteroid belt in the Ludugia system. According to her long-range sensors, they're chroniton particles."

Gomez's expression immediately deepened into a frown, the lines marking her normally smooth skin. Gold could tell just about everyone around the table stiffened at the mention of chroniton particles. Despite the rise of time-travel incidents over the last century, few seemed comfortable with the problems and paradoxes these opportunities presented. In fact, he had hoped to have nothing to do with time travel during the remainder of his career.

"Based on her readings, Starfleet was able to match their frequency to the waves encountered by the first starship to make contact with the Guardian of Forever. We're being asked to find a way to the chroniton source."

"You do understand what it means if a second Guardian is discovered?" Tev's expression was expectant, his dark, sunken eyes agleam.

All Starfleet personnel knew of the ancient Guardian, found over a century earlier, a device with artificial intelligence that could enable people to travel anywhere in the past. Given the problems it could cause should immoral people make use of the device, it remained one of the most carefully guarded items within the Federation. Unlike that object, this one was in a busy sector of space, near highly traveled space-lanes. Gold could only imagine what would happen should it prove to be true—the political fallout would be intense as well as the belief that if there were two, there might be more.

Tev interrupted his train of thought. "If I recall, the starship managed to enter orbit despite the temporal waves."

"Yes," Gold replied. "But these seem to be harsher and can pierce standard shielding. It's a navigational nightmare." The captain looked around the table. "We're a day out of the system, so until we learn more, everyone else can relax. I wouldn't stop your tournament, Doctor." To help the crew better integrate given the large percentage of newcomers, Lense had organized a board game tournament that had begun only a week earlier, shortly after their Venus mission.

"Well," Gomez said with a smile, something the captain had seen all too rarely since Duffy died, "I was about to trounce Bart. Permission to make two moves?"

"In your dreams, Commander," Faulwell said with a grin. "I'm just lulling you into a true sense of security."

"Then you're doing a very good job," Gomez deadpanned.

Gold added, "And you know Temporal Investigations has already caught wind of this." There were animated winces indicating the almost universal dislike of that particular division of Starfleet.

"Anything else we need to know?" Corsi asked.

Gomez said, "We won't be that far from the Ferengi Alliance. I'm sure there's a Ferengi or six who'll think this is a great business opportunity."

CHAPTER
2

A day later, the *da Vinci* neared the Ludugian system, with its small Type-O star. It had small planetoids circling it, plus the asteroid belt seventeen AUs from the star itself. Gomez stood at one of the aft consoles, Tev alongside her, as the captain instructed Wong take the ship out of warp a safe distance from the edge of the chroniton wave field. She monitored the readings, trying to figure out exactly what was being affected, when, and how.

"Commander Uthlonicam has cleared the area of all traffic, so we should be able to operate by ourselves," Gold said.

"Confirmed," Shabalala said from the tactical station. "Best guess is the last ship was in this area eighteen hours ago."

"I've never seen anything like this," Gomez admitted

softly. "Sir, can we ride the wave for better readings? It's a trick I learned on the *Enterprise.*"

Gold turned to look at his first officer with some measure of surprise.

Gomez continued: "I'm not asking to put the ship at risk, but sometimes you need to feel the problem as much as you need to study the readings."

"Tev?"

"Well, I for one don't see what we can learn, but I doubt we'd be in danger."

"Thanks for the vote of confidence," Gomez muttered. Tev was certainly taking some getting used to. It didn't help that he questioned her authority on their very first post-Galvan VI mission to investigate the Shanial Cabochon in San Francisco, never mind that Gomez's indecision following Galvan was affecting her abilities. She had enough to prove to herself without being put in a position of having to do the same with her second-in-command.

"Go ahead, Wong," Gold said. "Edge us closer so we can feel the distortion, but be ready to pull us back on full impulse."

The young lieutenant acknowledged the order and the *da Vinci* moved forward. Silence filled the bridge as the moments ticked off until finally there was a shimmy, building into a crescendo. Gomez felt the vibrations through her boots and instinctively grabbed on to the bulkhead to her right. The vibrations continued to grow until there was a visible distortion on the screen, and then they dissipated.

"Conlon to bridge. What's going on up there?"

"We're indulging Commander Gomez," Gold lightly replied.

"Good thing we're using new rivets. We should hold to-gether, but next time we could use a heads-up."

"My apologies," Gold replied. "We'll tell you the very next time we surf chroniton waves."

"Well, what did your finely tuned senses tell you?" Tev asked, looking directly at Gomez.

"I'm not sure yet," Gomez admitted through gritted teeth. She studied the readings from the sensors, fine-tuning two of the readouts. Before she could complete her next thought, the next wave arrived and it was faster and harsher than the one before.

"Time between waves?" Gomez asked.

"Thirty-seven seconds," Haznedl answered. "The second wave was almost double the intensity, plus it confused the sensor array with excessive radiation."

"Can you still steer us, Lieutenant?" Tev snapped at Wong.

"Helm's a little sluggish," Wong said.

"Pull us back," Gold said quietly. "I hope you've felt enough, Gomez."

"Me too," she said, and looked past the sneer on Tev's face to the viewscreen. The radiation and particles were not doing anything to distort the visuals. That told her something, as well.

Downloading the current readings to a padd, she said, "Captain, I'd like to check something with Lieutenant Conlon."

Gold nodded in approval, and Gomez headed to the turbolift. An idea was starting to form. . . .

Time, oddly enough, seemed to pass slowly with little change to the readings before them. Wong kept the *da*

Vinci far enough away that the chroniton waves barely caused the ship to waver. Starfleet Command called to inform Gold that the starship *Yeager* had been dispatched to follow up on the region once the *da Vinci* restored safe passage. They just had to solve the unsolvable and move on. *About like usual.*

Just then, the doors opened and Gomez emerged, a smile on her face. She went right to Haznedl's console and entered a set of figures from the padd she carried.

"We'll have to reenter the chroniton field and let the *da Vinci* absorb a significant amount of radiation," Gomez began.

"But chroniton radiation is harmful to living tissue," Tev said, interrupting. Gomez made a face at that and then redirected her attention to Gold.

"Yes, but as the *Voyager* discovered three years ago, you can neutralize the radiation with modulated antichroniton particles. I think we can blanket a portion of the asteroid belt with antichronitons and bring the ship to the source."

Gold nodded. His first officer had obviously been keeping up with the reports that had been coming in from Delta Quadrant ever since the Pathfinder Project—now Project *Voyager*—had made contact with Captain Janeway's lost ship.

"And has Dr. Lense signed off on the risk?"

"Not yet," she said hurriedly. "I wanted to see how much radiation we have to absorb before we can generate the antichronitons to open up the spacelane. Nancy thinks the rebuilt ship is up to some pounding."

"So, how much pounding do we take before we can move?"

"Presuming Songmin can keep us moving forward while being bombarded, about four hours. This is a particularly potent field of chroniton particles so the hull *should* absorb them quickly."

"And how long before you generate the antichroniton field?"

"Maybe twenty minutes later. We can continue to collect chronitons from the rear hull while emitting the antichronitons before us until we find the source."

"And do you think we can handle five plus hours of being shaken around?" The captain realized his voice was sounding incredulous, but he disliked the notion of banging up the ship so soon after the refit. They'd already taken a pounding from the Nachri and the Venusian atmosphere in the short time since being released from McKinley Station.

"Yes, sir, and Conlon agrees with me," Gomez emphatically added. She sounded convincing and clearly had worked out the science behind the scheme before returning to the bridge. It was at times like this the captain had to make a command decision less on the facts and more on his faith in the crew. And he trusted Gomez wholeheartedly.

"Begin your plans," he finally said. "Tev, have Dr. Lense do random checks to make sure no one is succumbing to the radiation. Also, let's have Soloman down at the computer core to make certain everything functions normally. We'll enter the field in fifteen minutes."

Everyone began busying themselves and the commotion made for a pleasant sound to the captain. He sat back, looking over Gomez's research and even indulged in reading the *Voyager* logs that held the answer to the current dilemma. The time passed quickly enough and Gold had already alerted the crew to secure loose objects.

"Entering the chroniton field now," Haznedl said. Gomez was standing beside her, hands braced on the console.

"Hull absorbing chroniton particles on schedule," Gomez announced after thirty minutes.

"Bridge to engineering."

"Conlon here, Captain."

"Everything holding together?"

"I guess they found tighter nuts and bolts at McKinley, sir, because we're airtight."

"Carry on," the captain said.

"Sir," Tev said some minutes later, "I've been able to track the waves back to their source. I'm forwarding the coordinates to the conn. We should be there in another three hours."

"Swell," Gold said through gritted teeth as the ship bucked under another wave.

Captain Gold was not at all surprised to see that the plan Gomez and Conlon had put together worked. It took the starship eighteen minutes longer than projected to absorb enough chroniton radiation, but there was finally a sufficient quantity to process the antichronitons required to spew forward, creating a clear passage. He was sure the entire crew was looking forward to a smoother passage to the asteroid Tev identified as the cause of the phenomenon. He now had to begin thinking about how to explore this root cause and who to send. When dealing with the Shanial Cabochon, he was on Earth, and when they helped out Pas Saadya's terraforming project, they were on Venus—he had the comfort of knowing backup was nearby. Here, once more among the stars, he was back to asking people to take risks without a net. Gold had lost crew before, he'd given commands that led to death, and he would again. Still, there was just a moment's hesitation, and he knew that he had to get past that to remain effective. Here, the hesitation was forgiveable; there was, ironically, time. But hesitate in a firefight, it might mean sudden death for both ship and crew.

"*Ready to transmit antichronitons,*" Conlon reported from engineering. She sounded confident, which pleased the captain.

"Transmit," Gomez commanded and then watched the viewscreen. In seconds, a golden haze filled the screen as antichronitons met, battled, and defeated their counterparts.

"The waves are breaking up," Haznedl said from her station. "We can proceed straight to the target asteroid."

"Let's go, then," Gold ordered. From the center chair, he could feel the bucking lessen and then vanish. Now he could fully concentrate on what lay ahead. "Shabalala, full sensors on the asteroid."

"Already on it, sir," he replied. Of course he was, Gold knew. No doubt, he was eager to see what was behind all this. "I'm reading one life-form, oxygen/nitrogen atmosphere, and an awful lot of technology. I don't recognize all the energy patterns, but whatever's in there is big and active."

"Tev?"

At the captain's question, the second officer studied his readouts, making some small noises that Gold realized were quite characteristic of his new colleague.

"It seems we have a new puzzle," he finally said. "I can't place the readings, myself."

"Okay, then, we'll need to beam over to investigate.

One life-form, lots of tech." He turned to Gomez and said, "Minimal away team to start, I think."

Gomez nodded and moved to the turbolift. "Lieutenant Commander Corsi, report to Transporter Room 1."

"Be careful," Gold called as the doors snapped shut.

CHAPTER
3

Gomez had Laura Poynter, the new transporter chief, beam them to a small chamber some ten meters away from where the life-form was located. There remained just enough radiation in the area to making identifying the race impossible. To be careful, Corsi opted to bring a phaser rifle rather than a pistol. Gomez had her tool case and a phaser tucked in a pocket.

The air was chilled, the security chief noticed. There were also two different mechanical hums working in harmony, both in the distance, heard beneath the floor plating. Gomez already had her tricorder out and began studying the composition. She shook her head at the readings, took more samples near the door, and then studied the results.

"This is at least five centuries old," she said.

"And still working," Corsi added.

Gomez nodded. "It's a metallic composite I can't pinpoint, but everything is uniformly manufactured. There's a lot of power running beneath us, a constant flow. It's not chroniton-based, but it probably powers the machine that creates the waves."

"What do I need to know?" Corsi asked, approaching the door, tightly gripping the rifle.

"None of this matches what we have on record for the Guardian," Gomez said, more to herself than her partner. "That means this is something very different—and a lot more recent. Everything seems to be designed to provide power to one main machine in the other room. I'm scanning a tremendous reservoir of pooled energy to prevent power interruptions."

"What about the person in the other room?" Her time on the *da Vinci* had taught Corsi to be patient and ask the right questions if she was ever to get anything resembling a useful bit of intel out of an engineer.

Gomez checked her tricorder again. "It's a Ferengi."

"Oh goody," Corsi muttered. Shouldering the rifle so it rested against her back, Corsi went to the door, examining it for latches or controls. Running an index finger around the frame, she found a depression on the left side and pressed.

Soundlessly, the door opened and the humming sounds grew in intensity and the air was even more chilled. For a moment, Corsi wondered how the Ferengi, with his sensitive ears, could handle such a high decibel rate. Perhaps he was using ear canal inhibitors, which would make it easy for her to approach safely.

They emerged into the larger, louder, cooler, and brighter room. Corsi, knowing her companion, paused to let the engineer take it all in. There were holographic projections with all manner of data scrolling past at three-meter intervals along two walls. The machine was directly before them. It was irregularly configured, with lots of jagged protrusions and no seating. You had to stand to control it all, and it seemed designed for a being larger than a humanoid. The Ferengi seemed to have built a platform to reach all the controls, which had pieces of tape, with the diagonal and oddly attractive Ferengi script stuck to almost every knob, lever, screen, and button.

Before the Ferengi, who was wearing the usual garish, closely tailored suits they favored, was a stack of latinum slips. He seemed to be counting and entering the information into a device. Numbers on a holographic projection before him kept rising, and he was laughing.

Corsi tapped him on the right shoulder with the phaser's tip and the Ferengi whirled about, a look of utter terror on his face. Spluttering, he said, "What are you doing here? It's mine; I found it by the rights of salvage."

"Well, we'll just have to talk about it aboard the *da Vinci*," Corsi said amiably.

"And leave all this?" he asked, gesturing broadly, trying to encompass every bit of machinery in sight. He really did think it all belonged to him.

"I'll give you a receipt," she said, her tone growing sharper.

The Ferengi hopped down from the platform and shrugged his shoulders in one of the recognized forms of groveling the race had mastered over the centuries. Corsi stood behind him while Gomez studied the readouts being projected in the air directly over their heads.

They had gone no more than three feet when the Ferengi ducked and bolted to his right, moving quite quickly. He reached the far end of the room and stood on tiptoe to grab at a spheroid object, hovering above a column, bathed in an orange light. Once it was in his hands, he stabbed at some hidden control and planted his feet firmly on the floor. By this point, Corsi was only a few meters from him, figuring there was nowhere for him to go and she didn't want to fire the phaser if she could avoid it, for fear of damaging the unknown equipment. If she did that, she knew Gomez would have cardiac failure. Engineers hated it when you broke things.

Red, pink, and orange sparks filled the area around the Ferengi, each glowing brighter by the second, and the air seemed to hiss. The sparks blended as they swirled around and around, gaining speed, until he was no more than a silhouette bathed in the light.

"Do I shoot?" Corsi screamed.

"No!"

Corsi expected the response and watched, just barely hearing the tricorder's distinctive tone. Gomez was capturing the readings, which should prove helpful, in some way. Corsi herself was breathing hard, annoyed at letting the Ferengi get past her.

And then he winked out of sight. The sparks flared once more and then they too vanished.

"What happened?" she snapped.

"Time travel," Gomez said, snapping the tricorder closed.

"Damn. I had a feeling you were going to say that."

The two walked over to the column above which the orb had floated. They heard the sound of machinery moving and within seconds, a new orb appeared from the column's top. Slowly it rose until it lifted off the column and floated, a perfect replacement for the one the Ferengi used.

Gomez studied it for a few moments and then walked back to the main console. Stepping atop the platform, she gazed at the readouts, occasionally comparing them with the ones recorded on her tricorder.

Finally, tired of the silence and the waiting, Corsi testily asked, "Well?"

"From what I can tell, that is a portable unit for going back into the past."

"This asteroid's past? Makes no sense."

Gomez fiddled with her equipment, tentatively reached out to touch some controls and then checked her readings. "This isn't just a time machine—it's a long-range transporter, too. Based on what the universal translator's telling me, it looks like the Ferengi has mastered how to send himself back a decade and to Ferenginar. Maybe that's why the chroniton particles appear richer, and denser, than the ones in the databanks. Which means—"

"Oh no," Corsi said.

"We might be able to saturate ourselves in the radiation, and also travel back to the same coordinates and find him."

"And we want to do that why?"

"Given that these coordinates are locked in somehow, he's clearly been going back to Ferenginar and doing something. By using the equipment, and I would guess he's only been doing it for the two weeks the navigational troubles have been noted, he's been manipulating something . . . for his own profit." She picked up a few slips of latinum and hefted the device he had been using.

"Of course he has," Corsi said. "And we have to stop him instead of Temporal Investigations because . . . ?"

"That's what we do," Gomez said matter-of-factly.

"Should he lose that node, and someone back then finds it, things could just spiral out of control. Wow, he's accumulated quite a bit of wealth in just a few weeks, if I read this right."

"Who built this and why?"

"I wish I knew, Domenica. Right now, though, we need to tell the captain." Quickly, the two women contacted the *da Vinci* and briefed Gold on the latest developments. While Corsi enjoyed action, she didn't like question marks. This equipment was one, and the Ferengi's motives an even bigger one. She was somewhat annoyed that Gomez seemed more worried about the lost technology, but then again, that's what she was trained to worry about.

"Before anyone goes anywhere, we need to find out what has changed. Let me send Abramowitz over to help you. Expect her shortly. Gold out."

In minutes, Carol Abramowitz, the ship's cultural specialist and closest expert on the Ferengi, arrived in the central chamber. By then, Corsi was studying the node that floated placidly above the column. Two other columns were inactive besides that one, and she had already figured out how to turn them on but left them deactivated.

Abramowitz, shorter than the others, with dark hair framing her face, nodded to her colleagues and began looking at the coordinates Gomez had translated and consulted one of several padds she carried with her. They worked fairly silently for several minutes, with Gomez occasionally explaining something about the technology. Corsi began to pace the chamber, at first looking for anything that resembled a defense system or hand weapon and then pacing because she had to do something.

"I think I have something," Abramowitz said softly. "He's been going back to the capital city repeatedly. No doubt he's been using his current knowledge to enhance his fortune on the Ferengi exchanges."

When she explained this to Gold, the next voice she heard was not his, but Songmin Wong's. The conn officer excitedly called out, *"He must be Lant!"*

"Who's Lant?" Gold asked.

"The darling of Ferengi commerce right now," Wong said.

"How the hell do you know that?" Corsi demanded.

"I inherited a few bars of latinum last year," he began. *"So I've been dabbling in the markets. The financial net is filled with stories about this Lant guy's amazing rise in prosperity. He hasn't made an investment mistake in the last six months."*

"And now we know why," Gold chimed in, sounding grim. *"Whatever he's been doing for six months worked, but for the last two weeks something's been wrong. This is bad and needs to be fixed. Gomez, can you program one of those nodes?"*

Gomez was already studying the tricorder translation of Lant's postings. As she did so, Tev spoke up:

"Captain, does this become a Prime Directive issue?"

Corsi's teeth started to grind. The only thing she hated more than engineering doubletalk was philosophical and ethical debates—especially from Tev, who, Corsi was learning, was more pedantic than the entire rest of the S.C.E. crew combined.

To the security chief's relief, the captain said, *"If they're going back only a short time, and after contact with the Federation has been established, then our away team will have some flexibility. But the Ferenginar of the recent past was even more male-dominated than it is now. You'll have to beam over and join the team. Assemble your equipment and head over there."*

Corsi had to admit to herself that adding Tev to the team made sense. Ferenginar had only recently begun enacting social reforms to undo countless generations of female subjugation. As she recalled, women couldn't hold much in the way of jobs and were usually kept out of sight except to family.

Abramowitz completed her look at the equipment and had called up data on that era of Ferengi society, even as the stout Tellarite beamed down. He held a satchel that seemed to be filled with equipment. His black eyes looked around the chamber, taking in the equipment, and he nodded to himself.

"Aren't you a bit out of uniform, Mr. Tev?" Gomez asked. Tev was standing with a bright orange shirt, open at the neck to show tufts of fur, with chocolate brown pants that tucked themselves into nearly knee-high boots. Slung over one shoulder was an all-purpose carryall, devoid of Starfleet markings.

"To blend in on Ferenginar, I can't be in uniform. But I am prepared." He opened up the collar of his shirt, and on the reverse side was his Starfleet combadge.

"What about the rest of us?" Gomez asked, but he ignored the question and proceeded with instructions.

"The captain wants us to go after Lant, find out where he caused the change in the timeline and undo it. We might have to ruin him financially in the process," he said. "But that's an acceptable loss."

"To you, maybe," Abramowitz said. "To Lant, that's possibly worse than death. They live and die by the deal and the size of their holdings. It was a heady time for these people. Formal contact had been made with the Federation not long before, and this was seen as the opening of a huge new market. The piracy of a century previous was curtailed, and people sought business ventures, partnerships, brokering, and whatever else could be used to earn a slip of latinum."

"What I don't understand," Gomez said as she programmed the node, "is how the Federation economy grew flexible enough to accommodate the Ferengi mercantile system."

"Ever take an economics course at the Academy?" Tev asked.

"No."

"Well, that explains that," he replied and turned his attention to a display on his right.

Gomez instructed Corsi to grab the first of the nodes, letting another rise for programming. The first officer repeated the procedure until all four possessed nodes, which were small enough to fit into Tev's bag.

"Gomez to Gold."

"Gold here."

"We're ready to head back after Lant. I can't tell you how long this will take."

"Let's be careful with time. Take twelve hours and check back in. Do your best and good luck. I'm sending Blue and Soloman over to continue studying the tech."

"Good idea," Gomez said. Corsi thought she caught a wistful tone in her voice. Corsi suspected that the first officer wanted to be the one studying the tech. However, Corsi preferred to have Gomez along on their time-travel trip—the alternative was to have Tev in charge, and Corsi wasn't entirely comfortable with him yet.

"Tell them I've picked up a few anomalous power fluctuations," Gomez added. "They might be the cause of the disruptions. I haven't isolated the cause as yet."

"Thanks, Gomez. They'll figure it out. Good luck."

"Tev, Sonya," Abramowitz said, calling attention to her studies. "Few Ferengi had seen humans by that point, making us a cultural curiosity. Tellarites were a little more common on the planet itself. We need to be prepared to be stared at, and doing anything unobtrusive will be almost impossible."

"Let's get started," Corsi insisted.

Abramowitz looked ready to say more, but seemed hesitant, which was not her nature, Corsi realized.

"What is it, Carol?" Gomez prompted.

"We'll be women. On Ferenginar."

Corsi and Gomez looked at her blankly.

"A decade ago."

"So?" Corsi asked, confused.

"You're dressed," Tev finally interjected. He waited patiently, letting the words sink in. Corsi's eyes narrowed with realization. Gomez caught the look, swung her head toward Abramowitz, who nodded in confirmation.

"We'll accomplish less than nothing while we're dressed," she said softly. "In fact, we'll be breaking social taboos and calling more attention to ourselves. We'll never get close to Lant this way."

"That's why the captain sent me over—to take point," Tev said. "I can be a . . . businessman, looking for some sort of deal with Lant."

"That makes sense. And three escorts will show you as prosperous," Abramowitz added.

Corsi shook her head. They were wasting time. She peeled off her duty jacket. Tev wisely said nothing, but simply opened his satchel.

"We have to?" Gomez asked.

"Sonya, let's just get this over with and grab Lant,"

Corsi said as she stepped out of her pants, folding them neatly and handing them to Tev. He silently placed them atop a dark console. He then withdrew a hand phaser and a strap. The security chief accepted it and considered for a moment before strapping it high on her right thigh. She hoped it looked decorative enough.

"When in Rome," Abramowitz muttered, pulling her shirt over her head. She too handed each article of clothing over to Tev.

"And what sort of businessman should I be?"

Abramowitz struggled with a boot as she replied, "Given our advanced technology, you might make favorable inroads by peddling new gear. But you can't really sell any of it or let them look too closely."

"Of course not," Tev said. "Still, I'll need money to get started, and it's not like we have any latinum in ship's stores."

"That's easy," Corsi said, strolling over to the main console and helping herself to the stack of latinum slips. "It's hopefully enough to get you in the door."

Tev placed the three pairs of boots below the console and then continued rummaging about, looking for the tools Gomez would need to handle the node and to impress potential customers.

Abramowitz continued, "We'll be your escorts, staying close. You have to make sure the Ferengi don't touch the merchandise. . . ."

"Or us," Gomez added. "It's going to be hard to use the tricorder if I'm just window dressing."

"We'll make do," Corsi said, her tone flat. "Tev, hand me the spanner."

He handed the device over with a questioning glance. Corsi merely undid her tight bun of blond hair and quickly wrapped her hair around the device, making it look like an accoutrement. He nodded in approval.

Gomez nodded and hit a control on the console that was marked in the Ferengi language. All four orbs hummed immediately. Within seconds, though, they began to glow the same way Lant's node worked, which made Corsi feel both relieved and more apprehensive.

On the *da Vinci* bridge, Gold had completed making an entry in his log and sat back. All the wheels were in motion: his people going back in time and more of the crew going to explore the device that made that absurd statement a reality. Time travel had always concerned him given the paradoxes posed by each such use. Still, with people popping back and forth in time going back to the days of the Temporal Cold War, it was no longer a fantastic notion. He still disliked the idea that a single accident could wipe out everything he knew and cherished. Sure, there were great tragedies he'd personally like to see undone, starting with losing half his crew, but he recognized that things happened for a reason. There *had* to be a reason, be it cosmic plan or divine intervention.

He looked at the banal image of the asteroid directly before the starship. Nothing about it looked artificial, but he knew better. And now he had four of his team risking their lives and the timeline to correct base greed. Was it worth it?

Speaking of worth . . . He looked at his conn officer. "Wong," he asked, "just how successful have you been with your new hobby?"

The lieutenant hesitated in answering, which just

made everyone on the bridge look directly at him. Wong finally swallowed and gave him a sheepish grin. "Well, I now own a pleasure yacht moored in dock around Risa, so you might say I've been pretty successful."

Gold let out a whistle and settled back in his chair. Some hobbies had better rewards than others.

CHAPTER
4

It was gray, Gomez noticed. Of course, on Ferenginar, anything but gray was considered unusual. She remembered Bart saying after their last encounter with the Ferengi on the *Debenture of Triple-Lined Latinum* that they had dozens of words in their language for rain, and they had almost as many to describe the lighting conditions. It was a light gray, she decided, meaning the sun was probably nearing the noon position. The air was tepid, and naturally damp. They were standing on a street slick with recent rain, some of it rainbowed from some oily substance that felt rather unpleasant on Sonya's bare feet.

The capital city was old and overbuilt. Their architecture was scaled for the shorter Ferengi physique, so their towers didn't seem as imposing as the skyscrapers back home on Earth. Still, there were some interesting styles on display that she would have enjoyed looking at in more depth under other circumstances.

Completely different circumstances.

She quickly surveyed the area and saw people approaching from the north. They were a crowd of Ferengi businessmen, all in motley attire, more interested in their padds than in the people around them. No doubt about it, they were going to stand out—a Tellarite and three human women.

"Now that we're here, can our nodes be fine-tuned to find Lant?" Tev asked.

Gomez shrugged as Tev handed her a tricorder and one of the nodes. She stepped deep into a gap between two buildings while Corsi kept watch at the entranceway. Despite light traffic, no one had bothered to glance their way.

As she worked, a pair of Ferengi walked by and eyed Tev, their eyes widening further when they spotted the women. Carol and Domenica met their gaze head-on, which caused the men to continue their conversation. Sonya was grateful, as it meant they were paying little attention to her.

"Each node works the same but has a distinct signature," Gomez finally said. "By screening out the four here, I've isolated just one . . . Lant's. He's due west of here, about a kilometer away."

Tev grunted in acknowledgment. "That's where the Tower of Commerce is and our starting point. Between here and there, we need to get our hands on some latinum; these few slips can get us in the door and that's about it. Let's get started."

He held out his hand toward Gomez, who blinked in surprise and then realized she needed to hand over the tricorder. She did so, muttering a curse. She could live without clothes if she had to, but without tools, she felt truly naked.

With that, Tev strode forward, turning left onto the street. Carol and Sonya followed, with Corsi taking up the final position.

No sooner had the *da Vinci*'s sensors showed the chroniton burst signaling time travel than Gold dispatched P8 Blue and Soloman to the asteroid for investigation. The chamber was silent as they materialized but was quickly filled with the whine from the Nasat's tricorder.

Soloman, built approximately the same size as a Ferengi, clambered atop the platform to study the master control panel. He nodded as he quickly took in the holographic readings from the idle equipment. With tricorder in one hand, Soloman gingerly sampled controls and waited to see what happened. Like Commander Gomez after Lt. Commander Duffy's death, one reason he remained with the S.C.E. after losing his bond-mate 111 was his desire to explore the new and undiscovered.

Even as he took in all the data through his dataport, Soloman glanced over his shoulder to see P8 Blue studying the chamber's construction. As the structural systems specialist, it was her job to find clues as to which species might have built the chamber and created the device. The supposition from the outset was that they were the same, but they needed to prove that beyond a doubt.

"It's half a millennium old," she observed, her tricorder waving in front of a support beam. "Basically sound architectural principals, some variations compared with about a dozen other planets but nothing that distinctive. In fact, it's so boring, even the Borg wouldn't assimilate it."

"Then maybe they spent all that time on their computer systems and time-travel technology. This is beyond anything I've seen before, and it's taking me some time," Soloman said. "Raw elements in the asteroid seem to be tapped to provide the tremendous amounts of energy required to power the equipment. What is the radiation shielding like?"

"Standard for space construction. They clearly were not concerned about chroniton radiation like we are. That explains some of the problems we were having with navigation. They just never screened it out. Perhaps I can do something about that with the shield modulations." Pattie used three of her eight limbs to feel around the architecture, testing the unit. Seemingly satisfied, she lifted herself up, scaling the machinery to get a better understanding of its construction and purpose.

"Interesting." With that, Soloman returned his full attention to the computer console. He had traced the connections to the backup systems and found the astronomical database. It seemed, at first glance, to be deeper and more complete than anything Starfleet had, possibly beyond the three dimensions used to map the universe. He determined a download would not be detrimental to the equipment, so he began setting up a link with the *da Vinci*'s mainframe.

As he worked, he considered one way after another to delve deeper into the programming. The algorithms used to access the time and place databases were inventively constructed, and he relished the challenge of cracking them. However, before he could begin his next area of study, he heard Blue let out a noise. Quickly turning, he saw her standing before a control panel tucked in an alcove opposite the node columns.

"Soloman, we have a problem," she said.

"Don't we always?" he asked innocently.

"Not like this," she replied. "This panel is some sort of fuel consumption monitor, and it appears that Lant has left the equipment on without a required shutdown period for automatic maintenance. As a result, an imbalance in the mineral admixture has developed and there will be an overload."

He considered that for a moment and then offered, "Could this be why the navigation has only been difficult these last few weeks?"

"That must be what Commander Gomez found before leaving," she added, nodding her head quickly. Soloman definitely preferred things that added up in neat sums, so connections like this comforted him.

"Can you stop it?"

"I don't even know what minerals are being tapped to provide energy, yet," she said, sounding exasperated. "If I read this right, it will become critical in about fourteen hours."

"That is after the crew is due back from the past," Soloman observed. "That gives us a two-hour margin, larger than usual."

"Assuming I read this right and the imbalance doesn't interfere with their ability to return home."

"You have developed the humans' knack for clouding positive news with negative information."

"Comes with the job, I think," she said. Then she tapped her combadge to report to Captain Gold.

CHAPTER
5

Tev led the away team toward the Tower of Commerce, and with every block the streets were filled with more and more Ferengi. Most stopped to point openly and stare at the women, many gap-jawed. Two even dared to pull out recording devices to take pictures, no doubt for private use and personal profit. The Tower's shadow fell upon the quartet, at which point the Tellarite consulted the tricorder once more, confirming Lant's signature remained ahead.

The Tellarite had quickly reviewed the historic database on Ferenginar politics of this time. Zek was still Grand Nagus, and it was prior to Ishka's influence on him for social reform. There remained strict adherence to the two hundred and eighty-five Rules of Acquisition, which he had also had downloaded, but had hoped Abramowitz was familiar with them in a pinch. They would need to get to the trading floor in the mammoth

Tower of Commerce, the largest structure on the planet. But to do that, he'd need more latinum to be taken seriously.

"Have any of you ever used the Exchanges?"

"It's not exactly on the tourist guides," Abramowitz replied. The others used silence for negative replies. "But we'll have to brave it. What will you do once we get in?"

"I presume we'll be given a line of credit and use that to build up a fortune, attracting Lant. He must come to us," Tev said.

"And if he doesn't?"

"Then, Dr. Abramowitz, you'll have to bring him to us."

"That'd be fun and a chance to mete out a little justice," she said.

"Now, now, he had no idea we'd find his fortune-building reprehensible," Tev continued. They were finally approaching the entrance to the Tower, which was truly a remarkable structure. Its top floors were obscured by low-lying fog and dense cloud cover. Etched in blocks carefully placed from the ground up, were the famed Rules of Acquisition. Ferengi wealth was literally built with these Rules, a lesson to all who entered the structure. The entranceway was brightly lit, bathing them in warmth and causing reflections to dance on the walls and high ceiling. Gusts of heated air buffeted them as they walked into the structure, which Tev assumed the women appreciated. A variety of house rules were listed on one wall, scrolling lazily down and then to the left as their language dictated. No one seemed to speak loudly, but there was a buzz of whispers that made Tev think he was surrounded by insects.

A man in what appeared to be a severely cut Ferengi

business suit with muted colors approached the group and gave them a long, leering look. After a few seconds' study, he put his wrists together, hands splayed outward, and bowed deeply.

"Welcome to the Tower of Commerce. I am Rheb, the floor manager."

Tev repeated the gesture and bowed, not once losing eye contact. "I am Mor glasch Tev, just in from Tellar." He hesitated for a moment, about to introduce his companions, but thought better of it. To Rheb, they were accoutrements and not worth knowing. *So be it.*

"I've come to negotiate some new contracts, but my meetings are not until tomorrow. But, as you say, 'Opportunity plus instinct . . .'"

"'. . . equals profit,'" they finished together. Rheb laughed insincerely and Tev chuckled to be a good sport about it.

"You must have good instincts to be so well attended." Rheb's very voice seemed to have a leer.

Tev reached out a hand to stroke Gomez's face, noting from the corner of his eye that she remained absolutely still. "I get by. My business is research tools, and now that you're doing more business with the Federation, I suspect you will need improved portable data storage units."

Rheb placed a withered knuckle under his chin and rubbed thoughtfully, refusing to take his eyes off Tev's hand, which continued to idly caress Gomez's chin. After a moment more, he nodded in agreement.

"Now, I fancy the Futures Exchange," Tev said forcefully. "If you'd be so kind as to open up a line of credit, I can—"

The wail from Rheb startled all four Starfleet officers, and Gomez stepped backward, breaking contact with

Tev. The Tellarite briefly glanced at the women and then back at their host. The look of horror on his face clearly meant Tev had made a major error.

"We do *not* give just anyone a line of credit," Rheb finally blurted out. "You can't walk in here, prosperous as you appear to be, and think we'll let ourselves be robbed blind."

"Now see here, Rheb," Tev said, trying to sound imperious. "There's no need for that sort of noise. Let's see what sort of an arrangement we can work out."

Rheb straightened his suit, quickly regaining his dignity as befits a floor manager. Puffing out his chest, he said, "Show me the color of your latinum and we'll be happy to make a place for you in the Exchange."

"You don't think I walk around with latinum to be picked from my pocket," Tev said, matching Rheb attitude for attitude. "This is a place of high finance, and I do not mean to insult you with a fistful of slips." Which, of course, was precisely what he had to his name.

"I appreciate you respecting this institution; I can see why you've been prosperous," Rheb replied, sounding magnanimous. "Still, our rules do not allow me to open up a line of credit without concrete proof of one's holdings."

"And how shall I do that since our two governments do not currently share economic data?"

Before Rheb could reply to Tev's question, Abramowitz sashayed past the Tellarite and bent low to whisper something in the manager's ear. She leaned in close, a fingertip tracing the rim of his right ear. The manager's eyes went wide and he suddenly seemed to be having trouble breathing, but Tev held still. When she was done whispering, Rheb reached into his coat and withdrew a slim padd. He tabbed a few controls and added a thumbprint to the bottom of the screen.

"Mr. Tev, an opening line of credit has been placed in your name on the Futures Exchange. I think fifteen bars should be a good start for you," Rheb said. "The Exchange is just this way, if you follow me."

He spun on his left heel and began briskly walking away from the group. It took Tev a few strides to catch up, and he heard the women behind him. When they were right with him, he turned to Abramowitz and gave her a quizzical look.

"I promised him delights no Ferengi had ever experienced," she said, a grimace crossing her features. "They may wheel and deal with their lobes, but men throughout the galaxy act fairly uniformly."

Rheb kept up his brisk pace as they moved deeper into the building, which seemed far larger than Tev would have imagined. People got out of the floor manager's way, many bowing in any number of prescribed Ferengi groveling forms. He knew each had significance but didn't want to slow down to ask Abramowitz for an explanation. There remained a tight time frame despite all the time-travel nonsense they had to endure. Instead, he snickered at the almost uniform reaction to his fellow officers. He pitied them but couldn't let it impede the mission.

Finally, Rheb turned sharply to his left and stood before a massive pair of doors. The Ferengi touched some control within his garish jacket and the doors parted, allowing a cacophony of sound to rush out. Tev had studied various forms of commerce while at the Academy, but nothing prepared him for the manic energy emanating from within. Rheb, though, took a deep breath, a smile plastered to his face. This was heaven to

the manager, or the Divine Treasury, as he believed the
Ferengi called their afterlife. To Tev, it was just noise
and desperation. Within, people were shouting at one
another, padds being passed back and forth, screens
flickering with information, and set against the far wall
was a clock ticking down to the end of the trading session. There had to have been hundreds of Ferengi
crammed inside, with movement being severely restricted. He noted the interior temperature was significantly higher than the hallway and for a moment
envied the women their lack of clothing.

"Tev, I think you will find everything you need if you
start with the room manager, Trotta. He'll take very
good care of you. Shall I escort your, ah, associates to a
waiting room?" His voice betrayed his desires, and Tev
smiled to himself.

"I think not," he replied. "No offense, mind you, but
we're new in town and I'd prefer not to misplace any of
my belongings."

The floor manager brought his wrists together and
bowed once more, backing out.

Tev returned his gaze to the dizzying room, as he
pulled out the tricorder. The node signature was still
nearby, probably in this very area, but he couldn't pin it
down further. Too many other signals were interfering
with the reading; he shrugged and pocketed the device.

Within moments, Trotta, a much younger Ferengi in
an even more garish suit, arrived and smiled toothily at
Tev. He even allowed himself a long look at the women
before speaking. After introductions were made, Trotta
escorted the group through narrow aisles until they
reached one particular station, its screens filled with a
constant flow of data and imagery. Withdrawing his
personal padd, Trotta sent a signal to the station, and

lights winked a few times before they all flashed a dull brown.

"Your account is now active, Mr. Tev," Trotta said, pocketing his padd. "I wish you good fortune."

"Thank you," Tev said and immediately ignored the man. He stared at the information coming across regarding grain production on Sherman's Planet. For a moment he marveled at how quickly the Ferengi adapted Federation information into their commercial world. Still, "adapt or die" was a universal law, although it might not have made it in so many words into the Ferengi's own Rule book.

He pulled out his tricorder once more and began placing orders with the man on the other side of the counter. For every order Tev managed to shout, the Ferengi surrounding him seemed able to get in five times as many. Still, a quick look at the account board showed he had placed seven orders in just under ten minutes, all of which would pay off in an hour. Based on the Federation historic database, he knew the outcomes but placed his orders conservatively, including two that would fail. This would allow him to repay his credit of fifteen bars of latinum and start his own nest egg. He would then parlay those resources into bolder trades that would be designed to attract Lant's attention.

He couldn't rush things, otherwise he'd raise suspicions. Instead, he'd have to waste precious time and he couldn't even dispatch the women to hunt down Lant. They had to play their part. He could already tell Corsi was simmering, ready to lash out at the first opportunity. They exchanged glances and she nodded once, reaffirming she knew her role and would play it for now. Tev suddenly felt the pressure of the twelve-hour window, the countdown to the end of the trading session and the now-lit fuse that would result in Corsi doing something that might jeopardize the mission. If only he could place bets on that. . . .

As Tev began the time-consuming task of building a fortune, Gomez, Abramowitz, and Corsi were left to stand around, being gawked at and little more. It sat well with none of them, especially the engineer. She disliked time travel and she disliked Ferengi culture and a woman's lack of place in it. Yet, here she was, a decade or so in the past, stark naked and surrounded by Ferengi, who would just as soon own her as look at her. She really wanted to go back to the starship . . . a feeling she hadn't had too often since Kieran died.

"Domenica," she said tentatively, "how're you holding up?"

"I'd prefer smacking every Ferengi who's looked at us, but I'm keeping my temper."

"Figure Fabe will get some mileage out of this mission?"

"He'll try and then he'll discover why they nicknamed me Core-Breach." Corsi actually smiled at the line, although Gomez winced at the image.

"How're things between you two?"

Corsi hesitated, uncertain of the answer, which was not her style. "I think we're okay. Once we got back to the ship we've been kept pretty busy. I'm not exactly used to this sort of thing."

"Shipboard romances? Me either, except for Kieran— but don't go by example."

A look of pity washed quickly over Corsi's face and

Gomez inwardly winced. "What you two had was great," the security chief finally said. "I'm not sure what I've got. Fabe might, but I'm still figuring it out."

"And it bothers you, I can see that," Gomez said.

"Yeah."

"The not knowing?"

"That and being involved with anyone," Corsi admitted. "I mean, who am I to suddenly have a man to complicate my responsibilities?"

"How so?"

"My duty is to Starfleet. It used to be to my father and mother, and now Fabian is part of the equation."

"It's not all math, you know," the engineer said with an accompanying smile. "If I know you, it's a little more like chaos theory."

Corsi laughed and actually started to blush at the comment. With a glance past Gomez, though, she saw the bewildered look on Abramowitz's face.

"What about you, Carol, ever have someone aboard ship?"

"No," was all she said, indicating a lack of desire to continue the conversation. In fact, Abramowitz turned away from the two and directed her attention to the big board of information.

Gomez and Corsi exchanged confused expressions, each shrugging their shoulders. But Gomez knew, as first officer, that something was troubling Carol; it occurred to her she didn't know her crewmate anywhere near as well as she should.

Before either could say anything else, they heard a slapping sound and spun around. Carol was backing away from a Ferengi, who was busily rubbing his cheek and cradling his left hand, awkwardly trying to do both at the same time. It was clear what had happened and equally clear that things were so chaotic that this was likely to occur again. The three huddled a little closer, trying to avoid any contact with rushing traders, floor-walkers, or even Tev.

"That's fifty-four bars to your account." The Ferengi sitting behind the desk spoke with a tone of amazement in his voice.

Tev accepted the padd back, making sure every slip was accounted for. He noted the processing fee seemed high and handed the padd back, tapping at the line of type with one well-polished and rather pointed black nail. The Ferengi looked at it as if he had never seen an error before and looked up at Tev while assuming one of the more popular cringes. The standoff continued for a few more seconds and finally the Ferengi acquiesced and corrected the deduction. Behind him, Tev noted a column of numbers seemed to shrink and he nodded to himself in agreement.

"Master," Carol began in a singsong voice. Tev turned toward her, an indulgent smile on his face. They leaned their heads toward one another to whisper sweet nothings into each other's ear, as far as the crowd around them was concerned.

"You're doing well, but Lant seems to be nowhere nearby."

"I noticed. I've been trading in the same sectors he has been from what Lieutenant Wong told us, and my successes should be matching his. Lant's obviously not stupid, so he's playing it smart and staying put. We just can't figure out where that is. We need to do something."

Right then, a new voice was heard and it wasn't a happy one. "What's going on?"

"Tev is having a good run," the morose man behind the counter said, ignoring the speaker and processing more trade orders.

"Very well," the other Ferengi said. He was an unpleasant-looking Ferengi with the most insincere smile Tev had seen yet. He was smartly dressed in a muted crazy-quilt jacket with a dull red shirt peeking through. By Ferengi standards, it was almost conservative.

"Ah, Mr. Tev, I see the fortunes are kind to you today," the man said. "I am Brunt, Trotta's adjutant. For new customers here on Ferenginar, we have a more comfortable room for you to use. Trotta suggests I escort you there. Maybe you and your, ah, party would like to accompany me." He didn't even wait, spinning on a heel and striding off, literally pushing people out of his way. The lack of reaction indicated this was typical behavior, so Tev refused comment, but did gesture for the others to follow him. They were led from the room to a private elevator, where a uniformed Ferengi youth stood. Brunt got in first, then the others, but before the doors closed, the attendant was expectantly looking from face to face. It was growing uncomfortable for Tev, who finally figured out the attendant was expecting some form of tip for performing his job. He glared down at Brunt, who was trying to ignore the look. Finally, he let out a small sigh and withdrew his padd. He beamed some form of latinum to the youth who heard a beep go off in his hip pocket. At that, the doors closed and the small elevator shot upward at a dizzying speed.

When they stepped off the elevator seconds later, Tev was amazed to see the comforts that awaited them: deeply cushioned plaid chairs, solid-color throw pillows the size of a bunk bed, tables laden with hot dishes of various tube grubs and a crowded bar. Beyond the bar, a handful of Ferengi were conducting business on communications devices or dealing with a far less crazed traders' desk. The noise level was decidedly muted, the tension less palpable. It was downright civilized to Tev's way of thinking. Trotta, concluding a conversation with two other Ferengi, saw them emerge from the elevator and came to greet them, a big grin on his face.

"You can continue your successful business from here," Trotta said. "Your, ah, women can wait in that corner until you're done."

"May I feed them?"

Trotta paused, and looking displeased, nodded once, a move echoed by Brunt. With a gesture, Tev indicated the women should help themselves from the food table. Trotta watched them appreciatively and commented, "You must be very good at what you to do to afford such fine creatures."

"I get by," Tev said noncommittally.

"I find it interesting you are finding success in the grain markets; that makes you the second one this month. Just the other week a man who didn't seem to have the lobes to pick his own clothes comes in and scores big."

"Really? A fellow countryman perhaps?"

"Mine, not yours," Brunt said. "His name's Lant. He's amassed quite the fortune, but maybe he's a savant. Absolutely no investment sense. He's been storing it all in long-term growth funds." He cackled at such a strategy. To Tev, it sounded eminently practical, but he had information Brunt didn't.

Corsi, her plate wriggling at her with the grubs and some salad, wandered by and was listening. "This Lant must have the lobes after all. Is he here today? He sounds fascinating."

Trotta looked at her with distaste. After all, Tev knew, women shouldn't be heard at all when out in public. Still, he was counting on some latitude, given the money he was playing with. He tried to catch Corsi's eye to have her stop but clearly her patience was almost at an end.

"He might be, woman," the manager answered. "Now please, chew Mr. Tev's food and give it to him."

Corsi took a step closer to Trotta, and it was clear she was the taller of the two, so he had to look up to meet her eyes. At first, he refused to look any higher than necessary but Tev cleared his throat, catching the older man's attention. Tev tipped his head upward, silently commanding respect for his property. Trotta finally looked into Corsi's smoldering eyes. He was looking more uncomfortable by the moment and Brunt backed up two steps. Tev was amused to note that sweat seemed to appear on his prominent forehead. Well, if he couldn't stop Corsi, he was going to at least wait and see how much more information she could get from him.

"Might isn't good enough," she said, steel creeping into her voice. "Tev wants to do business with him, business that might profit him, Tev, and even you. Do you know where Lant is?"

The circuits inside Trotta's mind were working overtime, Tev noticed. Clearly, he was looking for a way to benefit from imparting the information he had. A smile began to form on his lips, and Trotta stepped even closer to Corsi so there was barely any space between them. He leaned toward her ear and whispered, "Whatever information I have might be yours, if Tev would let you and me go to my office for, well, that is, for a little *oo-mox*."

Corsi's fist found Trotta's stomach before Tev could even tell her to stop. The Ferengi doubled over, air rushing out of him, and then he let go a squeal that had Carol and Sonya covering their ears. The security chief stepped over the kneeling Ferengi, grabbed his collar and hissed in his ear, "Lant. Now."

Brunt moved to help his superior, but Abramowitz and Gomez blocked his path. The others in the room looked up, stared, and then silently returned to their business. Clearly, there was no profit in participating.

"He completed trading about an hour ago and left the Exchange. He usually goes for drinks after a successful trading day."

"How successful was he?" she asked.

A long wheeze. "Very."

"Where does he drink?"

Trotta began to get off the ground but Corsi's bare foot pushed him into the carpeting.

"He's a hopper, starts at the Treasure Chest and goes from there. Now, don't hit me again."

"Not to worry. I think my master was planning to leave now." She gave Tev a look that meant it was indeed time to move on. Tev signaled the others and they all headed for the elevator, ignoring Trotta and Brunt. Corsi's glare stopped the pair in their tracks and let them leave the floor without further incident.

In the elevator, the attendant looked once more for a tip. Corsi stared him down until the car began to descend although at a slower speed than before. Tev looked angrily at his security chief. She looked back, defiant.

"She's right, we weren't getting anywhere," Abramowitz said.

"And time's a-wasting," Gomez added.

"I had things under control," Tev said with irritation.

"You might have a fortune in latinum, but Lant is still loose. At least now we have a trail," Corsi said. She turned to the attendant and demanded directions to the Treasure Chest. When he hesitated, she grabbed him roughly by the collar and glared once more. He provided the location and to his surprise, Tev sympathetically tipped him four slips.

Once on the street, he noticed the skies were a darker shade of gray and a breeze was kicking up. Rain was coming and he wouldn't be able to shield his companions, which would only make them cold, wet, and cranky. Another race against time, but he grudgingly admitted Corsi got further with a little strong-arming than two hours of trading, no matter how profitable. And it was fun, he admitted to himself. The question remained as to what he would do with his ill-gotten funds when this was all over. Pushing that thought to the back of his mind, he pulled out his tricorder. The readings indicated Lant was in the same general direction as the bar. Tev shook the random thoughts free and led the away team over several blocks west and then two north until they saw the bright yellow sign and animated image of jewels spilling from an old metal chest. He reached for the door and paused for a moment, looking at Carol.

"We'd be thrown out, so we'll just wait here," she said.

"Hurry, will you?" Gomez demanded. "And consider that an order, Commander."

Inside, it was crowded with businessmen having a late lunch. There were representatives of many races aligned with the Ferengi, but he was surprised to see a cluster of Nausicaans clearly concluding negotiations with a Ferengi. It appeared they were all enjoying liquid lunches and were acting very chummy; probably thinking each was getting the better of the other. Such were the ways of business on many worlds, he knew. The bartender was a Ferengi of indeterminate age, and he leaned over the counter to better hear Tev.

The Tellarite's padd was already out, and he keyed it to transmit ten slips of latinum. "I'm looking for a deal." The bartender's eyes lit up at that and he leaned farther over the counter, balancing on his hands. Tev reached down and held the hands in place, at the wrist.

"I'm looking for the answer to one question and these ten slips are yours. Prevaricate and you won't be able to mix drinks for the next week."

The bartender's eyes widened in fear and pain. He squirmed only a little before it became obvious Tev would prevail. He nodded once. Tev asked after Lant and got remarkably clear directions to the nearest branch of Frin's Taverns. Pausing long enough to transmit the ten slips, Tev hurried out of the bar and moved south, gesturing for the others to keep up.

As they moved down the street, he looked over at Corsi and smiled. "I tried it your way and found it remarkably effective."

"Thank you," she said through gritted teeth. At that moment, Tev noted the temperature had dropped noticeably since the skies grew darker. His pace increased.

Frin's was a brighter, cheerier establishment, with people of all walks filling the tables and lined up along the U-shaped bar. A laughing Ferengi was juggling five shot glasses, two of which seemed to be filled. Tev once more left his companions outside and was ready with the bribe to keep looking for his quarry. The tricorder had been ineffective in pinpointing Lant's signature, which proved vexing. Worse, Tev had to wait for the juggling bartender to finish his performance before being able to ask after Lant. He used the wait to scan the room, but no Ferengi was sitting by himself, so Lant was likely not here. He wondered just how far behind the time traveler he and the others were. An hour, half that?

It took him fifteen slips this time, but Tev at least got a time frame along with the information. They were fortunate; they were maybe fifteen to twenty minutes behind Lant, who had headed into an older quarter of the capital city. As they neared the third establishment on their hunt, Tev felt the first drops of rain moments before the curses came from Sonya. "Tev, give me your tricorder."

"Is that wise out in the open?"

"I don't care. I want to find this man, *now*," she said. He handed it over and she immediately began fine-tuning the signal. She tapped, waited, tapped again. Finally, with a grin, she handed it back to him.

"He's inside, waiting for you."

"How did you find him?"

"I narrowed the focus, screening out where he was not likely to be and then fine-tuned for the node's exact emissions—which only works in close proximity. Happy?"

"Enlightened." And he meant it. He had not been sure that Gomez was a worthy human to be serving under. He'd read her work, of course, and knew of her record, which was not of a certain accomplishment. Captain Scott had called her the best when he gave Tev the assignment, but Tev also knew that the captain was given to hyperbole, especially regarding human females. There was also the concern over whether or not the commander had recovered from her—to Tev's mind, totally inappropriate—relationship with Tev's own predecessor. However, she was starting to prove herself to be tolerably competent.

"If that's the case," Corsi said, "I'll circle around the back so he can't elude us again. Carol will come with me."

Tev considered for a moment and then nodded in agreement. He waved them off and motioned for Gomez to wait by the side of the small, run-down building. It was caked with some form of grime and seemed to actually smell. Half the lights proclaiming its name and its products were broken and he heard them buzzing. He crossed the threshold and there was a different, albeit equally unpleasant, smell within. People were huddled around tables, the bar was empty and the voices were hushed, going silent as they took note of the Tellarite's presence. As Tev's eyes adjusted to the lack of light, he scanned for Lant and sure enough, at a table toward the rear a man was hunched over a tall glass of something green fizzing and he was fumbling with something in his hands. He was the only one not looking at him. Cautiously, Tev stepped farther within the establishment and rummaged in his bag for a hand phaser.

The man seemed oblivious to Tev's approach, and the bartender remained silent. Others huddled down farther in their seats, drinking in silence, which made his footsteps seem amplified. His fingers gripped the phaser, and he tried to keep it out of sight. Finally, as he was ten feet from the table, Lant looked up and grinned stupidly. It was a mix of triumph and terror, telling Tev he wasn't being as careful as he had hoped. Lant stabbed at a control, and the node between his hands glowed with a shower of red, pink, and orange sparks. Tev threw himself at him, but landed atop the empty table, bruising his ribs for his trouble. He let out a Tellarite curse and snarled a little before getting up and checking his phaser. It was undamaged, so he stuffed it into the bag in favor of his tricorder and one of the nodes. Quickly, he rushed out the door and thrust both at Gomez.

"He's escaped in time. We have to find him."

CHAPTER
6

On the *da Vinci* ten years in the future, Dantas Falcão was finishing her meal in the mess hall when Bart Faulwell sat beside her. He carried with him a leather portfolio and a small satchel that he spread out on the table. She watched in fascination as he pulled out a sheet of parchment paper and an elegant pen. Setting it down, he rose and went to the replicator, returning a minute later with a plate of cookies and a mug with steam rising from the top.

"We haven't met," he began, a broad smile on his face. "I'm Bart Faulwell. You're Dantas Falcão, the new medtech. So tell me, how are you enjoying the ship?"

"How'd you know who I am?" she asked with some confusion in her voice.

Faulwell just grinned and returned to his letter.

Dantas frowned for a moment and then glanced at

the letter he was writing. "Wow, I haven't seen pen and parchment in a long time."

"Well, they say the old tools are usually the best tools," he said.

"Which they?"

Now Faulwell frowned at the simple question and took the opportunity to bite into a cookie. He finally shrugged and replied, "There's always a 'they,' I've been told."

"Who told you?"

He stared at her in surprise and then said, "You're messing with my head, aren't you?"

Dantas grinned at him and swiped a cookie from his plate, took a bite and chewed happily. Bart looked at her, his pen, the plate, and finally back at her.

"So, there's always a 'they' and someone's always telling you things. How long has this been going on?"

"What?"

"These voices? What does Dr. Lense say about it?"

"There are no voices," he said.

"Then who tells you these things?"

"What things?"

"Things like old tools being the best tools. You ask me, I'd prefer our computer interface to pen and ink."

Bart broke into a grin. "Ah, now there you're wrong! Ever since pen and ink and parchment came together on Earth, nothing has replaced it. Having something to hold, and keep, in someone's own hand is far more personal, and if I might say, romantic, than a voice on an isolinear chip. What do you find romantic?"

She paused, stopping a reply from being uttered. Clearly, she had thoughts on the issue, he noted, but he was willing to have her think this one through. He sipped from his mug and wrote out a few more words while she pondered.

"To me," she began slowly, "romantic acts are more spontaneous. A sudden present, a surprise for dinner, running away from home and going for a picnic. I guess my kind of partner acts more from instinct than careful planning."

"Well, I guess it's a good thing I'm taken," he said with a grin. She blinked at him in surprise.

Down on the asteroid, P8 Blue was shuttling back and forth between consoles, checking readings and tentatively triggering controls. Soloman knew she was increasingly concerned over the imbalance that was building on the schedule she charted hours earlier. There was less than eight hours to go before things grew critical and the asteroid was likely to explode.

"Soloman," Pattie called out. It was the first time she spoke in quite a while. "This new set of readouts makes me think things might implode instead. Something changed in the intermix." She scuttled up the computer a bit to better read one of the displays, and she seemed to be rechecking her work. The Bynar waited patiently even though he began to feel the sense of impending danger, a feeling he had grown accustomed to, but was never happy about it.

"The batteries are all drained and the computer is still active, so it's increasing its draw from the asteroid; that's what's making things change," she called out. "In fact, because of the constant drain, the asteroid is becoming less and less stable. Its increasing brittleness may cause the implosion."

"This is not a good thing," Soloman said, trying to keep things light. He had noted that his S.C.E. colleagues had been having more trouble doing so since Galvan VI, so he felt the need to increase his own efforts—especially in light of his own ostracism from mainstream Bynar society, underlined by the prejudice of the Bynar pair on the Ishtar project.

Time felt slow to him, which was odd given the countdown that continued inexorably downward. P8 Blue previously theorized the metallurgy employed by the race that constructed the chamber was uninspired, just a slightly different blend of ores than standard Federation construction.

"Pattie," Soloman called out. She turned toward him, lowering her tricorder. "I wanted to ask you about your visit home."

P8 Blue closed the tricorder and returned to the floor, obviously collecting her thoughts. While colleagues, the two were not close and he feared he was being inappropriate with the question.

"It was not what I had hoped for," she finally said, her voice sounding small. "My time in Starfleet has opened up my eyes and my mind, and suddenly my people seem a troubled lot."

"As I understand it, your opinion was discounted until it was almost too late."

"That it was," she agreed, coming closer. "The Citoac was believed a myth until physical evidence proved otherwise and my people had to adjust accordingly. They had forgotten their promises and needed to learn a painful lesson."

"Would you go home again?"

"Why do you ask?"

Now it was Soloman who grew silent. How could he explain what it was like, recently working with paired Bynar who then rejected him as aberrant? The pain of losing 111 was fresh again, and, coupled with the rejection on Venus, he seemed to dwell on his fate with increasing regularity.

"I am not sure I am welcome on my homeworld anymore," he finally said.

Pattie's expression changed to one of total sympathy. "Oh, Soloman, that can't be true."

"It might be, I don't honestly know. Unpaired Bynar are seen as unfit for society, and the bigotry I experienced on Venus makes me unsure about ever returning home."

"Do you regret the life you chose?"

"No, I do not," he said with conviction. "What I traded away in functionality I have more than made up for in life experience. It's just that I do not know if I would be welcome by the society at large."

"You and I, I think, are explorers and pioneers in our own ways. Our lives apart from our societies allow us to bring much-needed perspectives to the homeworlds. I had hoped that after the Dominion War our people would see a need for reexamining our place in the galaxy, but the conversation has not even started. However, there are more Bynar on Federation worlds and, I truly believe your people will come around once presented with the overwhelming evidence that there's more than one approach to life."

Soloman considered her words, taking comfort in them and in P8 Blue's willingness to open up. He had hesitated in even starting the conversation but needed to help crystallize his thinking. Before he could continue that thought, a flash of bright light caught his eye.

"There's been movement," Soloman called out. Pattie quickly moved to the main console and watched over his slight shoulder. He gestured at a small display on the right that seemed to pulse. "Lant's temporal node has advanced three years, two months, and eight days in the subjective future."

"You mean he's only seven years behind us now?"

"Exactly," he answered. "This is his first time in that period, if I read these screens properly."

"And that says he's still on Ferenginar?" She pointed to the adjacent screen that did not flicker, pulse, or change.

"It appears that way. But why would he do that?"

"A new market? Checking his bank account? He has a hot date? How should I know?"

His reply was interrupted by an alarm from Pattie's tricorder. She quickly looked at it and then craned her neck toward the fuel consumption monitor. Her look darkened and her soul shrank.

"The time jump changed the rate of decay, the imbalance has grown exponentially," she reported. "That's why the batteries ran dry before."

"But we still need to retrieve him," Soloman said, fingers tripping over themselves as he reprogrammed the command center. "It appears that I can send these new coordinates to the temporal nodes used by the away team and they can follow."

"And if they do that," she said slowly. "The rate will change again."

"How much time will we have left if the four pursue him?"

Pattie paused, doing mental arithmetic and entering other numbers in the tricorder. Slowly, she looked up at the Bynar, her expression pained. "Maybe an hour, and far less when all five come back here." She made one of the odd chimelike noises that characterized her species. "So much for the margin of error."

"It never lasts. You had better brief the captain," Soloman finally said. "I'll relay the coordinates."

In the past, Gomez was working with her node and the tricorder, attempting to lock on to the chroniton trail left by Lant's sudden absence as Tev paced back and forth. Abramowitz and Corsi huddled together for whatever warmth was possible as the light rain continued to fall, making the streets slick. She had to give the Ferengi credit for designing one of the best drainage systems she'd ever encountered.

Tev rubbed his sore ribs and seemed agitated, but she couldn't indulge his bruised ego for the moment. Now that the need for disguises was over, she resumed her command persona and concentrated first on the mission. Lant's node didn't transmit coordinates she could trace, but she had hoped to once more lock on to the particle signature and figure out where—or when—he went. She grew frustrated at the lack of success but refused to let on to her team.

A beeping sound caused everyone to turn around and stare at Gomez. She was studying her node carefully and then grabbed for the bag by her feet. Carefully, she removed the other nodes and the beeping sound increased in volume. Carol came over to watch and was given a node; another went to Corsi, and a third node went to Tev. All studied it while she concentrated on her node and the tricorder.

"Interesting," she said. "We've received entirely new coordinates. These things must be linked at all times to the asteroid's machines. Okay, we're back on the trail."

"What makes you think they can be trusted?" Tev asked.

"I'm willing to bet that these came from Pattie and Soloman. Yes, there's a chance these are from Lant and we'll end up in the middle of a prison riot, but I'm willing to take the chance."

"We stay or we go—those are the options, right?"

"Yes, Domenica."

"Then let's go," she said.

Sonya saw that Carol also nodded in agreement, which emboldened her. "Tev, Domenica, phasers out. Carol, you handle the baggage. On my mark, we jump to the future."

"How far forward?" Abramowitz asked, shouldering the bag.

"It looks like a little over three years," she answered. "I can't imagine he's doing this for any reason other than escape. He probably doesn't know half as much about how these things work as we do."

"But we really don't know that much about them, do we?"

"Actually, Carol, if we pooled our knowledge, the answer is yes. But if it were just you or Lant, I'd say things were pretty even."

Abramowitz made a face, which caused Gomez to smile for the first time in hours.

"Ready. Mark." Her right thumb triggered her node and the light show began again as her eyes shut. There was enough noise surrounding her that she suspected all four nodes were in use. Funny, she thought, the lights didn't generate any heat, nor could she feel them on her damp skin. And yet, they were bending the rules of physics and letting her slip through the years. It was enough to make her head hurt, which was one reason she tried to avoid temporal physics.

The blinking from the bright light stopped peppering through her eyelids and Gomez risked opening one eye. They stood on the same street as they had before, but it seemed even dirtier, if that was possible. The rain was harder than before and was even colder. Passersby who saw the light show begin were running away, some squealing in shock. Maybe a siren was going off in the distance, but Gomez couldn't tell. Both eyes open, she was pleased to note all four of them arrived together. Better yet, Lant was only a block or two ahead of them, running for all he was worth.

"Corsi, go!"

The security officer didn't need to be told twice and she was off like a beam of light. Her longer legs and grim determination allowed her to quickly close the distance. The engineer admired how the security chief managed to stay upright despite moving quickly, bare feet slapping on rain-slick streets. It wasn't even much of a race, and Lant was too busy running to even consider using the node to jump through time once more. With just a few feet between them, Corsi reached up and pulled the spanner from out of her hair. In one fluid motion, it came free and went flying directly between Lant's legs, tripping him. He went sprawling and then skidding on the wet street, making for a comical sight. No one, especially Gomez, felt like laughing.

Corsi sat on Lant's back, collecting the spanner and keeping her hand phaser pressed to the base of the Ferengi's enlarged skull. She was actually grinning when the others arrived. Carol crouched and collected the fifth node and stuffed it into the bulging bag.

"All right, Commander," Tev said, actually puffing a little from the exertion. "Can you program this to get us home?"

Gomez had been pondering that very issue, especially considering the amount of time she had to just stand around. Still, she speculated there was a simple return button rather than actual time and date to input. She was examining the device carefully and was about to ask Lant to confirm her hypothesis but the siren sound grew, breaking her concentration. Like many things that were seemingly universal, police sirens were among them.

"Everyone remain still. Let's avoid adding to our problems," Gomez said.

Sure enough, five Ferengi security personnel arrived in a vehicle, purple lights strobing. Their reflections off the street hurt Gomez's eyes, forcing her to squint. They each brandished hand weapons, although one had an energy whip out and ready. With a gesture, Gomez signaled for Corsi to get off Lant and let him stand. She nodded toward Tev, indicating he should resume a dominant role, and then prayed he could talk his way out of their predicament.

"What's all this then?" the lead officer asked, his voice deeper and rougher than any Ferengi voice she had ever heard.

"Well, this man—" Tev began.

"You be quiet. I'll hear from my fellow countryman first. Speak."

Lant was wringing out his jacket and trying to tidy himself despite the rain, taking a moment to collect his thoughts. No doubt he would try to extricate himself from the police despite the lack of temporal node. Finally, he placed his hands on his lapels and cleared his voice. "I am Lant, perhaps you've heard of me."

"Can't say as I have," the officer answered.

"Well, if you check the current accounts, you should see I am one of the Ferengi Top Fifty," he said with confidence. Gomez could only imagine how much wealth he must have socked away to be able to make a boast like that.

"And these . . ." he seemed at a loss for words to describe Tev and the women, so he took a different tack. "Any man of means, such as myself, is always vulnerable to common thieves, and worse, swindlers. I've used my fortune to tinker. I fancy myself quite the inventor and was attacked as I tried to bring my latest creation to the Commerce Council." He gestured toward the bag on Carol's shoulder.

"What is it?"

"What is it? What is it? Well, I'm not entirely sure you would understand something of such a complex scientific nature, Officer. In fact, I can scarcely describe it myself without all the schematics and technical specifications. Can't even think up a short enough name for the functions it performs. Truth to tell, I was hoping to work with the Trademark Board on coming up with something catchy." The Ferengi proceeded to spout double-talk for the next four minutes. All Gomez and the others could do was stand still, occasionally wiping rain from their eyes, and look as innocent as possible.

Finally, as Lant wound down, Gomez watched him casually reach into his jacket and withdraw his padd. She surmised that his patter lulled the police enough that such a move would not arouse suspicion. Worse, she fully expected him to bribe the police with whatever it would take to get free, *with the bag*. Frantically, she tried to think of an explanation that would exonerate them, or forestall the bribe.

"No doubt, your fine force is seeking additional funding to create better protections against Borg incursions," Lant began, entering a number onto the padd. Gomez did a quick calculation and realized that the Ferengi, like all other races in the Alpha Quadrant, had had their first serious taste of the Borg three years earlier—ironically, only a month or so after the time period when they were on Ferenginar last. A Borg cube had made it all the way to Earth, wiping out two score ships at Wolf 359 along the way, before the *Enterprise* stopped it. With a pang, Sonya realized that, even as she walked the streets of Ferenginar now, she was on the *Oberth*, having transferred off the *Enterprise* and broken it off with Kieran, still on the latter ship.

Kieran's still alive right now.

Lant's patriotic blathering brought her back to the "present." The Ferengi was offering the police a lump sum for them to do with as they pleased. She quickly turned toward Tev and widened her eyes, silently pleading with him to *do* something.

Tev cleared his throat, attracting everyone's attention. Once he had it, the Tellarite seemed uncertain and then finally plowed ahead. "Thank you," he began. "I think it's fair to note that we have yet to be given the opportunity to explain our side of the story. After all, I believe Ferengi justice acknowledges there are two sides to each negotiation. Before anything further transpires, perhaps our version of events will sway your thinking." Tev continued soothingly, sounding absolutely confident that his story would be more favorable than Lant's. As he chatted, Lant's arm lowered, and the police officer continued to look directly at Tev, eyes seeking something. Finally, it became apparent that Tev would be allowed to move, slowly, and he did so, taking his own padd out of his pocket. Quickly he tapped in a number and prepared to transmit it to the officer's unit.

Gomez prayed Tev was not going to be cheap about the bribe.

The officer thought for a moment and then signaled to one of his men to retrieve both padds. Once both were brought to him, he studied them thoughtfully and then handed them back to his colleague. A smile revealed well-filed teeth, and Gomez's heart sank. If they got out of this, she was going to kill Tev.

"I truly appreciate the fine contribution our otherworldly friend has offered our defense treasury," the officer began. "Perhaps his version of events would be fascinating to hear. But right now, with this rain, we have other safety issues to explore. I'll leave you to sort out your disagreement." He bowed slightly and turned away, signaling the men to return to the vehicle.

Lant stood in the rain, gape-jawed, while Gomez revised her plans toward the Tellarite. Quickly, she pointed at Corsi and the security chief once more stood intimidatingly close to Lant.

"He took both bribes!" Lant squealed.

"Can we go home now?" Tev asked.

"Actually," Carol interrupted, "we need to undo Lant's actions. His manipulation of the markets created wealth that never should have existed. The adverse effect on the Ferengi economy may be severe. I didn't have enough time to study things to make a determination, but we cannot take any chances."

"You mean we have to go *back* and lose all of Lant's money?"

"Exactly, Domenica. And we can't do it quickly, otherwise we'd set off a financial panic."

"Can't we just lose the latinum here and now, rather

than three years ago? Could it have that much of an effect?"

Tev had a point, and Gomez was wet and tired and grumpy enough to go with the simplest solution, rather than indulge in a discussion on the merits of temporal ethics. No doubt the away team would be sanctioned by the Department of Temporal Investigations—a debriefing she was *not* looking forward to—but right now, she didn't care. It was going to be her call.

"Lant, how much do we need to lose to return your accounts to what they were a month ago?"

The Ferengi mentally did the math, fearfully eyeing Corsi, who stayed right beside him. "I'd say about eighty-seven percent of my present holdings."

"And, to follow Carol's advice, how long do we need to properly lose the money without setting off a panic?"

"Well, if I lose half of it immediately, that should reduce my holdings enough so the Dominion War panic in a few years should wipe the rest out," he said wistfully.

"How long?" Corsi demanded.

"An hour, maybe two if I make lots of little buys."

"Let's go to the Exchange," Gomez said. She began leading the group toward the bright tower before them, only a few scattered floors obvious through the rain and haze. "The next session should be starting in a little while. First thing we do, though, is get dry."

"Amen," Carol said.

CHAPTER
7

Pattie noticed the chamber had grown warmer as she struggled with the workstation that was directly tied to the power processing machinery. She had been working with it steadily for fifteen minutes, coaxing the computer commands to reroute some of the building energy. Right after speaking with Captain Gold, she set to work on recharging the batteries. Soloman helped her to reestablish the links and then the Bynar took over, coming up with the commands that would get the mainframe to respond to Pattie's orders. It was tedious and slow, beyond what Pattie was used to, and she fretted over the time remaining. As it was, Fabian Stevens, back aboard the *da Vinci*, was monitoring the power outputs and had estimated that even with recharging the batteries, they had bought themselves maybe an extra hour.

It would have to do, Pattie concluded.

"Have your people ever done anything this reckless?" she asked Soloman. He looked surprised at the question, looking up from the master console. Unlike Pattie, he was looking uncomfortable. Bynars apparently didn't sweat, a humanoid trait she was grateful he lacked, all things considered. Still, after their chat earlier, she felt more comfortable around him than ever before. *Not bad for a couple of outcasts,* she mused.

"No," he answered. "While my people have studied and grasped the basic concepts of time travel, it is not something that we have found appealing. I remain amazed that humans find tampering with the timestream of any interest. The repercussions are enormous and, as we have seen, have changed the core timeline on more than one occasion. We have even theorized that the constant use of time travel threatens the stability of this core timeline."

"I've read some of the research papers," Pattie said, tapping a final set of commands. The holographic screens blinked with new data and everything matched Soloman's instructions. "The original Temporal Accord was strictly intended for research. While there are those who have used time travel to find out information lost to the ages, it has also been used to save a planet. There was an alien probe that sought information from an extinct species of marine life on Earth and some captain went back hundreds of years to bring back samples to answer the probe. Not only was the planet saved, but an extinct species was revived. The argument can be made that time travel can be used effectively."

"But what of the Temporal Cold War?" Soloman asked. "Technology from the future was handed to a race ill-equipped to handle it and there were disastrous effects felt throughout the quadrant for decades. It can be equally said that time travel can be used recklessly. Better we stay in the here and now."

Pattie glanced at the readouts, watching the alien characters change, obviously counting down. "Well, the here and now isn't looking that good to me."

Little had changed in the Tower of Commerce, Tev observed, as the odd group reentered the trading floor. It being three years down the line and later in the day besides, he hoped there was a different floor manager on duty. The fewer who recognized him and the women, the better. The level of activity seemed as cacophonous as before, but there were definitely fewer stares. The Ferengi were an adaptable people, he knew, and the sight of Federation citizens—dressed or otherwise—was more commonplace. *Good,* he concluded. Keeping close to Lant, he guided the hapless trader to a thin spot in the action and gave him a slight push.

"Okay, I just need something to lose on," Lant muttered. "Oh the pain. We're not supposed to try and lose our money, we're not built that way."

Tev snarled. "You are today."

"Of course I am," Lant said slowly, scanning the scrolling figures, catching on to the day's rhythms. He withdrew his padd, checked the account balance and then beckoned to a mauve-jacketed trader. "Ten bars on the *kanar* crop yield," he ordered.

"I can't stand that stuff," Abramowitz offered.

"Well, you're in luck," Lant said archly. "Blight decimated the annual crop on Cardassia and the reports should be coming through any minute. Prices went through the roof and I'll lose. Okay, that's one loss on the books; let's see what else is a sure thing. . . ."

Tev refused to let Lant move more than a foot away from him, and they inched closer and closer to the trading pit. The Ferengi's voice grew shriller as he placed order after order, ranging from octotriticale to trillium, as the greedy trader accepted them all without comment. As the first hour neared an end, it was obvious Lant was losing lots of money, but the traders said nothing. The pace was dizzying and Tev couldn't keep track of all the activity, but he watched Lant's padd and saw the numbers steadily decreasing. This time, no one was approaching them and offering a private room. Losers could remain in place, he concluded, and that was fine with him.

Tev did notice that even though human women were less an object of curiosity, they were nevertheless an infrequent sight in the Tower. Quite a few businessmen and traders strolled back and forth, sneaking peeks at Tev and his "assistants." The occasional expressions of disgust showed that social mores remained in place and most would prefer the women be kept at Tev's hotel, naked but still out of sight. He could tell from their expressions that they too shared the sentiment—but they could not separate now. Timing would prove critical.

The second hour passed and Tev grew impatient with Lant's rate of loss. It should have been over by now, but even a time traveler can be surprised. There was a forgotten rally in *kevas* that handsomely profited the group. Lant would have to make more transactions to dump the profit and each action seemed to take greater consideration or, perhaps, there was greater reluctance. Tev loomed over Lant and asked about the timetable.

"I'm going as fast as I can to avoid detection," he explained.

"Now, why would a fine businessman such as yourself want to avoid detection?"

The group turned to see the approach of a familiar-looking Ferengi who seemed to have a perpetual sneer on his face. "My name is Brunt, and I am with the Ferengi Commerce Authority. Have we met?"

"My name is Tev, and I am working with Mr. Lant here to make some investments to improve my portfolio."

A look of recognition crossed Brunt's face and he smiled wickedly. "If I recall, we met a few years back and you were quite successful. Has fortune abandoned you?"

"My business is my business," Lant snapped.

"Losses of your magnitude might become my business," Brunt responded. "You've lost quite a bit in several major markets. I've been dispatched to look into this in case this is a scheme of some kind. While it defies conventional theory, new ideas always seem to arrive that make us rethink economics, eh? Now, can you explain your goal here today?"

Tev anxiously looked at Corsi and nodded briefly. He wanted to avoid a scene at all costs, but an investigation by the officials would slow them down and possibly ruin their return. The security chief returned the nod, took a deep breath and sidled toward Brunt. She laced her fingers between those in Brunt's right hand and stroked his ear ridge. He tried to stifle a shiver and his eyes rapidly darted between Lant and Corsi, much to Tev's amusement. Corsi leaned into Brunt, whispered something into his ear, and squeezed his hand tight. Brunt let out a small yelp and looked at her with a touch of fright. She returned it with her Core-Breach stare that no one had managed to withstand, Brunt included. He withdrew his hand and stepped back.

"I'll ask you to leave the Tower in the next five minutes," he stammered and turned on his heel and moved quickly out of the area.

Tev looked at Corsi with a grin, but her stare remained.

"Don't ask," she said, and stepped back to the protective huddle of Abramowitz and Gomez.

"Have you lost enough, Lant?"

Glancing at his padd, Lant's shoulders sagged, which told Tev that enough damage was done to the fortune. While he excelled at most things, he was not an accountant and would have to trust that the plan would work. He'd have Wong do a more detailed analysis later.

"Win or lose," Lant said to himself, "there's always Huyprian beetle snuff."

"Personal credo?" Tev asked.

He shook his head. "Rule of Acquisition number sixty-five."

"Stupid rule," Gomez offered.

"Maybe," Tev said. "But our work here is done. Can you get us home?"

"Sure, just get me someplace private." She smiled at her colleagues and Tev knew they were all ready for this particular mission to be over. He led the group, with Lant tucked between himself and Corsi, out of the Tower and down the block. It was dark, and there was a chill in the air. Rain threatened, as usual. At the first alley, he gestured for them to step in. Abramowitz pulled out a light and Gomez quickly worked through all five nodes, inputting the return commands to make certain everyone would properly return. She checked them a second time and then handed them out.

"Say good-bye to Ferenginar, Lant," she said as she leaned over and activated his node. A moment later, she thumbed her own amid the lights blaring from the temporal ripples already being formed. The light show looked right to him as his surroundings shimmered, blurred, and finally winked from the cool street to the too-hot chamber.

CHAPTER
8

Soloman was bent over the master console, using his tricorder to trace an unusual circuit that captured his interest. He had done what he could and it would be a matter of, well, time, before the asteroid imploded or the *da Vinci* was able to leave. Rather than waste time, he wanted to learn as much as he could from the unusual computer before it was vaporized. He felt triumphant having gotten it to do as much as it had, given how long it took to crack the computer language. That in itself was worthy of study after the mission was over. Something about the computer code thwarted him, and he discovered he disliked being stumped by machine language. It felt . . . wrong.

Bright lights suddenly appeared all around the chamber, winking and blinking in no discernible pattern. Quickly, he presumed this was the temporal effect and closed the panel cover, just in case. Within seconds, five distinct shapes appeared and coalesced into familiar forms, although he was fairly certain he had never seen his crewmates naked before.

Pattie had seen the effect, but rather than watch, she had hurried over to a corner and grabbed up a handful of blankets and uniforms that had awaited their owners. As soon as the effect ended, she began handing out the clothing, receiving grateful grins from each of the women. Soloman was fairly certain he had also never seen Corsi smile.

Tev escorted the Ferengi toward him, and his expression indicated a mix of frustration and disgust.

"What's the situation?" Gomez asked.

Soloman glanced at the ever-changing readouts, and worry covered his expression. He rapidly hit several buttons and actually slapped once at an interface. The hologram readouts changed once more and then froze in position. "Lant caused a power imbalance that we've been forestalling, hoping you would return in time. We have less than fifteen minutes before this entire construct implodes."

Gomez was already back in her pants, struggling again with a boot, but knew enough to look worried. "Get us out of here, Soloman!"

"Soloman to *da Vinci*."

"*Gold here.*"

"The away team has returned intact. Beam us over, please."

Seconds later, the seven beings on the asteroid were snatched by a transporter beam. The chamber was suddenly silent, its holographic readouts continuing to chart the power imbalance. The heat grew more and more intense but there was no one to inconvenience. It did, though, cause the computer systems to begin malfunctioning, including losing control of the batteries. Unchecked, the batteries discharged their stored energy that hastened the overall collapse of the system. As a result, the entire asteroid imploded six minutes, twenty-five seconds earlier than Soloman estimated.

Later, the Bynar would note this was a final indignity heaped on him by the alien computer.

"And what's to become of me?" Lant demanded.

Corsi looked actually amused at the pathetic Ferengi, as he slumped lower in the chair. The two were in the lone brig, a small, cramped space that had been added during the *da Vinci*'s refit. To Corsi's amusement, it was the lack of anything to do with DaiMon Phug of the *Debenture* that led to Corsi's petitioning to have a brig installed on the ship, and now its first guest was another Ferengi.

The asteroid ceased to exist only minutes earlier, but the *da Vinci* had already cleared the system, safely away from any aftereffects. She was feeling comfortable for the first time in what seemed to her to be days. She rarely noticed her uniform but today Corsi liked how it fit her, keeping her warm and protected.

"For starters, we're doing a credit check to make certain your calculations were correct."

"I'm insulted."

"You should be," she agreed. "If you want to launch a complaint, I'm sure we can find someone from the FCA to help you investigate the situation. Or we could contact the Ferengi ambassador."

"I really don't think either action is necessary," he said hastily. Without the node or a stockpile of latinum, Lant reverted to the persona of a poor Ferengi, which was genuinely pitiful. As much as she wanted to care, she just didn't.

"What did you have in mind?"

"Now that you mention it, Commander, I was thinking of starting a new line of business and could use a pretty face to help present it to investors."

"Give it up, Lant."

"No partnership?"

"There was never a chance. Captain Gold, though, was thinking of returning you to Ferengi authorities with copies of our log entries. No doubt there are penalties for what you tried."

"They'll ruin me!" He buried his sizable head in his hands and stayed that way.

"From what Lieutenant Wong has determined, you were pretty much that way before you stumbled onto the asteroid. How long did it take you to master the computer?"

He snorted in disgust. "It took me longer to translate than anything else. Any idiot could have traveled in time."

Corsi smirked and figured justice would be served. She walked out, locking the conference room door behind her, feeling at last that something was completed.

Dantas entered the mess hall, her shift having just ended. At one table, Bart was once again sipping from a mug and munching on a plate of cookies. Carol Abramowitz was seated with him and they were having what looked to be an intense conversation. Still, she was surprised to see him wave her over. She was introduced to Abramowitz and invited to sit with them. Helping herself to a shortbread cookie, she sat next to Carol.

"I gather it was a pretty successful mission," she said.

"It had its moments," Carol admitted. "I was just telling Bart about it."

"It should make for a good letter," Dantas offered.

Bart smiled and shook his head. "I don't tell him everything. Besides, I wasn't needed once. The translations proved pretty simple, I gather."

"I'm not so sure about that. Soloman swears the computer kept changing things on him. And, well, it was embarrassing enough without having everyone on the asteroid."

"How so?" Dantas asked.

Carol shivered briefly with memory and then looked at the young ensign. "It's one thing to read about a culture, entirely another thing to be in the midst of it. Some of their mores are personally offensive to me."

"If I recall, they're pretty harsh to their women," Dantas said.

"True. It's better today under Grand Nagus Rom, but back then . . . well, I'd rather not be parading around nude for a race of leering capitalists."

Dantas's brown eyes grew wide and she felt herself blushing. "You had to be nude?"

"The entire mission," Carol said in distaste.

"Wow, it's a good thing you have the body for it," the ensign said. "Well, that is, I think so, not having seen you naked and all."

"We'll just keep it that way," Abramowitz said coolly. She and Bart exchanged glances that obviously conveyed a lot between the friends. How Dantas envied that kind of connection.

"I hear you think I'm hot," Bart said, changing the subject. "Thanks." Dantas looked at him, stunned silent. "Of course, I also hear you put me and Sabrina Simon in the same category. Clearly, that's not possible. I'm far more enchanting."

She continued to stare at him.

"I'm flattered, Dantas—"

"My friends call me Dani," she said. God, how'd she get herself into this conversation?

"Okay, Dani," Bart continued. "There's nothing requiring you to find a partner on the *da Vinci*. We're a small ship and such combinations don't happen that often. Just make friends and let things happen."

"Thanks, Bart," she said, her mind racing. A moment later, she was determined to get even with her gossipy roommate. Somehow, somewhere, she would.

"I can't believe it," Tev said as he entered the bridge.

"It's true," Captain Gold said. "We're being ordered to Starbase 410 so you can be debriefed by Temporal Investigations. They haven't had anything this juicy since. . . ."

". . . at least next week," Gomez added as she joined them in the command center. "I guess our tricorder records and log entries won't be good enough?"

"Not with that bunch," the captain admitted. "You both did superb work. From what we can determine, the extent of the tampering is negligible beyond some hiccups in the Ferengi economy. Lant is pretty much back to where he should be on the economic scale. He's maybe a few bars to the better, but nothing that should be of concern."

"I wish I had time to look at the chamber in depth," Sonya said. "Pattie tells me it was an odd construction. I'd much rather have been poking around that than wandering the streets of Ferenginar with nothing to hide."

"As hides go—" Tev began, but cut his comment off at the sharp look from Gomez.

COLLECTIVE HINDSIGHT

Aaron Rosenberg

CHAPTER
1

Stardate 53851.3

"Great, a runaway train."

Sonya Gomez found herself going through several emotional states at once. The part of her that was the first officer of the *da Vinci* thought, *Fabian's finally getting his sense of humor back. He's starting to recover.* But the part of her that was Sonya Gomez, the lover of the now-deceased Kieran Duffy, wanted to snarl, *How could you? Your best friend is dead! How can you joke about anything?*

She managed to put both halves aside and focus on what Fabian Stevens was talking about.

Captain Gold nodded his agreement. "That's a pretty apt description, Stevens. It's large, heavy, and moving at an alarming rate—in a perfectly straight line." He gestured at the viewscreen, which showed an image of the runaway ship. The image had been captured by a long-range sensor array as the vessel has hurtled past a Federation colony, and was too small to make out many details beyond the basic shape.

Sonya studied the image as best she could. The ship resembled an old Earth bullet-train, flat on the bottom and the back half of the top but curving down in front. Along the side stretched a long mirrored expanse, most likely a fuel nacelle. The entire shape emitted a soft glow, more orange and red than white and gold—almost like a wreath of fire.

"Well, I don't know that this means much, but I don't recognize it," Bart Faulwell said. He glanced at the dark-haired woman next to him. "How about you, Carol?" But Carol Abramowitz just shook her head.

"I don't either," Sonya admitted. "Not that I'm surprised—we've certainly seen our share of new ships, and new species for that matter, on this ship."

"One of the advantages to this job," Gold pointed out gently. "Always something new to see."

"We need to know what's in its path," Domenica Corsi pointed out.

P8 Blue waved an antenna. "Already on it. We've plotted its trajectory—easy enough, since it seems perfectly straight." She touched her padd, and a map of the quadrant appeared on the conference room's secondary screen. "Unless the ship changes direction, at least a dozen worlds lie directly in its path, three of them Federation members. And that's just the most immediate area—we have no idea how far this ship might go if it isn't intercepted."

"Then there's your job, people," Gold announced. "Intercept it. As quickly as possible. I'll get us near this thing, match its speed so you can study it. Just don't take too long."

At that cue, Sonya forced the S.C.E. leader portion of herself to take control. "All right, people. Tev, check our files—see if we have any data on this thing. Pattie, dissect that trajectory—we need to know how much time we have before it hits an inhabited world, or something near one. Fabian, start thinking of ways we might slow down this train. That's it, people—let's get to it."

"Okay, the train's a wreck."

Sonya walked over to the science station on the bridge where Fabian had taken up residence. She saw the long-range sensor display, which was now showing their runaway train. "A wreck?" she prompted.

"Yeah, it's taken a lot of damage. Worse, it's putting out a ton of energy. Way more than anything that size should—except for maybe a bomb."

"We're looking at a bomb?" Sonya shook her head. "That doesn't make any sense. Why fire a bomb this far from any possible target? And why make a bomb that big? More likely it's something on severe overload."

"Sure, but that doesn't make it any less dangerous." Fabian levered himself back to his feet. "Oh, and the energy—it's nuclear. Hydrogen and helium, most likely, though that's just a guess for now."

"Great, so now we have a runaway star instead of a train." Sonya sighed. "Okay, keep at it."

*   *   *

Tev was puzzled—and he hated the feeling. He liked to know what was going on, and usually did, but something was happening with this mysterious ship and he did not yet know what it was. During the briefing, he had been sitting across from Stevens and Blue, and had seen their reaction when Gold had put the image on-screen. The tactical specialist had paled and clenched his jaw, and the structural systems specialist's antennae had begun to quiver. Something about that ship had prompted a reaction. And they were not alone. Abramowitz had avoided Faulwell's question, nodding instead of speaking, which was uncharacteristic. Perhaps she was hiding something. Even the captain had seemed a bit more terse than usual. It was as if all four of them were in on some conspiracy.

The problem was, Tev couldn't find anything in the library computer for them to conspire about. The search for matches on that ship had come up empty. He had checked the files for that particular ship configuration, and found nothing. Then he had looked for anything resembling it. Also nothing. Next he had searched for ships known to have shields of that distinctive color and design. Nothing. He had even looked for vessels that traveled by way of straight lines alone, and drawn a blank.

No one knew anything about that ship. Or at least, no one was admitting to it.

Tev turned his formidable intellect to the problem of the conspiracy. If he could solve that riddle, it would lead him to the actual information he sought.

Oddly, though the captain, Stevens, Blue, and Abramowitz seemed to be involved, Commander Gomez and Faulwell had looked as puzzled as Tev was. As for Corsi and Soloman, they were more difficult to read; if they also shared the hidden knowledge, their faces had not revealed it. But if he assumed that they did, it provided an easy connection, for all of those involved had been on the *da Vinci* since before even Gomez had joined. In fact, they had all been here during . . .

Turning back to his console, Tev opened and launched a particular subroutine he had created some time ago, more for academic purposes than for real use. He had crafted the program with his usual efficiency, however, and it performed exactly as requested. A moment later a small smile crossed his face, and he transferred the information into his padd before rising to his feet. So much for being puzzled. But now came one of his favorite parts—the presentation. This promised to be . . . interesting.

"I've identified the ship."

Sonya glanced up at Tev's comment. She and Fabian had been going over the sensor data, along with Pattie. Tev waited until he'd received a nod before he continued.

"I scanned our files and got a match." Tev gestured toward the wall monitor with his padd, and the information he'd sent appeared on the larger screen. "The ship is called *Dancing Star*. I found its specifications in S.C.E. mission entry DV30193."

"Wait a second." Sonya looked back at Fabian, who was looking oddly sheepish. "DV30193? That's a *da Vinci* file! We've seen this thing before?"

"Well, not you," Fabian replied slowly. "It was back before you'd joined—just before, actually. It was—" He hesitated.

"—the last mission of Commander Salek," Pattie finished for him.

"Oh, great." Sonya leaned back in her chair and rubbed her forehead. Salek had been Gomez's predecessor as first officer of the *da Vinci* and head of the ship's S.C.E. complement. "So now we've got a runaway sun that's already killed one member of this crew. This gets better all the time." She looked back at Fabian. "During the briefing, neither of you mentioned this. Neither did Soloman or Corsi or the captain—and Carol out-and-out lied to Bart."

Fabian at least had the good grace to flush and glance at his feet. "We were under orders, Commander."

"Orders? What are you talking about?"

"What they mean is that the mission was classified." All four of them turned toward the ready-room door as Gold entered the bridge. "It was during the Dominion War, and all of those events are classified for security reasons." He glared at Tev. "I'd be *very* interested to know how you accessed those files."

Tev simply shrugged. "I performed a standard search. I did design the search engine myself—it must have simply bypassed the security measures. Starfleet might want to work on that."

Sonya reminded herself yet again to speak to Tev. The man was an excellent engineer, and an asset to the team, but his utter disregard for certain strictures and his contempt for anyone he did not consider an intellectual equal had already earned him several enemies. If not for his undeniable skill he never would have achieved his current rank—and if he didn't learn to behave with a little more respect, or at least circumspection, he'd never rise any higher.

The captain continued to glare at him for a moment,

and Sonya knew he wasn't fooled. Not much slipped past Gold. But finally he shrugged and walked over to the console.

"Actually, the reason I came in was to give you access to those files. I've cleared it with Starfleet Command—nothing in that mission is a security risk anymore, and you definitely have a need to know about *Dancing Star.*" He tapped a command into the console, followed by a security code, and the files appeared onscreen. Initially they bore the black band across the front that indicated they were sealed, but after Gold entered the code, the band disappeared. Sonya couldn't help but notice that Tev looked a little annoyed at this—it stole some of the importance from his accomplishment for Gold to simply hand her the materials a moment later.

But she'd deal with wounded pride later. For now she turned to Pattie. "Tell me about this thing."

Her Nasat crewmate nodded, antennae wobbling. "As the captain mentioned, it was during the Dominion War. There's a Federation outpost near Randall V, strictly surveillance, and they put out a distress call. A ship had appeared in their system, and it wasn't one of ours. Not one of the Dominion's either, but it was putting out an alarming amount of energy. We were sent in to investigate and get the new ship out of there before it could endanger the outpost. We also had a time issue—if the Dominion noticed the ship's energy output, they'd come investigate themselves, and that could expose the outpost."

Fabian took over. "We did disable it, ultimately, and the outpost was kept secure. But Salek was killed in the process."

Sonya nodded. She could see why the files had been classified—the outpost's existence and location would have been critical information during the war. The best way to keep that data from falling into the wrong hands was to simply seal the materials from everyone, and swear those involved to silence.

"Are we sure it's the same ship?"

"Would I mention it otherwise?" Tev tapped out a command on his padd. The wall monitor switched to an image of the runaway vessel, and a second image alongside it. "On the left is our current objective. On the right is an image from that earlier mission. The two are identical, including several distinct points of damage." Circles appeared on both images, highlighting several of those areas, which were then magnified and overlapped. They were a perfect match.

"Good work, Tev—you and your search engine. Okay, so it's the *Dancing Star*. But you guys disabled it once before. And Randall V is"—she called up a star chart and located the system—"well over a hundred light-years from here. What happened?"

Fabian shrugged. "I don't know. It was too big and too tough to dismantle the hull, and we were in a rush, so we disconnected the power supply. Then we tossed it into the sun. No way it should be here now."

"Well, it is, so find out why. Go back over your old mission files. Then reconstruct the mission for me. I need to know exactly what happened with this thing the last time we met it, so that I can deal with it this time."

"Time may be an issue, too." Gold had stayed quiet during the discussion about the ship, and Sonya had almost forgotten that he was still there. Now she turned toward him.

"What do you mean, sir?"

Gold frowned. "I've had a look at the charts for the area, and the mission logs of captains who've passed through here. One of them mentioned a strange ship at the extreme edge of sensor range. Unfamiliar design, somewhat boxy but not Borg, energy emissions of an unfamiliar kind. But not to us." He tapped a command into the console, and a new picture appeared over the twinned runaway. This one was an ugly squared ship, and one they all recognized instantly, for all that it was blurred from digital extrapolation.

"The Androssi are here?"

"Not necessarily right now," Gold corrected Fabian, "but they have been, yes. And that means they know this area. Which means they could be back."

"And this ship has an unusual energy system," Pattie supplied, "which I'm sure the Androssi would want to study and exploit."

"My thoughts exactly," Gold agreed. "And I'd rather not fight one of them if I can avoid it. So I'm afraid we need to solve this thing sooner rather than later. But that's par for the course, isn't it?" He moved to sit in his command chair.

Sonya turned back to her team. "Okay, this changes nothing. We need to figure this out sooner than soon, but we weren't going to dawdle anyway. Tev, I want you looking at options. Pattie, Fabian, start work on that reconstruction. Get Soloman to help you—he was here too, so he's another perspective. Plus, I want to know as much about this ship's operating system and data files as he can remember. Get going."

It wasn't until they'd walked out that she realized why Fabian had looked so sad about her order. Salek had been in command then, yes—Sonya had never met him, but she'd heard good things about the Vulcan commander. But Kieran had been his second-in-command. He would have been heavily involved in the mission, and she was setting herself up to relive that portion of his life. A portion she hadn't shared, just like all the portions she'd hoped to share and now never would.

She grimaced at herself. This was no time to break down. She had work to do. She could break down later, when the mission was over. Until then, she would just have to get through it.

"Okay, that should do it," Fabian said two hours later in the observation lounge. "We've collated all of our old materials on the mission—the official reports, sidenotes, personal entries in diaries and letters, everything we could find, plus our own recollections of anything we didn't include back then. If we'd had a little more time I probably could have set things up in the hololab, but . . ."

Sonya nodded. That might have been ideal, since it would have provided her with an actual visual replay of events, except for two things. First, they had a definite time factor. As it was, they'd reach the ship within a few hours, and by that point she needed to be up to speed. Even though the holo wouldn't have taken any longer to run, they'd have needed more time to program all the parameters into the systems.

The second reason, which Fabian knew as well as she did, was that listening to and mentally picturing Kieran would be bad enough. Actually having to watch him again would be far worse. She'd heard of people who had programmed their lost loved ones into holodecks, so that they could visit them at any time. But to her that sounded like sheer torture, the notion of watching Kieran and talking to him but knowing that it wasn't really him, that it was just a program. With a shudder she pushed the thought away. This option was definitely easier to handle.

"How long will it take?"

"Two hours if you let it run without pause," Pattie said from behind Fabian. "We condensed some of the less important elements so you'd get the basics first, and then could go back and call up the peripheral details if you needed them."

"Good thinking. Hopefully it won't come to that." Sonya blushed the minute she'd said that. Here she was, implying that their previous commander might have been so stupid he'd missed something obvious, and that they'd all been too dumb to catch it themselves. She saw from their faces that neither Fabian nor Pattie had taken it that way, but cursed under her breath anyway. She should know better than that, but lately she'd been saying a lot of things she shouldn't have.

Rather than risk insulting her friends and teammates again, Sonya just nodded to them and swiveled her chair to face the observation lounge's main screen. The swish of a door told her they'd left the room, but Sonya had already turned her attention to the monitors.

"Computer, engage program," she called out, and settled herself more comfortably. As the first report began, she winced but forced herself to listen past the sound of Kieran's voice. She tried thinking of the others on the mission, but that didn't help much. Based on the stardate, it was after Chan Okha was killed in action, but before he'd been succeeded by Bart. Replacing the ship's linguist wasn't a priority in the heat of battle, after all. It was also when 111 was still alive and working in tandem with 110, before the former died on the *Beast* and 110 became a literal Soloman. A Bolian named Tydoan was the ship's chief medical officer, not having retired yet. Drew, Barnak, McAllan . . . They were all still alive, too.

And so was Kieran . . .

Again, she forced herself not to think about it, put all the deaths behind her, and was eventually able to let her eyes lose focus and drift into the events, reliving them as if she herself had been there.

CHAPTER
2

"What do we know about this place?" Kieran asked, leaning forward to glance at Gold and Salek. "Randall V—I've never heard of it."

"Good," Gold replied. "If you had, I'd have to shoot you." The half-smile said he was kidding—mostly. "Randall V is classified, and what I'm about to tell you doesn't leave this room." He looked around, and everyone nodded their agreement. "Fine. It's not an important system, in and of itself—no habitable planets, no valuable ores or other substances on any of the rocks floating around that bloated sun. But it's strategic as all hell. On the far side of it is Cardassian space, and on this side is us. Most of the other systems around here are inhabited, and we've got bases or at least allies in half of them." He frowned. "They have the rest."

"So this one is the free zone, where anybody can pass through because nobody's looking," Fabian volunteered, and Gold nodded.

"Precisely. And both sides have agreed—without openly saying anything—that neither side will block this one system. It's the open channel, in case they want to negotiate or surrender." He didn't bother to mention the reverse option.

"But we can't just leave it like that," Fabian mentioned, half to himself, and once again Kieran admired his friend's perceptiveness. Fabe might not be the fanciest guy around, but very little slipped by him, especially if it had to do with tactics. "We've got to keep an eye on what they're doing, just like they'd want to keep an eye on us."

"Of course. Their method is to send a patrol ship through here every few days, just to make sure the system is still clean and safe." Gold grinned. "Ours is a little more subtle. Commander?"

At Gold's prompt, the dark-skinned Vulcan typed in a command, and an image appeared on the room's main screen. It looked like nothing so much as the stylized image of a large, pitted rock. "The official designation of this asteroid is R5-3791. It's one of over a hundred small asteroids in the system, composed of iron, lead, silicon, and carbon, with bubbles of nitrogen, hydrogen, and oxygen inside."

Kieran glanced over at Fabian, who'd started grinning. "What's so funny? It's a damn space rock!"

His friend shook his head. "You've got to start reading something other than those pirate stories, Duff. Sure, it's a rock—with exactly the right elements to hide a staffed base inside."

Silently Kieran cursed himself. Damn, he should have caught that! The air bubbles were the real give-away, and he noticed Pattie's antennae waving in good-natured laughter at his expense. At least Salek wasn't laughing—not that he ever did.

"Okay, okay—so I missed it. We're talking about a hidden outpost." Gold nodded for him to continue. "So we set up a station inside that rock, their sensors only see the chemicals already present, and we can watch them come and go. Nice. I take it something's wrong with the outpost?"

"The outpost itself is fully functional," Salek put in, "as are all of its crew. The problem lies beyond it, but within the system." He tapped his padd, and a new image appeared on the room screen. "Specifically, it lies here."

"Okay, now I'm stumped," Carol volunteered from farther down the table. "I've never seen a ship like that before." And Carol knew every major race's vessels, and a lot of the minor ones.

"No one has, as near as we can ascertain," Salek informed her. "The vessel does not match any record, nor even partial accounts. It is a complete unknown."

"Well, it doesn't look Cardassian, anyway," Pattie commented. "They'd never build anything without their typical nacelle configuration—it's too ingrained in their design philosophy."

"It's not one of theirs," Gold agreed. "And it's not one of ours. We don't know whose it is. But it's taken up residence there, and that's bad news. So your job," he glanced at Salek, then around at the others, "is to figure out whose it is, what it's doing there, and then make it go away. All before the Cardassian patrol comes back, sees it, and starts getting suspicious. Our number one priority is to protect the secret of that outpost."

"We will arrive in approximately two point seven-five hours," Salek informed them. "During this approach, Duffy will scan the vessel repeatedly, compiling information as our sensors pull in more details. Stevens will assist me in analyzing the data and creating as detailed a schematic as possible; 110 and 111 will scan the data for any transmissions, and will also institute a blocking protocol to prevent it from sending out any distress signals or other information. Blue will consider methods for contacting the outpost."

"What do you mean, contacting them?" Carol asked. "Can't we just open a channel?"

"We could," Salek agreed. "But if anyone else is within sensor range, that will pinpoint the outpost's location."

"Actually," Gold corrected him, "we can't do that even if we wanted to. The whole point to R5-3791 is that it can't be found. Not even by us. We don't know which of those asteroids it's in, and it's been designed to foil passive and even most active scans."

"Precisely." Salek tapped one long finger on the table. "But the outpost's own sensor array is exemplary, and will be able to provide a host of useful data on this vessel. Thus, when we arrive in the system, we must make contact with them, without knowing their location and without attracting undue attention. Blue, that will be your job." He glanced at his team. "In roughly two hours we will reconvene here to examine what we have discovered and plan the next phase."

Salek turned to go, and Kieran exchanged a grin with Fabian. In the months they'd been working together, no one had been able to convince their Vulcan team commander that the words "approximate" and "rough" did not go with precise time measurements. But since Salek was willing to put up with their little peculiarities, they suffered his as well.

Two hours later, the team met back in the conference room. A model of the unfamiliar ship rotated on the screen while they shared their findings. Next to it was the image of a small, cylindrical object. Fabian looked at it with admiration as Pattie finished her explanation of the changes she had made to the device in order to communicate with the base.

". . . so these radio beacons are now set up to send and receive short-range bursts in their immediate area. We'll deploy a bunch of them when we arrive, and they'll have overlapping coverage—we'll be able to hear the outpost's signal no matter where they are in the system. But the real key is this one." She tapped her padd and a section of the beacon enlarged, with a schematic beside it. "This links all of the beacons together, and any signal one receives is immediately echoed by all the others. They all broadcast on a low-level radio frequency that the Dominion isn't likely to pick up."

Kieran nodded. "So it's a mirror trick—with each beacon echoing the messages from the outpost, no one can tell which of them got the original data and which are just repeating it. That way they can't use the beacons to narrow down the location."

"Very efficient," Salek said, and Pattie sat back down, antennae vibrating with pride. "Now we can communicate with R5-3791 and share data with them. Stevens, please tell the others what we have determined about the vessel itself."

"It's big," Fabian said, and the others nodded.

In the year he'd been serving on the *da Vinci* he'd learned not to gloss over the things he thought were self-evident. Salek had told him early on: "Do not omit any detail, no matter how obvious or trivial. It may prove useful." So now he made sure to include everything, even something no one could possibly miss.

"About the size of a Cardassian battle cruiser, a little narrower but a little longer." Everyone nodded again as a battle cruiser appeared on the screen next to the model. It was an impressive display—one cruiser could carry two destroyers within its bay, and a destroyer could easily fit two *Sabre*-class ships within its own hangars.

Kieran took over. "The metals are a strange composition, though the elements are all familiar. Some type of titanium alloy, apparently, with a particularly high conductivity. Good for channeling weapons or shields, definitely. But the way the energy inside there is being damped out, it's got some pretty strong shielding as well."

"I've ruled out every race I can think of," Carol added. "This is somebody new." Fabian again admired the logic of whoever had first suggested a cultural specialist be assigned to the S.C.E.—along with a linguist, though they had yet to replace Chan Okha for that position. Both their insights into other races had proven invaluable more than once.

"No life signs are evident," Salek pointed out. "Though with a ship this size we would certainly expect crew. Docking bays and airlocks are visible along the exterior, indicating that it was built for entry, if not for sustained occupancy."

"The computers—" one of the Bynars began.

"—are active within—" the other added.

"—but are neither broadcasting data nor scanning the area."

Fabian shook his head. The way the pairing finished each other's sentences had taken a long time to get used to. It wasn't like with a long-term human couple, where one might anticipate the other's thoughts and finish what they'd been about to say. No, this was a case where the two Bynars were so linked that they basically had one mind. Neither possessed the sentence, and neither stole it—they shared it, with no sense of ownership beyond "us."

"So it's not looking or talking, but it is doing something?" Pattie asked, and the Bynars nodded.

"Not just—"

"—something. Its signal—"

"—is increasing in strength and frequency."

"So it's revving up," Fabian said, and they both nodded at him this time. "Okay, it's getting ready to do something. We just don't know what."

"Two other elements we must consider," Salek said. "First, the vessel shows no signs of damage. Its hull is structurally intact, with no more than the minor scrapes one might expect while floating within an asteroid-strewn system such as this one. Second, its energy signature is unique." A signal appeared beneath the model, with notations alongside indicating various benchmarks along the known spectra.

"That's not an antimatter signature," Kieran pointed out. "The pulse is all wrong, and it's at the wrong wavelengths. If anything, I'd say it was closer to a sun."

Salek nodded to him. "An excellent deduction. Yes, the closest match to the ship's energy type is that of a sun. Nuclear forces, caused by the fusion of hydrogen and helium particles."

"So this thing is harnessing a small sun as its power source?" Carol scratched her chin. "Isn't that kind of impossible?"

"As far as we know, yes," Pattie said. "A sun that small would have collapsed long ago, forming a singularity."

"But it could be solar-powered," Kieran pointed out. "Just absorbing stellar radiation and using that for power. Free fuel, essentially—and plentiful."

"That is the most likely possibility," Salek said. "But we will not know for certain until we have examined the vessel more closely."

He started to say something else, but Fabian held up a hand. "Hang on a sec. I know we need to find out what's going on here, and that will probably mean boarding it, but what if it's a trap? What if it's a bomb? High energy levels, active computer signals, strong shielding, no sign of a crew, no attempt to send out a distress signal, and it's sitting in the only free zone within ten systems during an interstellar war. That sounds like a trap to me."

Again, Salek nodded. "An excellent point. How do you suggest we proceed?"

Fabian sat back and thought about it for a second. "Well, we have to assume that it *is* a bomb, and prepare ourselves accordingly. The question with any bomb is, what's the trigger? If this thing is rigged to a timer, we're screwed—there's nothing we can do about it, short of getting in there fast and disarming or deactivating it before it counts down to zero. If it's got a stimulus trigger—it goes off if the air pressure changes, or the temperature, or the noise level, or if something is moved—we've got to make sure we don't affect any-thing."

"Easier said than done," Kieran muttered. "How can we get in there and look around if we can't touch any-thing? And if our own body heat could be the thing that sets it off?"

Fabian shrugged. "Nothing's perfect, but there are a few tricks we can pull. We should beam over in space suits—that'll help mask our body heat and will also keep us from altering the ship's atmosphere. We'll be breathing bottled air rather than touching and possibly shifting whatever's floating around in there. But ideally we'd have some way to hide our visible presence as well."

Pattie raised a pincer. "I can rig small holoprojectors to each suit. They won't run for long, but while active they can take whatever appears behind the suit and pro-ject it on the front, and do the same with whatever's ahead on the suit back. So it'll look like you aren't there. We'll have to move slowly, but I think it'll fool a ship's sensors."

"Great. That should take care of anything like light-ing, shadows, colors, etc. It will also fool lasers, which used to be one of the best ways to rig a bomb—link it to a low-intensity laser, and the minute the beam is broken the bomb goes off."

"Very well," Salek said. "Upon entering the Randall system, we will begin deploying Blue's modified radio beacons. That will put us in contact with R5-3791, so that we may receive and examine their data on the ship. Once we have collated that material with our own findings, Captain Gold will bring the *da Vinci* within transporter range. Blue will be beamed aboard the other vessel—her shell makes her more durable, and thus the most likely team member to survive an explosion. She will sweep the ship for any sign of danger. Stevens, you will monitor the situation, and alert us to any change in the ship's activity, and particularly in its energy levels. Be prepared for an emergency beam-out if you do detect an energy increase that might indicate an approaching detonation. If nothing is detected, Blue will locate a computer junction, and the Bynars will beam to her coordinates and interface with the ship's system. That should tell us whether we are facing a trap, a bomb, or a derelict. Duffy, you will begin developing scenarios for deactivating the ship's power source and disposing of it in some manner that will not call attention to this system." He stood. "We will enter the system in roughly twenty minutes. Blue, please begin preparing the holoprojectors and attaching them to our suits. Everyone else, prepare to release and sync the beacons." He turned and headed toward the door, leaving his crew to stand and follow him out.

Fabian caught Kieran's eye and pantomimed wiping sweat from his forehead, and Kieran nodded back. At least this time it wasn't the two of them walking into the proverbial fire like back on Lamenda Prime. . . .

"We've analyzed the data from R5-3791," Kieran reported an hour later. "The ship entered the system at warp three, then braked to a stop. At the time, the outpost registered over two dozen life signs on board, as well as an energy level of dangerous proportions. The ship began an active scan of the area. Immediately after that, its energy level spiked, and then dropped down to barely subsistence level. The life signs all vanished at the time of the spike. Since then, the energy has begun building again. No signs of life since, though."

"It is no longer a bomb, then," Salek commented.

Fabian, however, shook his head.

Salek's eyebrow rose. "You do not agree? The vessel had a much higher energy level, and then it rose suddenly before falling off again. If it was a bomb, it has clearly already been detonated."

"Not necessarily," Fabian said. "Sure, it did something, but that may not have been detonation. Some bombs have smaller explosions leading up to a larger one. They use the initial releases to catalyze elements, altering materials so that the final explosion will trigger a cascade effect from the now-radioactive surroundings. There's also the subterfuge factor. If I knew someone might be watching a bomb, I'd make it look like the thing had gone off prematurely by setting up a smaller explosion beforehand. Then, after letting it sit dormant for a while, they'd figure the danger was past and would wander in to get a better look. And that's when I'd detonate the real thing."

Kieran stared at his friend. "Y'know, Fabe, sometimes you scare me."

Fabian grinned at him. "What can I say, Duff? I'm twisted—it's what makes me such a good tactician."

Their commander nodded. "The ability to think like the enemy is a valuable one. You are correct that it is a possibility. We will proceed as planned." He gestured to Pattie and the Bynars. "Blue, 110, 111, suit up and meet me in the transporter room. Stevens, Duffy, please take your stations."

"Got it." Kieran watched him walk out, then turned back to Fabian. "Do you really think it's a bomb like that, with all those levels and safeguards and tricks?"

Fabian shrugged. "Honestly? No. But it's better to be safe, and survive, than get careless and die."

"I'll drink to that."

"Fine." His friend slapped him on the shoulder. "If we survive, you're buying."

CHAPTER
3

And, once again, having a shell gets me into trouble.

Pattie adjusted her suit, checked again to make sure the holoprojector was online, and then signaled Salek. He tapped a button, and vanished from sight as she was transported onto the alien ship.

Normally, the Nasat did not require a space suit—she could survive for prolonged periods in the vacuum of space. In fact, her first mission for the *da Vinci* involved repairing a communications relay by crawling across its outer surface. But there were other occasions when even her chitinous exterior needed protection—for example, the time they had to retrieve some equipment from the acidic atmosphere of Eridas IX—so Commander Salek had commissioned a specially modified suit to be fabricated for her.

Her first impression upon materializing was cleanliness. The corridor was spotless—gleaming walls of some sort, curving outward slightly so that the corridor was basically a tube with one side flattened for the floor, and a soft glow from the ceiling and walls providing light. No pictures, panels, or protrusions.

She checked her suit display. If it was right, the projector was working perfectly, and the corridor still looked empty. The suit had also shifted its temperature to match the area, which she noticed was near the upper threshold for human capacity.

"I'm in," she reported. "Hallway of some sort, completely empty. Be warned, guys—it's pretty warm in here. Not quite boiling point, but not too far off." She glanced around. "No sign of trip wires, lasers, or pressure plates. Also, there's no atmosphere in here."

Duffy's voice came through her communicator. *"We're not reading a hull breach."*

She checked her tricorder. "Neither am I. There's no pressure, and it's hot rather than cold. But there's no air—like somebody dumped it or purged it. Might have to do with the energy spike the outpost registered."

"We're not getting anything funny here, either. The energy buildup's continuing, but at the same slow rate. Your arrival doesn't look like it's had any effect. I guess Fabe's bomb theory may be a bust."

"And I'm happy to be wrong, too," Stevens chimed in. *"But it pays to be sure. And we won't know until the Bynars get a crack at the computer system."*

"Already on it," Pattie responded, moving slowly and carefully down the hall. She'd just rounded the first bend when she came across the corpse and cursed out a series of chirps.

"What's wrong?"

"I'm okay. Just surprised, is all. I've found one of the

ship's crew." She bent down for a closer look. "Dead, definitely. Humanoid, carbon-based—and extra crispy." She scanned the body with her tricorder. "No known match, but that's not really a surprise."

"Keep moving, Blue," Salek said. *"The primary goal is to reach the computer core."*

"Yes, sir." Pattie stepped around the body and continued on her way. A few paces later, she found what she was looking for. "I've got an access port, sir. Beam the Bynars a meter to my left."

An instant later, the Bynars materialized, their dataports clinging to the belts on the outside of their suits. The pair immediately opened the port and began speaking to the computer in that strange high-pitched singsong of theirs. Pattie settled back to watch—she knew that, at their speed, it wouldn't take too long.

Nor did it. She'd only been sitting for a minute or two, studying the material of the wall—some sort of ceramic, or ceramic-metal compound, she guessed—when 110 spoke up.

"We have gained access—"

"—to the ship's computer systems. This ship is known as—"

"—the *Nal'q'far*, or *Dancing Star*. Sensors confirm that—"

"—the ship has not been rigged with explosives, or otherwise—"

"—set to trap or harm visitors."

Pattie wiggled in relief. True, her shell could protect her from a certain degree of harm, but whatever had killed that crew member would have cooked her as well.

"Understood," Salek replied. *"Duffy, Stevens, and I will beam over momentarily."*

"Got it." Pattie left the Bynars to continue their talk

with the computer, and began analyzing the wall while she waited.

Salek materialized on the *Dancing Star*, and immediately took in his surroundings. Duffy and Stevens beamed in safely next to him. Blue was examining the wall with her tricorder, and 110 and 111 continued to inspect the computer core. Leaving the Bynars to their work, he approached Blue and asked after her scans.

"The wall's part metal and part ceramic," she said. "At a guess, I'd say it was built to handle intense heat."

"That would explain why this guy was roasted but the walls weren't even singed," Stevens commented, kneeling down by the body. "Whatever killed him struck hard and fast."

Salek was surprised at this pronouncement, since Stevens had not opened his tricorder. "Explain."

"Just common sense and a general understanding of how people work." He gestured at the body, which was blackened and shriveled. "The burns—and that's exactly what they are, burns from a massive heat source—are slightly worse in front. This guy was facing whatever hit him. But his face and chest are just as burnt as his arms. If he'd seen it coming, he'd have raised his hands to shield his face—it's a natural reaction, trying to protect yourself from danger. He didn't do that, which means he never got the chance."

"A sound deduction," Salek said. "Though it is merely conjecture, assuming this race would react in a way similar to your own, it is plausible. For now, we will consider it a working hypothesis."

"Sir, we have—"

"—accessed more of the ship's data," the Bynars reported.

Salek once again admired the way their thoughts intertwined, allowing them to alternate speaking without any hesitation. It was an impressive display of symbiosis. But they were still reporting.

"Much of the older data, including—"

"—the ship's origin point, have been purged."

"To keep the info out of the wrong hands, probably," Duffy commented. "That's what you'd expect from a military ship, certainly."

111 shook her head. "Except that this ship—"

"—has no weapons."

"No weapons?" Fabian straightened up from the body and stepped over to join them. "What about those funnels along the sides?"

"According to the ship schematics, those—"

"—are exhaust vents," the Bynars explained. "They also function as—"

"—maneuvering jets."

"An efficient use of excess energy," Salek said. "We will survey the ship quickly. Stevens and I will proceed aft. Duffy, you and Blue will head to the fore; 110 and 111, remain here and continue to analyze the ship's data. Have the *da Vinci* beam that body up to sickbay, so that Dr. Tydoan may examine it. Report in every five minutes." He set off down the hall, and a moment later Stevens caught up with him.

"I think the atmosphere got burned away," Stevens said. "The heat in here must have been pretty intense, judging from that body, and the fact that it's still pretty warm. I'm guessing it vaporized whatever air the ship contained, and that simply helped fuel the explosion."

"A valid conjecture," he agreed. "Given the scan of

that body, Dr. Tydoan will most likely confirm that the crew breathed an atmosphere similar to our own. Such elements would contribute to any fire, and be consumed by it."

They continued to follow the corridor, and Salek let part of his mind drift. This ship intrigued him in its sense of focus. No weapons, no security, energy vents that doubled as thrusters—it had been developed to use available materials to their fullest, and only for necessary purposes. If their mission had not been urgent, he would have been interested to study the vessel further and perhaps discover the builder's original intent.

Doors opened off the corridor, leading to small sleeping chambers, possible offices, and even what resembled a medical bay. Several of the rooms contained bodies, and a few were found farther along the hall as well. All of them matched the first corpse in general shape and in cause of death. Judging from Duffy's intermittent reports, the rest of the ship was much the same, which suggested a force not only powerful enough to char a body to the bone in an instant, but also one fast enough to sweep the entire ship in that same brief moment.

The corridor finally ended in a wide archway. Salek paused just beyond it, to take in the sight before him. It was a single vast chamber, easily large enough to contain the *da Vinci* itself. Lining the two side walls and the ceiling were flat panels covered in a slight sheen. More panels rested in flat racks that ran the depth of the room in neat rows. Conduits from the panels led to a fat column in the center, whose sides were inset with crystals. The crystals, for their part, were visibly throbbing, and the glow radiating from them lit the entire room easily. They also provided noticeable warmth that could be felt even through the cooling systems of the suits, making this room even hotter than the corridors beyond. Salek, who came from Vulcan's desert environment, actually found it comfortable, though he suspected the humans were not having as easy a time of it.

"The engine room, without a doubt," Salek commented, stepping inside and examining the objects all around him. He had begun to form a theory on how this vessel worked, after the initial scans, and now he applied the evidence against his theory to see if it held. It did.

"It would seem that Duffy's conjecture was correct," he announced. "This ship does use solar radiation for its power source. These are the storage units, and undoubtedly the larger panels we noticed along the hull, which we initially suspected were nacelles, are in fact the collectors."

"An entire ship powered by solar energy? Amazing." Stevens spoke in an awed whisper. Salek understood the sentiment. It was an impressive feat. But right now that was of no concern.

"*I'm on the bridge,*" Duffy announced. "*We've got more dead aliens here, most of them sitting in what look a lot like our own command chairs. I've yet to find anyone who wasn't killed the same way.*"

"Nor will you," Salek replied. "I believe the entire ship's crew died simultaneously as the result of an internal energy release."

"The ship vented excess solar radiation?" Stevens asked, and he nodded. "That would account for the burns and the lack of air, definitely, and if it had enough pressure built up the release would have flooded the entire ship in seconds. It fits."

"We will reconvene on the ship's bridge," Salek informed him and the others. "Now that we have more information, we can make sense of the larger picture."

Stevens followed as they left the engine room and moved down the hall, trying not to notice the charred corpses littering their path.

"Okay, so the ship runs on solar radiation, as your brilliant second officer deduced." Duffy smiled wryly from his perch on the edge of a console. He had not touched any of the corpses yet, and had no desire to move one just to gain a proper seat. No one else did, either. "It takes in too much energy, vents it internally, and kills its own crew. Anyone else see any problems with that?"

"Of course," Salek replied. "This ship was designed to handle such radiation—hence the conductivity of its hull and the shielding just behind that. A ship made to use stellar energies would have safeties preventing such an overload. Yet the cause of death and the internal damage"—for they had found some evidence of charring in side rooms, where anything not metal had been burnt away—"confirms that the energy was released in this manner."

"I don't think the lieutenant commander's arguing the what," Pattie chimed in, "more the why. Clearly whatever did this was extremely hot, and given the ship's power source, stellar energy makes sense. But the idea of an accidental overload seems odd."

Duffy nodded. "Exactly. We've got countless safety protocols for the warp core—why wouldn't they have the same sort of thing for their engines?"

"They do," one of the Bynars—Duffy thought it was 110—replied. "We have sorted through much of the—"

"—remaining computer data. This ship had—"

"—extensive safety protocols, including automatic cutoffs."

"Such an explosion should—"

"—never have occurred."

"Okay, so it couldn't have happened by accident," Stevens said. "What about on purpose?" The others all turned to look at him, and he held up his hands. "Hey, can I help it if I see the ugly possibilities?"

"You are suggesting sabotage," Salek said. "That is possible—certainly the safety protocols could be disengaged, and that would allow for the energies to be vented internally. A ship of this nature might even have some protocol for such an internal release, to flush away intruders or dangerous particles, and thus all that would be required is removing safety overrides and activating such a protocol."

"But if there was a saboteur," Duffy pointed out, "they'd have been killed along with everyone else. As near as we can tell, the energy poured through this entire ship in an instant. Nobody could hide from that."

"Could someone have set things up, then escaped beforehand?"

Duffy shook his head. "Not without being noticed. I've gone over the data from the outpost. They didn't see any other ships near it, no escape pods or the like, and no life signs outside it. So unless it was rigged before it ever hit this system, that's not what happened."

"What if the purpose was not to kill the crew?" Pattie pondered out loud. "We're assuming that it was either an accident or murder, but what if it was deliberate and the deaths were a necessary cost, not the end goal?"

Stevens paced about, hands gesturing. "So somebody on this ship decides to flush the energy from the ship's systems and does it internally, killing himself and every-one else on board. Why? Why not just flush it exter-nally, and not hurt anyone?" He paused. "What if somebody was going to get hurt either way? And the choice wasn't to hurt or not, but who would get in-jured? If these people valued other lives over their own, they might have sacrificed themselves to save the oth-ers."

"Which others?" Duffy asked him, and in response his friend stabbed a finger toward the front viewscreen, which showed the rocks floating beyond the ship.

"How about R5-3791?"

"They killed themselves to save the outpost?" Duffy was finding that one hard to believe, but the Bynars were both nodding, and speaking to the ship computers in that high-pitched series of whines and beeps. After a moment they switched back to more normal language.

"The computer logs indicate that—"

"—life-forms were detected somewhere nearby. The crew—"

"—knew that they were not alone in this system."

"Their engines can only handle so much energy at once," Salek surmised calmly. "From the brief glimpse Stevens and I had, the containment systems are limited, and are already close to capacity again. The ship must need to keep moving in order to bleed off what it has absorbed. It reached this system, and stopped for what-ever reason, intending to vent excess energy. But then the crew detected life nearby, and knew that, if they fol-lowed normal protocols, they would endanger those others. Instead they chose to vent internally, killing themselves but protecting the outpost from harm. It is logical."

"Yeah, except for one thing." Duffy tapped a few

equations into his padd, then showed the others the results. "The energy released in here wouldn't have covered the distance to most of these asteroids. Some of it, sure, but not enough to put the people on R5-3791 at risk, especially if they're holed up in one of the rocks along the system's outer edge. And we can assume this crew knew a lot more about solar energy than we do, since they worked with it constantly—they'd have known that the release wouldn't have extended far enough to hurt anyone that far away. So they killed themselves for no reason."

But Salek was not convinced. Duffy had noticed before that once his commander had settled on a hypothesis, he followed it until he was absolutely sure it was wrong. Often that meant he found something they might have overlooked otherwise but that proved the theory correct. Like now.

"You are partially correct," the Vulcan finally stated. "The outpost would not have been damaged by the energy's release. But that was not the true danger." He tapped a command onto the control console, and the viewscreen's image changed to show the area behind the ship instead—more rocks of various sizes, overshadowed by the system's massive sun. "That was the real concern." Salek typed in more commands, and beneath the sun an energy output graph appeared—even as they watched, the levels fluctuated wildly. "Captain Gold described the sun as 'bloated' earlier. He was correct. This sun is unstable, and most likely in the first stages of collapse. A release of energy such as this ship possesses could easily have hastened that process and caused the sun to go nova. Everything in this system would have been destroyed, including both the ship and the outpost. The crew knew this, and recognized that they would be dead either way. By internalizing the energy, they minimized the destruction, killing themselves but protecting their surroundings and sparing the people on the outpost."

Duffy considered that. It made sense. Once the ship had stopped here, the crew was as good as dead, and it was just a question of going out alone or taking the rest of the Randall system with them. They'd opted for the former, just as a Starfleet vessel would. Whoever they'd been, the people on this ship had shown a comparable respect for other life.

"We have more information now," 111 mentioned—she and 110 had continued speaking with the computer while the others had conversed, though Duffy knew they were also paying attention to the conversation. "The systems are rebooting as we speak. Apparently the—"

"—energy discharge knocked the computers offline, but—"

"—did no lasting damage. We have located—"

"—the command log, and can verify that—"

"—the captain disengaged the safety mechanisms and—"

"—vented the energy internally on purpose."

Stevens nodded. "So they saw the outpost, recognized what it was, realized the danger, and acted accordingly."

Salek looked pleased, almost a little smug, and Duffy didn't blame him. He'd been right about the ship's crew being killed by their own power supply.

"Now that we have solved that question," the commander announced, "we may proceed to the next matter. Duffy, Blue, examine the engine room more carefully. This ship is far too large for the *da Vinci* to tow, and it must be moved under its own power. I will expect a report on the engine's current condition, and on estimated time to restore it to operation. Stevens"—Salek seemed to straighten up slightly, if that was possible—"you and I will dispose of the crew."

"Dispose of them?"

"Correct." Salek glanced down at the figure in the command chair. "These people gave their lives to protect others. Despite the fact that we do not recognize their race, and thus cannot thank them properly, we will respect their integrity and courage. It is unfitting to leave them in such a condition. You and I will use our phasers to reduce the bodies to ash, which can then be released into space. It is a fitting end for noble starfarers."

Duffy was a bit surprised to hear his commander express such sentiments, but then reminded himself that Salek was not as rigid as most Vulcans. Sometimes he seemed almost human—though Duffy would never presume to mention that. Instead he sighed and levered himself off his perch. "Okay, Pattie," he told his Nasat teammate, "let's get to work."

"This material has me stumped," Duffy admitted an hour later. He and Pattie were in the engine room, examining every element both visually and with their tricorders. "It looks like oil, really, especially with that surface sheen. The chemical composition seems similar to oil, too, though not identical. But what I don't get is why it doesn't move at all. It's almost like an oil that's been solidified."

"How about fused?" Pattie suggested, checking her own tricorder. "Take a look—its chemical bonds are similar to glass, and these people are all about using heat. What if they found a way to make glass out of oil?"

Duffy slapped his forehead. "That's it! Glass is good for holding heat anyway, especially if you're using something like volcanic glass. They took an oil with high heat-retention properties, and then subjected it to such intense heat it fused into a glass. All the retention of the original oil, plus the added retention of glass itself, in an easy-to-use form. Nice job, Pattie."

She wriggled her antennae. "Just trying to look at it from their perspective."

Now that they knew how the containment grid worked, it was easier to trace the energy conduits and figure out the rest of the system.

"Solar energy is distributed throughout the ship," Duffy reported over his communicator. "They use it for warmth, for light, and to power all their systems."

"So this ship literally runs on starlight?" That was Stevens, finishing the last of the cleanup.

"You got it. The panels on the collection array absorb heat and light, and transfer that thermal energy to the containment system. It's designed to retain those elements for long periods, and the heat is then bled off as necessary."

"That matches what we just heard from Dr. Tydoan," Fabian said. *"The crew members definitely died from sudden heat—roughly five hundred degrees Celsius. That's more than enough to turn any of us to ash, but they apparently had a higher tolerance for heat—the doc guesses they came from a world much closer to their sun. But actual plasma from the sun would be ten times hotter than that, so they weren't actually scooping up bits of suns, or capturing solar flares. They used the passive heat and light instead—much less energy, but a lot safer."*

"*What is the engine's status?*" Salek asked. Pattie glanced at Duffy, who nodded for her to answer.

"Looks like we can have it up and running in another hour, sir. Not for long-range travel, maybe, but certainly enough to get it to the nearest Federation system."

"*Good. The Bynars have confirmed that the controls are also near restoration, so that we can direct the ship from the bridge. By the time you have the engines back online, we may also be able to program in a flight path. We will—*"

"*Gold to away team,*" the captain's voice interrupted. "*Salek, get your people out of there! The outpost's long-range scanners have picked up Cardassian energy traces. It's got to be their patrol ship, coming back early.*"

"They may have seen that energy spike," Pattie pointed out. "And now they're coming to check it out."

"*Whatever the reason, we need to get out of here,*" Gold replied. "*I want all of you to beam back now.*"

"*I strongly recommend against that course of action, Captain,*" Salek replied, and Pattie stared at Duffy, who looked back at her in shock. "*If we leave now, this ship will fall into the hands of the Cardassians. Not only can they try to adapt its technology for their own military efforts, but the computer registered the presence of the outpost. In addition, a detailed active scan by the Cardassians might reveal the outpost on its own. We cannot risk that.*"

They could hear Gold sigh over the link. "*Damn. You're right, we can't let the Cardassians find it. But we can't fight them off, either.*"

Fabian chimed in. "*Actually, maybe we can.*"

CHAPTER
4

*"S*tevens, report.*"

Fabian hit his suit's communicator to respond to Salek. "I've got the weapons array online." It had been simple enough, really. He'd mistaken the ship's exterior vents for guns, because they were clearly designed both to swivel about and to release bursts of energy. All he'd had to do was install a targeting system on the ship's computer, and then slave the vents to that program. It wouldn't have pinpoint accuracy, but it was good enough to lock onto and hit a ship the size of the *da Vinci*, and anything larger would be even easier. Plus, with the amount of energy the vents could release, it might only need to connect once.

"You have capped the release?"

"Affirmative." Fabian checked the displays again, just to be sure. "It won't vent enough to destabilize the sun." Part of him wondered why the original crew hadn't done the same thing—they could have limited the vent's capacity and bled off a little energy at a time. But maybe they hadn't thought of it, or hadn't had the time to let it vent in stages.

"Good work, Stevens. Report to the engine room to assist Duffy and Blue."

"Roger that." Fabian clambered to the nearest airlock and swung himself back inside. Then he shucked off his space suit and trotted down the hallway to where Pattie and Kieran were moving among the racks of collectors.

"Hey, need a hand?"

Kieran glanced up and grinned. "Back from your walk already? Sure, pick up a tool. We've got most of it running, actually—this ship really was built to withstand just this sort of radiation, so most of the important stuff wasn't too badly damaged. A few bypasses and some new components and the engine's back online."

"Great. Well, I've got the guns working, such as they are."

"The shields are up, too," Kieran admitted, then shook his head. "Sad, really. Here's this great ship, built without any need for attack or defense. And we come along and, in less than an hour, turn it into a warship." It was true—the shields had also been modifications from the ship's original design, taking smaller vents all along the exterior and syncing them together to provide a cohesive bubble of protective fire. The little vents had actually been designed to function as smaller thrusters, for fine-tuning the ship's movement.

Fabian shrugged. "It's a shame we have to do that to this baby, sure. And that we can so easily turn anything into a weapon. But better that than let the Cardassians do it. And definitely better than letting them hurt us, or the people on that outpost."

They worked silently for a few minutes, each of them going over an area of the engine room before moving to the next location. Finally, they met back near the central column.

"And here we come to the heart of the matter," Kieran muttered, and Fabian smacked him lightly on the shoulder. Even with Cardassians heading their way there was no call for a joke that bad. "Sorry. But it is." Kieran showed him and Pattie his padd. "Do you see what I see?"

Pattie nodded. "Definitely." She hit her communicator. "Commander, we have a problem."

"It's the engine, sir, she's gonna blow!"

Salek, having joined the team in the engine room, ignored Duffy's passable impersonation of Captain Scott and studied the tricorder instead. "Yes, I see." Then he spoke into his own communicator. "Captain, the team's estimates are correct. This ship is powering back up, and will reach danger levels again in approximately two-point-four hours. We had failed to realize that the exterior collection array was still active, and that Randall V's sun produces an unusually high amount of energy due to its own instabilities."

"So you're saying we have less than three hours before we've got the same problem that killed its first crew?"

"Affirmative, sir." Salek closed his eyes to concentrate. Two-point-four hours there, point-four hours until the Cardassians arrived, plus volume squared . . . yes, it would work. He opened his eyes and stood, tapping several new commands into the padd before returning it to Duffy.

"Captain, I have formulated a plan. Blue, you will disconnect the collector array immediately. Stevens, you will assist her; 110 and 111, you will return to the *da Vinci* and stand by the communications systems. Once the Cardassian vessel is in range, record their communications and decode their ship's identification signal. Duffy, you will accompany them. I have sent a series of commands into your tricorder, which you will relay to the transporter room. Then report to the *da Vinci's* bridge. Set our systems to broadcast the message I have included, using the Cardassian signal once the Bynars have isolated it. I will be on the bridge of this vessel."

"Wait a second, what are you going to do?" Duffy demanded, and Salek repressed the urge to reprimand him for speaking back to a superior. This was not the time or the place for that.

"I will do my job, Lieutenant Commander, as you will do yours. If my plan is successful, we will be able to deal with the approaching ship and protect the outpost from discovery. But only if we all do our part." With that he turned away, and waited until Duffy had beamed back to the *da Vinci* before glancing around again.

The humans are so—emotional, his sister had told him once. Salek occasionally wondered if his long association with them had in some way infected him with such irrational behavior. His sister's concern was, he believed, over that very thing, though Salek had dismissed it at the time. Certainly his current plan might seem irrational to some. But it was not. He had weighed the various factors, and selected the course most likely to succeed with the least risk to the smallest number of people. It was eminently logical.

He just hoped Captain Gold and the others would someday recognize that.

"What the hell is going on here?" Gold demanded as Duffy stepped onto the bridge. "What does he think he's doing?"

"Wish I could say, sir," Duffy replied, taking his place at one of the aft science posts. "I know Salek has something in mind, but he didn't bother to tell me what it was beyond my own part. He even encoded his instructions for the transporter room so that I couldn't read them. I do trust him, though."

"That's not the issue," Gold clenched the sides of his chair, trying to force himself to calm down. Duffy was too young to understand, even with the recent war. But Gold had seen a lot of battles, and he'd seen a lot of people throw themselves away, sometimes needlessly. Something in Salek's voice when he'd announced that he had a plan had reminded Gold of those others, and the chill it caused was still sliding down his spine.

But now was not the time.

"Cardassian vessel approaching, warp one and slowing," Ina Mar reported from ops. "Should be within visual range any second."

"Onscreen when it is," Gold ordered, and an instant later the warship appeared on the viewscreen. It was a *Galor*-class, as expected—far too big for the *da Vinci* to handle on its own.

"Salek, you picking this up?"

"*Affirmative, sir.*" The *Dancing Star* angled slightly, facing the approaching Cardassian. "*This ship is operational, and I am prepared.*"

Out of the corner of his eye Gold saw Duffy grimace. *What was that all about?* Well, he'd find out later—if there was a later.

"Fine, Salek. How do you want to play this? You've obviously got something in mind."

"Yes, sir. First we wait for the Cardassians to—"

"Sir, incoming from the warship," McAllan reported from tactical, and Gold nodded. An instant later the message was heard across the bridge.

"Unidentified vessels, this is the warship Grach'noyl. *You will power down weapons and shields, and remain in position until we can come alongside and board. Any attempt to do otherwise will result in our opening fire. You have one minute to comply."*

"Wong, prepare for evasive maneuvers," Gold ordered quietly. "McAllan, prepare torpedoes."

Exactly one minute later, the Cardassians opened fire. But their primary target was the larger *Dancing Star,* which was a good thing—judging from what he'd heard in the briefings, Gold figured it had stronger shielding than they did. Let them pound on the vessel he wanted destroyed anyway. In the meantime, the *da Vinci* was free to act.

"Wong, bring us around on its flank. McAllan, open fire."

The first salvo of torpedoes was launched, and at the same time *Dancing Star* released an attack of its own. Gold watched, awed, as a stream of fire lanced from the alien ship to flare along one entire side of the attacking Cardassian. It looked like nothing so much as a directed miniature solar flare, lighting the entire area with its brilliance, and they could almost see the warship shudder from the intense heat. Their own torpedoes hit the opposite side and did far less damage.

"Sir, the Cardassians' shields are down sixty percent," McAllan reported.

"Good," he replied, never taking his eyes from the screen. "He'll have to redistribute power, bolstering the area in front of Salek. As soon as the shields on our side drop, fire the second salvo." Then he glanced back at Duffy, whose fingers were dancing over the console. "Duffy, you know what you're doing?"

Duffy nodded absently. "Yes, sir. We needed that Cardassian message. Now I just have to wait until"—his console chimed, and he grinned—"the Bynars crack its ID code. And then we program our system to broadcast that ID." He glanced up. "You might want to warn the outpost not to get too alarmed if they suddenly hear the Cardassians again."

"Fine." Gold nodded to Ina, who sent a quick warning to the outpost via the radio beacon. Even if they hadn't been otherwise occupied, the Cardassians probably wouldn't have noticed. As it was, the warship was busy unleashing its full fury on the *Dancing Star,* with little to no visible effect. The jury-rigged shields on the large vessel proved more than adequate to melt the torpedoes and absorb the phaser fire before anything could reach the ship's hull.

"*Sir,*" Salek reported, "*I have programmed this ship's systems according to my plan. Whatever happens next, please do not interfere. Instead, when the Cardassians' shields drop, remove the* da Vinci *with all due speed.*"

"Salek, what—" Gold stopped as McAllan shook his head. The Vulcan had severed their connection. "Wong, you heard the man. Prepare to retreat at all possible speed, on my mark. McAllan, be ready with that second volley."

"Yes, sir."

"Sir," Ina reported, "I'm registering a third-party transporter lock. Someone has overridden our system and is redirecting the transporters for their own use."

"Don't fret, Ina," Gold assured her. "That would be Salek. Part of this *farkochte* plan, I'm sure."

An instant later, McAllan announced, "Cardassian shields reallocated, sir. Torpedoes away." They saw the torpedoes strike, and Gold could hear the excitement in McAllan's voice as he reported further, "Direct hit, sir! Significant damage!"

But what happened next made their attack pale by comparison.

First the *Dancing Star* unleashed its second attack. As with its previous strike, the funnel of flame struck the Cardassian ship full along the side, and they could actually see the ship's hull glow even through the shields. Then McAllan announced that the Cardassian shields were down.

"Sir," Ina announced, "transporters have engaged."

At the same time, Duffy shouted.

"Spike from the *Dancing Star!* No!"

The alien vessel seemed to glow from within—and then Gold realized that it was doing exactly that. Light was pouring from every seam in the ship, and illuminating every portal. They were looking at a small, metal-encased star, and Gold resisted the urge to look away.

It was a good thing he didn't, or he would have missed what happened next.

The Cardassian ship had also begun to glow, only its brilliance was more pronounced, as the section where the *Dancing Star* had struck it twice collapsed, pouring energy out from its side. Fortunately, the energy trailed off almost immediately, as the flames found nothing else to burn and so extinguished themselves in the cold of space. Even so, Gold understood why Salek had told him to move the *da Vinci*. If they had been too close, that release could have cooked them as well.

"I'm not registering any life signs, sir," Ina reported quietly.

"What about the *Dancing Star*?" Duffy demanded. "What about Salek?"

Ina glanced at Gold when she responded. "That was what I meant, sir. No life signs."

"Dammit!" Duffy slammed his hand down on his console, making several of the others jump. Gold had half expected it, and kept his seat. "He planned this all along! That's why he ordered us off the ship! That's why—"

"Duffy!" Gold let his own anger leak out, to give his voice the edge necessary to snap the younger man to attention. "Time enough for recriminations later. For now, finish the job your superior gave you."

"Yes, sir." The glance Duffy shot him could have come from the *Dancing Star*'s gun, but Gold didn't mind. Duffy would appreciate the need for focus later—for now it was enough to have him working again, and making sure Salek's sacrifice had not been in vain.

"Prepare to broadcast message along the requested frequency," Duffy muttered a few minutes later, and at Gold's nod McAllan set the comm systems to suit. A moment later, the Cardassian was heard once again on the bridge.

"*Grach'noyl to Cardassian Central Command. Anomalous energy reading identified as solar flare. The star is reading as unstable, and could prove dangerous. Ships are advised to exercise caution when—*" the message suddenly ended in static.

"That's it?" Gold asked despite himself, glancing over his shoulder. Duffy just shrugged.

"Yes, Captain. That's what Salek instructed us to send. Now the Cardassians will think the *Grach'noyl* got hit by a solar flare, and they'll chalk it up to a sloppy gul. No reason to suspect the presence of an outpost, although Randall V may not see as much traffic in the future."

"True enough, but not really our problem." Gold gestured to the screen, and the two ships floating lifelessly before them. "Those, however, are."

It was a subdued group that met in the conference room, and all of them avoided looking at Salek's empty chair.

"We need to get rid of both ships now," Stevens pointed out. "Not just the *Dancing Star.*"

"Yes, and we still have the same problem there as before," Pattie agreed. "That ship is too large for the *da Vinci* to tow. So is the *Grach'noyl*. And we can't wait for help—the Cardassians could decide to send a second ship, just to make sure that last message wasn't a fake."

Duffy shook his head. "They'll buy the message. It had the *Grach'noyl*'s ID stamp on it, and was in their gul's own voice. But you're right, they might still send someone—if for no other reason than to salvage anything left on the warship. So, any suggestions?"

Surprisingly, it was one of the Bynars who raised a hand.

"Go ahead, 110," Duffy told him.

"The Cardassian ship is badly damaged," the little Bynar commented, "but—"

"—the *Dancing Star* is not. Its systems—"

"—are offline again, but can be rebooted quickly, now that—"

"—we are familiar with the codes."

"Okay, so we've got one working ship and one that's been turned to slag." Duffy sighed. "Too bad we didn't find anything like a tractor beam on the *Dancing Star,* or we could use it to tow the *Grach'noyl.*" He knew there had to be a way, but his brain just didn't seem to be working right now. He was still too shocked by what had happened.

Fortunately, the rest of the team—now *his* team—was able to take up the slack.

"The Cardassians have tractor beams," Pattie pointed out. "We've seen them in use before. And that warship is big enough to tow the *Dancing Star.*"

Stevens nodded. "Right! And we can repair any damage to the tractor with our own parts. A lot of it's external anyway, so it might have escaped the brunt of the blow. If we can get it up and running—"

"—we can use that to hitch the two together," Duffy finished for him, "and then pilot the *Dancing Star* out of here, with the *Grach'noyl* trailing behind. Good call, people. The only question is, what do we do with them?"

He glanced at the conference room viewscreen, which showed the two ships floating in space—and the sun looming behind them.

"All set, Fabe?"

Fabian nodded from the console on the *Dancing Star.* "Just one more bit here, and—got it." He slapped the console shut and stepped away. "We're good."

"Right. Duffy to *da Vinci*. Diego, prepare to beam two back."

"*Roger that, Commander,*" said Chief Feliciano. "*Standing ready.*"

Kieran then said, "Pattie, how are you doing over there?"

Fabian watched his friend, and wished there was something he could do to help. Salek's death had shocked him, of course, but he'd only been on the *da Vinci* for a little under a year. Kieran had been here much longer, and so had worked with the Vulcan a lot more closely. The death had hit him a good deal harder because of it. But Fabian suspected that what had really upset Kieran was being left out. Salek hadn't bothered to reveal his plan to him, or to anyone, and Kieran felt betrayed by that. It was understandable, but that didn't make it feel any better.

"*We're good here, sir,*" Pattie replied over the communicator from the Cardassian vessel. "*Activating tractor beam—now!*"

A wide beam of dull yellow-green energy struck the *Dancing Star*, and Fabian felt the ship lurch slightly as the two vessels became linked together.

"Got it, Pattie. Good work. Now beam back. We'll meet you in a minute." Kieran glanced over at him, and Fabian tried not to let his own face show how awful his friend looked. "Ready to send this ship off on its final voyage?"

"Let's do it." They tapped in the commands, and the *Dancing Star*'s engines powered up. Without the collectors, and with all the energy it had recently released, the ship had little power left, but it would be enough. It wasn't going very far.

"That's it, then," Kieran muttered, and turned away.

"Let's head back." He tapped his communicator. "Beam us back, Diego."

As the transporter took them, Fabian couldn't help a final glance back, at the spot he and Kieran had both avoided on the bridge. The captain's chair—and the small pile of ash resting upon it.

CHAPTER
5

Sonya blinked and stretched, not surprised to realize that her back had gone stiff. Her eyes burned, partially from the strain of watching the screens so closely and partially from the tears she'd angrily brushed away. Those last few moments of the battle, when Kieran's anger and sorrow had come through so clearly—when he'd been both grieved at Salek's death and also furious that his commander had made such a momentous decision without him—had been too much for her. She'd had to pause the program for a moment and let her own feelings pour out, weeping uncontrollably and cursing the universe's sense of irony. But at last she'd gotten herself back under control, and had been able to watch the final portion of the reports with little more than a subdued sob.

Before her, the viewscreen still showed several panels of information—the last words of Kieran's official report, the schematics of the *Dancing Star*, and some theories on how the engines worked. But all she could see in her mind's eye was that gout of flame leaping from ship to ship, and the way both the *Dancing Star* and the *Grach'noyl* had glowed from within, like massive beacons in the night.

Salek had done the right thing, of course—the only thing he could have done, really. The ship had been powering up again, and in another two hours it would have overloaded, taking the whole star system. He'd needed to vent that energy a second time, and it had to be internal to protect the *da Vinci* and the outpost. So he'd made the choice to do it himself. He could have programmed the ship to vent, of course, but that would have left the *da Vinci* to face the Cardassians, and they would have been destroyed. So first he had used some of the ship's power supplies to weaken the Cardassians and knock down their shields. Then he'd set the *da Vinci*'s transporters to beam the contents of the *Dancing Star*, minus himself and any physical architecture, onto the *Grach'noyl*. And then he'd let the energy loose.

A lot of it had been beamed into the Cardassian ship, enough to kill everyone on board and to fry all of the ship's systems. But transporting energy wasn't an exact science, and a fair bit had still flooded the *Dancing Star*. Salek had known that it probably would, and that most likely the remaining amount would still be lethal. But it was still the best course of action. He'd died instantly, too fast to feel any pain, and had saved the rest of his team, the *da Vinci*'s crew, and the outpost.

The irony of it was that the *Dancing Star* itself had barely been damaged from the blast—it had already weathered one internal vent, and the S.C.E. crew had brought the ship back to full activity before the Cardassians had arrived. If they'd had more time they could have analyzed it more fully, perhaps, and tried to mimic the ship's energy collection system. But, since they needed to vacate the area as soon as possible, Kieran had led the team in sending the *Dancing Star* into the sun, where no one would ever find it again.

So what was it doing here now?

"Okay, I've been over the reports," she told the others a few minutes later, as they gathered around her. "Good work on the reconstruction, by the way." She'd been pleased to notice afterward that, once she'd gotten absorbed in the events, she had stopped realizing that it was Kieran speaking. Focusing on the details really did help ease the pain—or at least push it to the background. It had only been Salek's death, and Kieran's response to it, that had pulled the pain back to the fore. "But now we've got another problem.

"The thing is," she pushed her chair back from the table and stretched, "that Salek did a good job. No surprise there—from everything I've heard and read, he was an excellent engineer and a good commander. He considered the situation carefully, and based his decisions on the information everyone had collected. It all makes perfect sense, and I'm not sure I would have done anything any different."

"So why is that a problem?" Abramowitz asked. "It should be a good thing, shouldn't it, to know that you agree with his actions?"

"Yes, but clearly something was wrong. If not, the

Dancing Star would still be floating in the heart of Randall V's sun, unreachable even if it wasn't simply reduced to molten metal. Instead, here it is, light-years away and without a scratch on it."

"Which makes this thing even more valuable than before," Stevens pointed out. "Not only does it harness the energy of the stars, but it can dive into a sun and come back out none the worse for wear. The Androssi would kill to get their hands on it."

"Exactly." Gomez scrubbed at her forehead with one hand. "Which leads to another question. If you guys disconnected the collection array, why is it registering an energy buildup again? We know how powerful this thing can get, and I'll be damned if I'm going to let anyone here immolate themselves just to drain it off, but if we can't figure out why it's got more juice now we won't be able to stop this from happening again."

She sighed and resisted the urge to put her head down on the table. The S.C.E. had already been up against this vessel once before, and though at the time they thought they'd succeeded in disarming it, clearly in retrospect they had failed. So why should she think that she'd have any better luck this time around?

CHAPTER
6

"Clearly, the situation was more than they could handle."

Stevens glared at Tev across the table in the *da Vinci's* observation lounge, but the Tellarite ignored him. Gomez couldn't stop herself from sighing. The three of them sat along with Gold and P8 Blue, the former at the head of the table, the latter in her specially modified chair at the other end.

"It's not that simple, Tev," she said, wondering if her second would ever learn. "The original team did a fine job completing their mission, which was to remove the *Dancing Star* before it endangered the outpost or drew Cardassian attention to its system."

"With all due respect, Commander, I disagree." Tev always managed to make phrases like that condescending, and to turn her title into an honorific rather than something she had earned. "They were sent to analyze that vessel, determine its origins and nature, and render it harmless. The fact that it is here now, hurtling rapidly toward a planet, proves they failed."

"And I suppose you would have done better," Fabian shot back.

"Of course, Specialist."

"Well, now's your chance to prove it." Both of them stopped to look at her, which was something, anyway. "The bottom line is that we need to figure this ship out, and fast. And since Salek apparently missed something, we can't just rely upon his observations."

"He did figure out how the ship worked," Pattie offered, and Sonya nodded.

"At least well enough to get it operational, and to vent its fuel cells, yes. But he must have missed something. That doesn't mean he did a bad job—he didn't have a lot of time to study the ship fully. But we don't have to worry about giving away someone's position, and we don't have the distractions of a major interstellar war. Our job is to stop this ship completely, once and for all."

Gold leaned forward. "So how do you plan to do that, Gomez?"

"I'm not sure yet, sir. But I think, to start with, that we need a fresh look at this ship. Tev and I are the only two who weren't on the team the first time around, so we're going to beam over. I want to examine it fully, and build our own theories, based only upon what we find. We can compare that to Salek's data later." She glanced at the rest of her team. "While we're doing that, I want the three of you to go back over the original material. Look for anything you might have missed the first time, about where this ship came from and how it works. Find out why it was out here, who the captain was—anything you didn't feel was crucial to the mission then. Any bit of information could be the key we need."

Gold nodded. "Fresh perspectives, and a resifting of old material. Sounds like a plan. We should be within transporter range now."

"Pattie, how much time do we have before the ship hits something?"

The Nasat checked her padd. "Twenty-three hours, Commander. Then it slams into Riallon IX, which has a population of twenty-one million."

"Right. So we have twenty-two hours to figure this thing out and shut it down." She stood up. "Let's get to work. Tev, you're with me."

"I just don't like him," Fabian groused as he and Pattie headed back to engineering. "Sure, he's smart, but he acts like he's the only one with any brains, and the rest of us are all morons."

"He does have an ego, but that's mainly because he won't lie or conceal anything, including his pride in his own abilities." Pattie's antennae wobbled in the equivalent of a shrug. "If we put aside our modesty and talked about how good we really were at our jobs, don't you think everyone would call us arrogant too?"

"Maybe," he admitted as they passed through the door. "But it's not just that he thinks he's so good. It's that he thinks the rest of us suck. I know I'm good, but I know you and Commander Gomez and Soloman and Bart and Carol are too, and I'd never put you guys down or claim you were incompetent."

Pattie made a tinkling noise that was her equivalent of laughter. "Gee, thanks."

"No, I mean it. We're a team, right? And Tev isn't part of that, because he doesn't want to be. He's not willing to work with anybody else, because he's convinced that he's better than the rest of us and that we only slow him down."

"Well then, be glad that the commander is the one working with him, and not us."

He chuckled. "Oh, believe me, I am."

"It is unnecessary for both of us to do this, Commander." Tev's voice sounded in Sonya's ear as the pair of them, clad in space suits, started walking through the *Dancing Star*'s corridors. "I can analyze this ship while you attend to other matters on the *da Vinci*."

Sonya glanced over at him, saw her own helmeted face reflected in his faceplate. "I appreciate your confidence, Tev, but I disagree. You and I have different approaches, which means two different perspectives. I'd hate to think that we'd missed something here, and jeopardized our mission, because we were relying on a single viewpoint with all of its limitations and biases."

Her second drew himself up to his full height and thrust out his chin, which had the unfortunate result of making his beard jut out against his faceplate like a stiff brush. "I do not miss anything, Commander, and I resent the suggestion."

"Do you?" She resisted the urge to snap back at him, but also refused to coddle his ego any longer. Enough was enough. "Fine, then. Tell me what you see here." She waved her hand, and they both glanced along the hallway.

"A single corridor," her second replied immediately. "Cylindrical, though flattened at the bottom for easier passage. Indirect lighting. Doors spaced along each side, inset and with manual releases. Temperature of fifty degrees Celsius. No atmosphere."

She nodded. "And what does all that tell you?"

"Clearly this is the main corridor. The atmosphere has never been restored after it was ignited at Randall V, which indicates that the computers are either not fully operational or not programmed to provide air automatically." He glanced back at her.

"And?"

The hint of a frown appeared. "And? There is nothing else to be gained thus far."

"Not true, Tev. For example, you noted that the doors have manual releases. Judging from their shape, the crew must have hands and fingers like ours."

He sniffed. "We know they did. The autopsy reports—"

"But I didn't ask you what we knew from other data. I asked what we knew from what we could see right now. That's why we're doing this. Ignore everything you knew about this ship before we beamed aboard." She ran one hand along the wall. "This isn't metal, though it feels metallic. Looks more like ceramic, which would fit with the heightened temperature. Good heat resistance. The lights are actually tiny bulbs along a shelf just below the ceiling, with a lip that hides them but lets their light shine out. There's no carpeting—the floors are the same material as the walls and ceiling—and no decoration. This wasn't a luxury ship, or even a home. More like a science vessel or a military ship. Nothing here that wouldn't be useful. No time or energy for frivolities." She met his gaze and held it, and after a moment he shrugged.

"Point taken, Commander. Two views are more effective than one." For the first time since she'd met him, he said her title with a hint of respect, and she nodded back.

"Right. So let's get back to our viewing, shall we?"

CHAPTER
7

When the call came, Overseer Caldon was in his quarters. The message was patched through to him despite his orders to hold all messages while he slept, which meant that it must be important. The crew knew better than to disobey him without good reason.

The minute he heard the caller's voice, Caldon admitted that the crew's actions had been correct. He would discipline them for disobeying him, of course, but the punishment for withholding this call would have been far worse.

"I have a commission for you," his sponsor informed him.

"Of course, sir—I am at your disposal."

"Sensors in Quadrant Ten-Fifteen, Space Nine-Beta have detected a ship. Its configuration is unknown, though it is large—nearly of a size with your own vessel. I wish to obtain it."

Caldon's mind was already considering the problem. "Have other ships been sighted in that area?"

"Not recently, but Federation ships have been known to pass through there."

"Of course." He stood, knowing his sponsor could not see the movement. "I will depart at once." He hesitated—should he mention it, or wait for his sponsor to do so? The former could be considered presumptuous.

"Excellent." After a brief pause, his sponsor spoke again. *"You will, of course, be compensated at your usual rates, plus a bonus for a speedy resolution."*

Ah. He had been right to wait. "Thank you, sir." The call ended, and Overseer Caldon headed toward the bridge, to inform his crew of their new mission. And to punish them for disturbing his rest.

Soloman sat and stared at his screen.

"Something wrong, Soloman?"

He glanced up at Pattie, and shook his head. "No, I'm just accessing the data from the older files."

She glanced at his console. "Is that what you and 111 recorded from its computers?"

"Yes." He stared at it again, and felt as much as saw the Nasat crouch down next to him.

"What's going on? You can talk to me."

He thought back to their last mission, dealing with that strange time-travel device in the Ludugian system. He and Pattie had been sent to analyze the device while Gomez, Tev, Corsi, and Abramowitz had gone after the Ferengi they'd found taking advantage of it. While the two of them had worked, they had struck up a conversation, and both of them had revealed things they'd never mentioned to their other teammates. It had certainly brought them closer.

"I—I'm afraid," he finally admitted quietly.

"Afraid? Of what? The ship?"

"No, not physically afraid." He tried to put his thoughts into words—it was so much easier with numbers! "The last time we studied the *Dancing Star*, we had Commander Salek, and Lt. Commander Duffy—and 111." It still hurt just to say her name. "I was part of a bonded pair then."

"Ah." His teammate's antennae quivered with sympathy. "And you're afraid of reopening old wounds by looking at the data again?"

"It's more than that." He glanced over at her, then back at the screen. "It does hurt, of course, but I've learned to accept that. Though it's more painful than usual, reliving something we did together. But I'm also worried. I'm not 110 anymore—I'm Soloman now. I'm not part of a pair. I'm less than a pair."

All of them had gotten fairly good at reading Pattie's expressions, and he recognized this one with surprise. It was rage. "Is this about those two idiots on Venus?" The Bynar pair assigned to the Venus terraforming project, 1011 and 1110, had treated Soloman with contempt during the *da Vinci*'s mission to aid the terraformers, calling him a singleton, one of their race's worst insults. But he shook his head.

"No, I'm not worried about what they think of me. Nor about what any of my race think. But I am not as capable as 111 and I were together—that's a fact. I cannot process as well alone as we could united. And I worry that I may not be able to access the information as well now as we did then. What if I miss something because I can no longer read it as clearly?"

Pattie nodded and straightened to her full height again, which only put her level with him while he sat. "I know what you mean, actually. Fabian and I feel it, too. What if we've lost our edge now? What if we've forgotten something important, and are no longer sharp enough to catch it again?" She shrugged. "But I figure whatever we've lost in youth and eagerness we've more than made up for in experience. We're smarter than we were, and that includes you, Soloman. You may be less than the two of you were together, but you're a lot more than you were alone. You'll catch the important details. We all will."

She walked back to her own station, and Soloman glanced over at his screen again. He hoped she was right. But all he could do was his best, and that would have to be enough.

"Okay, how does this system work?"

Tev turned away from the collection array to glance at his superior. Was Gomez really so dense that she could not figure out the system herself? Then he noticed the look on her face. Ah, it was another test. No, he corrected himself. Not a test—a desire to compare data and conclusions. She was posing the question half-rhetorically and half as an invitation for him to share his own discoveries thus far. It was an odd approach, and not one he would have taken himself, but he had to admit that it was proving to be effective.

"This is the ship's sole power source," he replied, and wondered why she bothered to nod. He already knew he was right, or else he would not have mentioned it. Ah, but perhaps it was her way of verifying that she also knew this, and that they were in concurrence. Odd. "Stellar energy is gathered through the collection array on the exterior, funneled through these cables, and then stored in these panels." He glanced at the panels, which shimmered slightly. "I do not recognize the material, though it resembles both glass and oil."

"That's because it's oil that's been fused into glass." She showed him her own tricorder reading. "Very clever—it's comparable to our transparent aluminum, taking the best qualities of two different materials and combining them into a new structure."

"Of course. The energy is then drawn from these panels as necessary, either for fuel or to power other systems." He traced a conduit with one hand, following it back to the thick column at the center of the room, and tapped one of the crystals embedded within it. "This is the ship's actual engine. Power is pumped into these crystals, which magnify it and emit it through the thrusters placed along the hull. The tubes just beyond this store hydrogen and helium, which is ignited by the heat from the crystals. The sudden ejection of super-charged gases provides velocity, and smaller thrusts allow for course corrections."

"Right." Gomez tapped a few equations into her tricorder. "But there's a problem. If I'm right"—she showed him her calculations and he was forced to admit that she was—"these crystals should only enable the ship to accelerate to warp one. Maybe warp two, if the ship was running at maximum power and drained itself completely. But according to the logs from R5-3791, the *Dancing Star* was doing warp three when it entered Randall V's system."

"Impossible, given this data." Tev tapped one of the crystals again. "Nor has the engine been altered since its original discovery."

His superior met his gaze, and they both nodded. Something didn't add up.

"Let's get back to the *da Vinci*," she told him, "and tell the others. Maybe together we can figure out why this ship was going faster than its engines could possibly manage."

As they waited to beam back, Tev was surprised to realize that he did not begrudge sharing the puzzle with his teammates. Oh, he knew he could solve it on his own, given enough time, but he found himself curious to see what conclusions the others would suggest.

Gold shook his head as Gomez sat back down. The entire S.C.E. team—Gomez, Tev, Blue, Stevens, and Soloman, as well as security chief Domenica Corsi, linguist Bart Faulwell, and cultural specialist Carol Abramowitz—was gathered in the observation lounge.

"So you're telling me that this thing couldn't have been traveling at those speeds?"

"No, it clearly was—the outpost's data is very detailed, and their information on later events matches perfectly with our own logs, so we know their equipment was working properly. But those engines cannot produce that much acceleration." Sonya glanced at the rest of her team. "So, any ideas on how it managed that trick?"

"Could it have had a second engine?" Faulwell asked, but Stevens and Blue both shook their heads.

"We went over that thing top to bottom," Stevens told his roommate. "Nothing else even remotely like an engine. And nothing in the thrusters themselves that could have amplified the output to that degree."

"What about outside help?" Abramowitz said. "I know some races use delivery or launch systems for their ships—they have a much larger external engine that drops away after launch, or they have two ships linked together to increase initial velocity."

"A workable system," Tev said, and Gold kept the shock off his face. Had his second officer just indirectly complimented someone?

"The *Dancing Star* could have used such a system on its initial launch," Gomez added. "And it's currently moving at warp one-point-five, which suggests that whatever it used before wasn't available for extra speed this time around. We didn't find anything on the hull to suggest that extra engines were there, but that doesn't mean they weren't either." She glanced around again. "Good suggestion, Carol. Any other ideas?"

Gold nodded to himself. That was one of the things he liked most about his first officer. She was good with her team, she acknowledged contributions by her staff, and she kept her options open. This time it was Corsi who spoke up.

"Since we're talking about its initial launch system, do we know where this thing came from?"

Tev frowned. "I have computed its path, based upon its position within the Randall V system, its angle of trajectory, its speed, and an estimation of its travel time based upon the fatigue of its hull." He tapped a command into his padd, and the conference room screen displayed a star map. Randall V was circled, and a gold line ran from that off to one edge of the chart.

"That's the Delta Quadrant," Blue said, leaning forward to get a better look.

"Correct." If anything, Tev's frown deepened, which surprised Gold. Usually the Tellarite was smug about his discoveries. Why did he look almost displeased now? But that was quickly answered. "I have cross-referenced the location with the logs Starfleet has received from the U.S.S. Voyager, however, and have discovered a problem." Another command, and that portion of the map expanded. The line was now much thicker, and could be easily followed—as it ran right to a circle of absolute black.

"A black hole?" Stevens glanced at the chart, then back at Tev. "You're telling me this ship came from a black hole?"

"No, of course not." Now Gold knew why Tev was so unhappy—he'd been wrong. "Clearly it could not have originated there. But that is what the data suggests."

"What if it came from even farther away?" Faulwell asked.

"Then it would have been traveling for a longer period of time," Tev replied, "and it was not."

"Not if it was going even faster originally." They all turned to look at the slight, bearded linguist, who shrugged. "Since it was already going faster than it should have when it reached the system, what's to say it wasn't going even faster before that?"

"Makes sense," Gomez said. "Tev, extend the line farther out and let's see what we get." A moment later, the gold line projected past the black hole and off the far edge of the chart.

"Say, what's that over there, anyway?" Stevens pointed to a spot past the black hole, and Tev obligingly expanded that section—Gold was pleased to see that he didn't object or insult Stevens in the process. Maybe the man was learning, after all. With that portion enlarged, they could see a gold circle not far from the path, with a designation beside it. "That's a supernova."

"It's not on the path, though," Blue pointed out.

"Not right now," Fabian replied. "But if this ship really did pass that black hole, it would have been thrown off course by the gravity well." He worked with his padd for a moment, then beamed the information to Tev. "Does that look right to you?"

Tev glanced at it, then nodded. "Yes," was all he said, but even that was a step in the right direction, and Gold exchanged a smile with Gomez. Tev input the new information and the gold line shifted—it still ran straight from the black hole to Randall V, but now it angled as it passed the black hole. And ran right across the supernova.

"So you're saying this thing came from a supernova?" Gold asked.

"I don't think that was its point of origin, no," Stevens admitted. "But it did pass by this one. In fact"—he tapped a finger on the table absently—"what if it used the supernova for the energy boost Carol suggested?"

"You mean a slingshot?" Blue asked, and Stevens nodded. Tev had already begun typing commands into his padd, but Gold was lost.

"Hold on a second," he said. "Indulge an old man—slingshot?"

"It's a way to use the gravity of a sun or planet for momentum," Gomez explained. "The ship circles the object, entering its gravity well and gaining speed from the added force, then whips around it fast enough to break free of orbit. Cut it too close and you're trapped in orbit for good, too wide and you don't actually gain much, but do it right and you boost your velocity significantly, and with no real fuel cost."

Tev looked up and nodded. "I have calculated the effects of the *Dancing Star* slingshotting around the supernova, and believe that Mr. Stevens is correct." Gold was fairly sure that was the first time Tev hadn't referred to Fabian as "Specialist" or "Technician." "I have put the new information on the screen." The image had changed—now it showed the line starting a little past the supernova. "The ship's initial speed would have been warp one-point-three, well inside its capabilities. After circling the supernova, it would have reached a speed of warp nine-point-eight. It would have reduced that to three-point-one by the time it reached Randall V."

"Good work, everyone," Gomez stated, and Gold admired the way she had carefully included all of them in the praise—a subtle reminder that they could do more together than alone. "Now we know where it came from, and we've solved the riddle of its excessive speed. Let's keep doing what we're doing, reevaluating and reexamining, and see what else we can figure out."

She stood to go, and Gold watched them all file out of the room, sparing one last glance at the screen before he exited as well. A part of him was horrified by the notion that this runaway ship could move so fast, but the explorer side of him just thought, *Oh, to fly so far, so fast.*

CHAPTER
8

"Look at this input capacitor," Sonya muttered. She and Tev were back in the *Dancing Star*'s engine room, examining more of its equipment, and the more she saw the more impressed she became. "It's got a cascading valve structure—brilliant design. How much would you say this could take before overloading, Tev? Twelve gigawatts?"

He stepped over to examine it, then nodded. "Twelve-point-one, possibly twelve-point-two. Impressive design."

She gestured around them. "And this is just one of fifty like it. That's over six hundred gigawatts this ship can absorb at once. Amazing. Most cities can't accommodate that much energy!" She ran one finger lightly over the capacitor. "This ship could have slingshotted *through* the supernova instead of around it."

Tev glanced at his tricorder. "Yes, it could have.

Within the corona, certainly—it would have been able to absorb more energy that way, and still been far enough from the core to escape."

She nodded, thinking that one over. A ship that literally dove into a supernova for energy and acceleration! Amazing! The more she saw of this ship, the more it impressed her.

Another thought occurred to her, then. Salek's report hadn't mentioned the capacitors at all, or estimated the ship's absorption rate. He had noted that it used stellar energy for fuel, of course, but had suggested a more passive approach. Still, Salek's main concern hadn't been the ship's operating specs, just what it was doing there and how to get rid of it quickly.

As they continued their investigation, Sonya let herself wonder about the Vulcan she had replaced. She had never met Salek, of course, but she had read his files and his record, and had heard stories about him from Fabian, Carol, Pattie, and of course, Kieran. Salek had been a good commander, and his handling of the situation at Randall V had been exemplary, sacrificing himself to save everyone else.

Instinctively, she thought, *Just like Kieran did at Galvan.* She banished that thought quickly.

But Sonya found herself wondering about how Salek's mind had worked, particularly as an engineer.

She thought back over the re-creation she'd watched about the original encounter with the *Dancing Star.* Salek and Fabian had examined the engine room, just as she and Tev were doing now. He'd announced that Carol had been right about the ship running on solar energy, and had then told Kieran that he thought the crew had been killed by an internal energy release. But how had he known that so quickly?

"Fabian," she called out, tapping her combadge. His reply came immediately.

"What's up, Commander?"

"You were here with Salek during that first sweep of the engine room, right?"

"Yeah, he and I went that way and Duff and Pattie went forward, to the bridge."

"How did he figure out the ship's system so quickly? In the re-creation it seemed like he knew almost immediately how it worked."

"Well, that's just the way Salek was," Fabian replied. *"Actually, Carol had already suggested that it was solar-powered, so he was already thinking that way."*

"So he'd made up his mind beforehand?"

"No, but he had a theory already. Duff told me once that that's how Salek worked. He'd come up with a theory to fit the situation, and then see if it held up. Every time he got new data, he'd plug it into the theory. If it broke, he'd come up with a new theory. If it almost fit, he'd figure out where to bend the theory so they matched. And if everything fit: voilà!*"*

Tev nodded. "A sensible approach."

Sonya nodded as well. "So he always had a theory, for every situation?"

"Not instantly, no," Fabian replied. *"He'd listen to the initial data. Then he'd come up with a theory based on that, and he'd test it as he went."*

"Okay, thanks." Sonya thought about that. It did make sense. It was inductive reasoning, she realized. Salek had formed theories and then tested them against the data to see if they held true. A good, solid method, and excellent for an engineer. Any time he had to create an item, he could figure out what the device had to do and then break that down into specifics. If the first method he thought of wouldn't do the trick he'd try a different one until he found a method that would provide the necessary results.

That just wasn't how she thought, was all. She had a tendency to wait until she'd gathered all the data she could possibly get, and then try to piece together a theory from that. Deductive reasoning—from small to large, rather than the other way around. Her way didn't work as well for straight engineering—she got hung up on details too easily, and if she missed even one element she couldn't see the bigger picture, like trying to build a puzzle whose image you didn't know beforehand, while missing some of the pieces. But it was a perfect fit for most S.C.E. missions, because they involved reverse-engineering instead. And by not jumping to conclusions, by waiting until she had all the data, Sonya could be sure that she had everything necessary to reach the right conclusion.

Which gave her the advantage here, she realized. The problem with inductive reasoning was that, if all the data fit your established hypothesis, you assumed it was right—if you had already decided that the hole was square, and all the pieces fit through that hole, you would believe that the square was the answer. But if you looked at all the pieces first, and saw that they were all triangles, you'd know that the correct answer was the triangle. The square was the wrong answer because it didn't match, but it seemed to work because none of the triangles were too big to fit through it. So Salek's theory had seemed right because nothing had contradicted it, but he hadn't had all the facts beforehand. If he had been completely right the *Dancing Star* would not be active again, and they wouldn't be here. They had more facts now, more to work with, and were more likely to come up with the real answer, especially if they let the details form the answer rather than the other way around.

Hindsight, Sonya thought ruefully. Looking back now, they could see the things that the team had missed the first time around, and where they'd gone wrong. She just hoped that catching those past errors would let them find the real solution and make the right decision this time. It was unlikely that they'd get a third try at it.

Numbers scrolled across the screen, and Soloman lost himself among them. As was always the case when he worked with code like this, a part of him felt free, able to soar again—no more restriction to words or emotions, just pure logic and computation. But another part of him wept, because the numbers were trapped behind the monitor's glass while he was trapped within his own body. If he were standing at the actual computer access port on the *Dancing Star*, he could have switched on his belt unit and simply spoken directly to the computer, the code flowing between them with no barrier. And, when 111 had been alive, the three of them would have formed a perfect trinity, the numbers dancing back and forth in a rhythm he still ached to recapture.

But Commander Gomez had ordered him and Fabian and Pattie to go through their old files first, which meant he only had the data he and 111 had downloaded that first time.

While doing so, he noticed a line of code—he and 111 had found it before, obviously, or it wouldn't be in the recording now. But they hadn't paid much attention to it—it had not been relevant at the time. The commands embedded in it were so simple, so direct, and so restricted in their conditional trigger that it had been easy to dismiss them as unimportant. But conditions had changed, and they were all too applicable now.

Soloman's face burned, and his fingers almost twitched, which could have been disastrous—a single wrong keystroke and the entire recording might have been altered, or even purged. He had to pause to collect himself, which had the unfortunate result of leaving those particular lines of code sitting on the screen, staring back at him accusingly. He'd been so worried that he would not be able to perform as well now, as Soloman, as he and 111 had done before as a pair. He'd asked Pattie what would happen if he missed something now, or couldn't decipher something again, because of that lack. But it had never occurred to him that the opposite might be the case. That he might find something he and 111 had missed.

It scared him, making him wonder what else they might have missed, here and on other missions. Now that he knew that they had not been infallible, he found himself questioning all of the decisions they had made together, all of the data they thought they'd decoded. But another part of him, a part he was frightened to admit existed, was thrilled by the prospect. Ever since 111's death he had tormented himself with the conviction that they had been perfect together in every way, and thus by himself he could never hope to match that perfection. But they hadn't been perfect. And, while it might diminish his pride in what they'd had, it offered him hope that he could perform just as well by himself as they had together. Perhaps better—he had sacrificed speed, and the ability to have his computations double-checked instantly, but perhaps he had gained a bit more insight, and a bit more care in his work.

Pushing these notions away for later examination, Soloman rose from his chair. Time enough to consider such things later. For now, he had to bring this data to the commander.

"Okay," Sonya began. They were all gathered around the conference table again, several hours after their last meeting. Carol Abramowitz had spent the time studying the data, trying to figure out what kind of people they were dealing with, but it was difficult, given the lack of any indication of personal items. Of course, it was possible that any personal items were vaporized along with the crew back at Randall V, but that still left her with precious little to work with. She did know that these people had been honorable, and they'd valued all life. They'd also been more tolerant of heat, and had found new and impressive ways to harness solar energy. And they'd made a ship strong enough to dive right into a sun.

"So, what have we learned?" Sonya asked.

"Well, we know the ship's based on solar energy," Fabian said. "Not just propulsion but lighting, heating, circulation, everything. Its sensors actually operate mostly in the infrared spectrum, picking up heat signatures and translating those into three-dimensional image maps."

"Its shielding is mostly absorption," Pattie added. "The *Dancing Star* didn't have any weapons when we first encountered it, or any shielding against energy weapons. Instead it had a strong hull and a collection array to protect it from solar energy and then absorb that energy for its own purposes. That's why it could dive into a sun without harm, because the energy around it was siphoned off for the ship's use."

"The computer systems are efficient," Soloman said. "Not overly complicated, but very solid. Particularly resistant to heat and to vibration, even more than in most starships. The coding is not the most sophisticated, but it's very clean."

"The ship routinely used stars for both energy and acceleration," Tev said. "And the capacitors are built to handle exactly that type of massive input."

"It also went into a sun—all the way into one—and came out unscathed," Carol commented. She didn't get all of the technical details the others were sharing, but that fact had impressed itself on her.

Sonya nodded at her. "Good point. We also know that Pattie and Kieran disconnected the collector arrays after Salek's death and before launching the ship into the sun. Yet it has power now, and is approaching overload levels again." She tapped the table. "What does that tell us?"

"Was the array reconnected?"

Tev shook his head. "No, it is still isolated."

"So the ship was drawing power in some other way."

"Right. But what?"

Carol watched them all thinking. She wished that she could contribute more, sometimes. Then something occurred to her. "Um, Pattie said most of the ship's protection when it entered a sun was in its collection array, right?"

The others looked up at her, and Pattie wiggled her antennae in agreement. "Yes. There's some shielding material between the hull and the interior walls, to keep the energy from leaking through fully, but mostly it was the array that siphoned off energy before it could prove dangerous."

"But, with the array disconnected, how did the ship survive being inside Randall V's sun?" She leaned forward. "I mean, never mind its powering back up—why wasn't it incinerated?"

The engineers all looked at each other. Then Bart, her fellow nonengineer, spoke up.

"I've got a question, too. Pattie, did you just say that the ship has shielding between the hull and the inner walls?"

The Nasat nodded. "Yes. The hull is unusually conductive, and the shielding keeps energy from penetrating into the ship proper."

"But why make a hull conductive at all?" Fabian wondered out loud. "I mean, why not just put the shielding on the outside and be done with it?"

Sonya gasped, and everyone turned toward her. "That's it! Carol, you're a genius! The hull's an energy conductor! The entire ship is one giant absorption array!"

Everyone stared, then started nodding. It always amazed Carol that, even at times like this, they didn't just all start talking over each other. Instead, someone spoke and the others listened, with occasional interjections. This time it was Pattie who commented first.

"It all makes sense," she said. "The collection array was a supplemental power source, not the primary. So when we disconnected it, we thought we'd prevented the ship from powering up but all we'd done was slow the process down."

"And, with the entire hull absorbing energy," Fabian

cut in, "the ship can easily withstand diving into a sun. It's absorbing power from all sides, and all that energy gets sent through the capacitors and into the collection plates. The shielding makes sure none of it goes into the rest of the ship instead, and funnels it all toward the engine room."

"So when it was sent into the sun," Sonya finished, "it just used that to power up again."

"That still leaves one problem," Gold pointed out. "Duffy and Stevens programmed the *Dancing Star* to fly itself into Randall V's sun. They didn't give it any instructions past that. So what's it doing all the way out here? Even with its power restored, something made it leave that sun and launch itself in a straight line."

"I may have an answer to that," Soloman said. "Many of its computer files had been wiped before we found it that first time, but not everything was lost. I have been going back over it, and I think I've found the relevant command." He glanced down at his padd as if for confirmation. "Each internal vent knocked the computer systems offline, but they rebooted after a suitable period. An emergency protocol demands that if the ship's systems shut down twice within roughly one Federation week, the ship will immediately start a preprogrammed course. Most likely back to their homeworld, for repairs." He looked embarrassed, the first time Carol could remember seeing that expression on his face. "The commands were hardwired into the system, which may be why we missed it before."

Gold nodded. "Makes sense—if it's broken down twice in one week something's wrong, so it's recalled for servicing. And, between its crew's sacrifice and then Salek's, that was twice in a single day. So once it was online again, and had enough power, it headed home."

"Why is it close to overloading again, then?" Corsi asked. "Isn't it burning off the energy as it goes?"

"Not enough, apparently." Fabian thought about it for a minute. "Actually, I think I know why. And it's our own fault." He shook his head. "Salek disconnected the safety protocols so that he could vent internally that second time. I'll bet some of those protocols included commands for automatically venting energy to prevent an overload. Plus, I did retask some of its vents for use as guns—so it can't use those vents unless someone engages them from the weapons console I added."

"You had no way of knowing that it would reemerge," Sonya reminded him. "Why bother to reactivate those protocols if it's just going to sit in a sun forever?"

Gold glanced at everyone. "Well, I'm impressed, as usual. So now you know how it works, and why it's moving, and why it's overheating. What's next?"

"Now we deactivate it properly," Sonya replied. "We—" Whatever she was about to say was cut off by a call from Shabalala on the bridge.

"Captain, a ship just dropped out of warp and is heading right for us."

"On my way," Gold replied, standing up. The others followed suit. "Good work, people. Gomez, Tev, you'd better come with me."

As they all headed out, Bart leaned in toward Carol and whispered, "Genius?"

Carol just grinned back at him and, very maturely, stuck out her tongue.

CHAPTER
9

"All right, Shabalala, what've we got?" Gold settled immediately into his command chair, Gomez and Tev stepping to either side of him. To Wong, watching from his conn station, the move looked perfectly synchronized, as if they'd practiced it. He suppressed a grin at the image of the three of them blocking the move out late at night and turned back to his station instead.

"Single ship, sir," Shabalala said. "Configuration matches the Androssi."

"Oh, great," Wong heard Commander Gomez mutter. "Tell me it's not Overseer Biron again, at least."

"No, Commander, this ship isn't one we've seen before."

"Well, that's something," she said, but Shabalala wasn't finished.

"For one thing," he continued, "it's at least twice the size of Biron's."

"Me and my big mouth," Gomez moaned. "What else?"

"I'm picking up multiple energy readings, Commander. Each one matches the signature of an Androssi engine, but I've got three separate locations for it."

"Clearly they have installed multiple engines for increased thrust," Tev declared. Wong didn't much care for his tone, the "any idiot could see that" way he talked to everyone. Come to think of it, nobody on the bridge liked him much. But at least he was usually right.

"I've got something, too, Captain," Haznedl added from the ops console next to Wong. "Multiple communications readings as well. Also three of them, and they seem to be aimed—at each other."

"What?" Gold leaned forward in his chair—the crew liked to joke that they could remove the rest of the seat and he'd never notice. "Three engines, three comm signals? You're telling me—"

"Faugh!" Tev snarled, having stepped over to one of the aft science consoles. He tapped in a few commands, and an enlarged image of the Androssi ship appeared on one of the side screens. The multiple engines and comm signals were highlighted, as were the multiple weapons systems Shabalala had noticed but had not yet had the chance to point out. Then, at another command from the Tellarite, the image split into three separate components. Three equal components—each one with all the makings of a full ship.

"Captain, it's splitting!" Shabalala called out, and they watched as the image on the forward screen changed to match the one Tev had just created off to the side. "Now we've got three Androssi ships, each one roughly three-fourths the size of Overseer Biron's. And all three of them still making a beeline for us."

"How much time do we have, Shabalala?" It always amazed Wong that the captain could stay so calm at a time like this. He was perched on the edge of his seat, of course, but his voice didn't waver at all, and his hands were resting on the armrests instead of clenching them. *I doubt I could be that calm, with three Androssi gunning for me,* Wong admitted to himself with a shudder.

"At current speed they'll be within weapons range in three hours, sir."

"Fine. Gomez, you've got two hours to figure something out. I suggest you get to it."

"Yes, sir." Gomez and Tev left the bridge, again moving together as if they'd practiced it. Wong just hoped that wasn't the only thing their team had been practicing.

"Okay, we've got a problem," Sonya told the team as she and Tev entered the observation lounge. "The ship is Androssi, and it turns out it's some new modular design. It's split into three separate ships now, and all three of them are headed for us."

"If their sensors picked up the *Dancing Star* before this," Pattie said, "they would have known it was enormous. Maybe they figured they'd need three ships to deal with it."

"Could be," Sonya said. "But why they sent them isn't important right now. In two hours we're going to have all three in our face. What are we going to do about it?"

She turned toward Fabian, and he managed not to grin or sigh. It was nice being the team's tactical expert, and knowing they looked to him at a time like this. At the same time, he sometimes wished those expectant stares were focused on someone else.

"How big are these three, compared to Biron's ship?" That was the one they were most familiar with, having encountered it twice already.

"Seventy-five percent," Tev replied. Fabian wasn't surprised that the Tellarite would know the size of Biron's ship—he'd already demonstrated that he loved research, and that he'd read up on the S.C.E.'s previous missions, including the encounters with Biron at Maeglin and Empok Nor.

"Okay, so we've got three ships, each three-fourths of that size." Fabian got up and paced while he thought out loud. "No way we can take them ourselves—the *da Vinci* might be able to handle one, though we'd come away in bad shape ourselves."

"The *Dancing Star* dealt with that Cardassian ship, the *Grach'noyl*," Soloman commented.

"True, and it could probably handle at least one of these. But I doubt it could take two, and that'd still leave one for us." Fabian shook his head. "Sorry, Commander, but this is a fight we can't win."

"We can run," Tev said, and glared back at them when they all turned toward him. "Valor in the face of overwhelming odds is simple foolishness."

"No argument there," Sonya admitted. "But I don't think running would work. They've got three ships— they could send one or even two after us, while the remaining one or two lay claim to the *Dancing Star*. And we cannot let this technology fall into the Androssi's hands."

"Hell, they could focus all three on us," Fabian replied, "blow us away, then come back and pick over it at their leisure. A quick scan will show them that the

Dancing Star is unoccupied, so they'll know it's not a threat."

"What if we just scuttle it and go?" Pattie asked. "Toss it into the nearest sun and take off? They'll stop to see if they can retrieve it, which should give us the time we need to get away safely."

But Fabian shook his head again. "No good. They're too practical for that, and there are three of them. They'll leave one ship behind to watch the sun, and the other two will pursue us. Keep in mind that the Androssi would love to get their hands on Starfleet tech, too, and they've no compunctions about killing us to get it." He stopped pacing and glanced up. "I do have one idea, though. It's a bit crazy, but I think it'll work—and it'll keep both us and the *Dancing Star* out of their hands."

"You want me to do what?" Gold wasn't sure he'd heard her right, but Gomez repeated herself, with Stevens behind her nodding in agreement.

"We want you to move the *da Vinci* into the hold of the *Dancing Star.*"

"So that you can then—"

"Dive into the nearest sun, yes."

"Are you insane, Gomez?" He leveled a finger at Stevens. "You, I already know the answer. But you want me to take my ship into a sun? We'll be incinerated in an instant!"

"No, we won't, sir." Stevens had that mad gleam in his eyes, the same one he got every time he played a practical joke—or came up with an amazing engineering trick. "The *Dancing Star* is built for this—it can dive into a star without being damaged."

"In case you haven't noticed, son, this isn't the *Dancing Star*."

"No, but that is." Stevens stabbed his finger toward the viewscreen, which showed the *Dancing Star* sailing along beside them. "And its hold is big enough to fit this entire ship. Its shielding is designed to keep the heat and energy from bleeding into the inner compartments. Its crew survived sailing through a supernova, sir! We'll be fine in there."

Gold glanced at Gomez. "And you agree with this?"

She didn't hesitate, which convinced him that either she was right or that she'd also gone mad. "Yes sir, I do. We can't fight three Androssi at once, even with that ship, and we can't outrun them without leaving the *Dancing Star* behind—and possibly being cut down anyway. This is our only option."

He sighed. "You know, in the old days, I never had to worry about this kind of thing. I'd be sent to fight this ship or that one, or to carry this device from here to there, or to explore that area. No one ever asked me to fly into suns or through unstable rifts."

"That's true, sir," Stevens replied, and the gleam intensified, "but you probably didn't have nearly as much fun."

CHAPTER
10

"How are we doing with the *Dancing Star,* Tev?"

The Tellarite glanced over at his superior as she and Stevens entered engineering. "Computer systems online, Commander. We've reactivated the safety protocols, and have vented enough energy to prevent overload for another fifteen hours. We have also set its thrusters to begin braking—the ship is currently at warp one-point-two and decelerating."

"Nice work. Now, where are we going to put it?"

"I don't know," Stevens replied. "It won't fit in the living room." Tev stopped himself from rolling his eyes. What was it with humans that they always thought they were funny?

But Gomez, Stevens, and Blue had stepped over to study a map of the immediate area. Tev joined them.

"We've already passed through Sandion," Blue was saying, one antenna tapping a spot on the chart. "And we'd have to turn around to get back to its sun. The next system in our current path is Franjean," she tapped the chart again, a little higher up, "but we won't hit that for another four hours at current speed."

"We don't have four hours," Tev reminded them. "The Androssi will reach us in two-point-five."

"What about this one?" Stevens tapped the map. "Cardienne? We can reach that in . . ." he started to type into his padd, then glanced at Tev instead. At least he now recognized his inferior abilities!

"Two-point-three hours at present speed," Tev informed him. Stevens nodded at that—perhaps it was meant as an acknowledgment of his skill? Even after weeks of working together, he still found these people difficult to read.

"That's not in our path, though," Blue said. "We'd have to turn toward it."

"It's our best bet." Gomez spoke authoritatively—Tev was pleased to notice that she was finally making decisions the way a team leader should, instead of letting others make them for her as she had when they had first met. "Let's take a look at the *Dancing Star*'s thrusters and see if we can make this work."

Ten minutes later, all of them were frustrated.

"Faugh!" Tev announced, and Pattie nodded her antennae in agreement. The equations were clear.

"Steers like a cow," Fabian muttered. Pattie did not get the reference, but she agreed with the sentiment. The *Dancing Star* was too large to turn that sharply, particularly at its current speed.

"Well, what other option do we have?" Sonya demanded. "We can't leave it here, we can't fight, we can't run. We need to get to the nearest star, and that's the only one we can reach in time. So how do we turn something that doesn't want to turn?"

"The original crew used gravity wells," Pattie pointed out. "If we had a planet or even a large moon nearby, we might be able to use that to alter our course."

"Nothing within range is large enough to provide sufficient gravity," Tev informed her. Despite his brusqueness, Pattie was glad he was there—she might have been able to figure that out as quickly, but this way she didn't have to.

"So it can't turn on its own," Fabian mused, "and we don't have anything heavy enough to make it turn. But maybe we can bootleg it."

The others turned to look at him.

"Bootleg it?" Tev asked.

Fabian shrugged. "It's an old Earth term. Used to be bootleggers—people who illegally brewed their own alcohol, or moonshine, and then sold it to others. The cops would chase them all the time, and they got pretty good at making fast getaways. One of their techniques was called a bootlegger turn." He grinned. "Basically they'd throw a rope around a tree and use that to spin the car into a tighter turn."

"Like wheeling around a gravity well, but using a physical tether." Tev nodded with understanding. Pattie was momentarily overcome by an image of Tev, wearing overalls and carrying a shotgun, riding in an old Earth car as it spun around a tree with police cars in hot pursuit. Her tinkle of laughter was fortunately overlooked by the others.

"What could we use for the tree?" Sonya demanded, and they all scanned the charts.

"There," Pattie pointed out finally, enlarging a section and highlighting one spot. "It's an asteroid, twice the size of the *Dancing Star* and filled with heavy metals. Not enough to produce a gravity well, but with its mass the ship shouldn't be able to budge it. And it's between our present course and Cardienne."

"Right. So what do we use for the rope?"

"It's got to be a tractor beam," Fabian said. "Nothing else could withstand that kind of stress."

"But the *Dancing Star* doesn't have a tractor beam."

Pattie tinkled in laughter again. "No, but we do."

"I can't believe I let you talk me into this," Gold muttered as he and Sonya watched Shabalala steer the *da Vinci* into the hold of the *Dancing Star.*

"I didn't talk you into anything, sir," she replied with a grin. "You agreed that this is the best course of action."

"Being swallowed by a whale, which then hides within in a bonfire? What was I thinking?"

Sonya didn't bother to reply. Instead, she tapped her combadge. "Tev, how's the tractor beam coming?"

"Final attachments almost completed, Commander," came the reply. *"We will be ready in ten minutes."*

"Good. Report to the *Dancing Star*'s bridge as soon as you're done."

"And that's another thing," Gold told her. "We just got that new tractor beam, and now you're ripping it off and sticking it on some other ship. And it'll get turned to ash when we dive!"

Sonya shrugged. "Sorry, Captain. But it's either the tractor beam or us, and I'd rather give up the tractor beam."

He didn't have an answer for that, so he simply turned back to the viewscreen. It really did look like his mental picture of Jonah and the whale—the *da Vinci* sailed through the *Dancing Star*'s cargo doors without a problem, ample room on both sides thanks to Wong's deft handling, and settled into the middle of its hold. The ceiling soared above them, lost in the darkness, and the walls were so far away that they were also swallowed up. If not for the floor, it would have been easy to imagine that the *da Vinci* was still out in space, albeit in an area without any stars.

"All right, Gomez," Gold sighed as the thud of the closing cargo door echoed across the ship. "We're in. Now I expect you to handle the rest. I'll be here in my little minnow if you need me."

"Not to worry, sir," she called back as she headed for the door. "This whale's friendly. It's those three sharks I'm worried about."

"Everybody ready?" Sonya settled herself in the command chair, and Fabian had to suppress a wince. The last time a Starfleet officer sat in that chair, it was Salek. Fabian still remembered the sight of the Vulcan's ashes piled on the cushion before he and Duffy piloted the *Dancing Star* into Randall V's sun.

"All set here," he replied from the tactical station.

"Ready, Commander," Soloman called from the computer console.

"Good to go," Pattie chimed in from navigation.

"Of course," was Tev's only reply from ops.

"Then let's move some moonshine," Sonya said with a smile. "Distance to firing point, Tev?"

"Point-zero-seven light-years," came the immediate response.

"Current speed?"

"Warp one-point-one-five," Pattie said.

"Time to Androssi arrival?"

Fabian checked his monitors. "Point-eight-nine hours."

"Time to Cardienne, at estimated speed?"

"Point-eight-seven hours."

Sonya sighed. "It's going to be close. Tev, prepare to engage tractor beam, on my mark."

"Ready, Commander." It amazed Fabian that the Tellarite hadn't insulted anyone all day. *Maybe it's his time of month,* he thought wryly—and was glad he hadn't said it out loud.

"And, three, two, one—mark."

"Tractor beam engaged."

"Changing course," Pattie called out. "Speed dropping to warp one-point-zero-nine."

"Release tractor beam—now!"

"Tractor beam released."

"Now on course for Cardienne," Pattie announced, antennae waving. "Speed at warp one-point-three-nine!"

"Congratulations, people," Sonya said, leaning back in her chair. "It worked!"

"Yeah," Fabian couldn't resist adding, "those cops'll never catch us now."

CHAPTER
11

Overseer Caldon still could not accept what he had just seen. Upon dropping out of FTL, they had immediately detected not only the unfamiliar ship but also a Federation Starfleet vessel near it. Additional scans had identified it as the *U.S.S. da Vinci,* NCC-81623, a vessel that Caldon's fellow overseer Biron had encountered twice—and failed to dispose of each time. Caldon had been looking forward to correcting his rival's error when the *U.S.S. da Vinci* had moved inside the target vessel. Then this—

He stared at the screen, replaying the image in his mind. The vessel had been heading toward them, and had suddenly turned sharply to one side and accelerated. Given its size, such a turn should have been impossible, and the ship gave no indication that its engines had provided additional thrust to account for the change in velocity. Yet now it was moving more quickly, and on a completely different flight path.

Caldon frowned. Perhaps Biron was not a fool after all, and these Federation individuals were more clever than expected. No matter. His crew had already calculated their new path, and it led directly toward an uninhabited system—in fact, directly toward that system's sun. It was a simple matter for him to spread out his ship sections, one on either side and his main section approaching from behind. With the sun before them, the mystery ship was boxed in, and would be easy to capture. And the *da Vinci* had trapped itself within, which would prove to be their undoing.

Yet, even as he gave orders for the new vessel's acquisition and retrieval, Caldon could not help but think about that strange turn again—and wonder what else the crew of the *U.S.S. da Vinci* might do.

"He's right behind us, Commander."

Sonya glanced at the screen—half of it showed Cardienne's sun, whose outer edge they had almost reached, while the other half showed the view behind them. Two of the Androssi ships had moved to flank them, while the third traced their own path behind them. *He thinks he's got us trapped,* she thought. *Well, he's in for a surprise.*

"Distance to the sun," she called out, and Tev answered quickly.

"Ten minutes, Commander."

"All right—everybody get ready." She tapped her combadge. "Captain, we're entering the sun in ten minutes."

"Roger that, Gomez," came Gold's reply. *"We've got the marshmallows and hot dogs ready."*

"Don't forget the sunscreen," she said, then switched off and returned her attention to the screen. The sun filled the forward view completely, and a few minutes later it swallowed them up. The screen went white for a moment, then shifted into grays.

"What just happened?"

"The monitors operate on infrared," Soloman explained from his computer console. "Within the sun, that's useless—it's all hot. The systems have shunted to a different viewing method as a result. It's standard protocol for the ship."

"Ah. Okay." She forced her hands to release the armrests, and tried to convince herself that she was only sweating from anxiety and not from actual heat. She prided herself on being able to face any situation, but was willing to admit that deliberately diving into a sun wasn't the safest thing they'd ever done.

"What's our status, Tev?" she asked, and was pleased to see her second standing as calmly as ever. If something had been wrong, she had no doubt he'd be the first to tell her.

"All systems operating normally, Commander," he said instead. "Internal temperature has risen one-point-two degrees, and is holding steady. Hull intact, with no signs of damage." He frowned. "The tractor beam, however, has been demolished."

Sonya laughed. "Well, I did warn Captain Gold about that. Guess we'll have to put in at a starbase for a new one, once we get out of this. Which reminds me"—she glanced at the other half of the viewscreen again—"I wonder what our new friends think of our immolation?"

*   *   *

"Well, this is unexpected," Caldon muttered, standing beside his sub-overseer and watching the activity on the main screen. All of the reports he had seen of encounters with the Federation had indicated the same major weakness—a foolish overvaluation of all life, to the extent that Starfleet officers would not even dispatch a fallen opponent who would happily kill them if the situation were reversed. This behavior had proven useful in outmaneuvering them in the past—Biron had reported that they even valued workers, and would surrender rather than see one hurt! But clearly either Biron had been mistaken, or that behavior had been anomalous, or they had adopted a new strategy.

In a way, Caldon could not fault their decision. Clearly his own ships had outmatched them, and would defeat them in battle. Thus, the unfamiliar vessel would fall into his hands unless it was destroyed. He had not expected them to fly into a sun, especially with themselves still onboard, but it did prevent him from accessing the ship and its information.

"Scan for life signs," he ordered, and one of the workers did so quickly.

"Negative, Overseer," the worker reported a moment later. "We are not reading anything beyond the sun's energies itself. No evidence of the ship's engines or shields, or of any life-forms within."

Caldon considered. It was possible, of course, that this strange ship could survive such an experience, and that the Starfleet crew had known this. But they had not been present when the ship had first been sighted, less than a day ago, and to have discovered so much about it in so short a time was unlikely. They could have hoped it would survive, and gambled upon that, but all the evidence suggested that the Federation did not gamble with lives. Thus they must have resigned themselves to death in order to keep the ship from his hands. A valid decision, and one he himself might have chosen in their place. As it was, only quick handling by his sub-overseers had prevented them from following the ship into the sun, and even so their shields had sustained damage from its heat. A direct encounter would easily incinerate them.

"Sub-Overseer Rando, report," he ordered over the communications system, and received an immediate response from the officer in charge of the second vessel module.

"No sign of the ship, Overseer. It has not emerged from the other side, and we have no readings of it. It must have been destroyed."

"Most likely, yes. But you will remain here in case it somehow reemerges. I will expect daily reports. If the ship has not appeared again by the end of one week, you will return to base."

"Yes, Overseer."

"Sub-Overseer Mudat, report." Again, the reply was immediate—as expected. Caldon would tolerate nothing less.

"No sign of the ship here either, Overseer."

"Initiate linkage at once." There was no reason to leave the remaining two ships separate at this point.

"Yes, Overseer."

Caldon then turned his attention to his own sub-overseer. "As soon as the linkage is restored, we will depart. Set return course 36381. Set FTL at 15." At least he could tell Biron that he had disposed of the *da Vinci* for him. He might even be able to profit from that—surely Biron's sponsor would pay for the removal of such a persistent foe. And the fact that Biron had not accomplished the task himself would make it all the more sat-isfying.

"Okay, tell me the good news." Gold had finally given in to temptation and wandered up to the *Dancing Star*'s bridge, though he'd refused the command chair from Gomez—his was down in the hold, and sitting on this one wouldn't have felt right. Besides, she'd earned it.

"Two of the Androssi ships have left," Gomez replied.

"And the *Dancing Star* is holding up just fine," Stevens added from his station. Gold acknowledged that with a brief nod. It was true—the *da Vinci* was not experiencing any problems from the heat or radiation, and walking the corridors of this ship it had been a lit-tle warm but no worse than a spring day in San Fran-cisco.

"And the bad news?"

Gomez glanced away, and Tev took the opportunity to respond. "The third Androssi ship has remained behind, and has taken up a guard position just beyond the sun's outer corona." At least he didn't seem to be crowing about it—several times before the Tellarite had taken great pleasure in pointing out other people's mistakes. This time it seemed like he was just reporting the facts.

"Okay, so we've got one out of three left. That's not too bad. This ship can take him out, can't it?"

"Definitely," Stevens said. "But we can't risk it."

"Why not?" But he already knew the answer to that one, and held up a hand. "Let me guess—they've got an open comm line with the other two. So if we emerge and go after them, they'll have enough time to call it in before we can wipe them out."

"Right," Gomez said. "And those first two will come running back here. Plus, once they know this ship can survive in a sun, they won't be fooled twice. They'll just wait us out."

"How long can we stay in here?"

"Three-point-seven days," Tev said. "After that, the engines will suffer another overload and we will be forced to vent—a process that will incinerate all life within the *Dancing Star*."

Gold nodded. "Okay, so we've got one guy guarding us, he can call in reinforcements, and we can only sit here for a few days before we get deep-fat fried. Any more good news?"

"Well," Blue said, "at least power isn't a problem."

He considered glaring at her, but knew it wouldn't be worth it. Instead he turned back to Gomez and folded his arms. "All right, Gomez. You got us into the mess—get us out of it." He did smile a little to let her know that he wasn't really angry at her, but at the same time he wasn't going to let her off the hook here. Besides, if past experience was any indication, he knew she and her crew would think of something.

"What are we going to do, exactly?" Fabian tried to keep that from sounding like a complaint. He actually wasn't all that worried—they'd gotten out of situations worse than this before. Then he thought about the situation again, and decided that maybe they hadn't. But he was sure they'd find a way out again, as usual.

"We could take off when they aren't looking," Pattie said, but Tev shook his head.

"Their scanners have sufficient range to cover this

sun completely," he said. "Any movement would be spotted."

"And even if we could get clear without their seeing us," Sonya added, "without a slingshot this ship can only do warp two, max. They'd catch us."

"We could destroy them, though." Fabian waved aside Tev's look of scorn. "I know, I know—they'd call their buddies the minute they saw us move. Can we jam their signal?"

Soloman spoke up from his console. "Androssi systems are highly resistant to our interference, and with each new encounter they've upgraded to prevent previous methods from working."

"Right, hence Corsi's Androssi Protocols One, Two, and now Three," Sonya agreed. "Actually, that's not a bad idea." She tapped her combadge. "Corsi, can you beam up to the bridge, please?"

An instant later, the air next to Sonya shimmered, and Corsi appeared. Fabian was amused but not surprised to see that she was carrying a phaser rifle in addition to her usual type-1 phaser—even though the Androssi had never had a chance at getting onto this ship, their security chief believed in being prepared. He filed away a mental reminder to tease her about that later, when they were alone.

"Yes, Commander?" As usual, Corsi looked calm, collected, and ready to commit violence.

"We have a situation, Domenica, and I was hoping for your input." Sonya gestured at the forward screen— it was no longer split in half, and now showed a graph of the area around the star, including the red dot that was the Androssi ship. "That is the Androssi ship that's guarding us. We can't go after it because it'll just call its friends back. We can't run or it'll chase us—and call its friends back. And we can't just sit here, because the engines will overload eventually."

"In three-point-six-five days," Tev added. Sonya ignored him, a trick Fabian was still hoping to learn someday. Then again, it was easier for Sonya—she was Tev's commanding officer.

"So we need to take him out before he can send a message," Corsi said, and the others all nodded.

"Any ideas?"

Corsi smiled and sighted down her warp rifle, aiming it at the blip on the screen. "Of course, Commander. Taking out the bad guy is one of the things I do best."

Sub-Overseer Rando sat at the helm of his ship, watching the viewscreen. He was pleased that Caldon had given him this assignment instead of Mudat. Of course, circling a star in the hopes that some unknown ship had somehow survived diving into it was a waste of time. But that was Overseer Caldon's call, not his. If nothing had occurred by the end of a week, Rando would return and report, as ordered. If something did happen, he would be waiting and ready. Either way, he had done his job properly, and that would be reflected in his next promotion.

A brief flicker on the screen drew his attention. The surface of the sun was bubbling slightly, and a flicker shot out from it. On the screen it looked like a mere flame, but the computer showed the truth—that was a solar flare, easily a mile long and half that in width. It was impressive, certainly, but Rando had parked his ship five miles beyond the sun's corona, safely out of flare range.

"Any change?" he asked his crew, just to be thorough. They shook their heads.

"Still no life signs, Sub-Overseer," one of them reported. "And no activity not consistent with that of a star of this type."

"Very good." Rando sat back in his seat again and smiled. This would be an easy assignment. And when it was over, and he was back home, he—

Another bubbling occurred, and then grew. Even as Rando watched, still half-distracted, the bubbling erupted, and a massive tongue of flame shot forth. This was easily three times the size of the previous flare, and as he watched it, covered the screen—

—and Rando's last thought, as the solar flare engulfed his ship, was that perhaps Mudat had gotten the better assignment, after all.

"Nice shot, Corsi!"

Corsi nodded back and stepped away from the console. "Thank you, Commander."

Just then Gomez's combadge beeped, and they all heard Gold's voice. *"Gomez, report. What was the rumble we just felt?"*

Sonya smiled and tapped her badge to respond. "Good news, Captain. We've eliminated the Androssi ship. Coast is clear."

"Good. How did you do it?"

Sonya glanced over at Corsi, who was hefting her warp rifle again. "I asked Corsi for aid, sir. And she figured it out."

Gold's laugh came through clearly. *"Well, leave it to her to think of a way to shoot somebody while holed up in a sun. So, are you going to tell me the rest, or are you going to make me lie awake trying to figure it out?"*

Sonya gestured at Corsi, who shrugged and hit her own badge. "It was simple, Captain. This ship is built to absorb solar energy. We're inside a sun. So we're effectively invisible—their sensors would simply show solar activity while we were here. That meant we could move right up near the sun's surface and they still couldn't see us."

"Okay, but that's still a few miles from them. Even the guns Stevens rigged for this monster can't reach that far."

"No sir." Corsi smiled. "But its main engine can. We turned around and used the engine as a giant rifle. The blast looked just like a solar flare—which it basically is—and had more than enough range to destroy their ship. And it all happened too fast for them to react, much less send any messages."

"Nice work, Corsi. Now, Gomez, if we're all done here, let's take care of this ship once and for all. And I'd like to get the da Vinci *back where we can see the stars, if you don't mind."*

Shabalala glanced down at the command chair from the tactical station on the *da Vinci* bridge. "The *Dancing Star* has cleared the corona, Captain."

"Opening cargo bay doors," Haznedl added.

"Good." Gold leaned forward. "Wong, take us out of this beast, please."

"Yes, sir."

The *da Vinci*'s engines fired up, and the ship moved out of the hold and back into space. Gold couldn't help but sigh in relief. He wasn't normally claustrophobic, but having his entire ship inside another ship, and that ship inside a sun, had been a bit much. Being back out among the stars, where he could see their lights twinkling against the darkness, made him feel a lot better.

He tapped the comm unit on his chair. "Gomez, do you read me?"

Sonya replied quickly. *"Yes, Captain?"*

"The *da Vinci* is clear. How are you and your team doing down there?"

"Almost done, sir. Another ten minutes or so."

"Fine—let us know when you're ready."

Gold sat back and waited, and enjoyed the view. In what seemed like less than ten minutes—and, knowing this team, probably was—Gomez requested that she and her team be beamed up. Chief Poynter responded immediately, and reported to Gold a moment later that the full S.C.E. team was now back on board.

"Good. Mr. Wong, get us out of here, please. Set a course for Starbase 222."

"Yes, sir." And with that the *da Vinci* was moving again.

CHAPTER

12

"So it's all taken care of?" Gold asked as they gathered around the conference table again. Pattie thought he looked relieved, and it occurred to her that, for a starship captain, being confined and unable to see the stars was particularly torturous.

"Done deal," Fabian said, and the others nodded. "This time it won't be coming back."

Sonya explained further. "We disconnected the *Dancing Star*'s entire conductor array. All of the capacitors, the conduits, the crystals—everything. We couldn't take the hull off, since we were still floating along the corona's outer edge, but we did everything short of that."

"Which means it cannot power up again," Pattie added. "Then we vented all the energy in its cells, so the ship is now completely without power."

"I purged the computer systems," Soloman said.

"Nothing is left to start up again. I even removed the hardwired commands, like its directive to return home."

"And then we just beamed out and left it there." Gold glanced over at Fabian, and it occurred to Pattie that he might think Fabian was kidding. But one look at his face revealed what she already knew, that he was serious. This time.

"Wait a second, you left it there? Sitting on the outer edge of the sun, where anyone could beam on to it?" But the captain calmed down a moment later—perhaps because several of them were smiling.

"The sun's gravity has pulled the ship into its core," Tev said, even though Gold was already shaking his head. Of course, Pattie thought. He knows how gravity wells work—he just wasn't thinking about that at the moment.

"Has it been destroyed, then?"

Everyone glanced around, but no one answered. Finally, since no one had volunteered, Pattie spoke up. "We don't know, Captain. The *Dancing Star* was built to withstand the heat and energy of a sun. And even though we disconnected everything, its hull is intact. It could still be in there."

"It might always be in there," Fabian said. "Or at least as long as that sun survives."

"But it's definitely not going anywhere this time," Sonya added. "And nobody can get to it, unless they can already dive into a sun and survive—in which case they won't gain much from finding it."

"Well, at least it's not a threat anymore." Gold leaned back and looked around. "Did you bring back any of the pieces for study?"

Pattie couldn't help wriggling her antennae in excitement. "Of course. We have one of the crystals from the engine, and one of the capacitors, and one of the energy panes it used. Plus a sample of the hull, and the recording Soloman made of the computer systems."

Gold laughed. "Well, that ought to keep you all pretty busy, then." He stood to go. "Good work, team. I'll let Captain Scott know that the universe is safe from at least one runaway star."

"Penny for your thoughts, Commander?" Most of the others had filed out, but Sonya looked up to discover Fabian, Pattie, and Soloman standing before her.

"Sorry, Fabe, just lost in thought." She smiled a little. "I was just thinking about—well, about how funny life is."

"You don't seem to be laughing." Pattie's observation did make Sonya laugh, at least a little.

"No, not funny that way. More funny-odd. I mean, here is this ship, this amazing ship, and what do we do with it? We send it into a sun where no one can touch it." She sighed. "Plus it's a ship we've already seen once before, and now we're dealing with it again."

Fabian and Pattie exchanged glances. "Actually, Commander, we were thinking about that too, Pattie and I." Fabian sat down next to her. "The three of us"—he included Pattie and Soloman with a wave of his hand"—were on the original team. We thought we'd figured this ship out and shut it down, and now here it comes all over again. We couldn't help feeling like it was a ghost from our past."

"An old mistake, come back to haunt us," Pattie said. "And we wondered if, since we got it wrong the first time, we had any hope of figuring it out the second time."

"Especially since . . . we aren't who we were then." Soloman looked sad, and Sonya knew that this mission had hurt him at least as much as it had her. She'd been reminded of Kieran, but he had been reminded of 111, and they had actually been on this mission together, whereas she had not even been part of the team yet.

"But we couldn't have fixed this one without any of you." She looked at each of them in turn. "All of you contributed to this, and came up with things Tev and I didn't. We needed the fresh perspective, yes, but we also needed your ability to look back at it and see it again with more experienced eyes."

"I . . . was embarrassed," Soloman admitted quietly. "Embarrassed that 111 and I had missed that emergency protocol before. And I felt that I was tainting her memory by revealing that she and I had made a mistake." He lifted his head and met her gaze, and Sonya saw a strength there that she'd seen slowly growing since Venus. "But her memory is still there. We made a mistake, but now we've corrected it. And I don't think we, she and I together, would have caught the mistake this time, either. I think I caught it because I am no longer 110. I am Soloman. I have changed—grown—and that's made a difference."

"Pattie and I may not have changed so profoundly," Fabian said with a smile, "but we feel the same way. We were less experienced, less crafty. It's not that we were fools, just that we may not have had the tools we needed back then. Now we do. We're all better than we were before."

"And part of that," Pattie added, antennae waving gently, "is because we're part of this team. The old group was strong, but this one—this one is stronger."

"I know," Sonya said softly. "And it bothers me a little. As much as I hate to admit it, Kieran couldn't have done the things Tev did. Not that Kieran wasn't wonderful, and a great engineer, but his mind worked differently. We needed Tev for this."

"And we needed you," Pattie said. "You looked at the problem from a different perspective than Salek did, and saw what he missed."

Sonya stood, and Fabian did as well, the four of them clustering together. Like a group—like a family. "I think," she said slowly, discovering it as she spoke, "that I could see it because Salek had laid the groundwork for me. Because all of you had. He set things up, and that let me come in now and figure it out from there."

Fabian laughed, "You know, hindsight usually only works if it's your own."

Sonya met his laugh with one of her own. "Well, maybe, but on this team we share so much anyway, what's one more thing?" Then she shook her head and smiled. "I do feel good about it, though. I feel like this was a chapter in this crew's history, and we helped close it properly. And maybe now Salek"—she felt her eyes tearing up slightly, and this time chose not to fight it— "and Kieran and 111 and McAllan and Feliciano and Drew and Barnak and all the others who have gone before can finally rest properly, knowing that we've put it all to rights."

"Well," Pattie replied with a tinkle, "I don't know about all of it. What have we left to work on, then?"

"Not to worry, Pattie," Fabian told her as the four of them headed toward engineering. "I'm sure we'll find something."

THE DEMON

Loren L. Coleman & Randall N. Bills

CHAPTER
1

Captain S'linth tasted the air. The bridge of the Resaurian ship *Dutiful Burden* smelled of fear-sweat and musk. The hard plates inside his mouth secreted digestive juices that burned with an acidic taste at the back of his throat.

He stepped to the fore of the bridge, within striking distance of the massive viewing screen. Trusting his crew to navigate the spit, S'linth allowed himself a moment to stare into the Demon's face. Oblivion stared back. The maw opened wide as the Resaurian ship descended, the Demon snarling at the stars above, showing its hatred for all life. His *Burden* trembled as a new wave broke over the bow.

"Ten *ris*-units and closing, Captain," said First Navigator Th'osh. "Gravimetric tides are increasing. Perhaps we should make our offering now."

An idea that would not sit well with the ship's Council-appointed overseer. Looking back, he saw Suliss stir, rising out of his self-induced torpor.

S'linth pouched his neck muscles. "Your scales are dry, Th'osh," he snapped at the navigator. "Control your fear, or slither back to your quarters. Tradition dictates our offering to be given at no farther away than two *ris*-units."

Calming, Suliss nodded. Among Resaurians, tradition held the full weight of law. Th'osh bowed his head, nictitating membranes rolling over black eyes in a gesture of submission. "My apologies." The ship shook again, and Th'osh thumped his tail against the deck.

"Accepted," S'linth told him, not wanting to ruin the Resaurian by frightening him out of service. Th'osh was young, barely over his second adult shedding. By comparison, the soft scales on S'linth's belly were larger and darker than the armored ones on Th'osh's back. The youthful navigator had several centuries of life to look forward to, and would live better helping to maintain the small Resaurian fleet than he would coiled up in a planetside nest.

"Any other difficulties?" S'linth asked. His obsidian gaze roamed the bridge.

Only his communications officer, Lyssis, met his gaze. "I am still detecting the subspace signal on our emergency bands."

He faced back toward the front of the bridge. The signal again. It had bothered him ever since breaking orbit over Resaurus. An inconstant, open subspace signal. This was *new*. New always presented a problem. "No modulation?"

"No intelligent modulation, Captain. It continues to act like an open channel, except for the slowly shifting tone."

"It is outside of tradition," Suliss whispered. "Ignore it. We will make our offering, and return home."

But S'linth refused to ignore anything that might prove a hazard. Space travel was not for the hidebound. He continued to consider possibilities. A beacon. A nonstandard beacon, since the tone was not quite constant and would break off at irregular periods. An energy signature, warped by the gravimetric forces. Something about it felt familiar, but nothing S'linth could find in the traditions offered any help.

"Continue to monitor," he ordered. "Science station, prepare the offering."

The bridge crew functioned automatically, many following the traditional course of actions they had learned by rote. Science announced that the offering was ready. Navigation called down the distance as the *Dutiful Burden* crawled carefully out over the Demon's maw. This cycle, S'linth planned to take his *Burden* to zero *ris*-units. As the vessel eased to a halt over the promontory, he crossed arms over his scaly chest and spoke the Council's words.

"May our offering ease any suffering, shine hope in the darkness, and keep the forces within banished for another cycle."

Science station launched the Resaurians' offering as S'linth finished the traditional speech. A crash of metal against metal leaked up through the deck, followed by an electrical scream as the firing mechanism shoved the duranium-encased load out into space. On the viewscreen, it looked like a giant, faceted-nose bullet being shot down the mouth of the Demon.

Something . . .

"Tracking," Th'oth announced, busying himself with sensors feed. "Good signal. It looks as if the offering will be accepted with favor." He paused. "Signal is flattening out. Signal is constant." Softly, but not so softly that S'linth could not hear, the young Resaurian said, "Now we can get away from here."

Signal is constant!

S'linth coiled about, turning his back on the Demon. Weak legs pushed out from his belly to form a tripod with his thick tail, giving him greater stability. He pointed one muscular arm at his communications officer. "The subspace signal! The beacon. Over what range does it vary?"

Lyssis recoiled, then turned her gaze back to her panel. "Over what time?" she asked.

"Since leaving Resaurus."

"No more than twenty-five percent, plus or minus."

Slowly, he turned back around to stare into the abyss. The Demon stared back. "And it repeats. In between breaks, it must repeat."

"It shows no pattern in between breaks," Lyssis said, checking the logs. "No, wait. I see a repeating pattern between the fifth and eleventh, and the sixth and twelfth recurrence. And . . . now between the first and fifteenth. Captain? What does that mean?"

Suliss watched him intently, no doubt ready to argue that tradition demanded they return home. Now. S'linth tasted the air, and the fear-sweat was stronger. Once his people learned that the Demon was speaking to them, the scent would be overpowering. But tradition demanded that he tell his crew.

And tradition was law.

He nodded at the viewscreen. "I know what this is."

CHAPTER
2

"I know what this is," Sonya Gomez said, pulling her padd out of Tev's meaty hands. "I don't need help."

Having rescued her work from the Tellarite, Sonya carried it over to one of the *da Vinci*'s science workstations and relaxed into a chair, stretching her legs out, not caring that she blocked part of the aisle. She usually enjoyed the bridge during beta shift. On tired evenings when she wasn't studying the latest journals released from the Daystrom Institute, she often wandered up. Ensign Joanne Piotrowski was the duty tactical officer, and the two of them got on fairly well.

Sonya should have read more into the deadpan face Jo gave her when the turbolift doors whisked open, and never gotten off.

"I only commented that it looked familiar."

Mor glasch Tev had followed her. Hands clasped behind his back, with his monk's fringe of dark hair and frosted beard, he looked like one of her old Starfleet instructors about to deliver a lecture. The *da Vinci*'s second officer certainly never showed reluctance in offering his opinion. The fact that Sonya outranked him as ship's first officer and head of the onboard S.C.E. team did little to dissuade the Tellarite.

"Fascinating quantum degradation."

"I don't appreciate people reading over my shoulder either." She glanced up at him. "What I'm trying to say, in the nicest possible manner, Tev, is that I'd like to work on this *solo*."

If the Tellarite was capable of showing chagrin, she had yet to see it in his short time aboard ship. His porcine features were perfect for smugness, though. Or well trained for it.

The maddening thing was that, in general, she approved of Tev trying to be more of a team player. He'd started nicely on that road during the salvage of the *Dancing Star*. Now, though, he was going too far in the other direction, trying to be part of the team when she just wanted to be left on her own.

"All right. Let me know when you catch up." He snuffled. "But I'm guessing that signal has been bouncing around in subspace for close to one hundred years." He shuffled off with the air of a disappointed instructor who had just seen a promising student fail her first lesson.

Hah! This was actually a continuous signal being broadcast from only eighteen light-years distance. By subspace standards, that was barely next door. She considered pointing that out, but Tev was already back at another station working on whatever personal project he'd been on when Sonya arrived. Interpersonal Skills Assessment, maybe? She wondered what his face would show after receiving a big, fat "fail." The way Tev acted, you would swear he had never failed at anything his entire life. Well, maybe he hadn't.

Until now.

She wanted to point out Tev's mistake to someone. Not just for the petty pleasure it would give her, but it might go a long way to begin making him more tolerable to the crew. Little mistakes might help ease everyone into that transition.

Except that most of the second-shift crew were stringently watching their own consoles. No one had wanted to draw the Tellarite's attention, apparently, content to let their first officer act as the lightning rod. Only Rennan Konya from security met her gaze, and the Betazoid would already know her surface thoughts, wouldn't he?

Konya nodded, then waggled his head from side to side as if unsure whether or not to agree with her previous line of thought.

So much for that. She climbed out of her chair for a quick trip by the replicator, tucked her padd under one arm while making her selection. "Hot tea, Earl Grey."

With a light hum, the replicator materialized a bone china mug filled to the brim with her steaming beverage. She picked it up, warming both hands around the mug, blew steam from the top and sipped carefully. Perfect.

The Betazoid glanced over at her. "That's not hot chocolate, is it?"

From the other side of the security, Tev snuffled. "You are two meters closer than I. You must have heard her order. It is Earl Grey tea."

Sonya groaned. Her run-in with Captain Picard—quite literally—had taken on all the hallmarks of

Starfleet legend. *Yes,* she had spilled hot chocolate all over the captain of Starfleet's flagship while serving aboard the *Enterprise. Yes,* she had taken to drinking Earl Grey—Picard's favorite—as penance, and then discovered how much she liked it. Some days it had seemed the entire galaxy was bent on making her remember that awkward encounter, but the ribbing finally ran its course.

Then Galvan VI happened.

Two dozen crew replacements and months of grieving later, Sonya now wasn't certain what was worse: that the hot chocolate incident had resurfaced as a running joke among the crew, or that Tev couldn't even appreciate the humor.

She walked back to her station via security. "For a Betazoid," she told Konya, "you're pretty insensitive at times."

"Why do you think I opted for security?"

Of course, Sonya knew that wasn't really the truth. Rennan made a great security officer precisely because he was sensitive, in every sense of the definition.

Sipping her tea, letting the light brew slide down her throat, Sonya fell back to task, analyzing the signal the *da Vinci* had pulled out of subspace. She double- and triple-checked her results, chewed on her bottom lip for several minutes, and then kicked herself back out of the chair to find Tev.

The Tellarite was comparing the technical specifications of Romulan and Klingon cloaking shields. A little light reading, no doubt.

"Ninety-three years," she told him without preamble.

"Ah. Well, I only had a glance at the data, after all."

Sonya shrugged her apology. "The data is in the computer. You could have pulled a copy for yourself."

Tev turned away from his viewer, looking at her with his deep-set black eyes for a very long moment. "You are my superior officer. You made it clear—doubly so—that you did not desire my help."

"Right." She turned back for her chair, caught herself. No, dammit. She'd build a bridge over this river if it killed her. "Except we both see ninety-three years of degradation, according to the quantum shift, and the signal originates only eighteen light-years distant."

She had Tev's attention. He scowled. Another expression for which his heavy-jowled face was tailor-made. "The data does not make sense."

"That's what I'm saying."

Tapping commands into the touch-sensitive console, Tev brought up the communications logs and a variety of sensor readings. "Let us see if we can find your mistake," he said.

Sonya gritted her teeth.

But Tev could not find a way to reconcile the data either. A minor victory, and one that did not appear to sit well with the overachieving Tellarite. "Can we reconstruct the original signal?" he asked, a touch of wounded pride to his voice.

"I've been trying to do that," Sonya said. "At five hundred percent compression the signal approaches something that might be an audio waveform, though it's too far gone for the universal translator to match up with any known language files." She dumped her padd work back to the main computer and pulled up audio at Tev's station. It sounded like a lot of hissing, broken apart by a lot of static.

She supposed it could have been the other way around just as easily.

"Computer," Tev said. "Return to original signal. Repair using the Telek System and then recompress five hundred percent. Search language files and translate."

"Telek?"

"Romulan," Tev told her, and managed to do it in a way that suggested she should already know. "He made contact with *Voyager* several years ago. Through a wormhole. I told you the signal looked familiar."

"*Ready,*" the computer answered.

"Begin playback," Sonya snapped, annoyed at Tev all over again.

A wash of static burst from the station, followed by a raspy, metallic tone. "... *ellllf ... aussz ...*"

Sonya leaned in. If she had heard right ... "Computer, compress another twenty-five percent. Begin playback."

Close enough. The static was a sharper, more painful burst, but the voice clearer. "... *help uz ...*"

They had the attention of the entire beta-shift bridge crew. "Help us," Tev repeated, loudly.

Sonya nodded. "We have a distress call," she said, then tapped a lighted square on her console to summon Captain Gold.

CHAPTER
3

Captain David Gold had never been prone to nightmares, but the one he raggedly clawed his way out of left him gasping for air. Not trusting himself to speak for a moment, he remained in his darkened quarters, his deep, faltering breaths creating strange echoes that only heightened his uneasiness.

"Lights on," he finally managed and blinked rapidly several times as his quarters flooded with light. Though not large by any stretch of the imagination—he could cross corner to corner in about six quick strides, provided he didn't bump into his small desk or the bed—its familiarity nonetheless began to calm his nerves.

Glancing at the chronometer, he saw that its uncaring surface displayed 0300 hours; he'd only been asleep an hour.

Slipping his legs out from under the covers, Gold sat on the edge and rubbed both hands vigorously across his face, as though the effort would scrub away the last vestiges of the nightmare. He stopped when he realized that it still felt as though someone else were rubbing half his face. They'd told him that the hand replacement was almost a perfect match and that his mind and body would quickly come to accept it as his own. Yet, months later, on mornings like these, he could still tell. Holding out his hands, he saw they were still shaking.

"*Gevalt*," he said and slowly stood up. His wife Rachel might need multiple cups of tea, but once he was up, there was no going back for hours.

After a quick shower and shave he returned fully dressed and sat at his desk. "Viewscreen on," he said, and perused crew reports and duty rosters for the coming days on the small desk-mounted console. He continued on for some minutes before the realization struck that he was hiding from his nightmare. With disgust he turned off the screen and faced what had awakened him so early; he'd never backed away from the truth and he was not about to start now.

His granddaughter was just fine. There simply was no reason to believe otherwise. For a moment he pondered the possibility of actually contacting Rachel back on Earth, but then realized the ludicrousness of such an act. He couldn't help but smile at the thought of the ribbing his wife would give him for such a call. For a rabbi, Rachel had a mean streak in her. Better to face a Breen armada than years of that kind of torture, regardless of its good-natured fun.

But if Esther had been hurt . . . or was sick . . . No. Rachel would contact him at once.

A chime sounded, interrupting his debate. "*Gomez to Gold.*"

Clearing his voice with a rusty cough, he put on his

captain's voice and tapped his combadge. "Gold here. What's up, Gomez?"

"Sir, we have a distress call."

"I'm on my way," he said.

Looked like there was something to be doing after all.

Both Gomez and Tev were on the bridge when Gold arrived; as usual, his best officers were already on the case.

"What do we have, Gomez?" he asked before he'd even finished stepping onto the bridge.

Gomez punched up the signal and let it do the talking for her.

Static. Then, *"We are trapped inside the Demon. We are running low on resources. Help us."*

"The Demon." Gold tapped a finger against his chin. "Nebula? Plasma storm?"

Sonya glanced at Tev, then admitted something that was obviously difficult for the both of them. "We don't know."

"Well, it's a distress call. Why aren't we moving?" Another captain might already be reprimanding his crew for negligence, but he'd come too far and been through too much with the remaining crew after Galvan VI not to trust their judgment. Especially Gomez. If they weren't moving yet, she had a good reason.

"Because there is some doubt about its validity. It has a quantum flux that's right off the charts."

As usual, he waited for Gomez to continue; he knew when she had something further she wanted to say, but had not yet figured out how best to present it to a nonengineer. He stifled a yawn that threatened to crack his composure; he hid it behind a scratch of the nose and a quick glance around the bridge at beta shift's watch officers, who all looked calm.

He had a feeling that would change in a hurry.

Like he'd had a feeling that his granddaughter was in trouble?

"There's a resonating . . . no, more like a multiphase gradient to the signal that is causing the computer to determine that the signal, well . . . is about ninety-three years old . . . give or take a few months."

"Why is that so unusual?" Even in a quadrant filled with almost real-time subspace communications, there were still enough prewarp sentient races out there to have standard radio signals (some of which were distress calls) still crisscrossing the void with regularity.

"Because it's a subspace signal," Tev said with his usual bluntness.

Now that was unusual. Subspace made for almost real-time space communications. To discover one that the computer actually tagged as being a century old . . . didn't make much sense at all. He had a vague recollection of a course in the Academy where the professor had droned on and on about the theory of a subspace signal retaining its cohesion and field strength in a self-renewing loop that would allow it to travel across quadrants, if not across the entire disc of the galaxy.

Could they have stumbled across such a signal, originally from an unimaginable distance away at the outer rim of the farthest side of the Milky Way?

As he continued to look at Gomez, he realized she had something more to say and was waiting for him to assimilate the first bit of news. He was never sure whether this habit of hers annoyed him or amused him.

He quirked an eyebrow. "What's the rest of it?"

"The signal degradation puts the point of origin at only eighteen light-years away." She glanced down at the screen as though to verify the information once more.

"Even I know that doesn't make any sense, Gomez." He moved to his chair and immediately began to warm up to the problem. "What do we know about the region of space around the point of origin?"

"The sector is designated 221-H. It is close to the recently fallen Thallonian Empire," Tev spoke up as though the question had been cast for his ears alone. Gold saw a flicker of annoyance wash across Gomez's features and vanish as quickly. Tev, while continuing to speak, was not even looking in their direction. "It is a region of space the Federation has not been welcome in for very long. I believe there are now two Federation starships assigned to the area."

"The *Excalibur* and *Trident*," Gold said. "And they're hip-deep in local politics. Anything else?"

"Tellar dispatched a science vessel toward this sector to study astronomical anomalies, which is as detailed as the Starfleet report gets on the subject. But they will not arrive on station for another six months or more."

"So we know virtually nothing about this sector. No Federation outposts or colonies, and the region's littered with astronomical anomalies that have so far defied the Federation's ability to define. Would that sum it up, Tev?"

"That is correct, sir. Until the Tellarite vessel arrives."

If one thought about it in the right light, such comments were almost amusing. Gold glanced at Gomez, and saw that she hadn't found this new way of thinking yet.

"What about the message itself? What language did it arrive in?"

"The language banks mark it as Resaurian." Tev shrugged. "There are no immediate references available in the computer's archives."

"Well, regardless, it's a distress signal and we're obligated to respond. Even if we end up being one hundred years too late."

"Nintey-three," Tev reminded him.

Gold swiveled his chair toward the Tellarite. "Yes, of course." He swiveled back. "Rusconi, set a course for that destination point, maximum warp."

The conn officer answered with a professional, "Yes, Captain." She adjusted their course with efficient movements. Gold took a moment to glance out the forward viewscreen. Stars chased themselves through the slipstream wash. He hoped he never tired of the beauty of warp speed.

He turned back toward Gomez but as usual, she was already ahead of him.

"I've already got my people working. Carol and Bart are digging into the computer, looking for any files related to the Resaurians. Fabian has a theory that the signal itself may have been caught in a subspace-generated stasis field that only recently ruptured, allowing the signal to continue. I'm not so sure that is the case." She glanced at Tev, almost as though waiting for him to interrupt. "The quantum degradation is simply wrong for . . . um . . ."

Gold knew that he was becoming very adept at appearing to be interested in the technobabble of his engineers, but with Gomez, he just couldn't seem to fool her no matter how often he tried.

"Sorry Captain," she interrupted herself with a slight

shake of her head. "We'll get right to work, and see what answers we can pull in for you before we arrive."

"Thank you, Gomez."

With that, she departed with Tev in tow and Gold moved with purpose. He needed to inform Starfleet that they'd be delayed in their current mission.

CHAPTER
4

Sonya shook her head. Amazing the difference only a few hours can make.

Rather than the quiet annoyance of sharing beta shift with Tev, the *da Vinci*'s bridge was now full of activity and energy. Alpha crew, alerted to the situation, had taken over early. Domenica Corsi stood guard over security, pulling down files on every known race from this corner of the Alpha Quadrant, searching for threats and discussing quietly with her deputy chief Vance Hawkins, Rennan Konya, and the tactical officer, Anthony Shabalala. Songmin Wong helmed the ship, and Susan Haznedl sat next to him at ops. They were still engaged in their mental game of tri-D chess, whispering moves back and forth when they assumed Captain Gold wasn't listening.

At least they were accomplishing something.

Sonya and her team had spent several hours trying to

pull additional information out of the signal, all to no avail. The best they'd managed was to clean up the audio, and being able to drop the transient intermodulation distortion to zero was no consolation.

Her one bright spot should have come with seeing Tev just as frustrated, but he never wavered. Tellarites supposedly wore their emotions on their sleeves, but either she simply couldn't register his agitation or he hid it well. He was still certain that he would figure it out before they arrived (and likely before anyone else). It wore very thin on Sonya.

Fortunately, she finally had something new to report. "I'm starting to measure appreciable gravimetric waves." She quickly ran through several algorithmic models to verify what she already knew. "They are centered on the signal's origin."

Gold nodded, glanced at Tev. "Astronomical anomalies."

Or something. Sonya glanced again at a side monitor and was surprised at her findings. She'd allowed the computer to continue running models of what they might find, but the primary screen was displaying an increase in gravimetric waves that dwarfed her models; her parameters had simply been too small. They were increasing now at an exponential rate!

"Captain, we may have—"

She was interrupted by a severe jolt as the *da Vinci* suddenly dropped out of warp, unscheduled. Crew members grabbed for armrests, for the edge of panels, as the inertial dampers failed. Sonya caught herself against the command pit railing. She saw Anthony Shabalala sit back with a gash bleeding over his right eye.

Gold had stuck to the captain's chair as if strapped in.

Now he was up, moving fast, standing over his conn officer. "Wong, what just happened?"

The conn officer was already bent over his panel, fingers flying over the interface. "No idea. One moment we're fine, and the next we're at impulse."

Sonya bounced back to her station. "We hit a gravity well. Those gravimetric waves were merely on the leading edge of it." She chewed her lower lip, trying to make sense of the data streaming across her viewer. The captain was waiting on her. "Maybe a rogue planet, or a cosmic superstring . . ." Something with enough gravity to drag them out of warp.

"Damage report?" Gold asked, stabbing a direct look back to Shabalala as the ship trembled again.

The tactical officer shook his head. "Nothing major, Captain. Reports of minor injuries so far."

"Distance to signal origin?"

Haznedl checked sensors. "Estimated one hundred fifty million kilometers, approaching at one-quarter impulse."

"*Captain.*" Nancy Conlon interrupted from engineering. "*Warp drive has been knocked offline. I'm reading severe gravimetric wave buildup. It's interfering with the containment field.*"

"Looks like we've found your astronomical anomaly, Tev." When no response was forthcoming, Sonya looked over to find Tev still as a statue, his head barely moving as he glanced between the viewscreen and his own tricorder. She wondered why he'd use a tricorder instead of simply tapping into the *da Vinci*'s sensors through another work station.

"Lieutenant Conlon." Tev lowered his tricorder, typed some input. "We appear to be approaching some type of anomaly that is emanating massive gravimetric waves.

Their concentration is beyond the scope of what we originally believed as we entered the region."

He didn't look in her direction, but Sonya still felt the sting of a reprimand. Who said Tellarites can't be subtle? She redoubled her efforts and began running additional simulations, expanding her parameters.

"When will you have warp drive back online?" Gold asked Conlon.

"I'm not sure, Captain. A warp containment field can act pretty crazy around gravimetric waves of sufficient force. I'll give you an update in an hour, but the best course of action would be to get us away from the problem."

"That is not a possibility yet, Conlon. I'll let you know as soon as I can comply with that request." A slight tone of humor crept into the captain's voice.

"I'm sure you will, sir. Engineering out."

Sonya clenched her fists as the simulation she ran failed to match what they were experiencing. Perhaps she was simply looking at it wrong. She'd increased her parameters significantly but that didn't have the effect she was looking for either.

Start at the basics. She began poring over the readings coming in. The gravimetric waves were increasing. Right. Was anything else increasing? Background radiation? Any neutrino spikes? What wasn't she seeing?

Suddenly she realized why she was clenching her fists. She took a deep breath and called out, "Tev, what have you got?"

She might as well have been talking to the wall. He continued to input data into his tricorder.

"Tev!" she called in as close to a shout as she'd had to use with any subordinate in years. Gold glanced sharply in her direction, and Sonya's ears burned.

Tev finally looked over. "Yes, Commander?" he asked, a placid look on his gruff face.

She gritted her teeth. Did he truly not hear her before, or was he just now willing to listen? She unclenched her fists slowly. She would make this work.

"What have you got?" She began fresh, trying to immerse herself fully into the problem, leaving behind, for now, any problems with Tev. "I've been running simulations and they simply aren't generating what we're seeing. We should expect to see energy level increases across the board with this much gravimetric force washing through."

"Commander, there is no increase elsewhere." He paused for a moment, as though waiting for an answer. Then he shrugged. "There is a significant decrease, however."

"What?" she asked, startled that she had not delved into that possibility.

Tev stepped over to her station and passed his tricorder to her. She noticed immediately that it was not standard issue, but had been altered subtly; it operated as a remote station, tapped directly into the full power of the *da Vinci*'s sensors. Impressive work, actually.

"The ambient energy level in the entire region is draining off. There's also a spectral distortion that we've just picked up, centered on the signal's point of origin."

Sonya finally understood. Of course her simulations were failing. Regardless of how many times she'd increased the parameters, they'd not be increased enough. Not by a long shot.

"Captain," she said, wondering why Tev had not spoken up as he'd obviously figured it out before she had. She made a quick decision; it may not matter to Tev in the slightest, but it mattered to her. "Sir, Tev's figured out what we're up against."

"Of course," Tev said, as though answering her.

She fought against grinding her teeth. She'd given it to him and he'd pushed it in her face. Sonya tried to relax. Just his way. Captain's waiting.

"Looks like the signal is originating from a black hole."

CHAPTER
5

The *da Vinci* rocked slightly, buffeted by gravimetric forces, as Mor glasch Tev stomped into the briefing room. He was aware of every pair of eyes that glanced at him in that uncertain way humans (and so many humanoid races) used to prejudge what they did not understand. They were already making assumptions that would never hold up under direct evidence. Relying on prejudice over scientific method.

Carol Abramowitz glanced back toward the door. "Glad you could make it, Tev."

Bartholomew Faulwell, sitting next to the cultural specialist, eating from a pile of individually wrapped candies, smiled. On the other side of the long table the Nasat, P8 Blue, chittered in her way of approximating human laughter.

He did not bother to consult a chronometer. "I am

four minutes early," he stated clearly. Abramowitz flushed, and shifted uncomfortably in her seat.

Captain Gold half rose from his chair at the table's head. "It's a figure of speech, reserved for when someone is late, *or* is the last to arrive."

Tev snuffled at the air, the Tellarite equivalent of a sigh. "I shall make a note of that, Captain."

"Please do. No need to get your back up over a simple pleasantry."

His back wasn't up over anything. He had just said that he would try harder, hadn't he? He would not even complain that Fabian Stevens had taken Tev's seat across from Sonya Gomez. He would save instruction for later, when he could speak with Stevens alone. He grabbed the empty chair in between Faulwell and Chief of Security Corsi.

With a nod from the captain, Gomez rose and stood at the front of the room. Stevens brought up the latest scans on the black hole, including what the S.C.E. team had found inside. Tev all but felt his mind *twist*. It looked odd, even in a universe as varied as one that could produce cities encased in static warp bubbles and warheads to ignite gas giants into small stars. Such challenges there still were to confront!

"As near as we can tell," Gomez began as very rough schematics flashed up on the screen. They showed a wedge-shaped construction that displaced two cubic kilometers of vacuum. "The distress call originates from this station that we located *inside* the black hole, which we're currently calling the Demon—the name from the transmission."

The screen froze, pulled down into the bottom right corner, and was replaced by magnified images of the *da*

Vinci's approach to the black hole. A large dark circle expanded in the center. The stars around its circumference warped away at improbable speeds, as if reflected over a concave surface.

Which, in effect, they were.

"Am I seeing double?" Faulwell asked. "There's a diamond-pattern of stars in the upper-left quadrant, and a smaller set just like it to the Demon's lower-right?"

Of course, as a cryptographer, Faulwell would be adept at recognizing patterns and repetitions. Tev knew about the effect, but the language specialist had beaten him to seeing it. Inexcusable. "That is an illusionary effect known as an Einstein Ring. What you see is light from the same four stars, pulled around the far side of the black hole. You will see a better example in just a moment."

The star field slowed its expansion. "Ten thousand kilometers," Sonya intoned. Now the *da Vinci* crawled forward. A moment later it stopped. "Five thousand. This is highly magnified. As large as this singularity is, about one hundred times the solar mass of Earth's sun, its photon sphere is only nine hundred kilometers in diameter."

Several stars looked bloated, highly magnified from being dragged around the back side of the Demon, which stared straight ahead like the dead eye of some malicious entity.

The same metaphor suggested itself to Abramowitz, who shivered. "I keep waiting for it to blink," she said.

The sky shifted as most stars tracked to the left. "The *da Vinci*," Gomez continued her narration, "orbiting the Demon." Her voice held a touch of awe, and Tev could hardly blame her. "At this distance, we're fighting approximately six hundred gravities to maintain station."

Marvelous. Tev noted several tense reactions around the table, though no one could tear their eyes away from the screen. It was an odd sky, the kind most explorers never dreamed of seeing (nor wanted to). The stars continued to track left, most of them, bending outward to flow around either side of the black hole. Except in a thin ring surrounding the void where the mirror images trapped in the first Einstein Ring counterrotated in the exact opposite direction.

The vessel finally came to rest, and the sky remained stable.

The table was silent for a moment, everyone lost in their own thoughts. There was a space station down inside that hell. What would they see? What kind of technology permitted them to survive? Tev's hands itched to find out.

"This space station?" Dr. Lense asked. She sat at the other end of the table, and had remained very silent up to now. She often had just as much trouble following the engineer's explanations as Faulwell, or Gold. "By 'inside,' you mean falling into?"

Gomez shook her head. "No. It is definitely anchored within the photon sphere, at approximately one-point-three Schwarzschild radii." Lense frowned and Sonya explained further. "A Schwarzschild radius is equal to the radius of the black hole's event horizon—the point where gravity goes to infinity. The photon sphere is where light can no longer escape, at one-point-five radii." She smiled grimly. "That is the point where, if you look along the plane of the Einstein Ring, light would be perfectly bent around the black hole and you could see the back of your own head."

The concept weighed heavily over the room for a few seconds. Faulwell skated a candy across the table to

Lense. He pushed another over in front of the Tellarite. "So if this station is within the photon sphere, how can we see it?" he asked.

Tev ignored the candy and stifled the urge to lecture. It was not his discovery. Even though the process had been fairly rudimentary. Gomez nodded to Stevens, who took up the narrative from his seat.

"Probes. We threw one in orbit around the Demon, and then sent it and another into its mouth. Our subspace connection deteriorated rapidly, but by forming a kind of relay system from Probe One to Probe Two and back to the *da Vinci*, we managed to get those basic images. They also helped us pinpoint the gravitational anchor."

Tev could not take it anymore. His large hand trapped the candy Faulwell had slid in front of him just to have something on which to concentrate. A twist of cellophane dumped out a greenish rock of square candy. "An anchor had to exist," he said, looking at the strange emerald in the palm of his hand, "or the station would have fallen into the event horizon decades ago. Even accounting for time dilation."

Gomez nodded. "Right," she said, stealing back the floor. "Of course, there was another large sign, when we finally noticed. The gravimetric waves. You would expect them to radiate out in a fairly uniform manner. But they don't." She tapped the console in front of her, and the display shifted into a bluish tint. The black hole roiled with energy. Now it looked more like a mouth, chewing.

"This is the Hawking radiation evaporating off the Demon. It shows a large disturbance centered here"—she pointed it out with a wave of her hand—"where there is a discontinuity in the tidal forces. The station is somehow anchored to space far outside of the photon sphere, which has kept it safe. It has also created a mostly stable channel for approaching the station where the gravitational pull is far less than it should be."

"How much less?" Lense asked.

Gomez's voice was very small. "Somewhere around the order of one point five million gravities, as you approach the photon sphere."

"And the gravimetric waves?" Gold asked, bringing them back on topic.

"Backsplash," Tev said. Gomez glared at him, and he popped the candy into his mouth.

"Backsplash is actually a good way to look at it," she allowed. "Take an ocean tide, rolling waves near an atoll. One of those waves starts to shallow, and crest, and then strikes a large rocky protuberance."

Apple flavor washed the inside of Tev's mouth as the candy began to slowly dissolve. Tart. Almost sour. "Momentum has a lot of force to it when interrupted," he said, adding to Sonya's explanation. Why not? He had tumbled to the source of the gravimetric waves before her, after all. His mouth puckered as the taste built up, and he swallowed, catching the candy between his teeth to hold on to it. Remarkable.

"Apple Rancher," Faulwell said, leaning aside to whisper the candy's name. He skated one to P8 Blue, who declined. Abramowitz grabbed it instead—the cultural specialist went through them like, well, like candy.

Captain Gold leaned back into his chair, steepling his fingers in front of him as he looked at some point on the wall over Tev's head. "So we are proceeding on the assumption that this was a deliberate attempt to place some kind of outpost—a research station perhaps—inside a black hole. But now something has gone wrong?"

Abramowitz nodded. "Details on the Resaurians are sketchy. A few brief mentions in some corrupted old logs of a pre-Federation Earth ship captain named Archer, and not much else. Without more cultural details to go on, a research station seems the most logical choice. Except—"

"Except what?" Gold pounded on her hesitation right away.

"Well, the images we have of the station itself. I spoke with Pattie earlier," she nodded to P8 Blue, "and there don't seem to be any escape pods. Near as we can tell."

"Or if there were any," the structural specialist said, "they have already been used."

The ship rocked again, and Gold waited until it passed. "Communications?" he asked. "Life signs?"

Stevens again. Tev shifted uncomfortably. "Unable to be sure. No answer to our hails, but given the nature of their distress call, I'd say no." He leaned forward, resting against the table with hands clasped before him. "They piggybacked their anchor, using it as a kind of transmission medium, or antenna, to escape the black hole. Life signs . . . same answer. Our probe's sensors couldn't penetrate the station's shielding, except on a very specific band."

This was new. Tev straightened up, eager for more data. A few seats down, Gold did the same. "And that is?"

"Transporters," Stevens said. "The shield harmonics are meant to allow transport."

"Transporters?" Gold frowned. "Through that kind of gravimetric interference?" Gold might not always understand the engineering side of things, but he knew his ship well. Tev had to give him credit for that. "Risky." He leaned forward, waving a finger in the air. "Didn't *Voyager* fall into a singularity recently?"

The logs that had been coming in from Project *Voyager*—which had managed to make contact with that ship in the Delta Quadrant, where it had been all but stranded for six years—had made for fascinating reading for the entire S.C.E. team, Tev knew. They had encountered some phenomena that almost defied belief.

Stevens answered the captain's question. "Their chief engineer rigged up a dekyon beam to reopen the 'rift' by which they entered. Nothing like that will work here. I think transporters are our best bet."

Gomez nodded reluctant agreement. "I was thinking that Tev might be our answer."

He was? Tev swallowed, the hard rock of candy forcing its way down his throat with reluctance. He coughed into a large fist, and Faulwell hit him on the back. He shrugged away from the affable linguist, able to recover better on his own. Faulwell looked wounded. "You want me to transport over?"

"I want you to rig up a transporter relay system that can get a team over there. We'll take pattern enhancers, which should aid in recovery of any trapped crew."

Tev blinked in surprise that Gomez was acknowledging his expertise. "A relay?"

"Through a series of probes. You wrote a paper on the miniaturizing of transporters, didn't you? Can you rig up some kind of circuit that will pass through our patterns, without distortion?"

He snuffled. He should have thought of that. One of his specialties, in fact, and Sonya Gomez handed it to him as a favor! She certainly hadn't wanted to share the credit, as competitive as the S.C.E. team always seemed to perform. "Yes. It can be done. Quite easily, I should think."

"I'll want a trio of security personnel to escort any away team," Corsi said.

Lense nodded. "I'll join it with medical supplies. There might be injuries over there."

"Let's set it up," Gold said. "But I want it well tested before we commit any live personnel to it." He pointed at the screen, where the Demon was frozen in timeless pause. "That is one of the most destructive forces in the known universe. We treat it with great, great respect at all times. Clear?"

Sonya answered for the team. "Yes, Captain." She looked them over. Shrugged. "What are you waiting for? Get to work."

Tev felt that last comment aimed right for him. It didn't matter what he had solved yesterday, or even this morning. What mattered was what he contributed now. Commander Gomez had made that amply clear.

He stood, waiting while Gold and Gomez left first. He would have been third out of the room, by seniority, but he paused. Faulwell was gathering his wrappers. When the language specialist looked up, he found Tev standing just inside the door. They were the last two left.

"Dr. Faulwell, I was wondering?"

The slight man rubbed at his beard. "Yes, Tev?"

The Tellarite glanced back into the hall. No one. He snuffled. He needed to get back to work. He would have to try even harder. But first . . .

"May I have another piece of candy?"

CHAPTER
6

Gold kept his finger on the pulse of his ship, constantly in touch with engineering and the transporter room. The bridge was a beehive of activity as Tev diligently worked to become a miracle worker and transport the away team down to the station through a relay system, circumventing the titanic forces of a black hole.

The captain snorted softly. It would almost be worth interrupting Tev to see what his oh-so-dry response to "miracle worker" would be.

"Captain, I've definitely verified it's an ion trail," Shabalala said.

"How old?"

Shabalala tapped his screen with practiced efficiency. "I'm not sure. Our sensors are still catching massive interference. The best I can say is three to five days; just can't narrow it down any more. I'm sorry, Captain."

"That's narrow enough." He shifted slightly in his

chair (would they ever make one of these that actually felt comfortable?) as he tried to accept what that meant.

"Captain," Shabalala began as he turned a concerned look toward his captain, "that means—"

"It means that ship must have detected the signal and yet . . . what happened? Did they depart? Go in?"

Shabalala looked down at the sensors for a moment before answering. "The gravimetric waves, not to mention the massive flux of Hawking radiation, are making it very difficult to analyze the ion trail. Hell, we spent how many hours here before it was even detected?"

Gold tried not to read too much into the defensive tone, but his own lack of sleep had him on edge as well.

He leaned back in his chair, staring out the viewscreen at the awesome maw before him and tried to think through the sensor readings. He began to knead the muscles of his neck when his skin prickled with the knowledge that this flesh did not belong to him; Gold almost shivered when an echo of his nightmare shimmered before his eyes, as though part of the maw itself. He stood abruptly and walked around to Shabalala's side at the tactical station behind his chair, trying to hide his agitation; that had never happened once he was fully awake. Though he felt the need to face down this specter again, he set it aside for another day.

His crew and his ship needed him right now.

He laid his hand comfortably on the lieutenant's shoulder. "What *can* you tell me about the trail?"

The gesture and tone of voice seemed to work, and he felt the tension draining out of Shabalala's muscles. "I can place it about three to five days ago. There appears to be a second trail—almost a mirror image—but that could simply be an echoing effect: a version of the Einstein Ring, where the trail is duplicated."

"There's no debris?"

"None."

"Then I'd say that leaves us with two possible answers. One: a ship approached, drew almost to the photon sphere, perhaps hearing the distress signal, and then departed. Two: a ship approached, heard the distress signal, and attempted a rescue by actually taking the ship beyond the photon sphere."

"Captain," Tev interrupted. Gold turned to see the Tellarite standing almost at his shoulder, snuffling.

"Yes."

"Your second hypothesis is incorrect. If the ship traversed the photon sphere, our sensors would still be able to locate its presence—or the *absence* of its presence. As such, for the craft to simply have vanished to the point that our sensors refuse to reveal its location, it would need to pass through the event horizon, not simply the photon sphere." The black orbs of Tev's eyes reminded the captain of the black hole: light, matter, even emotions, seemed to vanish into those depths without a trace, without a reaction from Tev in the slightest.

"That would, in effect, be the same thing, wouldn't it?" Gold could feel the shaking of Shabalala's shoulders as the tactical officer attempted to repress his laughter. *Poor Tev. We humans can be more difficult to understand than Klingons or even Romulans. Nothing we say can be taken literally.*

Gold's words finally seemed to affect Tev as he raised his bushy, foliage-quality eyebrows, as though shocked his own captain could be so dense. "Of course it is different, Captain. Though I could explain it in detail, the most telling difference would be the location of the ship.

With the right knowledge and technology a ship might survive crossing the photon sphere. No ship could survive crossing the event horizon."

Gold raised his hand. "I'm sorry, Tev. I know what you meant. What *I* meant is either the ship stayed, or it passed and simply vanished. Either way there is no trace of it and we've still got our team heading across that same barrier."

Tev snuffled loudly, and Gold suddenly realized this must be a Tellarite way of clearing their throat before speaking. Could Tev actually be nervous about something?

"Captain," Tev began. If he was nervous, it didn't show. "The modifications are completed. I'm leaving now to monitor a test directly from the transporter room as we send a probe into the Demon. As soon as it succeeds, the away team can be sent."

"Excellent."

"You know that it should be me leading the away team. My theories and ultimate application allowed for this success. My knowledge and experience on this matter are greater than any other crew member's."

"Exactly," Gold said. "Which is why Gomez wants you to stay on the ship. If there's a problem, your knowledge is the only lever we have."

"It will not fail, Captain."

"Of course it won't. But other problems are likely to arise, and you're the one needed *here*."

Tev snuffled and then bowed his head ever so slightly; orders were still orders. He shuffled off, and Gold watched him head toward the turbolift.

"And Tev?"

The second officer stopped and turned. "Sir?"

"The composition of the away team is Commander

Gomez's decision. You have a problem, talk to her. Don't think you're going to accomplish *anything*—with her *or* with me—by going over her head. Got it?"

"Yes, sir."

"Good."

As the Tellarite entered the turbolift, bound for the transporter room, Gold hoped Gomez was having better luck with Tev than he seemed to be.

Sonya did not care for environmental suits. The bulky outfits weighed on her like a straitjacket. Stiff. Claustrophobic, even without the helmet on. And they always smelled of feet, though the maintenance crews promised her that just wasn't possible. To her engineer's eyes, they needed a good redesign. Maybe she'd take her hand to it, after this mission, but for now there was no way around them. Without any idea of a breathable atmosphere over on the station, the suits were a necessary evil.

She shuffle-stepped to one side, clearing a path to the transporter pad. Elizabeth Lense and Fabian Stevens waddled past. P8 Blue, in her self-designed suit, marched past on all eight legs, low to the ground and moving much faster than a humanoid might. Pattie carried pattern enhancers strapped to her back, which Tev didn't feel necessary but, as he'd finally allowed, "Couldn't hurt." She considered it a minor victory pulling that concession from him.

Sonya still wasn't certain if the Tellarite's extreme confidence in himself was his greatest failing, or his greatest strength.

And she wasn't the only one. As each member of her

away team reported in to the transporter room, they came by to check with her that she felt confident in Tev's transporter relay system. Second, they offered whatever piece of advice they thought was prudent, or asked for clarifications based on the latest data.

Domenica Corsi was the exception. Hauling a pair from security in her wake, the intimidating blonde planted herself in front of Sonya. "We'll take a three-point perimeter on beam-over. If we split up, I want one security guard present at all times." She glanced back. "Everyone got that?"

Konya simply nodded. Next to him, a thick-necked man carrying a phaser rifle in one hand and his suit helmet in the other shrugged his arms out as if loosening up. "Ya got it, sh-weetheart." His accent was nasal.

Corsi glared. "Don't make me tell you again, Vinx."

"Absolutely, doll—er, Commander." He put on his helmet and winked, an exaggerated expression that took half his face to do. Propping the phaser rifle one-handed up to his shoulder, he sauntered up to the transporter pad.

Sonya couldn't see how the man pulled it off, sauntering in an environment suit. And living through calling "Core-Breach" Corsi "sweetheart."

"Did we take out an advertisement?" she asked, *sotto voce.*

Corsi shrugged with her eyes. "Iotian. He's having troubles, ah, assimilating." She glanced up at the nearly packed transporter stage. "Are you sure—"

The doors whisked open, and Tev stormed in with a thundercloud darkening his face. Corsi looked over at the Tellarite, and asked the question with a raised eyebrow.

Sonya nodded. "He hasn't dropped the ball yet." Even

if she wished he would. Just not this time, thank you very much.

"No engineer out of sight." Corsi reminded her. "Ever."

Sonya nodded. "No pairing up with Stevens."

Corsi started, and Sonya smiled. She hadn't been completely sure about the two of them being a couple. On the other hand, given her and the late Kieran Duffy, she was hardly in a position to object. On the third hand, look how that relationship ended. "Relax, Domenica. It's me."

"If you three are ready," Tev said from the control panel, "my probes are nearly in place."

Corsi and Konya moved past her, taking up position on the pad. Sonya stepped up onto the stage, fastening her helmet down, making certain she had good air flow. She inhaled her first breath. Feet.

"Phasers ready," Corsi ordered, drawing her own.

"Packin' heat." Vinx held his phaser rifle at waist level.

"Ready," Konya answered, though Sonya saw that he had not drawn his weapon. The security guard still persisted in finding noncombative solutions. So far, no one had room to complain.

She looked over to Tev, but the command "energize" never made it past her lips. The Tellarite took it upon himself, and started the transport sequence on his authority. A high-pitched hum filled Sonya's ears, and the transporter's energy matrix cascaded over the away team . . .

. . . falling away as they rematerialized inside a dimly lit space. Shadows moved around them, lunging forward quickly.

Bright lights stabbed into the back of Sonya's eyes. "Do not move!" a rasping voice ordered.

She adjusted quickly. Not that there was much she could do. They were surrounded by a dozen beings from a reptilian race, with dark scales and glassy-black eyes.

And each one held a makeshift energy weapon pointed at the S.C.E. team.

CHAPTER
7

The fear scent was overpowering.

Captain S'linth snapped his jaws shut to close out the olfactory overload, to keep his anger scent in check. Then again, he doubted Suliss would even notice. His fear overpowered everything.

Slowly reviewing his crew, S'linth made a decision and rocked back on his tail, opening his jaws wide and puffing his neck muscles. Let Suliss scent his anger. Let his crew know of his displeasure. The *Dutiful Burden* was *his* vessel, and no Council-appointed overseer would change that. Outside of the blessed Council, if ever there existed a place where a Resaurian could be first egg, then by Demon, this was it!

"Captain," the communications officer spoke up. Rotating his head toward Lyssis, his tongue flickered; she was as uncomfortable as the rest of the crew and yet, despite her third shedding, she performed her duty. If

Lyssis moved for a challenge in the next cycle, she would have his support.

"Yes."

"The alien ship continues to broadcast communications on numerous bands. I'm still working on translations, but there can be no doubt that most of those signals are aimed at the Demon." Her tongue did not flicker once as she spoke the name so many, including the Demon-cursed Suliss, could not utter without a head-sway of fear.

S'linth did not need to glance at the overseer to feel his panic as a physical presence; he probably wishes to curl up in a nest with his females. *Why does the Council burden me with such shedding leavings?* S'linth's anger pulsed once more, and he brazenly puffed his neck to expel his displeasure into the already torrid air.

So often S'linth had been forced to put up with the foolishness of Suliss; the Demon-cursed nestling carried his fear on his tongue. Now, as S'linth was on the verge of discovering the greatest change to occur in the last thousand cycles, Suliss could only sway with fear, his obsidian eyes almost completely obscured with multiple membranes. As Suliss's fear moved toward terror, driven by changes he could not accept (the subspace signal from the Demon *and* the arrival of an alien vessel) S'linth's anger moved to rage. He knew Suliss would attempt to block all moves of contact; S'linth had never been so close to baring fangs on his own bridge.

The tableau was interrupted as Third Councilman Sha'a slithered onto the bridge. All rotated heads toward Sha'a and bowed, nictitating a single membrane; as captain, S'linth need only bow his head, yet he nictitated as well. S'linth needed to bleed off anger; it was not appropriate in Sha'a's presence. The Third Councilman would know of the emotions on the bridge regardless, but continued anger would only knock his own tail out from under him. Additionally, S'linth truly respected Sha'a. The councilman had been a full supporter of the captain's crèche for long cycles. What's more, Sha'a had to know fear from this travel (only his second departure from Nest) yet no fear scent hovered about him. This was a Resaurian to nictitate to.

"Third Councilman," S'linth said.

"Captain."

"We requested your wisdom due to the presence of a strange vessel over the Demon."

The councilman slithered sinuously toward the giant forward screen. S'linth noticed he moved entirely without the use of his front legs as he navigated the unfamiliar decking through the bridge; such grace was in high contrast with the stumbling movements of Suliss. Coming to rest, Sha'a settled back comfortably on his tail, his flowing carmine robes gathering around his form as a second skin.

"What has been learned, Captain?" S'linth had noticed no overt flickering of Sha'a's tongue, but was confident he knew all that had occurred. There was no hiding in the Nest from a councilman.

"Communications has verified that most of the signals broadcast by the strange vessel are cast into the Demon."

"And?"

S'linth paused for a moment, tasted the air to see if he could find Sha'a among the emotions that clogged the bridge (it was impossible, the councilman was too adept at keeping his own glands in check). "I would approach this strange vessel and make contact."

"And?"

Shaken from his trance, Suliss stumbled into the conversation. "Councilman . . . our traditions! This alien ship cannot be contacted. Other ships have come and gone, as regular as sheddings. This too shall slough. There can be no doubt. There can be no contact." He speared the ship's captain with a glare. "There cannot be another Klingon."

S'linth firmly closed his jaws, but could not keep Suliss's fear from coating his tongue with its filth. His lips trembled to peel back. To bare fangs.

He held his anger in check. "I am versed in our traditions. The captain's crèche, as it has since hatched, knows its duty and the laws. But never has the Demon spoken. And now the arrival of this vessel . . . The two cannot be independent. The one leads to the other. You must see this."

Sha'a did not even rotate toward S'linth, but the captain instantly knew he had overstepped his boundaries. This was a battle that required submission as much as aggression.

"I'm well aware of our traditions, and of the gravity of this situation," Sha'a began, as though unaware of the raging scents around him. "However, I do believe this ship is tied to the strange occurrences within the Demon; we shall not depart until it does."

S'linth had an overwhelming urge to peel back his lips and puff his neck in triumph; such an unseemly display was not worthy of a captain, especially in front of a councilman, and he withheld.

"Nevertheless, we have no scent of this ship. We must know more before a decision can be made.

"We shall wait."

*   *   *

"What the hell are they waiting for?" the captain asked, staring at the alien ship that hung on the viewscreen.

Shabalala divided his time between the screen and his panel. A gravimetric wave rocked the *da Vinci*, upsetting the delicate sensor balance he had achieved, but he corrected for the disturbance with a light touch. The alien vessel was not going to slip away from him. Especially since verifying that its ion trail was a perfect match for the vessel that had recently visited the black hole.

The vessel was wedge-shaped. An uninspired design—with poor warp drive characteristics, he'd bet. But it had slipped up behind them, and now sat between the *da Vinci* and open space.

"Shall I hail them, Captain?" Shabalala asked.

Gold tapped his chin in thought. Whatever was on his mind, he held it close to the vest. Shabalala liked that about the captain. No histrionics. Just good, solid leadership.

"Give them another few moments," Gold finally said. "I want to see what they'll do."

Another tremor shook the bridge. Shabalala corrected sensor calibration again, but noticed that a wash of static lapped at the edges of the main viewscreen. He sighed and hoped the captain did not wait out the aliens too long.

What did Commander Gomez do? Tev sniffed the air, as though his superior olfactory sense could span the distance from the *da Vinci* to the space station and aid him in determining what error the away team made.

How did they cause his system to fail?

Sucking on a piece of Faulwell's candy, worrying it between his teeth, Tev studied the transporter interface. His large, almost pudgy fingers moved over it with grace and ease. For what seemed the hundredth time he recalled all data surrounding the transport and could find no anomalies of which to speak. He sent a query down through the probes and back again with no difficulty.

All systems nominal.

Nevertheless, after initialization of the energy matrix and the successful transport of the away team, he'd instantly lost transporter lock. What's more, the *da Vinci* had been unable to even contact the away team.

The captain, of course, was upset by this turn of events.

Tev had tried to explain that the system was in perfect working order; the tests had worked flawlessly, and he found no reason to believe that the away team had not arrived safely onto the station. Though he could think of nothing Gomez and her people could've done to disrupt the system's ability to track them, he nevertheless conceded that humans had surprised him on numerous occasions with their ability to derail the simplest protocols. This was likely the case.

Suggesting this had seemed to anger the captain. Why should the truth be difficult to accept? Tev had been slightly disappointed with Captain Gold at that moment. Especially when the captain offered to send down another crew member to help.

The man would only have gotten in the way.

He bit down on the thinning wafer, finishing off his candy with a satisfying crunch and wash of flavor—a sticky, sour but not unpleasant aftertaste that not even a drink of *jota* could fully banish.

Perhaps if he sent down additional probes, he could boost the signal and then triangulate the away team's positions? He idly pulled on his beard. Perhaps a thermal print. . . .

Tev put the transporter station on standby, surrendered it to the duty chief, and jogged toward the door. He tapped his combadge. "Transporter to bridge. Captain?"

"This is Gold. What've you got for me?"

"Captain, I believe that I can drop additional probes, setting up an imaging grid to sweep the station, triangulating on their thermal print. As the station is probably long dead, their thermal signature should be easy to locate."

"What if the station's not dead?"

Tev summoned the lift, organizing his thoughts as the doors whisked open and then closed. "Bridge," he ordered. Then, "Even if the station is fully operational, with numerous active targets, the thermal print of a Nasat is rather unique. It should help us pinpoint their location."

"Make it happen, Tev. We've got a situation of our own up here—stand by to hail them, Shabalala—so let's get our people back. Inform me when you've gotten a lock. Bridge out."

Tev did not bother to inform the captain he was already en route to the bridge. From where else did you program probes? Gold *had* sounded distracted, though. Hail them? Hail whom? Still trying to contact the station, which had ignored every attempt at communication since the *da Vinci*'s arrival?

Not exactly. As the door to the bridge slid open, and Tev stepped out of the lift, he was just in time to see a wedge-shaped vessel dissolve from the main viewer, to be replaced by a static-laced view of an alien bridge with half a dozen reptilian beings staring back with glassy eyes and wide, blunt-edged mouths.

Captain Gold should have informed him about this! How else was Tev to render him the best possible service and advice?

But he had his orders. As Captain Gold opened a dialogue with the aliens, Tev moved to an open science station and set about reprogramming some probes.

CHAPTER
8

Rennan Konya sensed the hostility and the fear that surrounded him, scoring his psyche like twin barbs on the same lash. Part of him recoiled from the contact—had seemed to feel a shimmering of revulsion even before materializing, though intellectually he knew that was not possible. The stronger part of his Betazoid mind embraced the pain, made it a part of him, and searched for a way to turn it into a strength.

He picked up no coherent thoughts, but within seconds of materializing he already *knew* that the two reptilian beings nearest him were far too afraid to pull their triggers. Many of the others were strangely ambivalent, afraid to fire but resigned to do so if they found it necessary. Two of them were eager to resolve the situation with action.

Far, far too eager.

One of these stood within reach of Rennan, holding a

metal rod that bled red sparks from its front end. Some kind of converted plasma welder. She covered Commander Gomez and Fabian Stevens, weapon swinging back and forth as if deciding which one should be shot first.

The other snakelike being with violent emanations stood opposite Vinx, competing in a stare-down contest with the Iotian security guard. Vinx egged him on with not-so-subtle gestures, poking toward the alien with his phaser rifle. "Are ya talkin' to me?" Vinx taunted, his voice only slightly muffled by the environmental suit's helmet.

"Drop the weapon!" The alien held some kind of pistol-style weapon.

Apparently Vinx wanted to get shot. Louder, he asked again, "Are ya talkin' to me?"

This could not have a good end.

One of the uncertain beings tried to defuse the situation. "Hold," he ordered the one facing off with Vinx. Though a head shorter than his larger companion, the alien's raspy voice held the unmistakable air of authority. He leaned forward, catching his man in a glassy-eyed stare. A tongue licked out, tasting the air. "Rhyss, I said hold!"

Too late. Rennan's special training allowed him to tap into the motor complex of the brain much easier than the thought process. He felt fingers tightening on triggers, knew that the leader could not stop his two makeshift warriors in time. Not both of them. As the leader lunged forward, tucking his legs back to strike snakelike toward his own man, arm coming up to grab the pistol, Rennan slid in low and sideways toward the alien who had finally decided to start with Commander Gomez, the closer engineer.

It all happened in the brief span of two seconds. The pistol-like device discharged into the ceiling, raining a shower of sparks and molten droplets over Vinx and P8 Blue. The Nasat curled into a protective ball, rolling forward out of reflex to bowl over both aliens.

The second trigger-happy alien had sensed Rennan's approach, swinging her plasma-dripping rod around to skewer the Betazoid. Using a specialty he referred to as proprioception, sensing the alien's actions and using her movement against her, Rennan dodged in, spinning to one side. His environmental suit made it harder, but not impossible. His left hand grasped the rod just forward of its makeshift stock, yanking it free, while his right arm snaked up and around the back of the alien's neck, putting her into a reverse choke hold that effectively neutralized her as a threat.

Fear roiled off the two skittish aliens, and Rennan quickly assuaged their worry by throwing the plasma weapon at their feet and holding up his empty hand in a (fairly) universal sign of neutrality. His empathic ability confirmed that he had done the right thing as the aliens hesitated, and then backed away.

Commander Corsi had her phaser out, covering a trio of aliens who aimed back in a very lopsided standoff. She tapped her combadge. "Corsi to *da Vinci*. Corsi to Gold!" Nothing. She swore under her breath. "Get a grip on yourselves, people. Vinx? Vinx!"

The Iotian stood over the two reptilian beings that Pattie had knocked over, his phaser rifle levered from his hip. "Piece of this action? Huh? Ya want that?" A lot of mouth but no real anger, Rennan was satisfied to note. The Iotian was in full control of the situation. The leader of the small alien band lay there, arms raised in another fairly universal gesture.

Releasing his captive, Rennan stepped over and prodded Vinx back away from the two fallen aliens.

Stevens already had his tricorder out, taking readings and occasionally tapping his combadge to see if the *da Vinci* answered. Gomez made placating gestures to the aliens at the team's rear, where Rennan had left the back of the team open to possible attack. Sonya couldn't know that the Resaurians were more afraid of being wrong than they were of being threatened.

Pattie partially unrolled, looking out to see if the situation had resolved itself.

For the most part, Rennan felt that it had. No one was in immediate danger of firing a weapon. More importantly, no one was hurt. Violence had been avoided.

That was security's job.

CHAPTER
9

As the image materialized on the viewscreen, Captain Gold shivered. And immediately felt abashed. Humans had been exploring the galaxy for centuries, and yet the collective fears of millennia continued to haunt them like a plague.

Why did they so fear snakes?

"I am Third Councilman Sha'a of Resaurus," the figure on the screen hissed. He was difficult to see, as the ambient light on their bridge was low. The alien's reddish hued scales blended so well with his clothing that it took Gold a moment to realize that Sha'a wore a clinging carmine robe. The councilman's tongue flickered to the right, *"This is Captain S'linth of the* Dutiful Burden.*"* He spread his arms wide and bobbed his head slightly once more. *"We welcome you."*

Interesting that the civilian spoke in place of the captain of the ship; Gold understood right away where the real power lay.

Resaurians, as they identified themselves, looked like a thick-bodied snake with nearly vestigial legs but strong arms. Coal-black eyes stared forward with a hypnotic gaze. Gold tried to shovel his childish fears aside. Perhaps Resaurians got the willies when looking at humans. The thought helped.

"Third Councilman Sha'a," he responded, trying not to trip over the glottal stop in the name. He stood up and took his best "we are friendly and hope you will be too" stance. "I thank you for your welcome." He paused for a moment, wondering if he should bring Abramowitz up here. No time. "As your ship approached ours, I would ask what your intentions are?"

Looking not unlike a thin tapeworm squirming for life, Sha'a's tongue flicked in and out several times before he responded. *"Captain, it would seem that you have picked up a distress signal emanating from this black hole. We would like to share with you what you'll find."*

"We welcome any assistance, Third Councilman. May I offer the hospitality of my ship?"

A whitish membrane slid over Sha'a's eyes for a few heartbeats. Then the councilman nodded. *"We will shuttle over, Captain."*

"No need. Our matter transference system can beam you quite safely aboard."

Another long blink. Then, Sha'a nodded. *"There will be three of us,"* he said. And communication broke off from their side.

Perhaps the Resaurians were not so comfortable either.

*   *   *

Gold walked along briskly, with Carol Abramowitz attempting to match his stride; a security detail would meet them in the transporter room.

"What have you got for me?" he asked.

Carol paused before responding, trying to juggle keeping up with the captain as she consulted her tricorder. "The Federation has had a few brushes with the Resaurians, but nothing in long decades. I've tagged one or two references. The computer did come up with some corrupted files from that old Earth ship I mentioned, but not much beyond that."

"Soloman was no help?"

"Not so far. Even Bynars have their limitations when it comes to computers, sir."

"So, for all intents and purposes, this is first contact?" Of all the things going on right now, he had to run into this?

They entered the turbolift and descended smoothly down.

"I'd not call it that. More a recontact. However, indirectly I dug up some additional information. Not from our archives, but from a Klingon source." Carol sounded very satisfied.

"Klingon?"

The doors whisked open and they headed toward the transporter room.

"Yes. It seems that our allies subjugated the Resaurians for the better part of a century, using them for their large mineral deposits. A very hidebound and slowly developing people, according to the files. Traditions were given more weight than laws, which caused no end of difficulty with their overlords. The Klingons kept them in virtual slavery, and then discarded them and moved on once the most accessible resources had been tapped out."

Gold heard the disgust in her voice and couldn't bring himself to dispute it. He knew many Klingons that he respected, but as a race . . . "How long ago was this?" he asked.

"The dates aren't translating well, but when Captain Archer made first contact, the Resaurians were already long since free of the Klingons, and that was two hundred and twenty years ago."

"So, what does that mean for us?"

"I'm not exactly sure on all points, but at the very least they are likely to be hostile toward any new race. Their encounter with the Klingons had to be devastating and they'll most likely do everything in their power to prevent something like that happening again."

"So why are they being so open? So friendly?"

"That's the gold-pressed latinum question, all right."

They arrived at the transporter room, where a trio from security already had phasers drawn and ready.

"None of that," Gold said, motioning their phasers away. He turned toward Chief Poynter behind the transporter console. "Energize."

The hum and light show commenced, with the energy pulsing, coalescing into three forms: that of Councilman Sha'a, Captain S'linth, and another whom Gold did not recognize.

Up close, the impression of a snake was even stronger, as their tongues flicked madly and their heads rotated back and forth, swaying, almost hypnotic. Gold immediately took a step forward. He noted a scent of dry, bitter musk.

"Third Councilman Sha'a, welcome to the Federation Starship *da Vinci*," he said and then turned slightly to indicate Carol. "This is our cultural specialist, Dr. Carol Abramowitz, Transporter Chief Laura Poynter," he said, indicating the transporter chief, then pointed at the security guards, "and Chief Vance Hawkins, Ellec Krotine, and Madeleine Robins from security."

Sha'a bowed his head slightly in both their directions. His arm swung out to indicate his own companions. "This is Captain S'linth, introduced previously." The third Resaurian, "This is Suliss, overseer of the *Dutiful Burden.*"

Gold wondered what the difference was between a captain and an overseer—and who outranked whom. Normally a tone of voice or a facial expression could give something away, but these Resaurians were too alien for him to pick up anything. He'd simply have to proceed as he could.

"Please, we've a room ready for our discussion," Gold said, still mulling over how to address this trio, and led them toward the observation lounge, which Carol had readied from what scant information they did know.

"Your hospitality is gracious, Captain," S'linth whispered in the Resaurian's hissing style of communication. "Of the first egg." Several different types of refreshment and liquid had been laid out, and each of the Resaurians found something apparently to their liking. S'linth, though, seemed to be the only one enjoying himself.

"You are most welcome, Captain S'linth."

After several minutes of pleasantries, passed mostly with S'linth, Gold allowed the silence to lengthen. Councilman Sha'a obviously wanted to discuss the topic on his terms. Gold steadily drank from a glass of cold water while Carol sat patiently, waiting. Finally, Sha'a spoke.

"Captain, it has come to our attention that you have

received a distress signal from within the Demon. This black hole."

"As you said earlier, Third Councilman." Gold would not get drawn into a long discussion. His people could be in trouble.

"Yes, and I'm confident, from what I've seen, that you have already verified that there is a space station anchored within."

"That's correct. How do you know this?"

"Because that is a Resaurian space station."

Gold blinked as he took that in. From the startled reactions of both Suliss and S'linth, it appeared to be news to them as well. He traced a circle through the sweating liquid from his glass that marred the table. Despite his misgivings, he began to hope.

"If that's your station, then you'll be able to help us."

"I'm afraid, Captain, that is quite out of our capabilities."

Captain Gold slowly pressed his hand down against the tabletop, reined in his anger.

"Why?"

"Because the station has been abandoned for over several centuries and we allowed the technology . . . to languish."

He leaned back and tried not to let his distress show. Had the away team found nothing? Were they trapped and dying down there alone? What was happening?

"Several centuries? And it's still there? Why did you abandon such an impressive research facility?"

"Yes," the Resaurian said in a slow hiss, "a research facility." He paused. "There was a plague on the station, one which drove the . . . the researchers toward insanity. Tradition dictated that we not allow it to affect the rest of our people if we could help it."

Gold grasped suddenly that he distrusted the Councilman, though he could not pin it to anything; he didn't believe himself shallow enough to distrust simply based upon those dead, holelike eyes, or the dancing black tongue that quivered. It was by far the more human traits. The hesitation. The vague answers. Sha'a was hiding something.

"Did you pinpoint the source of this plague?" Carol finally spoke up. Whether she did so of her own volition or because she detected his unease, Gold couldn't tell.

"No. It remains a mystery to us even today. But considering the danger inherent to this area of space . . ."

Carol nodded. "The black hole?"

"Unable to do anything, we were forced to abandon the station, however much it pained us. We have never returned."

It made sense, and yet still something seemed off. Gold looked toward the other two Resaurians and found nothing; they might as well have been statues for his ability to read them. He'd been on the point of informing the Resaurians about their away team, but now demurred. He simply had to find out more about this race. Of a sudden he stood, uncaring if he might be breaching protocol.

"Sha'a, it has been a pleasure. More, I appreciate your candor on this subject. Nevertheless, there are urgent matters that I must attend to."

"Then you shall be departing?"

"Very soon, I hope. Very soon."

Carol stood beside the captain as the Resaurians disappeared through the door, escorted by security. "That was abrupt."

"We've got to find out more about them, Abramowitz. They're not telling the truth."

She turned toward him with a quizzical look in her eye. "How can you tell? I've had an easier time telling what a wall feels than those Resaurians."

"I'm not sure, but there's something. . . ." He arched his neck, as though to stretch his mental faculty past the cobwebs that angry chemical spiders were weaving at a furious pace; he had to get some sleep.

But not until his crew returned.

"You and Soloman get back to work on those corrupted files you mentioned. There has to be something in there that can open a crack on these Resaurians."

CHAPTER
10

Sonya's job description rarely included such tasks as first contact procedures. That was left to ships of exploration, like her first posting on the *Enterprise*. They came through, initiated protocols or not, made a tangle of things or not, and then moved on to the next mission while the diplomatic corps or S.C.E. (or both!) moved in to clean up after them.

She felt fairly certain, however, that most of those protocols did *not* involve staring at each other over drawn weapons. Wars could begin that way. And had.

Fortunately, this S'eth did not appear to harbor a grudge. Just the opposite.

"Once again, I wish to apologize, Commander, for your reception." S'eth had greenish black scales from the leading edge of his blunt-nosed face to his coral-tipped tail. His chest scales were smaller and lighter, almost an emerald green. He rested back on a thick coil, his legs propping himself up on either side. It made him look smaller than he actually was, nearly a head and a half shorter than Sonya. "Your matter transference beam caught us by surprise."

The Resaurian certainly sounded apologetic. A discreet glance at Rennan Konya, who shrugged and then nodded, confirmed that the Betazoid at least felt comfortable with the alien's contrite attitude. Rennan went back to intently studying some scorch markings on a nearby wall.

For her part, Sonya was simply relieved to be out of the bulky environmental suits now that they had ascertained that the Resaurians breathed Class-M atmosphere. She glanced around the operations center where Tev had inserted her team. Panels with actual keystroke pads lay open with jury-rigged components bleeding out onto the metal decking everywhere. Lights flashed on monitors here and there. Most screens had large dark spaces that again told of age and neglect—or maybe just of an inability to repair. More than a few bulkheads and workstation hatches had carbon score marks that might have been from ruptured systems, and sloppy welds could be counted by the dozen, as if the Resaurians had been learning repair procedures as they went.

Only the main viewer seemed to work perfectly, looking out of the photon sphere. High above, the universe was compacted into a small circle of stars surrounded by bands of blue-shifted light that marked each progressive Einstein Ring.

The rest of the "sky" was dark. Nothingness.

Checking on her team, Sonya saw Corsi and Vinx standing together, talking, shoulder to shoulder and facing opposite directions so that one of them had full view of half the bridge at all times. Fabian crawled halfway into a large, darkened workstation, and Pattie inspected a welded door that looked as if it once fronted the opening for a lift of some type. Lense ran intense scans of one of the Resaurians, pausing every few seconds to recalibrate her tricorder. Of the thousand survivors who S'eth assured them still remained on the station, they had so far seen perhaps twenty. In singles and small groups they wandered in, offering a hand and answering any questions put to them.

Caught by surprise or not, the Resaurians cooperated with great eagerness now.

"Your shields were designed for transporters to penetrate easily," she noted. "I would have thought that our arrival method would be quite common."

"It was. It was. Once upon a time. But we haven't had such an occurrence, well, in decades."

Decades! "How long have you been trapped here?" she asked.

"A lifetime, it seems." S'eth scratched behind his right shoulder, picking loose a scrap of dried skin that had been wedged in between some of his scales. He tasted the air, black eyes gazing about the bridge. "How long depends greatly on the time dilation, of course."

Of course. Decades to the Resaurians trapped within this station could, objectively, translate to centuries outside of the black hole's influence. How much time was her team losing, right now, separated from the *da Vinci*? "I don't suppose a Federation stardate would help?"

"Not unless you can translate it into the time it takes Resaurus to orbit its sun," S'eth rasped.

"Without the *da Vinci*'s computers, I'm afraid not. Fabian," she called over to her tactical systems specialist, "any luck?"

"Nothing," Fabian told her, head still stuck inside the cavernous workstation. He pulled back out, squatted against the station's corner, and laid his head back against a nonfunctioning keypad. "This is all local station comms. I can't find a subspace transmitter here. I'm not even certain how they sent their distress call."

Sonya looked to S'eth. "Much of this station was automated," he explained. "We have retaken manual control over as much as we dare."

"And your subspace communications?" she asked.

"On a lower deck, I imagine. It was never a part of the main operating systems."

Sonya couldn't put her finger on why she thought the Resaurian had just hedged on the truth. It simply felt not *quite* right. Either way, it was damn strange.

"Can we triangulate on the transmission?"

Fabian kicked his tricorder, sitting on the deck, all but forgotten. "Useless. Or damn close. The shields around this station have a dampening effect on this side. It limits the range and effectiveness of our best equipment. Which is likely why we lost communications." Fabian exhaled sharply. "And transporter lock."

With no comms and no emergency beam-out after two minutes, Sonya and the rest of her team had already come to that conclusion. "Pattern enhancers?" she asked.

"Still need a basic site-to-site signal." He nodded toward where Pattie had already set up the pattern enhancers around a clear section of deck. Vinx's combadge, donated to the cause, rested in the exact center. "On the off chance that Tev somehow manages to work around that shortcoming, we've recorded a status update that will help us coordinate a rescue." There was no talk of *if* a rescue would be made. Only *when*.

Sonya had good people under her. They took quite a bit on faith, which was unusual for by-the-math engineers.

"Can we drop the shields?" she asked as Rennan and Lense walked up to join the small gathering. "That would give Tev his chance. We can easily absorb the radiation, can't we?"

"For a time," Lense said, nodding, but S'eth disagreed.

"Cannot be done. Our shields work in conjunction with our gravitational anchor. We drop our shields, and the Demon swallows us."

Which Sonya translated as a complete loss of integrity as the black hole's tidal forces ripped the station apart. "Poor engineering design," she stated bluntly.

"Or a very good fail-safe," Rennan said, not the least bit surprised, apparently, to hear about the integrated systems. "If you never want the station, or its inhabitants, to see the light of day again."

"What are you saying?" Sonya inhaled sharply, turned on S'eth. "This station, and all aboard her, were sunk into the gravity well *intentionally?* With no way out?"

S'eth hesitated, then nodded. "That would be the case, Commander."

"Why?"

S'eth did not appear to want to say. Embarrassed or disgruntled, Sonya wasn't sure. But Rennan Konya had the answer. The Betazoid had waved over Corsi and Vinx, who gathered in cautiously, alerted by some signal. He nodded at the Resaurian, and then let his gaze take in the half-wrecked operations center around them. "It makes perfect sense," he told his commander, "if you are designing a prison."

CHAPTER
11

Tev wondered what this meeting was about as Soloman took a seat opposite him. With the captain to Tev's right, Abramowitz to the captain's right, and Faulwell to his left, they could commence.

The captain looked strained. Stretched thin. Just plain tired. Nothing showed in his voice, however, as he spoke.

"You called this meeting, Abramowitz. What have you dug up?"

Tev sniffed at her lack of preparedness; she took a whole four heartbeats to begin as she checked a few last notes on her pad.

"Actually quite a lot. Thanks to Soloman's efforts, we've decoded most of that corrupted Archer file." She nodded at Soloman, who managed to look slightly embarrassed at the praise. If he'd succeeded, why not take appropriate credit?

"It was a simple matter, Captain," Soloman began in his strange cadence. "After Carol met with the Resaurians, I spoke with her at some length to extract additional information that can only be synthesized in a face-to-face interaction." He nodded right back at Carol, bestowing mutual credit. "Once I had those additional data bytes, I constructed a new set of algorithmic search patterns and set it to work on the corrupted files. Once I'd extracted the first bytes and reincorporated them into the search parameters, the rest quickly fell into place, building a cohesive whole. Carol simply took that information and distilled it into what we have now."

"Enough with the back-patting already," Gold said with a tired smile. "Get on with it."

Abramowitz cleared her throat. "Yes, Captain. What we appear to have is a race that is steeped in tradition; traditions hold more importance than law. In fact, most traditions become laws by default. They are slow to develop and slow to adapt. Nevertheless, a progressive faction appears every few centuries and the Resaurians suddenly leap forward in their development: culturally, scientifically, technologically—really across the board. However, this doesn't last long. As a natural equilibrium reinstates itself, the progressive faction simply dissolves as their goals come to fruition and then centuries of slow, almost torporlike progression begins again."

"Okay, but how does that help us? That's a fine history lesson and we might use it to our advantage, but I'm not sure what that has to do with the station or our current predicament." For the first time that Tev could remember, Gold actually sounded slightly annoyed.

"I was getting to that, Captain," Abramowitz responded, speeding up her delivery. "This cycle progressed for who knows how many centuries. Until the Klingons."

Everyone, except Soloman, leaned back slightly as though that were the answer to everything. How many times had the Klingons been the problem? Tev could name numerous instances where he'd personally been involved in Klingon problems, much less history in general.

Abramowitz nodded her head and continued. "The Klingons practically enslaved the Resaurians for decades—I can't tell for sure how long, unfortunately, but enough time to thoroughly alter their society. When the Klingons departed, they left a hole that apparently was filled by another progressive faction. However, as upheavals tore at the very fabric of the Resaurian society, progress in sciences and technologies, most of it gleaned from the Klingons during their occupation and taken from their castoffs, spiraled out of control, advancing beyond the attendant advances of culture and the moral fiber to know how to deal with such technology."

Tev leaned forward to place meaty palms onto the table, finally able to join the conversation. "This progressive faction, so enamored of technology, did not dissipate as had occurred previously. This required the traditionalists to finally rise up and remove them from power?"

Abramowitz stared, chagrined, at Tev. She was not the only person to study societal behavior. Dealing with bizarre alien species such as humans, Cardassians, and Ferengi had forced him to such lengths, even if it was simply a small side hobby. It had neither the clean lines nor the pure form of engineering and mathematics, but the probabilities study of a sentient race's reactions to stimulation could be interesting in its own right.

"That's right, Tev. That's exactly right." She turned to look at the rest of those present, as though to assure herself she'd not been the only one to hear his words. He'd be offended if Abramowitz wasn't so far beneath his station.

"For perhaps the first time in Resaurian history, a violent overthrow of a movement occurred." She paused, as though done with her recitation. "After that, well, it would all be conjecture. I've no idea what occurred with the progressive faction, or how the traditionalists dealt with something so unprecedented. More importantly, I've no idea if the Resaurians found their equilibrium again, or whether the imprint of the Klingons was simply too powerful and the appearance of the progressive faction occurs more frequently and with more violence than before."

The captain finally leaned forward, resting his elbows on the table, and ran his hands back through his hair before raising bloodshot eyes to the room.

"Which still doesn't answer our question of why they've been so open," Gold said. "If everything you say is true, then our first impression should've been correct. They should be adamantly opposed to encountering new species."

Faulwell finally spoke up. "Could this Sha'a you met be a part of the progressive faction? Perhaps they've turned up once more."

The captain shook his head. "No. Of course, it's hard to read the Resaurians, but if ever I saw a traditionalist, Sha'a was it. S'linth, the captain, might be something different, but it looked to me like Sha'a is calling all the shots."

"What if—"

"Captain, this is the bridge."

Tev snuffled—he *hated* being interrupted.

"Gold here."

"Captain, we're receiving a message from Commander Gomez."

CHAPTER
12

"A prison?"

Sonya Gomez wandered through one of the lower corridors, between a hydroponics bay and the auxiliary generator that provided power to what remained of the functioning operations equipment. She was beginning to see a great deal more insidiousness in the welded doors and the carbon scoring that marred the walls everywhere she went. "All of this to lock up a group of political dissidents?"

"Dissidents!" S'eth shook his head. "We were free thinkers. Progressive diplomats, teachers, and engineers. The Council quaked in their nests when our eggs hatched."

Corsi, Vinx, and Konya had taken up sentry positions, guarding the small S.C.E. team as they continued their survey of the station. They held off all Resaurians except for S'eth. Corsi shook her head. "Why not space you? A whole lot easier."

S'eth recoiled as if bitten. "Resaurians have a long life span. To shorten it would be an inconceivable crime. Not that other races haven't shown a tendency to do just that." He had already told Sonya of the Klingon oppression of his race nine hundred years ago. "After experiencing that kind of brutality, we were more devoted than ever to the tradition of the sanctity of life."

"And warming to the concept of cruel and unusual punishment." Sonya adjusted her tricorder, fighting against the dampening field that limited its range to mere meters. Power fluctuations on the deck below. Thermal signatures in the next room—more Resaurians standing posts in the auxiliary power room, most likely. "A life of confinement, spent inside a black hole?"

"Technically, we might never die." S'eth shrugged. "And the station had every possible convenience. With holographic technology, we might pretend that life was fairly normal."

"A silk prison," Fabian said. Everyone looked at him. "Old Earth history. Feudal Japan. Carol was telling me about it after that mission to the Kursican orbiting prison. You create a palacelike prison, as a show of respect for your prisoners."

Pattie shook her antennae in a negative way. "The Resaurian definition of 'palace' leaves a great deal to be desired."

S'eth slithered along next to Sonya, ducking his head in repeated apology. "It was a grand station, originally. But the . . . century of wear and use have stripped it down to the most basic elements. A large metal cage thrown into the darkest pit around."

Trust was going to be a long time in returning, Sonya

knew. If the S.C.E. team didn't *need* S'eth in order to complete their survey and find a way to reestablish comms with the *da Vinci* . . . She pointed out some welded doors, and the weld scorches that slashed the walls nearby. "Looks more like vandalism to me. Or damage from some of your ad hoc weapons."

"Most of that kind of damage is what is still left over from the riots. The early years were not easy ones on the twelve hundred who were cast away. We became our own small world, with factions and struggles and even a dictator who was prepared to risk everything— all of our lives—for a mad chance at freedom."

Lense hugged her arms, shivered. "I think I might have agreed with him."

"Es'a, the nest-breaker, was insane," S'eth said adamantly. "Even among the progressives, his thoughts were too radical. We looked for a saner method of escape, or of rescue."

A century, and meanwhile nearly eight hundred years had passed outside of the Demon. The conversion of Resaurian cycles to Federation years wasn't hard once they had the common Klingon calendar as a frame of reference between them. And it was just as easy for Sonya to calculate the time dilation (assuming a fairly constant standard) between the away team and the *da Vinci*. One hour on the station. Eight hours aboard ship. The captain must be tearing out what was left of his hair by the handfuls, if he hadn't already ripped his clothes and buried them.

No. Not David Gold. He wouldn't give up hope until he saw cold bodies. Maybe not even then.

Sonya slowed, dropping back for a moment to speak with Rennan Konya. The Betazoid security officer held on to every word spoken by S'eth. It was starting to unnerve her. "Everything okay?" she asked, perhaps a bit louder than required. She didn't want S'eth worried about the S.C.E. team. They still needed allies.

Rennan nodded slowly. "This is one of the rare times I wish I had a greater gift for telepathy. S'eth believes what he is saying. And I don't sense any immediate danger. But there is still something he's not telling us." He shook his head. "Like why they still have so many weapons if these riots took place so long ago."

"We've seen one hydroponics bay that might feed a tenth of the population he claims still lives on this station." Sonya glanced at some more scoring along the walls. "There is quite a bit our host isn't telling us." She drifted back forward, smiling as if Rennan had just given her good news.

"Don't worry," she said to the security guard. "We'll get out of here yet."

"Are you certain there is a chance to contact your ship?" S'eth asked.

Fabian glanced up from his own tricorder screen. "If we can find the transmitter array being used for your distress call, yes. With luck, we can modify the system and alert the *da Vinci* of our status."

"And without luck?" Lense asked.

Without luck, it would be ninety-three years before their change in the message worked its way up out of the black hole. Everyone knew the answer. Vinx simply shrugged. "I can create a fizzbin deck and teach you to play. It's good for passing time."

Sonya smiled. Not much got the *da Vinci* crew down for long. "I'd rather believe in a universe that contains luck," she said, paraphrasing James T. Kirk.

"Then you will convince your Captain Gold to climb down the anchor and, how did you say, 'bump shields' with us? That will let you transport everyone off the station?"

"It may take a few trips, but yes. We can manage that, I believe."

S'eth shook his head, pouching his neck muscles in what might have been a shrug of exasperation, or defeat. "I think it sounds like you are asking for the impossible as well."

She bristled, but it was Pattie who came to her rescue against S'eth's pessimism. "We're the S.C.E.," the Nasat said. "'Impossible' is our stock-in-trade."

Taken right off the lips of the S.C.E.'s overall commander, Captain Montgomery Scott, but Sonya couldn't have said it better herself.

Fabian could. Smiling, he walked over to a nearby wall hatch. Pulling his phaser, he didn't bother with the niceties of dismantling the hatch but instead sliced through the hinges. It fell into the corridor with a metallic clang. Behind the panel, an energy conduit pulsed with a modulated energy wave.

He snapped his tricorder off.

"Impossible takes an extra ten minutes," he said.

CHAPTER
13

The triumvirate of Resaurians faced the viewscreen, as inscrutable as ever; strangely, they were the only individuals on the bridge. Gold knew it was simply a problem of communications, but he couldn't help but think their emotionless faces were an act—a conscious move to hide their true emotions behind a façade.

It only enraged him further.

"So, this is how it went down," he said, uncaring that the endless hours of frustrating failures to bring his crew home were hemorrhaging into his voice. "For millennia you've peacefully passed through cycles of quick progression, followed by centuries of slow evolution. Until the Klingons came. They subjugated you, enslaved you, and after thoroughly altering your society, cast you aside. With more technology than you could possibly hope to deal with, your equilibrium shattered, the progressives came into power and held sway for a hundred years. Upheavals continued as you tried to come to terms with technology well beyond your cultural or moral development. Finally, in an act of desperation, the traditionalists overthrew the progressives and removed them from power. How am I doing so far?"

Gold couldn't care less about his sarcasm-laced words, as the trio continued to stare at him as though watching a bug they found fascinating, but ultimately would eat. He knew Abramowitz was probably having a conniption right about now, but he couldn't care less about that either. They'd lied to him. Lied to him on his own ship, while his crew was stuck in that hellhole they'd created.

"So, you'd overthrown the most powerful of the progressives, but you didn't know what to do. You couldn't kill them—the Klingons may have erased much of your culture, but that was one tradition that you'd jealously kept—so you constructed a prison inside the black hole and threw them. How long have they been down there? How long has this secret been kept?"

He stared daggers across the electronic gulf, and for the first time noticed something different. Sha'a had remained a statue during his rant and Suliss only less so, nodding once in a while as though to confirm and support everything he'd said. Captain S'linth, however, appeared agitated. If the councilman had not been so still, perhaps holding himself from giving anything away, Gold probably would not have even noticed S'linth's movements. Now, however, the slight sway of the head, the twitch of the arms, the quiver of the lips: they all added up to a captain who was receiving the surprise of a lifetime. *He's been lied to as well. Can the whole Resaurian population be blind to this but the councilmen? Or perhaps the overseers to each ship that the Council appoints?*

Gold looked again at those obsidian eyes and had his answer. "Councilman, answer me. You threw them into that hole for eternity."

"We did not kill them," Sha'a finally answered.

"What?" Gold launched himself out of his seat and moved to stand close to the screen; it changed nothing, but psychologically it was good to appear closer to them. "That's your answer? You didn't kill them? You for damn sure might as well have. It's been nine hundred years since they were tossed into that *mishegos*. The whole galaxy has changed in scope and then some since then. It would've been better to slit their throats and be done with it."

Finally, he seemed to reach the councilman, as his tongue wiggled for several long seconds. The Resaurian suddenly leaned forward and rested onto his legs for the first time in Gold's presence.

"Captain, it matters not what we did. Nor, by the egg, does it matter to you. This is our business and our station. You cannot interfere."

"Like hell I can't. That may be your station, but my people are on it." Gold was gratified to finally see some real emotion from Sha'a, as the councilman rocked back onto his tail and wove his head back and forth, quickly. That had taken him by surprise. "This may be Resaurian business, but you forgot to stick up a sign saying 'no trespassing.' We received a distress signal, we moved to assist, and now I've got seven of my crew trapped on that tin can. I'm going to get them out."

"You cannot do this."

"You don't seem to understand, Sha'a. My people are down there and I'm going to get them out. If that requires I pull out the entire space station and hand you back your exiles, so be it."

With that he motioned and the front screen went dark.

Time to bring his crew home.

Captain S'linth's lips ached from the act of not baring his fangs in dismay. He'd gone seven cycles on this bridge. Seven cycles of unfailing service to the Nest and the joy of exploring the astronomical wonders in near space; how had it come to this?

Suliss and Sha'a were bent in a whispered conversation, while he stood on the side, forgotten. He'd known that the real power behind each ship was the Council, regardless of how much a captain flexed against his overseer, but only now did he understand what a figurehead he truly was. A figurehead to be cast aside when necessary.

S'linth tasted the air and found a raw, blood harshness that demonstrated a will of iron. A will to do anything to accomplish what must be done.

He did not like it. Did not like it at all.

Could what the aliens said be true? Could their ancestors really have done something so terrible? Could the Council know about it? Could the stalwart councilman (ever the captain's crèche supporter) know of this?

He stabbed the air multiple times, drawing in as much sensation as he could muster. Try as he might, he could not deny what stood before him.

Against all tradition, he slithered forward, intruding, spoke.

"Third Councilman Sha'a, what will you do?"

Suliss, the nictitater, so afraid of the events transpiring before, rose up in fury and righteous indignation with power at his side, only to be cut off by a small gesture from Sha'a.

"Captain," he hissed softly, "what do you feel should be done?"

"I simply don't know, Councilman. I don't know."

He hissed laughter. "That is what I've always appreciated about you, Captain. Your are unfailingly truthful. However, I know what we must do. There really is no question." He turned to look back toward the now black viewscreen. "They must be stopped."

CHAPTER
14

Fabian and Pattie had worked a small miracle, one of several, routing the phased communication array back to the station's bridge. Cannibalizing a pattern enhancer for its amplifier circuits and reverse-engineering one of the station companels to meld it to Federation technology, they now had a working station that allowed for an only slightly distorted audio signal between the away team and the *da Vinci*.

Of course, it would never have worked without Tev's network of probes, forming a strong enough reception grid that the away team did not need to rely on the Resaurian method of a ninety-three-year transmission, but that's what teamwork meant. Didn't it?

A burst transmission squealed over the speakers. Sonya captured it, pulled it out over a better length of time.

"Waiting on your order," Tev told her.

"We're still getting ready here. Wait one." Sonya reminded herself to keep it short. Due to the time dilation, which was closer to two hundred percent than the eight hundred they had believed from S'eth's story, Tev would have to capture and speed up her sentences. If she bothered with many more long-winded reports, it would be another several hours of time on the *da Vinci* before they could attempt the rescue operation.

Another of Tev's inspirations—and a good one—was realizing that the gravitational anchor could be grabbed onto from the ship. Rather than skating the *da Vinci* down its length, worrying the entire time if they could make the careful rendezvous and then climb back out along the extremely narrow channel, Tev would use a modified dekyon beam to uproot the anchor while Gold "threw the ship into reverse" to haul them out like some kind of shuttle-pull event.

She had not been stinting with her praise, either.

"Tev, that's ingenious." It didn't matter that Fabian had provided the initial genesis of the plan with his story about *Voyager*'s run-in with a small singularity. He had put it all together and delivered a sound and only seemingly impossible plan. The hallmark of an excellent Starfleet engineer.

His answer? *"Of course."*

Self-righteous prig, she thought. How many times would he knock away her hand, even when it reached out to give him some applause?

"How are we doing?" Sonya called out, checking her team's status.

Lense stood by near Sonya, no doubt hoping her services would not be needed but ready nonetheless.

Security held positions at the operations center's only two entrances, keeping a low profile as they watched for anything that might resemble more of the Resaurian's makeshift weapons. So far, things looked on the up and up.

Pattie and Fabian tore into another of the workstations. The one kept in the best working order by S'eth's crew. Three of the Resaurians hovered over them, worriedly wringing hands and making small ducking motions with their sinuous necks. This was the gravitational anchor control station, working in direct concert with the station shielding as S'eth had promised. The S.C.E. team had no intention of dropping the shields, however.

They were working to strengthen them.

Pattie scuttled out from behind the panel's open back, trailing some waveform guides that she had managed to remove in favor of Federation EPS conduit. Amazing what one could salvage from an environmental suit.

"Fabian just about has it. If we can strengthen the shield harmonics, we can hopefully 'lighten' the displacement of the entire station." She said that loud enough for any Resaurian ears. Quietly, the Nasat added, "And for all of S'eth's complaints, we are not the first ones to do this. You wondered why the time dilation was only two hundred percent? Because the shields are already running at double strength."

So the Resaurian prisoners had lived through four hundred years of captivity? Their life spans weren't that long. Or was the modification more recent? Something on the order of one hundred years? About the same length as the distress call? She looked for S'eth, and found him slithering a narrow box around Fabian's work area. What more wasn't the Resaurian leader telling her?

Mysteries to be solved later. Fabian came squirming

out from under the smaller access panel. "Good as we're going to get," he said. "I got us another twenty-five percent. Any more and we might overload the circuits."

S'eth held himself rock-steady. "I would not recommend that."

Sonya could almost feel sorry for the Resaurian. "Neither would I," she said. "Let's do it."

Fabian went back to the anchoring station, Pattie to the main power supply junction in case the heavy power demands required a quick reroute. Lense moved a bit closer to Sonya, who stayed at her post at the communications panel.

Domenica and Rennan smiled their support. Vinx was picking his teeth with a small metal toothpick, slouching back against the wall as if it were just another day for an Iotian.

Sonya opened a channel. "Ready as we're going to be," she said, echoing Fabian's report. And because she couldn't resist: "Pop the clutch, Captain."

Gripping the sides of her station, she spared one more glance behind her. "Everyone might want to grab hold of something."

Tev sniffed contently. Satisfaction radiated from every pore. A flow of organized chaos spun itself around him on the bridge as almost every crew member present moved to his strings. The only mar on the moment: the absence of Commander Gomez, whose attitude usually revolved around the question of what Tev had done for her lately. She would not be here to see him in his best form.

Then again, she would be rescued by his orchestration, and that held its own appeal.

"Tev." The captain greeted him as Gold strode onto the bridge. "Well, it appears that things are well in hand." Tev only nodded in response, too absorbed in the execution of his plan to be truly aware of extraneous details.

His pudgy fingers moved swiftly across the interface, bringing the final bits of information in. Though the away team would not be brought back without him, he admitted to Gomez's aid in collecting and transmitting *some* key data. Specifics on the gravitational anchor, gleaned from this S'eth, being the most important. She'd been of some use, at least.

"Ensign Haznedl," Tev spoke abruptly. "I need that final data analysis immediately."

"Yes, sir. I'm finishing up the compression now."

The operations officer didn't have the proper deference in her voice while speaking to a superior, but Tev simply couldn't spare a moment to instruct her. As with so many on this ship, he'd take her aside later and inform her of her error.

"Got it. Looks like the team peaked the yield at twenty-six-point-seven percent. They've got a good grip." The ensign shot the data over to Tev's workstation only after her commentary.

Pulling in the last of the data, Tev trusted nothing to the analysis of someone else. He reviewed it himself, and pulled it into shape. The puzzle finally fit . . . and the whole resonated within his mind at its magnificence.

A plan well thought out and about to be well executed.

"Captain," he said. "The system is ready when you are."

Gold ordered Shabalala to sound yellow alert and to

be ready to go to red alert should the Resaurians attempt to interfere. As if that ranked higher in importance than his mission; why had the captain not waited for his statement?

"Captain," he said louder, standing up to formally gain notice.

A few more frustrating moments passed as the captain finished debriefing tactical and then turned toward Tev.

"Yes, Tev?"

No contrition whatsoever! "Captain, the system is stabilized and ready to initiate."

"I know you told me once before, Tev, but humor an old man and explain it again. In as simple terms as possible."

He had no compunction about explaining it again, though he thought the captain must be attempting human-style humor again; he *had* explained it simply before.

"I have precise measurements on the gravitational anchor being extended from the station. Our modified dekyon beam will act as a grapple, uprooting it and binding it to us instead of local subspace. The probes I'd previously deposited not only established contact with Commander Gomez but are now acting as a regulating grid within the photon sphere, helping to inhibit the blacksplash of gravimetric waves around the station and the anchor as well." Tev realized he was almost sweating with the effort of simplifying his explanation. "This will allow us to latch on to the anchor and, using the probes to synchronize the energy levels and minimize any stress waves, it will be a simple matter to pull the entire station past the photon sphere and ultimately out of the black hole's gravity well."

"It appears as though you've got every base covered."

"Of course I have," Tev responded, surprised.

"Do you see any reason not to engage?"

Tev furrowed his brow, wondering if the captain was calling him on something. Had the captain noticed something he had not? Or was this simply Gold's way? "No, Captain, there is no reason to delay whatsoever."

Gold sat down in his seat and surveyed his crew. Then with a firm nod, he said, "Good. Engage."

Tev nodded in return and seated himself once more. With satisfaction he initiated the sequence.

Power flowed down computer systems and ignited the dekyon tractor beam. Transmitted signals flashed down relays to the probes, igniting their own sequences, energy pulsing and meshing into a cohesive whole to bring the station out.

Data readouts confirmed all systems nominal, and the *da Vinci*, without even a tremble, began moving backward. Data streams from inside the photon sphere confirmed the displacement of the station from its anchored position for so many centuries; it began to gain altitude above the event horizon.

Settling back, content, Tev knew there really was nothing further to do but allow the computer to execute his masterful plan.

The tension on the bridge, held at a peak for several minutes, now began to ease as long seconds passed and success seemed imminent. Just as Tev readied a vocal transmission to Gomez, a fluctuation on his data terminal caused him to pause momentarily. It had been entirely within his stress parameters, but he could not deny that it bothered him. There should not have been—

Vertigo stretched a sickening hand across the bridge,

and Tev's inner ear complained. The ship lurched horribly, flinging crew around like a crazed giant tired of its playthings. Tev, wedged tightly in his seat, survived the worst of it, his grip iron-strong on the edge of his workstation, eyes bolted to the readouts.

—an entire crashing of waves splintered and shattered across his terminal—the beauty of his order shattered by chaos.

CHAPTER
15

This could not be happening.

Tev frantically punched up data readouts and yet each contained the same information. As the crew scrambled to secure the ship and the pounding it was taking from the horrible backsplash of gravimetric waves, Tev sat as an island of one, wholly concentrating in an effort to save his beautiful, ordered plan. The gravitational anchor that he had snared, uprooted, was loose, and slipping through subspace as it clawed for purchase. Tev fought to reestablish a hold on it with his dekyon grapple. Missed.

The captain's call to him finally intruded on the third try and Tev turned to look in Gold's direction.

"What happened?!" The discourtesy of the yell did not even penetrate.

"I do not know, Captain."

"What do you mean, you don't know?"

"One moment, the dekyon beam and the energy grid through the probes inside were stable and the next . . . chaos." For the first time in his life, Tev stared defeat in the face and it left him speechless.

"Tev!" the captain yelled once more to overcome his shock. "This is why you are here. You're the only one who can tell us what happened. You! No one else."

The praise sank in and stuck, pulling enough of him out of the stupor to ignite his fierce intellect.

Fingers once more probed for electronic answers. They had to be here. The fluctuations he'd seen were not from the ship. He could not verify that they did not originate from the station, but if he *assumed* competence on the part of Commander Gomez . . .

Tev hardly noticed another breaking wave of gravimetrics that tossed the ship about like a cork in the surf, sending Lieutenant Shabalala straight into a bulkhead.

If not the ship and not the station . . . Tev remembered the captain's conversation with tactical. He reset his parameters, searching . . . found it!

"Captain," Tev said.

"What?"

"I've found the anomaly."

"And?"

"The Resaurian ship, Captain. Its tractor beam is attempting to latch on to our ship."

The *da Vinci* tumbled, and an EPS conduit blew sparks out from beneath the operations console. Ensign Haznedl fell out of her chair, her uniform scorched and torn.

Gold hung into his seat with white knuckles and a furious glare for the cause of this chaos. "Did they cause this?"

"I think it could be," Tev said. The admission was difficult. This fit the parameters, but he couldn't be certain. "Such interference could easily have shattered the dekyon beam."

Rage suffused Gold's face. As the captain dealt with that news, Tev turned to a strident alarm from his interface; the anchor was slipping farther into the gravity well, toward the photon sphere.

Which meant that the space station was falling toward the Demon's event horizon.

Power failures began in the jury-rigged communications station, cutting Sonya off from the *da Vinci*. She had all of three seconds' warning. Enough time to begin, "I think there's something—" and then a shower of sparks exploded from the primary power relay being guarded by P8 Blue.

The Nasat chirruped an alarm, sprayed down the junction with fire retardant chemicals, and then leapt for the secondary relay to work on a quick power transfer. It blew up just about in her face, shooting flame and globules of hot molten steel toward her eyes. Pattie curled up into a protective ball, and was still.

Resaurians reacted quickly, shouting for S'eth and swarming toward the gravitational anchor controls as well as to either exit. Corsi disappeared within a rush of snakelike bodies, carried with them into the corridor beyond. S'eth was one of those congregating around the anchor controls, worried that the overloads might dump power to the most critical system on the station.

Fabian stayed with him, monitoring, calling out the shift in shield harmonics. "Down ten percent . . . twenty-five . . . forty!"

Which meant the anchor characteristics were changing by the second, as was the station's subjective displacement. Sonya had turned toward Pattie, but Lense was faster and she was needed here, to get back in touch with the *da Vinci*. Yanking open the maintenance access cover, she reached in to grab hold of her team's work.

Which was when the first gravimetric wave slammed sidelong into the station, bucking the deck beneath Sonya's feet. She stumbled, fell sliding. Lights died all across the operations center.

Slamming against the corner of an abandoned workstation, Sonya caught the edge against the side of her head, and stars exploded in her vision.

Resaurian alarms rang out over the bridge, sounding like metallic rattles. The Resaurians themselves slithered and ducked about in the near total dark, backlit only by one of the small electrical fires or the main screen that still, with all the failures, showed the bright circle of stars clustered at the top of the Demon's gravity well.

Another gravimetric wave shook the station roughly. Sonya's sense of balance swam before her eyes, and she felt heavier, awkward. Gravity fluctuated—or maybe that was just her head that pounded to the sound of large spikes being driven into her brain, burning where she had clipped the station corner. Rolling to her hands and knees, she tried to shake her head clear.

Nearly fainted.

"Commander!"

Rennan's yell was close by, but she couldn't see him. Blood oozed from the wound, trickling past her ear and down into her hair, over her face. A smear burned at the corner of her left eye. The sound of shots, phasers, welders. She smelled the acrid scent of hot metalwork, looking up in time to see one of the bridge's welded doors spit a fury of angry sparks around three sides. It fell inward with a large crash, and more Resaurian bodies crashed through into S'eth and Fabian.

Then rough hands seized her, hauling her forward.

And nothingness finally claimed her.

They had lied to Gold on his own ship and now the Resaurians had apparently doomed seven more of his crew to die. Captain David Gold did not entertain violent thoughts; few Starfleet captains did, or they'd not be in command of a vessel. But at this moment, as he suddenly found himself facing Galvan VI all over again, the idea of several photon torpedoes was somehow comforting.

"Captain." Tev interrupted his bloody fantasy. He turned and shucked himself of such delusions. There would be time for recompense later. Rational recompense. Right now, he had to rescue his crew.

"What have you got, Tev?"

"The anchor has completely torn away. The station is falling."

Not on his watch it wasn't! "Is there any way to grasp the anchor before it vanishes beyond the photon sphere?"

"No, Captain. A dekyon beam is not a lasso to grasp a moving target. It was only a viable option against a rock-steady target." Tev snorted. "Even then, it really was only viable because of the addition of the probes and their dampening effect. There is nothing to stop the fall of the station."

Gold nodded, his mind working furiously. A shadow walked across his grave, and he shuddered, knowing what he had to do.

He stood like a sailor of old, rock-steady on his deck as his ship bobbed among the gravimetric waves and he stared his nightmare in the face. His granddaughter had never been in danger. All along it had been he who faced death. Of course he had always known and accepted that, but never had it seemed more personal than right this moment. Gold might never see *any* of his grandchildren again. Might never see his beloved Rachel again, or listen to her harsh but loving ribbing.

For an instant, he wavered. He'd lost twenty-three of his crew not so long ago and he'd be damned if he'd lose seven more. If that meant he never saw his own loved ones again, then so be it.

Such was the price of wearing the red.

"Tev, we need to cross the photon sphere."

To his credit, the Tellarite slowly blinked without a word, as he considered all the ramifications and other possible solutions before nodding. "It is the only way to secure the station and recover the crew," he agreed.

Gold breathed deeply. For a brief moment he'd hoped that Tev might have another plan. Another idea that would save them from this. But there wasn't.

There was only the Demon and the best damn crew he'd ever had the pleasure of commanding.

Looking around the bridge, his eyes came to rest on Wong, who looked expectantly over his shoulder at him. Gold saw no doubt in the young lieutenant's eyes.

"Take us in," he said. "Straight into the maw of the Demon."

CHAPTER 16

Sonya Gomez came back to the universe slowly. Echoes of the Big Bang rolled around inside her head. Flashes of formless light slowly took shape as her consciousness struggled against the cobwebs that entangled it. Like a ship fighting against the clutches of an inescapable gravity well.

Seizing on this thought, her mind brought her back to the Demon.

The plan, she reflected, had been half-perfect.

Tev's half, no doubt, as the Tellarite would certainly explain smugly if she ever made it back to the *da Vinci*.

Sonya groaned. Whether from the possibility of another insufferable lecture by Tev or due to the painful jog of footsteps that pounded through her brain, she couldn't be certain.

Footsteps!

Sonya opened her eyes and tried to sit up and reached for her phaser, all at once. The result was not pleasant. Pain hammered at her temples. Her arm slipped out from beneath her, tingling with numbness, and she collapsed back against the cold steel deck, striking the side of her face and shooting fireworks off behind her eyes. About the only thing she accomplished with her action was a brief glimpse of one of her captors.

Resaurian. So far she had seen Resaurians with coral red scales, others with greenish black, and even one of dull gold. This one had looked pale blue—almost an Andorian coloring—and sat-stood with typical Resaurian posture, resting back on a thick tail and using thin legs for tripod stability.

Sonya also thought it had looked a good deal smaller—only three or four feet tall—but that was hard to tell from the floor.

Cautiously this time, she opened her eyes. No one.

She lay on a cold steel floor, her face bruised and aching along her left side. The deck was filthy with a thick dust of dried skin from Resaurian shedding mixed with metal granules and filings. The sound of footsteps and the scraping brush of scales against deckplate came from behind her and above her, and every few moments the entire station trembled a deep shudder. Her tongue felt swollen. She dry-swallowed several times, tasting old blood.

Still alive, though. Always a step in the right direction.

She stared into the open bay of an old transport lift. Somehow she simply *knew* the lift shaft ended behind a welded set of doors on the station's bridge. Near where she had been, her team working with the *da Vinci* to haul the station out of the black hole. The doors had blown inward.

Weapons fire.

Shouting.

P8 Blue had been knocked across the room and Sonya had . . . she'd . . .

Stop this, she ordered herself. *What do you remember? What did you see?*

S'eth had shown the engineers the station's upper levels. Rigging a way to contact the *da Vinci,* using a relay system of probes set out by Tev, a plan had been formed. Two plans, actually. The first, hers, had involved sliding the *da Vinci* along the gravitational anchor, bringing the vessel down into the Demon to bump shields with the station and transport survivors aboard. It would have taken several trips, with over a thousand lives to save, but possible. In the Starfleet Corps of Engineers, a can-do attitude was not just a help. It was required.

Tev, of course, lived and breathed that ideal. He one-upped Sonya's plan by coming up with a way to uproot the station's gravitational anchor from outside the black hole, and then use it like a lifeline to simply haul the station up and out.

Simple. Direct. Brilliant.

Disastrous, as it turned out.

Everything had gone wrong so very quickly, it was still a jumble in her head. Her team's efforts to keep a stable field around the station had failed as power relay stations blew under the stressed load. The anchor slipped, caught, and then slipped again.

And then the attack came.

No other explanation. The old, welded-shut doors had burst inward—under directional charges, she guessed—and Sonya had been caught in the concussive force. After that, it all turned hazy.

She remembered the shouts. Seeing Konya swept back away from an arcing panel . . . and Corsi going down under an assault of weapons fire.

Hands grabbing at her shoulders and legs. Lifting her. Carrying her into the old lift.

Taking her prisoner.

"What kind of mess have we fallen into this time?" she asked aloud, her words breaking inside a parched throat.

"Very bad mess," a soft voice hissed from behind and above.

She hadn't expected an answer. Especially one from so close. Sonya blinked hard, banishing the last of the fog from her vision and thoughts. With a great deal of effort she rolled onto her back.

A Resaurian crouched over her, looking very tall and unhealthily thin, with mottled, red scales and dry, dead black eyes. She felt at her hip. No phaser. "But I'm still alive," she said aloud, as if confirming that fast.

"Yesss . . ." The Resaurian nodded. "But not for much longer," he said, reaching down for Sonya. She tried to fend him off, but he was quick, striking down to grab her under both elbows, hauling her to unsteady feet.

"Not unless you do as Es'a says."

CHAPTER
17

The backsplash of gravimetric waves continued to pummel the *da Vinci*. A tough vessel, able to weather a harsh pounding, the ship nevertheless felt the immense stress as the Demon attempted to wrench it from its position and pull it down to oblivion.

Tev snuffled, his fingers dancing over the console. Only five minutes ago he'd faced the specter of failure. When the station's gravitational anchor had slipped from the *da Vinci's* grasp, he'd considered it the low point of his otherwise bright career. Captain Gold's quick action, taking the ship deeper into the black hole's embrace, had given him a second chance. Instead of grabbing at the anchor again, which just was not possible, he'd used a modified dekyon beam to "spear" the anchor into place. A tense and troubling moment.

One he would never face again if he had any say.

He leaned forward against the console to help balance against a particularly harsh wave that slewed the ship one way and whipped it back another. Even Tev found it difficult to believe the dekyon beam held. Then again, Tev found it difficult to believe most of what had occurred in the last short while. He'd never been in such dire straits, with ten things demanding his attention and all of them critical to success. His mouth felt like sand had been scraped across his tongue and his eyes ached as though he'd been staring at an A6-class star without polarization filters.

"What have you got for me, Tev?" Captain Gold's voice interrupted. Tev continued to stare at his monitors, drawing their information like a poison from a wound: analyzing, detecting, compartmentalizing, scrutinizing. However, the more he looked, the more he realized that to fix an error, he might have made a worse one.

"Tev?" The captain's voice rang loud, filled with all the years of command at his disposal. The Tellarite blinked once, and looked up at the captain.

"What?"

Gold slowly stood and walked over to within a foot of Tev, an amazing feat considering the ship slewed twice. "Tev, I need you here. Now. The ship needs you. My people on that station need you. You stopped the station falling; now I need to know how to pull us back out."

The physical intrusion of the captain into his space, along with his rude comments, simply didn't scratch Tev's exterior. Only the tone of voice and the look in Gold's blue eyes left an indelible mark. Later he would admit (only to himself) that at that moment, Gold had had a more commanding presence than any Tellarite officer he'd ever served under.

Tev blinked, his coal black eyes giving none of this

away. "I had to reroute power from the rear shields, Captain, but by increasing the dekyon beam threefold, we seem to have 'speared' the anchor in place."

"If it's speared in place, how can we pull it out? If you unspear it, won't that simply allow the anchor to slip once more?"

"That is a problem," Tev admitted. "Though I believe I've found an answer." He didn't mention that he still believed even this answer to the problem would only make it worse in the end. The proverbial cure that is worse than the disease.

Gold stared hard at Tev. "Out with it."

He'd simply waited for a command. Why had the captain's tone changed? "I'm going to attempt to split the dekyon beam into two streams. The first will stay attached to the anchor, while I'll attempt to spear a second beam into subspace .0025 light-seconds farther above the photon sphere than the first beam. I will then remodulate the beams, creating a synchronic sine wave that will merge the two beams. Provided the modulation is correct, the wave will merge the first beam to the second, not the other way around, and leverage the station and anchor approximately seven hundred fifty kilometers farther out of the gravity well. Obviously this will need to be repeated numerous times; I should be able to increase the distance between the two beams before merging, the higher above the event horizon I drag it, accelerating the process."

Only after finishing did it dawn on Tev that he'd actually used an if/then statement. For the first time since his cadet days, he'd given a qualified answer about whether the modulation of the dekyon streams would be successful. He realized with irritation that if Commander Gomez had been present, she would have already verified his findings. With so much splintering his concentration, such a confirmation would have been welcome, even from *her*.

"Bootstrapping. *Gevalt*. Only you would find a way to bootstrap a station out of a black hole."

What did a boot—or a strap for that matter—have to do with what he'd just said? He raised his bushy eyebrows, continued. "Captain, the only real issue is one of power. I already had to redirect most of the power from the rear shields just to increase the dekyon beam enough to spear the anchor. To create two streams with sufficient intensity for our needs, I'll need to divert most of the power from all the shields, as well as drawing from life support."

The captain paused and glanced toward tactical, where Piotrowski had relieved Shabalala after the latter had been taken to sickbay. The tactical officer had been thrown into a bulkhead by the wash of gravimetric waves after they *(admit it, Tev, after you!)* had lost the anchor. Tev knew what the captain had to be thinking. If the shields were lowered to such a level, it would leave them open to a possible attack by the Resaurian ship.

After a review of the data, Tev no longer believed that the Resaurians had tried to disrupt the first rescue attempt. A failure on the station also fit the circumstance, and additional data pointed more strongly toward that solution. Still, the aliens had shown themselves unhappy with the *da Vinci*'s interference, and the fact was that dampened shielding might tempt them into a permanent solution. Gold would be laying the vessel bare for the fire and spit. Tev didn't envy the captain at this moment.

Not at all.

The ship lurched and yawed as though it had struck a sandbar; only the lightning quick reflexes of the captain in snagging the edge of Tev's console kept Gold from stumbling. The rest of the crew had strapped themselves fully into place after realizing the inertial dampers simply could not compensate for the awesome forces being unleashed by the black hole's backsplash. Even so, Gold still found his feet almost above Tev's head for a moment, before he dropped like a stone to the deck and stumbled to one knee.

"That's it. Haznedl, divert all shield and life support control to Tev's command. We will not lose that station. Piotrowski, you will keep your eyes glued to that Resaurian ship. If they even so much as turn on a landing light, I want to know about it."

"Yes, sir," came the instant responses.

A quick shifting of schematics on Tev's monitors showed Ensign Susan Haznedl's competence as the shields and life support controls were handed over.

Gold glanced at Tev and nodded. *Go.*

With a deep breath and another stab of annoyance that Gomez's absence meant he could not reverify his calculations, Tev reached out and began to massage power away from the shields. At thirty percent power, he halted; any further and they might not hold up to the thrashing the gravimetric waves were handing out with relish. Verifying that the specified cargo holds contained no personnel, he locked them down and drew additional life support power.

Having reached his predetermined requirements, he fed the algorithmic calculations into the computer. The tension of the moment, his own frustration at losing control of the situation and at Gomez's absence began to ease as the computer took his finely crafted formulae and extrapolated them as necessary. After a final deep breath, Tev tapped another interface, and a brilliant beam of ghostly energy tore through near space and punched a hole into subspace. Though no visible distortion could be seen on the main viewscreen beyond the beam's simply ceasing to exist, the subspace monitor went haywire as overlapping energy fields showed the displacement of local subspace and the terrible forces the dekyon beam poured into the region.

Though separated by .0025 light-seconds, the interference between the two beams caused whorls in subspace that began to show that his initial assessment, regardless of his wish to deny it, had been correct. His fingers rekeyed the modulations and initiated the sequence to draw the two beams together.

As the beams began to slowly merge, his worst fears were realized. The distortions in subspace, along with the initial spearing of the anchor by the dekyon beam, were beginning to shred it. And try as he might, Tev simply had been unable to determine the anchor's makeup, much less how he might replicate it.

"Captain," he began, while his fingers keyed back the dekyon beams and cut off the secondary stream of energy; how much additional damage he'd just done he did not know. However, he did know with absolute certainty that if he'd continued, the anchor would've torn apart completely, leaving them absolutely nothing to use in stopping the fall of the station.

"What, Tev? Why'd you stop?"

For the second time in a day, failure reared its ugly head: a bitter pill that tasted vile going down. If Gomez had verified his calculations, he would've been able to determine the extent to which the gravity anchor's structural integrity would be affected. Bitter tonic for hindsight.

"The anchor is shredding, Captain." He took a deep breath, stood, and faced the captain. His to take responsibility for. "My solution is no solution at all; it has only further damaged the already weakened anchor. The twin streams are no longer a viable solution."

"What are our options, Tev?" Tev could feel the disappointment radiating from the crew.

He tried not to gag on the words. "We should follow Commander Gomez's original plan. Transverse the photon sphere and overlap our shields with that of the station and transport the lot of them. And it must be done quickly, before the anchor shreds away to nothingness."

CHAPTER
18

Rennan Konya leaned out over the dark, gaping shaft, one hand wrapped around the emergency ladder, the other holding a tricorder up to his face. Faint tones whistled and lights danced on the dark screen. The readings were faint, and might not have been much more than an interference spike peeking through the station's dampening fields. They might also be life signs. Human.

Sonya Gomez.

A rope tugged at his waist. The lifeline Vinx held. "In a moment," Rennan said. He leaned farther out over the abyss. A tremor shook the station, and the ladder trembled.

The rope tightened and hauled him away from the drop. Rennan felt the physical move coming at his shoulder, ducked, and sidestepped right, falling back into a ready stance.

"Easy, Konya." Lieutenant Commander Domenica Corsi frowned, dropping her hand back to her side.

Vinx stood behind her, the sturdy Iotian still holding the safety line. Off to one side Fabian Stevens conferred quietly with P8 Blue. Stevens went back to work over his own tricorder, inputting data. The Nasat returned to her study of the lift mechanisms. She rose up on her back four legs, half-crawling up the wall to study the weld-cuts that had sliced open the doors.

"S'eth would like to speak with us. I want you there." Corsi's gaze strayed to Rennan's hairline. "You should get that looked at."

Reaching up, he probed carefully at the large swelling peeking out of his dark hair. Pain answered every light touch. Dried blood flaked off beneath his fingers. "I'm fine, Commander."

The *da Vinci*'s chief of security looked torn between ordering him to see Dr. Lense and physically compelling him. Her rank gave her command with Sonya Gomez missing in action. She was also quite obviously spoiling for a fight. No Betazoid training was required to detect *that*. He saw it in the angry flush spreading out of her blond hair, her shorter breaths, and the hard set of her blue eyes.

She also might have the juice to take him. They worked out together occasionally, aboard ship, and so far his Betazoid touch had barely been able to keep pace with her reflexes and greater strength. But this was not the time or place for a contest.

"There's too much to do," he said.

She exhaled sharp frustration. "All right." Backing off, she waited while he untied the safety line and handed it to Vinx. "Keep an eye on things," she ordered the Iotian.

Vinx set the coil of line to one side, unslung his phaser rifle. "You bet, doll. I got the drop on 'em." He took up a position near the two engineers, making sure that any nearby Resaurians could see him.

Rennan felt Corsi tense with the familiar address, an involuntary response to the Iotian's freewheeling attitude, but she overrode the need to correct her subordinate here and now. Instead, she gestured Rennan to follow alongside her as they left the alcove.

The station's bridge was still in shambles. The wounded sat against one wall, tended by Elizabeth Lense and one of the snakelike Resaurians. Blood stained the doctor's uniform, though none of it apparently her own. Resaurians slithered back and forth, bringing tools and replacement parts to damage control teams. The station trembled again, and everyone stopped, looked down, as if waiting for the end to come. When it did not they rushed back to work. Panels lay out in the middle of the floor, away from antique workstations where Resaurians burrowed back into nests of wiring and conduit to reach damaged components. These stations had not looked in prime condition before the attack, showing many dark screens and jury-rigged repairs. Now, piles of smoking circuit boards and twists of blackened fiber-optic cable littered the deck. The ozone stench of electrical fires and suppressant powder hung in the air, left an acrid taste in the back of his throat.

Or maybe that was the taste of failure.

Everything had happened so fast. The power relay station blowing up into a fireball, throwing Pattie across the bridge. That was when Gomez went down. Rennan managed to dodge two Resaurians armed with crudely made cutting lasers, trying to reach her side, but a third swung a simple bar of metal into his path.

He didn't duck quite fast enough.

"How much of a read do you have on the Resaurians?" Corsi asked, quietly. She nodded toward where S'eth directed repairs. The Resaurian leader stood near the main viewscreen, which looked out of the black hole's photon sphere. Stars gathered in a small, intense circle in the middle of the screen. Bands of blue-shifted light marked each Einstein Ring. The rest: nothingness.

Rennan slowed, buying time to think. Explaining Betazoid training was difficult in most textbook cases. His position was more unique.

"My skill is in tapping the motor reflex area of the brain, not the thought process. I knew before that our 'host' was keeping something from us, and I communicated that to Commander Gomez, but he never exactly lied."

"What does that mean, 'never exactly lied'?"

"If S'eth believes what he is saying, even if he shades his explanation, I cannot distinguish between a fervent wish and the truth."

"Wonderful."

Corsi separated slightly from him, giving both of them free space in case sudden violence became necessary. Rennan wasn't too certain that it would not. There was a great deal of hostility in the Resaurians now. And fear. He felt both in their muscle twitches and agitated pacing. The two never mixed well.

S'eth saw them approach, tucked his legs back and slithered over, meeting them halfway. Greenish black scales protected him from blunt-tipped nose to tail. His vulnerable underbody usually had a more emerald cast to it. Rennan saw that those scales had paled to a pea green. Shock, blood loss, or something else? S'eth had a shoulder wound from the earlier fighting, bandaged quite efficiently by Dr. Lense.

"Lieutenant Commander." He bowed low, nictitating membranes rolling up to protect his coal-dark eyes. "Have you found any sign of your Commander Gomez?"

"Other than a blood trail and some impressive damage to the wall back there? No." Corsi did not sound in any mood for diplomacy. "Maybe you should tell us what we're up against, S'eth. Why did your people attack us?"

"Not my people!" He reared back, much like a snake preparing to strike. Rennan tensed, but S'eth simply rested back on a thick coil. "Es'a, the nest-breaker."

The name sounded familiar. Rennan remembered hearing the Resaurian mention it before. "Maybe you should give it to us from the top," he suggested, playing "good cop."

S'eth hissed a long, drawn-out sigh. "For decades, our . . . we . . . thought to escape. Equipment was dismantled and reassembled. We learned. We planned. But the traditionalists were careful. Our theories always fell short of resources, and we slowly resigned ourselves to our fate. This became our world.

"Except for Es'a. He . . . was a young engineer, and insane. He would risk all our lives for any mad gamble to escape. His plan involves major alterations to the shield generator controls, which are all that anchor us inside the Demon. To prevent this, several decades ago we seized the bridge and many upper levels, including life support. Es'a and his followers control the lower levels—most of our hydroponics and our fusion reactors. We have a stalemate. We survive."

"Yet you worked with us to escape," Rennan said.

"You have outside resources. The risk seemed acceptable."

Did it? Then why did S'eth's muscles contract tightly as he said this? Rennan felt the Resaurian's tension, but sensed no impending hostile action. He nodded, and Corsi asked, "Why did Es'a take Commander Gomez?"

"So that he too may control new resources. The nest-breakers will let us know his demands." He ducked his head, in apology it seemed. "We will not bow to him. I am sorry."

Rennan stepped on Corsi's impending outburst. "So are we," he said calmly, nodding his commander back and leading her away from the Resaurian leader. When she started to speak, the muscles in her jaw loosening, he simply shook his head. *Not yet.*

Not until they were back at the lift shaft. Vinx stepped back, letting them pass. Then he swung back on guard like some kind of brute enforcer, with a Starfleet-issue phaser rifle. Stevens and Pattie waited for them in the alcove. The sounds of repair from the main floor were slightly muted inside the alcove, and the smell of burnt wiring not so prevalent.

"What?" Corsi demanded shortly.

"He lied to us. For the first time I can be certain. Right there at the end. But I can't say what he lied about."

The intimidating blonde looked ready to march back in and wring answers from the Resaurian. "Is he dangerous to us?" she asked.

"Everyone is dangerous, Commander. You know that. It's only a matter of what pressures set them off, and how they choose to act." Rennan shook his head. "I am certain that he will not help us recover Commander Gomez. We will need to mount our own rescue attempt."

Corsi gestured to the engineers. "What have you got?"

Pattie shrugged. For a Nasat, the gesture involved multiple sets of legs and a lowering of her antennae. She had examined the lift doors carefully, but had very little to report. "Obviously the doors were cut away," the structural specialist said. "Some kind of torching compound, hot enough to cut through steel but without the concussive force of shaped charges."

Stevens agreed. "I saw it come down. Right in the middle of the attack." He ran fingers back through his short-cropped black hair. "Welding sparks drew fast lines around the entire edge of the door."

Rennan had seen the same. He'd been on the move, to assist Pattie. If he'd veered over in time . . .

"Fabian?" Corsi asked. "What about the station? Where are the repairs?"

"No one is saying much, so it's hard to say." That had to be hard for the engineer to admit. "The damage is extensive. There are many redundancies built in, but the way the power grid selectively blew . . . I don't know. I'd almost swear it was done deliberately."

Corsi nodded. "The timing of the assault came right on the heels of that first power rupture. It certainly is suspect."

"Well, we have some time," he said. "It looks like the anchor grabbed hold again. But the station's trembling has them worried. We may be slipping farther into the black hole. Or the shields may be failing, which means that gravitational tides will rip us apart. We've no word from the *da Vinci,* and zero fail-safes if that anchor gives way."

"We have to assume that Captain Gold has the rest of the ship bent toward rescuing us. In the meantime, I want options. How do we reestablish contact? What can we do on our own? S'eth mentioned that the lower-decks faction had a plan to use the shield generators in a plan to escape. Look into that."

"What about the commander?" Pattie asked. Like Rennan, her concern seemed to be with the recovery of Sonya Gomez. "We could split into two teams—"

And though he knew it wrenched at Corsi's gut, the security chief shook her head. "We have no way of knowing where she's been taken. It's a big station, and our tricorders are all but useless with the shields' dampening effect. Commander Gomez would agree that our first priority is to get free of the Demon."

"I don't know," Fabian said. He squirmed, obviously uncomfortable speaking against Corsi. His attraction to her was just as plain (to Rennan) as his respect for the chain of command. "Sonya would be the first one on point if it were one of us missing."

"You mean she'd be running solo while the rest of us worked on the problem at hand. But we don't have the resources. We can't spare you and Pattie from the repairs. Dr. Lense won't leave her patients. And you all need security to watch out for trouble." Corsi stared them all down. "I don't like it either, but that's where we are."

Slowly, sullenly, Stevens and the Nasat peeled away to head back to work. Which left Rennan with his superior officer. "It should be me," he said.

Corsi blinked. It was her only physical reaction, and the lack of response itself was enough to convince Rennan that he was right. "I don't know what you mean," she said.

"I felt your muscles ease when you mentioned Commander Gomez running off alone. And you are clamping down on your own fight-or-flight impulses even now. You're going off after Gomez. Or you think you are. But it should be me."

Corsi glanced back from the alcove, checking that Fabian had moved far enough that they would not be overheard. "No. It shouldn't. Our responsibility is to the engineers still here, still working to get us home. Ordering out a solo security guard would be irresponsible."

"And going it alone is not?"

"My career," Corsi said. "My choice."

Rennan took a step closer. He sensed that this might come down to physical action, and wanted to negate Corsi's longer reach. "I have the best chance to find her. You know that. Tricorders aren't reliable. Now you have a choice. Try to stop me, or not."

He waited for her to make the first move, felt it building in the sudden flood of adrenaline in Corsi's system, but then a slight easing as she deliberately pulled herself away from the edge. Captain Gold did not suffer fools, or a chief of security who gave in to blind aggression, it seemed. He stepped away from Corsi, giving her his back and putting a hand on the shaft's emergency ladder.

It was a long, long way down.

"Do you even know if she's alive?" Corsi asked. He did not need to look to know that she had not turned to watch him go.

He paused for a moment. Corsi, he knew, would prefer the truth.

"No," he said. "But I feel it."

CHAPTER
19

The broken power coupling sparked. A shower of splintered light cascaded across half the bridge, briefly illuminating the dimmed region. Flicking his tongue, Captain S'linth tasted the dread; it coated his tongue like the vilest skin leavings of an unproductive. Another gravimetric wave inundated the *Dutiful Burden,* and the inertial dampers, already stressed beyond their means, failed once more; scaled bodies vaulted, landing in disheveled heaps of silent pain. Only one hiss spoke of anger. Of desire to overcome.

Using his tail to rebalance, S'linth's tongue flicked: First Navigator Th'osh. The rest of the bridge crew were almost incapacitated with the stunning events that had upset their carefully controlled lives. For cycles they had traveled in near space to the nest, tasting the fruits without the labor. Now the predator had come calling and most of his crew's colors showed loud and clear.

Except for Th'osh. He *knew* the First Navigator had the spark within him.

"First Navigator. What's our situation?"

Within moments Th'osh regained his seat, his nose buried in his sensors.

"I believe the worst of the gravimetric backsplash has abated, for the time being. We've lost partial power, with most sensors off-line. Shields, however, are holding at fifty percent."

The taste of smoke tinged the air; intolerable on his ship. "Science, I want full power within five minutes and this cleared immediately." He jabbed his hand into the air for emphasis.

"Yes, Captain." Weakness. The voice held terrible weakness, but she had responded. A start.

"First Navigator, where's the alien ship?"

"She's still five thousand *ris* units off our bow. Sir, their dekyon beam has ceased."

S'linth stiffened. "Get the main screen on." He nictitated several times, still annoyed with the acrid stench of slightly burned plastic housing. Within moments the screen burst to life, only a slight distortion showing the damage it had sustained. Th'osh magnified the view several times without prompting. Yes, Th'osh would do well indeed.

The alien vessel appeared to be listing. To his trained eye, the vessel had obviously suffered damage as well. Where before the bright stream of energy had cleaved the darkness, now only the ship remained.

"Why did the beam stop, and where did the backsplash originate from?"

"I cannot say, Captain. What I can say is that the dekyon beam appeared to . . . flounder . . . almost immediately. They lost their hold on the gravity anchor, which is when the backsplash began. Twenty-eight seconds later, the ship emitted a dekyon beam of a different modulation; one that interacted with subspace in a way I do not understand. A second dekyon stream emitted, then stopped."

S'linth gazed into the void, wishing his tongue could span the distance and taste the alien air. Feel their emotions. Find what drove them. What had happened? "You said they halted the other beam. Why?"

Behind him, S'linth could hear a rustling of robes and scraping of scales on deck as someone approached close to his command chair. Only one person had the audacity to approach like that; he ignored him. He'd pay the price later.

"I cannot say, Captain."

"Is the ship dead in the void?"

Lithe, clawed fingers moved smoothly across the console—clenched in frustration. "I'm sorry, Captain, but full power has not yet been restored. Most of our sensors are still offline."

S'linth glanced once more at the ship that to all appearances looked dead. Another, very slight gravimetric wave rolled and yawed the *Dutiful Burden*. Barely enough to notice. The alien vessel, much closer to the original location of the gravity anchor, tossed about more actively.

A silence descended, broken only now and then by the whisper of scales on metal. Reviewing all that had come before, he made a decision. "Ahead, one-quarter impulse." A rustle of clothing and scales exploded; terror turned to horror on the air, forcing him to snap shut his jaw or choke on the miasma of feelings.

A hand descended to touch his forearm. He could no longer ignore the presence. Turning his head, S'linth brought Third Councilman Sha'a into view. The reddish hues of his polished scales blended almost seamlessly with the carmine robes he wore. The way he carried his neck spoke of power and authority, of one accustomed to being deferred to without question.

Only hours before, S'linth had not only bowed his head, but had nictitated as well. No requirement for such a show of respect, but Councilman Sha'a had been a champion of the captain's crèche for cycles. But now, too much had come out from under the rock into the harsh afternoon light. He had come to know that his ancestors had built a station within the photon sphere of the black hole called the Demon, and had left political opposition there to rot for all eternity. What's more, they had kept it from the general populace. The entire Council, along with their hated appointed over-seers for every starship, knew this truth. All the years of sending gifts into the Demon's maw were a sub-terfuge, a blatant lie.

No. He would incline his head as a dutiful egg of the nest, but respect? He no longer had that for Sha'a.

The councilman snapped his tongue against his nose several times. "Captain S'linth. What are you doing?"

He ignored the rebuke. "The alien vessel appears to be in distress. We will render aid."

"No, Captain, you will not."

S'linth's attempt at not stiffening failed miserably. In the course of events in the last several hours, he'd run up against the brutal truth that he held a figurehead status on his vessel. The real power lay with the Coun-cil. However, in the past, the overseers, even the hated Suliss, had managed to couch their orders in sugges-tions, leaving the captain, and more importantly, his crew, with the illusion he held power on his ship. Without such illusions, only chaos would follow. Now, the truth had bared its fangs and revealed itself to his crew as well.

From the egg, Resaurians were taught to obey the Council; it was almost a genetic imperative. Not even the Klingon occupation of their homeworld had interrupted this devotion. But this? How could he obey this command? When a distress call went out, you responded. A code beaten into every aspirant within the captain's crèche. The two necessities warred within him.

Sha'a casually turned away and began to move sinuously to where Overseer Suliss had begun to collect himself from the pitiful heap he'd collapsed into.

S'linth looked around the bridge at the crew members who would not meet his gaze, until he found First Navigator Th'osh. He had moved soundlessly to his tail and now stood upright, meeting S'linth's gaze with a firm one of his own. S'linth tasted the air and felt the conviction of trust. Sha'a would notice any moment; Th'osh bowed his head deeply, nictitating several times to S'linth. Not to the councilman, but to his captain. Only a moment's more hesitation and S'linth tailed to his full height, radiated an affirmation of reciprocated loyalty, and turned toward the third councilman.

"First Navigator, I said ahead one-quarter impulse."

Sha'a stopped and slowly turned around; he did so gracefully, considering this may have been the first time in his life someone had directly contradicted one of his orders. Beyond him, Overseer Suliss had begun to shake and hiss; overzealous fury washed the room, and he began to spit.

"How dare you. You cannot—"

"Third Councilman," S'linth began, ignoring the nictitator, "that ship appears dead in the void. I have a sacred obligation to come to its aid."

"Don't ignore me, Captain. You will answer—"

"What's more, if we do not go to the aid of this vessel, we will ignore what we are. It does not matter that they are aliens. All our codes will mean nothing if we knowingly let the helpless die."

"You will be—"

"We will be no better than Klingons."

The last phrase fell like a photon torpedo, detonating and sweeping all other conversation into nothingness. The occupation had ended nearly a millennium ago, but still the Resaurians remembered. S'linth kept his eyes locked on those of Third Councilman Sha'a. He had no need to taste the air to feel the malignant hatred of Overseer Suliss. The tableau held for several heartbeats until Suliss had mastered his emotions enough to once again begin his tirade.

"Treason!" Suliss spat at him. But like a thrown switch, Suliss cut off with a small raised hand from Sha'a.

"Captain, I have always admired you for your truthfulness and integrity. However, those are strong words you speak. And once spoken, they cannot be taken back. Once the fang has punctured, the poison is set, regardless of regrets. I believe I gave you a—"

"Captain," Th'osh interrupted. Both turned to find out what could possibly have driven him to interrupt a councilman. "The ship, Captain. We have partial sensors back online, and she is hurt. Badly. However, she's attempting to move into the photon sphere."

"What?" Twin voices echoed.

"I cannot tell you anything else, but she's limping down toward the photon sphere."

"Is it a deliberate move? Or is she falling into the gravity well?"

"I cannot say."

S'linth turned back to Sha'a, but spoke to Th'osh. "Ahead one-third impulse, and prepare the tractor beam."

Suliss shook as though preparing to molt into another stage and started to speak, only to be cut off once more.

"By all means, Captain, proceed." Sha'a's words might as well have emerged from the Demon for the confusion they caused.

S'linth knew Sha'a had been on the verge of ordering him to remain clear of the alien vessel. What had changed? "Proceed?"

"As you say. You have a moral obligation. A 'sacred trust,' I believe you called it." The councilman smiled. "We'll save the humans, even from themselves."

CHAPTER
20

"Wong, take us in." Captain Gold couldn't help the shiver that prickled his skin and left his fingertips tingling. Try as he might, he could not banish the nightmare that had been dogging him before this whole mess had even begun. However, though he liked to pretend he was not superstitious, he could almost hear his beloved wife putting on her rabbi voice to tell him it had nothing to do with superstition at all.

He'd been given a premonition, and shouldn't he be thankful?

In his nightmare he had been worried about the life of his grandchild. Now, as the photon sphere approached, he knew the premonition had been for himself. Perhaps even for his crew. Or even for the *da Vinci*. He had to keep reminding himself that other starships had managed to escape the depths of black holes in the past. But with the ghastly mouth of the universe's most awesomely powerful force ripped wide to savage anyone stupid enough to get caught in its maw . . . well, he found it difficult indeed not to feel very, very stupid right now.

But there were seven of his people across that fearsome barrier he would not let down.

"Yes, sir. I can only get one-quarter impulse right now, sir."

"Then that's what we'll use." Gold turned toward Tev and found the Tellarite with his nose buried in his instruments. Considering the devastated look on his face (which meant it had to have been a scream for a human, since Gold couldn't read his face any better than he could a Vulcan's) following the failure of Tev's bootstrapping idea, he found such dedication impressive. Comforting. Even in distress this crew, even the newest member, pulled together.

"Tev, how does it look?"

Without his usual pause, or the need to be asked twice, Tev responded. "The gravity anchor appears to be holding, but I cannot say for how long. However, when I managed to spear it, it had almost reached fifteen Schwarzschild radii."

Gold shook his head for a moment. "Remind an old man—Schwarzschild radii?"

Tev glanced up, snuffled, and said, "I'm sorry, Captain. One Schwarzschild radius is the size of the event horizon. For a black hole of this size, fifteen RS is four thousand five hundred kilometers."

For a moment Gold almost didn't hear what Tev had said as his surprise blocked it out. Tev had *apologized*. The captain tried to remember if he'd actually heard the Tellarite apologize before. He didn't think so. Could he be coming around, finally? A member of the crew? Perhaps this hell would have a silver lining.

If they could get the away team home.

"The station?"

"With the loss of our probes during the backsplash, I cannot tell for certain; too many sensors are still off-line. However, I calculate the station is still a safe sixty kilometers above the Demon's event horizon."

"Safe!" Gold couldn't help the guffaw.

"Why, yes, Captain. There is no reason to believe that the shields on the station are not still fully operational. It has held itself against the tidal forces for several centuries now."

Gold smiled. Leave it to Tev to break up the tension. And do so without even knowing. "I trust your calculations completely, Tev," he said, cutting the Tellarite off. He ignored those raised eyebrows that reminded him of the hairbrush his sister had used so many years ago.

The ship lurched and stopped, almost spilling him to the floor. He regained his feet quickly. "Wong, that didn't feel like a gravimetric wave."

"Captain," Piotrowski interrupted. Gold turned.

"What?"

"It's the Resaurians. One moment they're holding off at a distance, and between one eye blink and another, they've closed and have us in their tractor beam."

Gold was suddenly all business. "Are we certain this time?"

"Yes, sir, and they've got us tight."

"Tev, the tractor beam. Can we break it?" Though Gold noticed a moment's hesitation as he asked Tev to break his concentration in midstream and fly in a new vector, the Tellarite moved with the flow.

"Not right now, Captain. As I said, most of our systems are still offline. Even if we could, they've a strange tractor configuration I've not seen before. If I took some time, I could break it." He looked up expectedly.

Gold hid his smile. *There's the arrogance we've grown to love.* "Get working on it, while I see if I can talk to our friendly neighborhood Resaurians." He turned toward the viewscreen; he noticed peripherally that Ensign Haznedl had come at Tev's call. "Piotrowski, get me that ship."

"Hailing frequency open, Captain."

"Captain S'linth, this is Captain Gold of the *da Vinci*. I would appreciate knowing why you've latched on to my ship with a tractor beam." He knew full well why the captain had done it, but he remembered Carol Abramowitz's briefing on the Resaurians' trouble in trusting other races after being conquered by the Klingons. He tried to moderate his tone, keep it civil.

The viewscreen sputtered and then materialized to show the dim interior of the *Dutiful Burden's* bridge. A crewman or two were in view, but Third Councilman Sha'a captivated the attention like a siren song. *Regardless of how alien he might be, he's got* chutzpah. *Power.* Standing in his carmine robe, he had one hand casually resting on the back of the empty captain's seat.

It took an instant longer for the import to set in. *What's this? Where's Captain S'linth?* The casual way Sha'a touched the captain's seat could not hide his possessiveness. Gold finally spotted S'linth standing at the back of the bridge, head bowed but back ramrod straight. Gold's job had just become a lot harder. The one Resaurian he might have been able to reach, one captain to another. Gold shuddered at the idea of a slimy politician seizing control of his own vessel.

"*Captain Gold.*" Once again Gold felt the revulsion most humans have for snakes. However, this time around, he didn't feel shame. Not for this particular snake. *"Captain S'linth will not be dealing with you directly at this time. However, I'm here to answer any of your questions."*

Politician's words. "Why have you latched on to my ship with your tractor beam?" Gold didn't feel like bandying words.

"I told you why. This is our station. Our internal affair. You have no right to interfere, Captain. I sympathize with your plight. You attempted to rescue a station you felt was in need and have crew there now. For such actions I thump my tail. However, I simply cannot allow you to go any farther."

Gold felt his temper spike even harder. He glanced sidelong at Tev, and then shook his head. "We'll see about that," he said.

"We simply don't have the power to break the tractor beam," Tev said in a low, frustrated voice at Ensign Haznedl's continued optimism. The sound of the captain's voice, raised in anger, a static in the background.

"Okay. What about the dekyon beam? Could it be modulated to splinter the tractor beam? Or weaken it?"

"No, tractor beams don't work that way. The dekyon would have no effect." Tev snuffled. What did they teach at the Academy if *this* was an example of their education?

Then a thought bloomed within Tev, spreading like a virus and engulfing his intellect. Quick as firing synapses, he had the solution. "A second dekyon beam! We don't have sufficient power for the warp drive to attempt a forced break. However, we do have enough energy to create a second dekyon beam, which can be modulated to ensnare a gravimetric wave on its sine toward the black hole."

Haznedl blinked confusion, but then seemed to catch on. She began to calibrate a second beam.

Tev approved. "Captain," he called back, and nodded once, decisively.

Gold interrupted the useless argument with the councilman to turn toward Tev. The Tellarite nodded once and Gold smiled. Tev may have been kicked, but now he was kicking back. Gold nodded in return; Tev would be ready.

He turned back toward the councilman. "Third Councilman Sha'a. This is my last warning. Release my ship, or suffer the consequences."

"Captain, there is no reason to resort to fang-baring. We are both civilized. Nevertheless, you cannot rescue the station. It does not need rescuing."

Gold didn't know exactly what to expect, but just in case, he made sure he sat back down and held on. "I think, Councilman, if you asked those on the station, they just might have a different opinion from yours."

"That is no longer a worry," Sha'a said.

"But I think it is. Tev, engage."

A slight keystroke and nothing happened.

If it were possible, Sha'a's grin grew wider on his reptilian face. *"As I said—"*

Both ships lurched forward with horrific speed as the hand of the universe smashed them down into its maw.

CHAPTER
21

Standing inside a crawlspace conduit, Sonya Gomez leaned out from the open maintenance hatch, sweat stinging at the corner of her eyes as she strained to reach the microspanner that lay among a spread of tools on a nearby table. Her fingertips brushed the narrow handle, shoving it a few millimeters farther away. In her other hand she clutched at a pair of power regulator feeds, pinching them together at just the right place, and she dreaded the idea of letting them go now.

Eyeing one of the nearby Resaurians, she licked her dry, chapped lips. "A little help here?"

Ulsah turned away from her own workstation, uncoiling very carefully and moving slow. She saw which tool Sonya needed, picked it up, and gingerly handed it over as if it were the most delicate thing in all the world. The grip felt odd in her hand, created for the more delicately boned fingers of a Resaurian. She would make do.

"Thanks."

Ulsah nodded. She glanced nervously at her station's panel of displays, hugged herself around her middle with long, thin arms. It was a familiar gesture. "Is there anything more I can help with?"

Sonya wiped sweat from her brow with the back of her hand. Her skin felt greasy, and far too warm after an hour in this oven of an engineering space. "Iced tea?" she asked. Ulsah studied the tool spread, as if trying to figure out what that might be. "Never mind. Not until I need another tool."

Delays like this were costing her, in time as well as a rising frustration level. Her engineering sense told her that the tool tables were mounted perfectly for the wide Resaurian shoulders, accessible from any one of three possible maintenance panels. Sound ergonomics, really. But she was also used to her equipment being laid out a certain way, where she could snag the exact tool she needed without looking. She needed an assistant, but hadn't thought to ask for one at the time. And other than Ulsah, only the guard at the door with his plasma welder wasn't extremely busy.

Hopefully he would remain that way.

Bending back to task, all of her aches and bruises protesting, Sonya fused the power regulators together in a way that their small electromagnetic fields would complement each other rather than work in competition. A small victory, yet a possibly vital one. She bit down on the spanner's handle, holding it in her teeth while she used a small tester from her back pocket to test the output. Perfect.

The tester went back into her pocket. The microspanner she let drop from her mouth, and then licked the taste of machine oil from her lips and spat dryly. "Dirty job." But someone had to do it.

Es'a waited at her shoulder when she turned back. Sonya started at the appearance of the frail-looking Resaurian, then swore. "I wish you wouldn't do that."

"We learn to move silently," the alien lisped. His voice was frailer than most, full of a hissing accent that reminded Sonya of a serpent's warning. "It is hard to give up." He took the spanner from her, replaced it on the table, and handed her a fusion cutter when she glanced at it. He was very good at reading body language.

"Thank you. Have you learned anything more about my friends?"

"No. Reports from the upper decks come down slowly. We have no time to waste. This must get done before your friends alter the shield strength again."

That much Sonya agreed with, especially as a new tremor shook the station. The station's fusion reactors provided power along one of three different trunks. If she could not calibrate their flow patterns to within a micron, Es'a assured her, bad things would happen. She turned away, using the fusion cutter to open a flexible conduit along its entire length. The work was slow, but not taxing. "You know, you could try talking with S'eth. Make him understand your position."

"More than one hundred years, my people struggle against his people. No talking is possible."

Sonya shook her head. A century of stubborn refusal to negotiate. A hostile stalemate where each faction waited for the other to make a mistake. S'eth in control of life support and the shield generators. Es'a with foodstuffs and the fusion reactor rooms. What kind of division could turn a people so savagely against each other? "Is S'eth really so unreasonable?"

"He listens to none of us. His way is to keep things as

they have always been. Our way is to search for a better life. To improve and to grow and to escape!"

"And another generation of traditionalists and radicals are born," she said.

She felt S'eth recoil behind her. "What is that you say?"

Sonya handed back the fusion cutter. She felt the frown hang heavy on her face, wondering why what she had said bothered the Resaurian so much. Surely they had seen this for themselves. "I said that you've created here the exact same situation that caused you all to be banished in the first place. The overly cautious. The determined forward-thinkers. Only this time, instead of Klingon occupation throwing your culture out of whack, you did it to yourselves."

Es'a looked ill. Not that he ever looked extremely healthy. The Resaurian hung his head low, letting it sway back and forth. Membranes rolled up over his eyes, giving them a white cast. "They did this," he admitted. "We have done this as well."

It seemed an odd choice of phrasing, but Sonya had too much work ahead of her to puzzle it out now. And she needed a break. Climbing out of the crawlspace, she brushed her hand against a torn and filthy uniform. She had long since discarded the jacket and was now wearing only the undershirt. Soon, the gold engineering color would be completely lost to a pallor of grease and dust-gray.

"You are finished?" Es'a asked.

"Refresher station." She held her grimy hands out, then nodded toward the door. "Getting hard to hold tools properly. I'll be right back."

He nodded. And the guard at the door stepped aside when she thumped him on the shoulder.

Down a short, dimly lit corridor she found facilities

meant for the Resaurians, but she managed adequately. As well as washing out some of the grime burning at the corner of her left eye, Sonya used a handful of water to slick her hair back, wetting it as protection against the humid engineering spaces. She stared into a mirrored wall, seeing the dark circles under her eyes, knowing that she had only hours to find Es'a's problem and help fix it. Part of her mind worked on the repairs that were likely to be needed—necessary—if anyone on the station hoped to see real space again. But another part kept turning over the small clues she'd picked up over the last few hours.

"They did this," she whispered aloud, repeating Es'a's words. "We have done this as well."

Ulsah's behavior. Her awkward shyness.

A new generation of traditionalists and forward-thinkers.

No!

Sonya pushed herself away from the mirrored wall. She hit the door hard, slamming it back with a bang, and sprinted for the engineering space and its maze of conduits and workstations. Her feet pounded an alarm against the steel deck. She knew what it was that S'eth—and Es'a—had kept from her. The stakes were going up, high enough to force either side to take the most drastic action available if they could not be brought to some kind of arrangement. She had to start things moving right away.

Which was the last thought to race through her mind, before arms reached out of an open doorway, grabbed her by her shoulders, and pulled her into a darkened room.

CHAPTER
22

The long, laborious climb down the lift shaft and the following search had taken a great deal out of Rennan Konya. He considered himself in great shape with his regular security training. But the emergency ladder's rungs had been set too far apart for a non-Resaurian, and the frequent tremors shaking the station forced him to keep a death grip on each rail.

By the time he began exploring the lower levels of the station, his thighs already felt tight and his shoulders ached severely. He spent a great deal of effort working his way around the many watchstations set out by the Resaurians and avoiding their patrols. Alerted to their presence by his ability to tap into the motor reflex of other beings, he was always able to find a hiding place inside empty rooms or in the overhead pipes that ran along many corridor ceilings. But the constant effort to keep his own screens down and feel every twitch and strain in those moving near him, around him, in decks beneath him—it demanded a toll as well.

So when he finally sensed the familiar ache of a human's lower back pain, he tracked in on it slowly but with a measure of relief.

Down a spiral staircase and through a large steam heat distribution venue, he approached with care, waiting to discover the guards set on Commander Gomez. He'd seen her on the way to the refresher station, but held back in the shadows while keeping an eye out. He spotted no furtive demeanor in Gomez's movement; she certainly did not look like an escaped prisoner. He had to assume she was under some kind of surveillance. He still hadn't spotted it by the time she decided to return, running as if there would be Resaurians chasing her, armed to the fangs. Chancing his own discovery, he clapped a hand over Gomez's mouth as he pulled her into the room, wanting to take her from the corridor quickly and quietly in case anyone was close. His Betazoid training sparked a warning as Gomez drove her elbow back violently, relying on conditioning long since ingrained as a natural reaction. He barely had time to shift his weight before she buried her elbow into his midriff. Air rushed out in a desperate exhale.

"Commander," he wheezed. He caught her next blow as she came around with a right hook, wrapping his arm around hers, trapping it. "Commander, it's me."

She jumped back, startled at his appearance. "Rennan? What the hell are you doing down here?"

"Keep it down," he whispered, glancing into the corridor. "Where are they?"

"Who?"

"The Resaurians chasing you."

Her black hair looked disheveled and dirty, streaked with an oily grime and slicked back from her elfin face. There was a smudge on her left ear that he wanted to wipe clean, so unbefitting an officer but quite appropriate for the engineer in her. Decorum did not stop him. The puzzled frown and the following exasperation did.

"Oh, for . . . Rennan, I don't have time for you right now. Come on." She grabbed his arm and pulled him into the corridor, heedless of their discovery. He felt her urgency in the tense set of her shoulders but no sense of panic. The flight-or-fight response was definitely missing from her posture and also in the way she put herself in front of the plasma welder brought to bear on him as the door opened to a new engineering space and a Resaurian guard snapped to feral attention.

"Easy," she said with unnatural calm. "He's with me."

Rennan hated having to carry a phaser. Weapons were too often relied upon by security, when diplomacy and fast thinking should have sufficed. But the danger he read in the reptilian faces, and the tightening grips on weapons and tools, made him suddenly glad for his sidearm. He moved on the balls of his feet, hands always in view but ready for quick and decisive action. A panel operator coiled away from him. Her abdomen muscles spasmed, and he jumped away from her, thinking that she had tensed herself for an attack. Instead, she wrapped arms protectively around herself and slithered back several meters.

The Resaurian who waited for them did so with ill-concealed impatience. He shifted from foot to foot, his thick tail lashing out behind him. "Should this make me nervous?" he asked with a wheezing hiss. "You did not leave here with a friend."

"Blue," Gomez exclaimed. Rennan looked around, saw no sign of that color. It was the first thought, though, that Gomez decided to challenge this Resaurian with. "Es'a. The small Resaurian you had watching me earlier had smaller scales, and blue! Where are they?"

This was Es'a? The nest-breaker? Rennan felt the alien's sickness, the fire raging within his body, burning up his strength. This did not feel like the strong leader S'eth had made him out to be. Leaders paled over the years, of course. But the Resaurian did not move as if he possessed a mature body taken over by the ravages of age. His muscles, his joints, they felt more like a stunted youth.

And his flesh crawled with a desperate flush.

"What is it you mean?" Es'a asked.

"You know what I mean. If you're willing to go to such lengths for them, S'eth will be as well. It's going to bring disaster. We've got to get this sorted out, and I mean now."

"It will not change anything," he said, glancing at the nearby Resaurian who hovered protectively at the edge of the conversation.

Rennan was still behind, but catching up fast. First and foremost, he now knew that Gomez had not been kept as a prisoner. No matter how she had been taken from the team, she had remained voluntarily. Given her appearance, there were obviously engineering concerns she felt important enough to mitigate other concerns. Es'a's reaction told Rennan that there might be one other thing going on that the Resaurian might consider even more critical. The security agent followed the alien's gaze to the nearby panel operator. His abdomen hitched and jumped with sympathetic spasms.

And he knew.

"You're pregnant," he announced.

Gomez was right. This changed everything.

CHAPTER
23

Gold watched, in a detached way, as Carol Abramowitz and Bart Faulwell entered the bridge and stopped dead in their tracks. Abramowitz's mouth might just have fit a half-dozen tribbles. He'd called her to the bridge to be present when they had their next run-in with Third Councilman Sha'a. She must have been with Faulwell, who had tagged along, no doubt feeling useless in a crisis with no call for his particular skills in cryptography or symbolic analysis.

Abramowitz, however, was still in her element, as Gold wanted backup from the ship's cultural specialist in his next dealings with the Resaurians. He had no doubt he'd be hearing from the councilman soon enough, providing that the *da Vinci* crawled back from the brink of the Demon's event horizon. The *Dutiful Burden* doggedly maintained its tractor lock, though it trailed the *da Vinci*'s fall by several hundred kilometers.

Pointless, as both vessels were caught in the inexorable grip of the Demon.

He had another reason for wanting Abramowitz on the bridge, though he'd never admit to it. She was a good barometer and adviser for situations where his bridge crew would be too by-the-book and an engineer would simply default into technical jargon. There were times, Gold had seen, when being a scientist robbed one of the ability to simply sit back and observe the beauty or terror unfolding around you.

Gravimetric waves increased in frequency and strength the farther in they fell, rocking the ship with more fervor. Gold had become so used to the turbulence he'd almost forgotten about it, but not even a drunk Klingon could ignore the thrumming vibrations that rang through the whole vessel. And the farther they fell, the slower the ship moved as more and more power was dedicated to the structural integrity field. Each gravimetric wave had to be registered on sensors, and the ship maneuvered in this high-gravity soup to take the brunt along solid shield facings.

"Wong, how are we doing?"

"If Tev's numbers are correct, we'll be transversing the photon sphere in moments." All eyes fixed on the main viewscreen.

The *da Vinci* crawled forward at a bare kilometer per minute. And that was still far too fast. They watched as a perfectly round hole sliced through the very fabric of existence, tunneling into . . . nothing. Even in the farthest depths of the quadrant Gold had found existence. Comets. Nebulae. Protomatter. Ejected coronas of supernovas. Even space dust. Though much of the matter could be clocked at millions and at times billions of years old, it still existed. This, however, could only be called the antithesis of what life meant. No, Gold corrected himself. Not just life—too narrow a definition. Existence itself.

Gold knew his wife would chide him that God made everything. However, if He'd made black holes, they were the largest drains in existence, where He flushed anything He no longer needed.

Like Gold's crew, if they were not careful.

The ship continued its descent. The forward viewscreen showed absolute darkness, as though the ship were nudging into the universe's largest tar pit. Only one where the dinosaurs were still alive somewhere in its depths and their angry kicks sent crushing ripples expanding out in every direction.

"Sidescreen." If the front showed nothing, he wanted to see what they were passing through. Abramowitz gasped and Gold himself felt tingles rippling along his skin and setting his fingertips afire.

The universe had begun to crush itself. God's drain, no doubt about it. And at the bottom, the universe's trash compactor. The ultimate plunger rammed and thudded against existence, squishing the universe down into a thin band. What had once been the visible universe in front of them, now stretched in a concentric circle perpendicular to the orientation of the *da Vinci*. Not just the visible universe in front, but from behind them as well.

Einstein Rings. The words rang in Gold's head and he chased after it, latching on to it with all his might. That's what Tev had called them in a meeting that had occurred in another life.

Glancing over at Abramowitz, he could see the fear, naked on her face, a fear to match his own. Here they were, peeling back the very fabric of reality to show the skeletal underpinnings, and everyone immediately backpedaled in fear. Too awesome. Too grand. Too terrible. Too . . . simply *too*.

Perhaps all scientists, regardless of their outward façades, or their intellect, when they brushed up against such terrible magnificence, had to take refuge in their science. In their words and their calculations and their theories, or they'd simply collapse in fright.

Another sickening swaying lurch of the ship and the wonders of the universe continued to unfold. A second ring. Now a third. Gold had heard numerous accounts of bubble universes and other dimensions. He'd even spoken with respected, trusted comrades who had such experiences, and yet he'd never really been able to bring himself to believe.

Now, as he witnessed not simply the compacting of the universe, but its very replication as easy as one-two-three, he believed.

"Captain, there's another ship following us in."

"That's the *Dutiful Burden*."

Wong checked his readings one more time and then turned to look at Gold over his shoulder. "No, Captain. There is another ship besides the *Dutiful Burden*."

"What? Center the viewscreen on that location." The forward screen changed to show a familiar-looking vessel at some distance.

"Magnify." The screen zoomed forward several times, and Carol's was not the only gasp.

The *da Vinci* floated before their eyes.

"What's going on? That can't be right."

"Of course it can," Tev said.

Everyone looked toward him and for just a moment he felt irritated. Had they not been at the briefing? Did all humans have such short-term memory?

He snuffled. "We are passing through the photon sphere. The very name should explain what we're witnessing." He paused and another wave of irritation swept through, like the gravimetric waves that continued to increase in severity and duration, at their blank faces.

"Light. The photon sphere is the distance above the event horizon when the force of the black hole's gravity bends light into a perfect circumference. Our ship is sensing our ship; the forward sensors are picking up the visible light bent around the perimeter of the black hole, showing us the rear of our own vessel. If you stood outside at this moment, you'd look forward and only see the back of your head." A look of strangeness glazed most of the bridge crew's faces.

The ghost-image of the *da Vinci* disappeared. The stars continued to be eaten up from beneath by the encroaching black.

"Aft screen," Gold ordered. His voice was solid.

The screen switched viewpoints. Above them, the visible universe filled a shrinking hole, with outer darkness stretching across the *da Vinci*'s side and in front. Tev turned back to his sensors.

Magnificent.

Most of the bridge crew only attempted to assimilate this experience with the weakest sensory input at their disposal. Vision would never scratch the surface of what he experienced. Looking down at several monitors, he could see the full glory.

The gravimetric waves were pulled in from every direction, across unimaginable distances, to crash and thrash. He normally did not give in to such imagery, but Tev admitted that the rage of lines on his monitor reminded him of nothing so much as living tentacles, thrashing, stretching, attempting in a futile frenzy to save themselves from the inevitable plunge into the event horizon.

Another screen glowed almost incandescent with a fountain of energy that shot millions of miles out into space from the direction of the black hole, cascading out in every direction. Hawking radiation blazed as though it desired to create a sun to compensate for the destruction occurring on such a fantastic level.

Yet another screen showed the Einstein Rings, along with measurements depicting how much relative time occurred outside the photon sphere, compared with their current position; at each forward movement, the time dilation increased.

Commander Gomez would appreciate the mathematical perfection of this event.

That last thought troubled him for a moment. He shifted uncomfortably in his seat and felt the pull of his uniform across his chest. Tev didn't like emotions and thoughts he could not pinpoint. After a moment, however, it became painfully obvious. His irritation at the crew had nothing to do with their inability to grasp the splendor around them. Of course they'd be unable to. What irritated him was that he wished Commander Gomez were here. Not simply so that he could impress her, to show that "this" is what he'd done for her lately. No, he simply wished to share this moment with an equal.

He started. An equal.

Bartholomew Faulwell slipped up near Tev. "I wish there was something I could do," he said.

Tev nodded. He had found himself thinking along similar lines in the last few hours, and he didn't like the feeling of that one bit. "You shouldn't be on the bridge," he said, but low.

"Yes. That's likely true." He was also just as obviously waiting for Tev to order him away.

Tev shuffled awkwardly from one foot to the other. He honestly did not want Bartholomew to leave. At the last few briefings, Bartholomew was the only crew member to actively press for Tev's friendship. Most of the crew did not seem to know how to approach the Tellarite, and Tev was equally stymied when it came to social relations. He wished Gomez were here as an equal. Bartholomew should be allowed to stay as a possible friend.

"If you are going to stay," Tev said, never taking his eyes from the screen, "you might find me one of those apple rancher candies you seem to enjoy carrying about."

Bartholomew smiled, reached into a pocket, and pulled out two twists of clear cellophane. Inside was a hard, green candy. He set one carefully on the edge of Tev's panel, where the Tellarite could reach it when he wanted, when he could. He unwrapped the other for himself.

Tev reached for the candy, but then stopped when a screen lit with red tones and an incessant beeping warned of a drastic change in status. Tev's mammoth eyebrows rose alarmingly.

"Captain?"

"Yes, Tev?" His voiced sounded as though he were not really paying attention; the Demon simply held too much power. That would change fast.

"The Resaurian vessel has unlatched its tractor beam from the *da Vinci*."

"Why is that a problem?"

"Because it's latched on to the gravity anchor." Tev looked up to find Gold's full attention focused on him.

"But that means—"

He nodded. Why did events conspire against his every plan? "The anchor will self-destruct even faster."

Faulwell paled. The cryptographer shook his head in denial. "But . . . but do they realize that?" It was a good question, and Captain Gold nodded that Tev should answer.

"I do not know."

"They just might," Abramowitz said. Tev looked to find the cultural specialist's composure had returned. Only a slight wildness to the eyes indicated she stood on the bridge of a ship inside the photon sphere of a black hole.

"Remember how traditionalist they are. From what you told me, Captain, it looked as though this Captain S'linth may have been deposed by the councilman and the overseer." Another wave caused everyone to stumble. Abramowitz grabbed on to a seat and immediately continued.

"With such a desire to keep this knowledge from the general populace, they might just sacrifice the entire space station, perhaps themselves as well, to see that secret kept. How many centuries have they kept it till now? Quite easy to take it to the next level."

Tev hated it when politics intruded upon the beauty of his scientific universe, but he could not fault Abramowitz's logic. It made all too much sense.

"Tev, how quickly will we reach the station?" Gold said.

"Not quickly enough, Captain." He turned to verify with his monitor, his hands grasping the edge of the monitor as though he could pressure it into giving a different answer. Commander Gomez was on that ship.

"Wong, ahead one-half impulse."

"Captain!" Tev interrupted, rising to his feet in alarm. "You cannot do that."

Gold turned stormy eyes on Tev; one did not countermand the captain's orders.

"The gravimetric waves are too strong. Right now, at a quarter impulse, we are pushing the limits of our shields." Tev thought furiously, trying to find an analogue the captain would understand. "Imagine a boat pushing full forward through a heavy water storm. The hull would smash into the wall of the waves, instead of flowing with the movement; the hull will shatter."

Gold continued to stare angrily at him for a moment and then shook his head. "Then we've lost."

"No. I believe there is a way we can actually reach the station even faster. However, there is inherent risk—not as much as pushing forward with impulse engines, but more than what we risk now."

Gold chuckled and leaned back in his seat. How had he amused the captain?

"Tev, we're in a black hole. *Everything* we do is a risk. What is it?"

"Currently we are using the impulse engines to move forward, but it also keeps us at a set speed; a velocity we can manipulate. If we cast ourselves adrift, we will ride the gravimetric waves. This will create a jarring ride, but one that we should survive. One that should get us to the station before the gravity anchor disintegrates."

"Flotsam, eh?" Gold said. He looked speculative for a moment and then nodded his head. "After everything we've done, this is no crazier. Wong, I believe you heard the man."

"Yes, sir. And, Captain—I never thought I'd be trying to grab a good wave with a starship."

"I don't think any of us did, Wong. Not at all."

CHAPTER
24

This part of the station was the best kept, Sonya noticed right away. Clean and in good repair. Corridors painted in bright and cheerful yellows, soothing greens, and sky blues. Branching corridors ran off to either side, with the doors to living quarters standing open in warm invitation to neighbors, to friends. A warm, spiced-meat aroma filled one passage, and she knew that someone was cooking a meal nearby. Actually cooking—no replicators here.

Several Resaurians stood around talking, seemingly oblivious to the danger they were in. They evidenced little surprise seeing a pair of humanoids under escort through their living area. Only when the station shook with a new tremor did they glance around self-consciously. As if wondering what they should be doing to help.

"They don't know how bad it is, do they?" she asked Es'a.

"They know. But we've lived with the fear of this day all our lives. Panic will help no one." He gestured to an open double-wide archway. "In here."

They passed from the corridor, stepping out onto grassy lawns, looking up into an ochre sky. Fruit-laden trees spread thick branches overhead, offering rest to a number of brightly feathered birds and shade from the blazing orange sun to the Resaurian young who slither-ran and played on the pale grasses. Sonya stopped in amazement. This was the largest space-born arboretum she could remember seeing in her career, obviously coupled with holographic technology to complete the illusion of a true outdoor park.

Rennan Konya found his voice first.

"Dozens. Hundreds." He counted the smaller Resaurians with their blue-green scales and slender upper bodies. Nearby a larger youth picked at the beginnings of his shedding. Beneath a dull, waxy peel of skin, his scales were coming in dark and coral red. Rennan watched with fascination. The full implications were just beginning to hit. "There are no survivors from the original prisoners, are there?"

Sonya knew the answer, but let Es'a take it. "No," the Resaurian admitted. "Finding a way to lessen the time dilation was one of our first priorities. It gave our forebears a chance to escape before too much real time passed on our homeworld."

Ulsah slithered up and nestled against him. He wrapped an arm around her. "We solved our infertility problem not long after."

And then dealt with overpopulation concerns, diminishing resources, and the very real stress of raising families in such a contained environment. Sonya glanced over to a picnic spread where two youngsters ate food while playing atonal music from a small portable device. It looked so normal, it tempted her to smile. "You've kept everyone conditioned for an indoor-outdoor life, in case escape ever happened." She approved.

"So what is the issue?" Rennan asked her. "We get back in touch with the *da Vinci,* and you engineers work your miracles and get everyone out of the Demon." He looked to Es'a. "You tell your people not to sabotage the attempt *this time,* and we get you home."

Sonya shook her head. "For a Betazoid, you can be fairly dense at times, Rennan. Es'a's faction did not sabotage our escape efforts. S'eth's faction did. For the same reason they originally resisted the attempt to use the station's anchoring shields to attempt an escape. They will not endanger their children, no matter how strong their drive for personal freedom."

"It is worse than that," Es'a explained. "Our forebears were the forward-thinkers of their generation. Many of us—most of us—remain true to that predisposition. But some traditionalist behavior creeps back into our culture here. S'eth fights to preserve what he has known his entire life."

"And there is a real danger," Sonya admitted. "S'eth's father discovered it. The power distribution system is set up in a carefully calibrated manner that any radical change in gravitational pull *outside* the shielding will cause harmonic fluctuations and force a feedback surge into the fusion reactors."

Rennan looked at Sonya. "Let me guess. Boom?"

"More like a fizzle. Lights out." Which meant shields dropping that suddenly exposed the entire station to the full gravitational effects of the black hole. "The tidal forces would rip the station to pieces. That's what I've been working on for the past few hours."

"About done?" he asked with a wry smile.

Not asking for much, was he? Sonya felt a sudden urge to punch the man. She did smile this time, when Rennan stepped back into a wary stance. She also liked the way his hand came up to protect his gut, where she had earlier slipped in an elbow. Served him right.

"Just about. I'm using an application developed by La Forge and Brahms. I think it will hold up."

"You think?"

She nodded. The station shook again. Was it her imagination, or were the tremors getting worse?

Rennan shifted uneasily, then shrugged. "Good enough for me," he decided. Reaching out slowly, he rubbed a thumb against the outside of her ear. It came away dark with grease. "Since you're going to play the diplomat," he said, "you should look the part. What's your plan?"

Sonya rubbed the flat of her palm against the same ear, making certain the last of the smudge was gone, and helping hide her flush of embarrassment. Turning to business, she looked to Es'a, who waited patiently with his mate and a growing number of Resaurian adults.

"I think," she said slowly, her plans forming even as she spoke, "we should arrange for a reunion."

CHAPTER
25

A wild ride. That was all you could call it.

Captain Gold, clinging to his chair to avoid being dumped to the ground once more, enjoyed it. He could admit that. He'd never been surfing before, but after this, he just might take it up.

"Engineering to bridge."

Gold reached up and tapped his combadge. "Gold here. Go ahead, Conlon."

"Captain, we've almost got full power restored. This ride has actually given us the time to take the warp core off-line momentarily, recalibrate, and restart. That did the trick for most of the systems. The rest, unfortunately, are burned out and will likely need to be replaced at the source."

"Good. Keep me posted."

"Yes, sir. Conlon out."

Gold turned toward Tev. "Tev, how we looking?"

"We are closing in on the station even now; estimated contact in five-point-four-five minutes."

"And the gravity anchor?"

"I cannot be certain when it will fail, but its density is fracturing. There can be no doubt failure is imminent."

"I understand, Tev."

The Resaurian station now filled the forward viewscreen: an insignificant piece of flotsam desperately clinging to existence above God's drainpipe. Just over a thousand meters long, the station was a large one indeed. Two cylindrical objects rose perpendicular (above and below) toward its stern, while several large extensions thrust down from amidships. A particularly large extension sat amidships on the starboard side.

"Captain, we're now within fifty-five seconds of the station."

"Wong," Gold said in response to Tev's warning, "prepare to engage impulse power upon my mark." Gold leaned back, rubbed his hands on his face, and then roughed his hair. How many hours had he been without real sleep?

After all they'd been through, it looked as though they just might be on the verge of saving the ship from falling farther. Of course the problem he'd been ignoring for some time now would no longer be kept in abeyance. He sighed and glanced over at Tev again.

"Tev, when we latch on to the station, we can keep it from falling farther toward the event horizon, correct?"

"Yes, Captain."

"But how do we get out again?"

He noticed Tev straighten slightly, a small smile creasing his porcine face. "The previous plan I had for saving the gravity anchor will be able to pull us back out of the gravity well and past the photon sphere. I'm confident the twin dekyon beams—the bootstrapping you called it—will be more than adequate for the task."

"You say it will be adequate to rescue the *da Vinci*. But will it rescue our vessel and that mammoth station?"

Tev's eyebrows lowered until he almost couldn't see the Tellarite's coal black eyes. Obviously he hadn't made considerations for that, and it irked him. "No, Captain, it will not."

"I know you'll come up with something."

If possible, Tev became even more stiff. "Back to the drawing board, Captain."

Gold nodded, keeping his emotions tightly leashed. The worry that had plagued him as a nightmare from the start of this whole mess reared its ugly head once more. He'd lost so many people at Galvan VI. Now, it appeared as though those events might repeat themselves, with much more dire effect. The team he'd ordered onto the station had to be rescued. Had to be. But at the cost of the rest of the crew? Had he been determining his course of action based upon those dead ghosts that called to him? Had he put himself, and more importantly his ship and crew, in danger to try to make up for what had gone before?

The sinking sensation in the pit of his stomach warned him that that might be exactly what had occurred.

And in his next thought, he felt the *right* of it.

"Captain," Tev interrupted his reverie, "the gravity anchor has torn away. Both the station and the alien vessel have begun a freefall."

"Wong, engage at one-quarter impulse immediately. If we take a beating, the ship can handle it. We've got to make it to the station now!" Against the tidal forces at work, they would need to be right on top of the station if they hoped to stop its plunge.

As his ship thrummed with power and leaped forward, Gold couldn't help but continue his earlier line of reasoning. He began to understand the enormity of what he'd done. Gripping the edge of his seat, he swore if they actually managed to get out of here, the dead would be laid to rest at last. Rescuing members of his crew necessitated risk. And when that risk passed beyond the pale and threatened to kill the rest of the crew? Who among them would say no?

It came with the uniform. It came with the job. Gold had allowed doubts to eat away at his convictions of duty. But not again.

"Captain," Tev said, "we're close enough."

Gold stood up, unable to contain the sudden energy that flowed through him. "Engage tractor beam."

"Tractor beam engaged. We've got the station. I'm punching a reinforced dekyon beam into subspace . . . now!"

The *da Vinci* rocked precariously over on its starboard side, as if wrenched by an invisible hand. A power conduit blew beneath the tactical station, flames licking out. Piotrowski grabbed an extinguisher and fought down the small electrical fire. But the vessel held.

"Matching shields," Tev announced. "We're synchronized, Captain."

Gold tapped his combadge. If wishes could be turned into energy, she'd hear him even across the event horizon. "Gold to Gomez, come in."

*   *   *

As reunions went, Sonya had heard of worse. Among a family of feuding Klingons, for instance.

Es'a and his small party from the lower decks were searched and put under immediate guard as soon as Rennan led them all into the upper decks that fell under S'eth's dominion. The intervening levels had had the look of a battlefield, which they had been several times over the past century. Plasma-scarred walls, ruptured steam pipes, and exposed power conduits bore witness to that, along with the musty odors of dust mixed with old machine oil. It was a no-man's-land through which Resaurian battled Resaurian over the fate of their children: to be raised inside the Demon, in relative safety, or risked to bring them home.

Sonya allowed nothing to slow down the small group, however, even waving about her phaser (recovered from Es'a) a few times to make her point. Rennan shook his head over those theatrics, but they got the job done faster than his personal style of calm argument.

"We'll try your way next time," she promised, heavy on the cynicism. Neither of them believed that, but it kept him from complaining aloud.

From the final corridor leading up to the bridge, Sonya wondered if there were ruptured steam vents ahead as well. A great deal of hissing rolled together to make a crash of white noise. The equivalent of Resaurian shouting, she realized a moment later, as her universal translator finally made headway against the static.

Panicked shouting.

The bridge was a beehive of frantic activity. Resaurians slithered and ran, coiled into the backs of panels, and labored to rush replacement parts where they were needed. The ozone scent of electrical fires stung

Sonya's sinuses. Her eyes teared up from the acrid smoke. Even as they arrived, another junction box blew out in a storm of white-hot sparks. Pattie swarmed over with an extinguisher held in each of her forward legs, spraying down the box with heavy, one-two doses of dry powder.

"Commander!" the Nasat exclaimed, seeing her commander lead the small contingent forward.

Dropping one canister and throwing the other to a nearby Resaurian, P8 Blue swarmed forward on all legs to wrap Sonya in a stifling embrace. Being hugged by a five-foot-long pill bug was no small matter. It took Sonya a moment to extract herself, trying all the while to flag S'eth over so she could calm him before he noticed for himself. Too late. One of his patrol guards made it across the room first.

"Nest-breaker!"

S'eth's hissing shout was enough to momentarily halt most of the work on the bridge. But engineers would be engineers no matter their race. The repair teams fell back to work, leaving the matter to S'eth, who abandoned his perch near the blackened main viewscreen to slither forward with reinforcements.

Rennan had caught Corsi and Vinx by now. Stevens had heard Pattie's shout, and come running with Lense. The team was back together, and everyone tried to talk at once and louder than the quarreling Resaurians.

"Your fault!" S'eth accused Es'a. "It must be your fault. Our anchor is deteriorating and it is accepting no reinforcement."

"Us?" Es'a recoiled. "You cause intentional power failures when you know the condition of our systems, and you blame us?"

Sonya held up a hand for silence. Didn't get it. She

pointed her phaser at the overhead and squeezed off a quick shot, scoring a trail of red sparks. Everyone ducked except for Rennan and Sonya. Bickering ceased.

"I wish you wouldn't do that," he said with a forced calm.

"I know." Holstering her weapon, content to let Vinx and Corsi cover the assembled group, she held up her hands again. It was the work of a moment to explain to the rest of her team about the young Resaurians, and the sabotage perpetrated by S'eth's people in their first attempt to free the station from the black hole.

"Whatever your past difficulties," she said, "you have to put them aside." The station shook, violently. Some of the children Es'a had brought with them cowered behind him. "Obviously the station is no longer stable. If it cannot be fixed, we have to get it out of the Demon. Now."

"Impossible," S'eth hissed. "The phase variance in our power distribution system will overload the reactors. We cannot disengage the safeties." He glared at his rival. "You are as impatient as your father."

"I've already made a start at solving that problem," Sonya told him, heading off any further shouting. "I'd be done by now if I hadn't worried that you might blow up something else as a means of delaying our escape." As if caused by her words, the bridge lights flickered uncertainly, then brightened again. "I think we can stabilize your systems, and hold them steady long enough to get out of the black hole."

"You think! Long enough!" S'eth waved away her promises. "That is not good enough, Commander."

"Okay. Then we can all stand around here glaring until the Demon swallows us whole." It was a sobering thought. One which shut S'eth up for a moment, and allowed her to outline the basics of what they needed.

Stevens nodded at once. "You're using the La Forge-Brahms matrix. I can handle that." He retrieved his personal tools. Es'a directed one of his people to take Stevens below. Corsi so obviously wished to follow, but sent Vinx with them instead.

"It's at least another hour's work," Sonya said. "Which means Fabian can do it in thirty minutes. Can we hold on that long?"

S'eth shook his head. "Not at this rate. We've blown three junction boxes trying to reinforce the anchor. It will fail at any moment."

"Then we need to invent a new anchor. And we need to contact the *da Vinci* to update them on our situation."

"It cannot be done," S'eth told her, though he seemed more subdued than hostile this time.

Es'a scoffed. "Always ready to quit. Duck your head into your nest and hide from the universe."

S'eth puffed out his neck muscles. "Our communications equipment is beyond salvage. We have even lost our main viewer. It is not possible."

That worried Sonya. Her team could work miracles at times, but three impossible tasks in thirty minutes seemed beyond even her current best estimates. Just a little help would have been welcome.

"*Gold to Gomez, come in.*" Captain Gold's voice, loud and insistent, spoke from her combadge.

Smiling with her first measure of relief since arriving on the station, Sonya held a hand up to her badge, tapped it to open a channel. "Gomez here, Captain. You have no idea how good it is to hear your voice. We have serious problems, please stand by for update." Tapping the channel closed for a moment, she gave S'eth a heartening smile. "We're the S.C.E.," she reminded him, and herself as well. "Impossible just takes an extra ten minutes."

CHAPTER
26

With a sensation similar to the genetically imprinted memory of the egg, the *Dutiful Burden* fell toward the station and, beyond it, the event horizon. Though the overseer's bowed head and twitching tail signaled his dislike, S'linth found he rather enjoyed it. A return to the universe's womb—a permanent one, if he and his crew did not find a way to arrest their descent.

S'linth purposefully moved around the bridge. Unlike the sinuous, graceful movements of Third Councilman Sha'a, or the halting, timid steps of the nictitator, he strode with confidence: proud, almost boastful leg-to-tail, tail-to-leg steps. The thump of his tail was a strong counterpoint to the anxiousness that had prevailed on the bridge for too long. Now, he provided an anchor for his crew. He portrayed confidence, and for him, his crew returned it.

He came to a stop just outside touching distance of the science station. "Science, report."

"Captain, I simply cannot replicate it. I've tried numerous different energy matrices, all with what I believe to be identical signatures. Yet, each time I attempt to incorporate the energy within the matrix, it collapses, its cohesion vaporizing before it can fully solidify. I simply cannot re-create the anchor." Frustration wafted off the Resaurian (no fear, now; a victory!), but underneath it, a hard core of determination to support his captain.

In addition to demonstrating strength to his bridge crew by stopping by each one, he also was able to taste the emotions of each and determine where their full support rested. Though some wavered, the underpinning of their emotions radiated a quiet confidence. A willingness to follow their captain wherever he led.

"If I had a cycle or so to study," Science continued, "I might be able to understand what the ancients accomplished. But right now . . ."

S'linth radiated confidence. He'd known from the moment the gravity anchor failed they were doomed; the science officer simply did not have the expertise to attempt to replicate the anchor. Like so much, this too had been lost to the conservatives.

Step-thump; step-thump; step-thump. S'linth continued his prowl around the bridge, all the while keeping Third Councilman Sha'a and the nictitator from direct visual contact. The rasp of S'linth's scales across the deck was a soothing susurration to the commanding impact of his tail. He stopped at Tho'sh's seat.

"First Navigator. Report."

"The *Dutiful Burden* is one point four *ris*-units above the event horizon."

"The alien vessel?"

"Point seven-four-three *ris*-units."

"And the station?

"Point seven-three-nine *ris*-units."

"So close?"

"Yes, Captain. I'm surprised at how quickly the alien vessel managed to close with the station."

"How did it accomplish this?"

"I cannot say, Captain."

"And why? Why close so quickly with the station? To what purpose? Even if they stacked the station's occupants nose to tail they could not transfer but a fraction."

"What does it matter, Captain?"

Sha'a's voice slicked the air. Though no scent accompanied the pronouncement, S'linth still felt as though he'd been immersed in brackish liquid. The sudden heat of hate radiated from Tho'sh at Sha'a's voice. Though he reciprocated, such blatant scents were extremely dangerous. S'linth shockingly brushed a fingertip quickly across Tho'sh's shoulder. The first navigator reined in his pheromones and bowed his head slightly in acknowledgment.

"It matters a great deal, Third Councilman." He tried with difficultly to keep his voice neutral. Too much baggage was now attached to their relationship for the easy respect of the past. S'linth turned, too sharply, to gaze at Sha'a. "If the aliens find a way to escape the Demon, we may be able to replicate it. If the solution involves the station in some way, then understanding it is also important."

"The captain wishes to rescue his crew, just as he said from the beginning. He's determined to continue to interfere in Resaurian affairs. His maliciousness in dragging us across the photon sphere is proof enough of that."

So, revisionist history. S'linth almost shook his head

in disgust. *Is this how it happens? Did the councilmen millennia ago also wish to hide their heads in the nest and casually change what really occurred?* The thought sickened him.

"I believe the alien captain dragged us across the photon sphere because we held him against his will. It shows determination and amazing ingenuity. I have to respect him for the one and admire him for the other."

"You admire him?! How dare you—"

Lucky for the nictitator, Comms interrupted. With everything that had occurred, S'linth had reached the point where the unproductive—it had taken crossing the photon sphere of a black hole for him to see the Resaurian in his true light—would not be allowed to make such statements on his bridge without consequence. Even with the councilman aboard.

"Captain, the alien vessel is hailing us."

S'linth moved to the side of his command chair. "Respond to the hail, Comms. Captain Gold, this is Captain S'linth. How may I be of assistance?"

The bridge of the *da Vinci* materialized and the strangeness of numerous alien faces greeted his eyes. Their monochrome, too-smooth skin almost made his skin crawl, until he remembered what he'd witnessed. Commitment, honor, determination, mercy. Aliens they may be, but they espoused everything the Resaurians claimed to stand for. *In fact,* he thought darkly, *more so than some.*

"We've managed to latch on to the station with our tractor beam. However, though we've found what I believe to be a very workable plan to save ourselves and the station, we cannot do it alone. Since it appears you too are in dire straits, I feel we can pool our resources and save all of us."

Sha'a butted into the conversation with an imperious manner. "What if we wish not to see ourselves saved?"

The rage of hate engulfed S'linth with a suddenness that snapped his jaws shut tight and sent his tail tip quivering. It had all become too much. The vapid overseer could've broken the fang all by himself, but for the councilman to behave as though the captain were not even present? That tunneled the nest. A nest-breaker could not be allowed to remain.

The thought cooled his heat with a splash of frigid ice. Could he really be thinking of breaking centuries-old traditions?

"Then you'll be dooming yourselves to death. We've got the key to escape and unless you've figured it out, which I doubt since you're still falling, you're going to die. I'll gladly share it with you, provided we work to save everyone. If you don't, not only will you condemn yourselves, but you'll be murdering those on the station and killing innocent aliens as well. You espouse peace and acceptance and yet you show yourselves to be as callous as the worst Klingon. Uncaring of the devastation you leave behind due to your traditions."

The words sank into S'linth like mating fangs: incessant, hot, irresistible. Though the captain spoke to Sha'a, S'linth felt as though the words were tailored for him and him alone. The echo of his previous sentiments only enhanced their barbs, making them impossible to ignore.

Sha'a continued to speak; his tone made it sound as if they were discussing the price of fertilizer in a casual afternoon meeting. "You don't know the first thing about our culture. Your specialist has scanned a cube or two about us and now you profess expert knowledge? You try and stretch a skein across a skeleton that does not fit. This is Resaurian business, Captain. I told you at the beginning, Resaurians deal with Resaurians. Even those who've spent millennia on the station would agree. Even unto death."

S'linth knew nothing of humans, but the small upward stretching of the lips looked exactly like baring of fangs. *"And I said at the beginning, Third Councilman Sha'a, you should speak with them before making such a blanket statement. You see, I have spoken with them, as have my crew. And they've a very different opinion of this matter. Those grandchildren have been working alongside my away team to save the station you consigned to oblivion."*

The creasing lips did indeed turn into a baring of fangs, albeit small ones; the captain's words spiked in intensity. *"That's right. Grandchildren. The aliens you put on the station have been dead for centuries, and their children and grandchildren have been toiling on a prison barge that has lived centuries beyond when it should've been decommissioned. Would you like to see those children at work?"*

S'linth felt as though a disemboweling fire claw had struck, spilling his insides onto the deck.

When no Resaurian moved, the alien captain shook his head in disgust and slashed his hand in the air. A new image materialized on the viewscreen. Though in slow motion and incredibly fuzzy—in a detached way he realized the recording had occurred across a time dilation—S'linth easily picked out the Resaurian young. Their size gave them away immediately. Nevertheless their blue scales stood out like neon. Young. True Resaurian young.

A miasma of disgust washed through the bridge, practically choking all. That they'd participated in keeping Resaurian young in fearful, dangerous servitude for endless cycles made them all physically ill. It didn't matter that they'd not known. The guilt hung around their necks like months-old skin sheddings, and would not dislodge.

Captain Gold's face appeared once more. *"Would you consign the children to death as well?"*

Fang and claw, the words struck at S'linth's soul.

"I will not stand for this deception," Sha'a finally responded, his voice low and dangerous. "There are no young on that station, and that you would use such against us shows the monsters you are. It will be my pleasure to see you destroyed in the Demon."

A deep, long hiss burst from S'linth, forcing every Resaurian in hearing to puff out his neck muscles in a reflexive defense. Hiding in the nest when you don't like what your eyes lay plain before you. The humans knew nothing of Resaurian young and could not have replicated such a fine forgery. All they had said had been the truth from the beginning.

With a suddenness he'd become known for on his rise to captaincy, S'linth made his decision. Though it felt like shifting the weight of the nest, he moved forward and spoke words he never believed it would be possible to say. "No, Councilman, you will do no such thing."

"What?" Suliss slithered forward. "How dare—"

S'linth whipped his head in the nictitator's direction, bared his fangs, and piled out the hatred and rage that had built hour after hour. The spitting hiss caused the nictitator to stumble backward and cower against the wall; he had no wish to accept a challenge he would lose.

"Security, remove this unproductive from my bridge immediately." He turned away before watching for a response; he did not doubt his crew.

Sha'a did not realize when he'd lost. "So, you betray me. After all I've done. You would violate every tradition of our people. Betray them for aliens." At a genetic level, the voice of the councilman pulled at his loyalties. However, S'linth had witnessed too much for his conscious brain to give in to such directives without question anymore. He no longer felt under the command of the councilman.

"Security, remove Sha'a from my bridge as well. Keep them in separate holding cells until we return to the nest." He turned away without once acknowledging Sha'a. To do so would only give some validation and leave a crack open for his crew to doubt.

With the most difficult part past, S'linth turned back toward the viewscreen to find wide eyes and open mouths on the aliens; he couldn't be sure what it meant, but at this point it didn't matter.

"Captain, I believe you hailed me with an offer?"

The captain slowly nodded, closing his mouth.

"If you will trust me with your plans, I swear, we will help bring our children home."

CHAPTER
27

Sonya Gomez stepped through, onto the bridge of the *da Vinci*, before the lift doors had fully whisked open. Bart Faulwell and Carol Abramowitz met her on the upper landing. Both of them threw protocol out the airlock and folded her into an awkward three-way hug. "Welcome home," Bart whispered. His breath was warm against the side of her face, and smelled of apples.

Sonya smiled thinly. "Good to be back," she told them both. Even if this wasn't over, it did feel good to have the familiar feel of the *da Vinci* around her again. A swaying feeling of vertigo washed over her, but she held her footing. "You might want to clear the bridge," she said.

"We were on our way out," Carol told her. She broke away first, headed for the lift. Bart followed after a final, brotherly squeeze on both arms.

The bridge felt tense, but together in a way Sonya

had never felt on the station, with warring factions and secrets being kept. Joanne Piotrowski nodded a greeting from tactical. Even Tev's natural surliness seemed light by comparison to what she had lived through, though he did not welcome her back with the same enthusiasm that her friends had. He merely grunted at her arrival.

David Gold was no more forthcoming with his feelings. "Let's get the hell out of here."

Of course, with the main viewer open onto the bridge of the *Dutiful Burden,* she expected her captain to maintain a respectful distance. The three-way alliance he'd put together was built on intimidation and the threat of imminent death for all concerned. He did shift around in his seat, looking back at her. "Keep it smooth, Gomez," he said, *sotto voce.* "Not too many bumps." And he tipped her a casual wink.

The confidence in his gaze, regardless of what he might feel inside, warmed her. "Yes, sir."

She moved to the main panel, pulled up readings on the Resaurian station, the *Dutiful Burden,* and the *da Vinci's* position within the black hole. A small, green candy sat on the edge of her lower panel, still in its twist of wrapper. From the side, a hand covered in coarse, brown hair crept in to pluck the candy from its resting spot.

"That's not exactly regulation," she said, seeing in her peripheral vision that the Tellarite still stood there.

"Faulwell," Tev said, as if that explained everything. In a way, it did. "He rode across the photon sphere on the bridge."

She glanced sidelong at Tev. Most times, the stodgy engineer would have demanded nonessential personnel to stand clear of the work areas. Then again, there had likely been a great deal more to worry about than a quiet cryptographer and a cultural specialist standing nearby. "What was it like?" she asked. She did not need to specify, Sonya knew. Not with Tev.

"Magnificent." He nearly let it rest with that, then, "You should have been here to see it."

Sonya nodded, sensing that the Tellarite had just offered her a very left-handed compliment. "I'll see it on the way out," she told him. "Ready?"

"Always, Commander." He moved back to the science station, unwrapped his candy, and popped it into his mouth.

Sonya checked in with Stevens, who continued to monitor the power systems aboard the station, and Pattie, standing by aboard the station bridge. Both reported they were as ready as they could be. "All hands report ready to go, Captain."

"Can we pull anyone else off first?" Gold asked, a measure of concern laced into the request.

"Fabian can't leave the reactor distribution venues, in case new calibrations become necessary. Pattie insisted on staying behind as well. This three-way anchor is our weak link, especially given the station's sheer bulk. She'll make it work, sir." She didn't bother to tell Gold that Corsi was unlikely to leave the team unattended on a station surrounded by potential hostiles without anything short of a direct order, and perhaps not even then, and Rennan and Vinx were backing up their superior.

"Make it happen, Gomez."

Sonya passed along her orders, and Tev loosened the da Vinci's grasp on the station just enough to allow the vessel to climb against the Demon's intense gravitational pull. Using his "bootstrapping" technique, he punched one dekyon beam into the curved wall of space-time, then another farther up, and slowly merged the two. The extra pull allowed the *da Vinci* to struggle along several dozen kilometers.

"Hang on, Tev. *Dutiful Burden,* go."

The Resaurian vessel performed the exact same wall-climbing maneuver while the *da Vinci* anchored the station in place. Once they were at an equal position, the anchor was tightened and the station slowly dredged up from the Demon's maw.

It was working!

This time she gave the Resaurian vessel the lead position, sending them scaling up the warped space-time ledge. Like a pair of rock climbers hauling an injured partner up a cliff face, first the *Burden* edged its way back toward normal space, then the *da Vinci,* and again the station levered itself up once both vessels had hammered in their dekyon pitons.

At one point during its turn at hauling, a gravimetric wave broke over the bow of the *da Vinci*. The small *Saber*-class vessel weathered it as though it had been a large sneaker wave crashing over the prow of an old ocean-going vessel; the ship gave a shake and a roll, and then burst forward with an extra kick from the engines.

At one-point-four-five Schwarzschild radii the raw gravitational force had lessened to the equivalent of twelve billion Earth-gravities. Lessened! Sonya almost laughed at such an idea. The gravitational tide between vessels and station was approximately two hundred million gravities. The *da Vinci* groaned and labored against the pull, but up the station came.

"Coming up on the photon sphere," Tev called out.

Sonya spared her engineer's curiosity only ten seconds, glancing between her monitors and the main viewscreen. She saw the Einstein Rings bulge out from the compacted starscape. The troika of vessels now hung on to the division between eternal night and a universe of possibilities.

Another gravimetric wave slammed into them, bucking the ship.

The Demon was reluctant to release its prey.

"Not my ship," Gold muttered, his deep voice carrying across the bridge. "Not today."

Slowly, painfully, the starscape crawled down toward the bottom of the viewscreen. Sonya watched, coordinated, and worried. The irony did not escape her. Starfaring vessels, each capable of traveling across light-years in short order, clawing and scrabbling for simple kilometers. Ten here. Twenty there.

At three complete Schwarzschild radii, an impressive nine hundred kilometers from the singularity's center, she began to breathe easier. Tension eased from her shoulders, and she dry-swallowed some life back into her throat.

At five radii the ships had shed two orders of magnitude in gravitational pull, and she lengthened each leg of the journey, allowing the *da Vinci* and *Dutiful Burden* to eat away a full hundred kilometers on each stride, then a thousand. Soon they were able to drop the dekyon beams and proceed under normal propulsion, fighting their way past an orbit of one thousand kilometers, a simple fifteen thousand gravities. Gold passed the word to bring his own people back from the station, and then shifted screens aft.

A dark circle of night shrank from the *da Vinci* as stars reclaimed the sky. And from out of the Demon's mouth came the Resaurian station.

"Gravitational pull falling past one hundred fifty G's,"

Sonya reported at three million kilometers' distance from the Demon. Both vessels were under full impulse, racing away, the danger past. She used the back of her sleeve to pat the sweat from her brow. "Let's not do that again anytime soon, please."

"No promises," Gold said, but he was grinning ear to ear. "Not in the S.C.E. Wong, put us in a very distant orbit around the Demon, please." He thumbed open an all-hands circuit. "Stand down from alert, investigate all spaces and make damage control reports to the bridge." To his main bridge crew he said, "Rest easy, everyone."

Haznedl slapped Wong on the shoulder. Piotrowski kept to herself at first, though she whooped a moment later when Corsi led Konya and Stevens out of the turbolift.

"Everything's in okay shape on the station," Stevens reported. "A bit bouncy, but we made it through."

"Lot of engineers and extra security crowding my bridge," Gold complained with a smile. There was no mistaking the relief in the captain's voice. "Why don't some of you get cleaned up and rested?"

Sonya nodded wearily. "I volunteer for that duty." She felt grubby and bone weary, but also a great deal of pride in a job well done against overwhelming odds. After a shower, she expected to feel even better.

Tony Shabalala entered the bridge, a small bandage on his head, but otherwise apparently fit for duty; he relieved Piotrowski, who followed Fabian and Rennan toward the lift. Sonya trailed, and was stopped briefly on the upper landing when Tev put a large hand on her shoulder. "Yes, Tev?"

The Tellarite paused, shuffled from one foot to the other, then snuffled a short laugh. "Good to have you back, Commander."

Sonya smiled, felt it reaching up into her eyes. "Thank you." She headed for the lift, still looking forward to that shower.

But she doubted it would make her feel any better than she did right now.

CHAPTER
28

Gold stood in the transporter room and felt like a cloth bag of loose bones that might break if he set any one angle down wrong. How long had he been up? His mind had passed beyond caring.

Before him, Captain S'linth and the frail station leader Es'a both stood on the low stage, ready to transport to the *Dutiful Burden* and the fate that now stood before them. They both looked at him expectantly.

"Captain S'linth," he began, trying to ignore the film of too many hours awake on his teeth and the oily feel at the tip of his hair. "I must say, I can only imagine what it is you've done today, and yet it impressed the hell out of me. I also know a captain is only as good as his crew, and for them to follow you into what surely will be trouble speaks even more about you."

The Resaurian closed his eye membranes and bowed slightly. "It is I who am honored. You showed me not all aliens are to be feared, or despised. You have shown the Federation holds its morals in deeds, not just actions. This has brought me hope for our future, as we continue to explore the regions near the nest."

Gold couldn't help the raised eyebrow. "You think you'll be able to continue to explore space with all you've done? Don't get me wrong, I'd love to run into you at any corner of the quadrant, but . . . just seems like you've stirred up a hornet's nest and a whole heap of trouble to boot."

"I don't know exactly what a hornet's nest is, but trouble, yes, I believe I have broken the egg and then some."

"Captain," Es'a interrupted. "There will be troubles, no doubt, but please do not worry. I and those with me shall see the Council is far too busy to deal with Captain S'linth." Though the Resaurian was frail and unassuming, Gold immediately changed his mind about him. A lot of steel there, no doubt about it.

"Then good luck to you both, and I wish you well in the new world you're about to create."

After their departure, Gold found himself walking down the corridor of his ship, satisfaction radiating its usual warmth of a job well done. It was the kind of warmth that might carry over into solid, dreamless sleep. He stepped out of the turbolift to the bridge. Looking around, he saw that beta shift was on watch. Ironically, that meant that Piotrowski, having already done a chunk of alpha shift substituting for Shabalala, was now back on duty. The captain almost stepped back inside and then decided he might as well sign off on his log entries for the day. As he crossed to his ready room, he noticed Gomez and Konya, standing together at the rail, watching the Demon get smaller on the viewscreen.

It was the work of moments to pull up the log entries regarding this incredible day, and copy his signature over them. He passed back through the bridge on his way out. "When you're comfortable, Rusconi." The instruction to the conn officer was his only order. It was enough.

Sometime later—it actually unnerved him that he'd never recall how much time later—he sat on the side of his bed, having just finished prepping for sleep. The warm embrace of the bed called to him, and for once in a long while he knew there would be no dreams. The nightmare that had awakened him so many hours ago would not trouble him. Just as the ghosts of lost crew would no longer trouble him either. He'd finally come to terms with it and laid them to rest. Where they should be.

With a sigh of contentment, knowing his ship (and of course his granddaughter) were safe, Gold closed his eyes and fell asleep before he could even command the lights off.

Having watched the turbolift doors whisk shut behind Captain Gold, Rennan Konya relaxed, resting forward on the bridge's upper landing rail next to Gomez. The commander had refreshed herself since their time on the Resaurian station. Her black hair was neatly back in place. She smelled of soap and had donned a clean uniform without grease smudges or dusty cuffs.

A small abrasion on her temple and a split fingernail seemed to be her only physical reminders of the entire adventure. Rennan had a good-size egg on his forehead from the steel pipe, and a nice bruise over his solar plexus to remind him that it just wasn't a good idea to grab Sonya Gomez unannounced.

They'd all gotten off easy.

On the main viewscreen, the Demon looked over the bridge with its dark, baleful eye. "I've never been one to endow inanimate objects or stellar phenomenon with human traits," he said. "No 'happy suns' or 'hostile weather.' But I would almost be willing to swear that it hates us." Almost.

Gomez shrugged. But it was an uneasy shrug. "Back on Earth I once had a motorized scooter I named Lucifer. It was always breaking down and stranding me someplace. I'd take it apart and put it back together, trying to make it work. And it would, for a while."

"How old were you?"

"Twelve. I knew very early that I wanted to be an engineer."

At the conn, Robin Rusconi plotted a course back to their original assignment, ready to go to warp once all gravitational effects from the black hole had diminished to safe levels. Piotrowski was back at tactical. She looked bored, and was resisting the urge to crane around to look at Gomez, ask her about the station, or just simply gossip. No Betazoid training necessary to detect that; Rennan had seen the two women get along well on and off the bridge. And beta shift was rarely an exciting time.

If Gomez had shown any desire for it, he would have turned back to his security station and left her to entertain the young ensigns. But the commander seemed perfectly content to relax with him. Wanted something from him, in fact, he sensed. A shield, perhaps, to prevent her from having to talk about the event so quickly.

Of course, it could also be a piece of wishful thinking.

He could delve into her surface thoughts, see if it happened to cross her mind, but just now he preferred to have his nice, safe little mystery.

"I never did thank you for coming to look for me," she said suddenly. "Did I?"

Rennan shook his head. "Now that you mention it, no. Though at the time you were most forceful with your . . . opinion."

"Sorry about that."

Silence reigned for a short time. The Demon's eye shrank down until it could hardly be discerned from the dark voids that fell between stars. Rennan finally shrugged off her apology, then asked, "What about Lucifer? That motor scooter? Whatever happened to it?" It wasn't that important. It just seemed a good piece of trivial conversation.

"I finally took it apart and never put it back together. So I guess I got the last word in, didn't I?" She laughed, low and throaty. "But it kept its secret to the end. That was one of the other things I learned early on. Some things we just aren't meant to discover."

"That seems a fairly odd sentiment for an engineer."

She smiled a secretive little smile. "I never said I liked the idea." Gomez glanced sidelong at him. "For that matter, you're not typical security either, you know."

"I know."

"Well, for what it's worth, I'm glad. Leaves any haphazard shooting that needs to be done to those of us who don't know better."

That sounded like another apology. And a heartfelt one, he knew.

"Commander," Ensign Rusconi called out. "Ready to go to warp."

"Go ahead," she said. "Get us the hell away from that thing."

Stars stretched out for a brief moment, then snapped into fast-paced light that slipped away quickly toward the *da Vinci*'s stern. The Demon was gone. And Gomez breathed a heavy sigh of relief. "I appreciate it, Rennan," she said, then turned for the door and an escape from the bridge. "Good night."

Rennan watched her leave, hands still braced around the upper rail, until the lift doors slid shut. Then he shoved himself off the rail and toward his own station. So she had wanted company until she saw that the Demon had been vanquished back among the stars. Maybe borrow a bit of his companionship, but nothing more. Did that help her feel safe? Or simply not so alone? He glanced back at the retreating stars once more. Either way, he decided, that was fine by him.

That was security's job.

CHAPTER
29

Tev stomped down the corridor and wondered if he was making a mistake. He'd thought long and hard about this decision. However, logic seemed to play a much lesser role in this situation than he found comfortable.

Instead, his feelings demanded the overture, regardless of what his rational mind tried to say. Hence he stomped down the corridor, disgusted with his inability to simply say no. The simple fact that he had begun arguing with himself appeared to be a good indicator that he needed some type of resolution. But could this be what he was looking for?

He had already tapped the chime for the cabin Bartholomew Faulwell shared with Stevens before he could back out of it. A moment later Bartholomew stood before him, surprise spreading his features into a ridiculous parody of human emotions.

"Tev? What brings you here?"

Tev stepped from one foot to the other. "Well, if you don't want me here, I'll be going."

"No, Tev. Please. That's not what I meant. You just—you surprised me. That's all. Please, come in." Bartholomew's tone, from what little Tev had been able to determine about humans in his time among them, appeared to hold no hidden agenda, just pure sincerity. As Tev entered the room, the cryptographer happened to catch a glimpse of the small package the Tellarite carried.

"What's that?"

"This?" Tev said, raising the small box up. Why had he wrapped it? It made no sense. It didn't change the value of the gift in any way. Nevertheless, it had felt important to do so. Like so many subtle things he'd missed in his time so far aboard the *da Vinci*, he'd begun to realize that sometimes the little things were important too. Just as a point oh-oh-five fraction of variance in a warp field could have devastating results, so too could coworkers have difficulties if they were not calibrated appropriately.

And sometimes such calibrations required a brightly colored bow.

"Here," he said, without more preamble.

Bartholomew responded with an easy smile as he tore into the box.

"It's nothing. Really. But, you've been nice enough to share your candy with me. I felt it appropriate to share something with you. A present, if you will."

The human laughed. Not the brash harshness of mockery, but the hearty, good-natured laughter shared by friends. "You really didn't need to do this. We're friends."

Tev felt a small warmth spread within him and realized it came of this small step of acceptance. Eventually he'd understand how to take such steps with Sonya Gomez, and with others. In the meantime, little steps.

Bartholomew finished opening the box and pulled out the chip. "Um, I don't mean to sound dense or anything, but what is this?"

"I know that you enjoy writing letters. I also happened to hear from Dr. Abramowitz that you've created a program that will allow you to generate a replication of your letter. Well, this program will allow you to dictate the letters like a log entry, and when they replicate they'll do so in your own handwriting." It had been such a little thing and yet he felt immense pride.

The cryptographer held it up and smiled that easy grin again, then chuckled. "Tev, I appreciate this. I really do. But, well, it kind of does away with the whole reason for writing a letter."

Tev blinked in surprise. It had never occurred to him that the human might actually enjoy such a laborious process as writing on paper when there were so many other ways to communicate.

Bartholomew spoke again, as though the silence made him uncomfortable. "Tev, I really do appreciate this. I know what you meant and I accept it."

Tev smiled back. "Thank you, Bartholomew." He reached out in the human gesture of a handshake. As he departed the room, he felt optimistic. He'd not quite gotten it right, but he'd tried nonetheless, and his error ratio had only been off by a small margin.

If he kept trying, he'd nail it.

ABOUT THE AUTHORS

At the age of five and a half, **Christopher L. Bennett** saw his first episode of *Star Trek,* believing it to be a show about a strange airplane that only flew at night. As he continued watching, he discovered what those points of light in the sky *really* were. This awakened a lifelong fascination with space, science, and speculative fiction. By age twelve he was making up *Trek*-universe stories set a century after Kirk's adventures (an idea years ahead of its time), but soon shifted to creating his own original universe. He eventually realized he did this well enough to make a career out of it. Meanwhile, Christopher made two separate passes through the University of Cincinnati, thereby putting off real life as long as possible, and earned a B.S. in physics and a B.A. with High Honors in history in the process. Christopher's other published works include "Aggravated Vehicular Genocide" in the November 1998 *Analog*;

"Among the Wild Cybers of Cybele" in the December 2000 *Analog*; " . . .Loved I Not Honor More" in the *Star Trek: Deep Space Nine: Prophecy and Change* anthology; "Brief Candle" in the *Star Trek: Voyager: Distant Shores* anthology; one of the eBooks in the *Star Trek: Mere Anarchy* miniseries; and the novels *Star Trek: Ex Machina, Star Trek: Titan: Orion's Hounds,* and *X-Men: Watchers on the Walls.* More information and cat pictures can be found at http://home.fuse.net/ChristopherLBennett/. The author is not the same Christopher Bennett whose father is *Star Trek* movie producer Harve Bennett, though he is apparently a cousin of paleontologist Chris Bennett. You can see why he uses the "L."

Randall N. Bills began his writing career in the adventure gaming industry, where he has worked full-time for the last eight years. His hobbies include music, gaming (from electronic to RPGs to miniatures to all those wonderful German board games), reading (of course), and, when he can, traveling; he has visited numerous locations both for leisure and for his job, including moving from Phoenix to Chicago to Seattle, numerous trips to Europe, as well as an LDS mission to Guatemala. He currently lives in the Pacific Northwest where he continues to work full-time (and then some) in the adventure gaming industry, while pursuing his writing career. Randall has published four novels; this is his first published *Star Trek* work. He lives with his best friend and wife Tara Suzanne, precocious son Bryn Kevin, utterly adorable daughter Ryana Nikol, and an eight-foot red-tailed boa called Jak o' the Shadows.

Loren L. Coleman wrote fiction in high school, but it was during his enlistment in the U.S. Navy that he began working seriously at the craft. Discharged in 1993, he went to work as a freelance fiction writer and eventually became a full-time novelist. His first novel, *Double-Blind*, was published in 1998. As of the end of 2006, he has written and published over twenty novels, a great deal of shorter fiction work, and been involved with several computer games. Some of his recent works are *Fortress: Republic*, set in the MechWarrior: Dark Age universe, and the *Age of Conan* trilogy *Legends of Kern*. *The Demon* is his second foray into *Star Trek* fiction following the publication of the short story "All that Glisters . . ." in the *Star Trek: New Frontier* anthology *No Limits*. When he isn't writing, Loren plays X-box games, collects far too many DVDs, and trains as a black belt in traditional Tae Kwon Do. He has lived in many parts of the country. Currently he resides in Washington State with his wife, Heather Joy, two sons, Talon LaRon and Conner Rhys Monroe, and a young daughter, Alexia Joy. The family owns three of an obligatory writer's cats, Chaos, Ranger, and Rumor, and one dog, Loki, who like any dog is just happy to be here. His personal website can be found at www.rasqal.com.

Robert Greenberger is no stranger to *Star Trek*, having written about it or for it since he was in ninth grade. He was a longtime editor of the *Star Trek* franchise for DC Comics before moving on to become a contributor to the world of *Trek* fiction. He has collaborated on numerous projects with Peter David and Michael Jan Friedman in addition to several solo efforts. In 2004 he wrote *Star Trek: A Time to Love* and *Star Trek: A Time to Hate* as part of a nine-volume series, and he's published stories in the *Star Trek* anthologies *Enterprise Logs*, *Tales of the Dominion War*, *New Frontier: No Limits*, and *Voyager: Distant Shores*. His most recent forays in the *Star Trek* universe are the *Corps of Engineers* adventure *Troubleshooting*, published in eBook form, and a short story in the *Star Trek: Constellations* anthology. Additionally, Bob has written ten young adult non-fiction books on a range of topics from the *Nature of Energy* to *Lou Gehrig*. Bob makes his home in Connecticut with his wife of twenty-five years, Deb, and their children Kate and Robbie. A lifelong Mets fan, Bob obviously likes suffering.

Andy Mangels is the coauthor of several *Star Trek* novels, eBooks, short stories, and comic books, as well as a trio of *Roswell* novels, all cowritten with Michael A. Martin. Flying solo, he is the best-selling author of many entertainment books including *Animation on DVD: The Ultimate Guide* and *Star Wars: The Essential Guide to Characters*, as well as a significant number of entries in *The Super-Hero Book*. He has written hundreds of articles for entertainment and lifestyle magazines and newspapers in the United States, England, and Italy. He has also written licensed material based on properties from many film studios and Microsoft, and his comic book work has been from DC Comics, Marvel Comics, and many others. He was the editor of the award-winning *Gay Comics* anthology for eight years. Andy is a national award-winning activist in the gay community, and has raised thousands of dollars for charities over the years. He lives in Portland, Oregon, with his long-term partner, Don Hood, their dog Bela, and their chosen son, Paul Smalley. Visit his website at www.andymangels.com.

Michael A. Martin's solo short fiction has appeared in *The Magazine of Fantasy & Science Fiction*. He has also coauthored (with Andy Mangels) several *Star Trek* novels (including the first two *Titan* novels *Taking Wing* and *The Red King*; *Enterprise: Last Full Measure*; *Excelsior: Forged in Fire*; *Worlds of Star Trek: Deep Space Nine* Book 2: *Trill: Unjoined*; *The Lost Era: The Sundered*; *Deep Space Nine: Mission: Gamma* Book Three: *Cathedral*; and *The Next Generation: Section 31: Rogue*), stories in the *Prophecy and Change*, *Tales of the Dominion War*, and *Tales from the Captain's Table* anthologies, and three novels based on the *Roswell* television series. Martin was the regular cowriter (also with Andy) of Marvel Comics' *Star Trek: Deep Space Nine* comics series, and has written for Atlas Editions' *Star Trek* Universe subscription card series, *Star Trek Monthly*, *Dreamwatch*, Grolier Books, and WildStorm/DC Comics. He lives with his wife, Jenny, and their two sons in Portland, Oregon.

Aaron Rosenberg writes role-playing games (including the Origins Award-winning *Gamemastering Secrets*), novels based on games (*Starcraft: Queen of Blades*), S.C.E. eBooks (besides the story herein, he's also written *The Riddled Post* and co-written *Creative Couplings* with Glenn Hauman), short stories ("Inescapable Justice" in *Imaginings: An Anthology of Long Short Fiction*), educational books, and anything else people want to pay him for. When not writing, he runs his game publishing company Clockworks (www.clock-worksgames.com), reads comics, watches movies, or spends time with his wife, their children, and their cat. Every so often he sleeps, just for variety.